A Thin Shee

Pippa Beecheno

First published by Endeavour Media Ltd in 2018.

Table of Contents

Beginnings	9
Cordless	16
Heart Rip	29
Black Thursday	39
Friendship	55
Love	68
Witness	80
Determination	93
Torn	108
Confrontation	117
Madrid	130
Foreboding	142
Mission	162
Failure	167
Cracks	176
Collapse	187
War	200
Recovery	207
Relapse	222
Hope	238
Grandad's Poem	248
Afterword	251

'It is the evil things that we shall be fighting against – brute force, bad faith, injustice, oppression and persecution – and against them I am certain that the right will prevail.'

Neville Chamberlain, 3rd September 1939

'In our age there is no such thing as "keeping out of politics". All issues are political issues, and politics itself is a mass of lies, evasions, folly, hatred and schizophrenia.'

George Orwell, *Politics and the English Language*, 1946

A Thin Sheet of Glass is dedicated to my great-aunt, whose life was tragically interrupted, and my grandparents who loved her and wanted us to know her story.

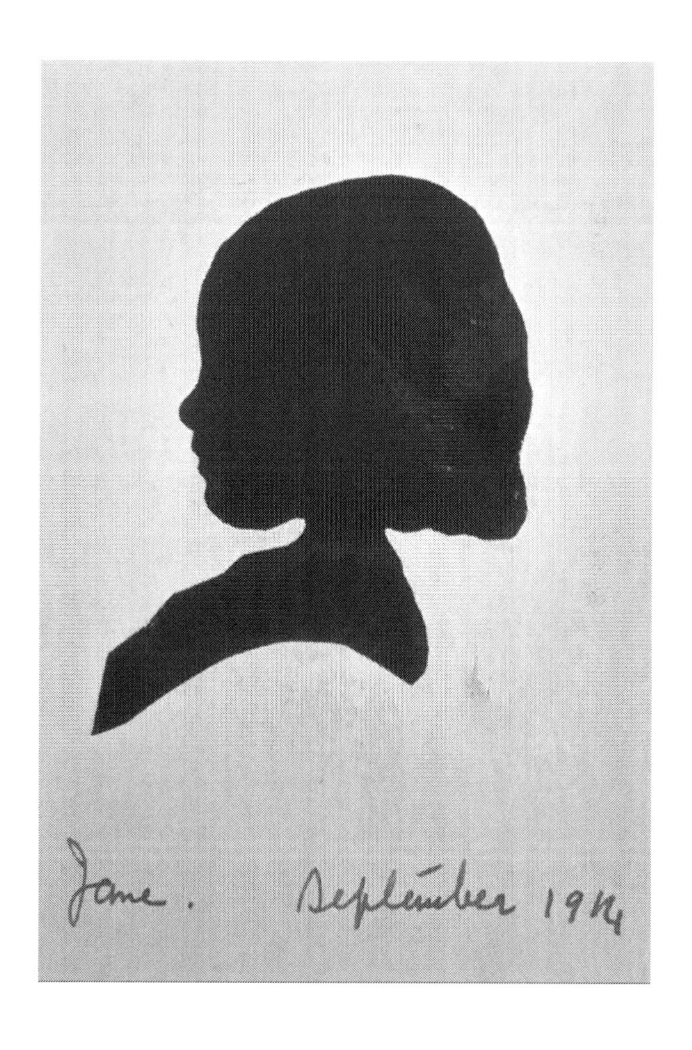

Beginnings

18th September 1940, 7pm
Bloomsbury, London
Jane is twenty-six

'Get away!'

She screamed until her throat cracked and her lungs jammed against her ribcage, and ran.

They want to take me back.

She took the stairs two at a time, down and out the front door.

I won't go back.

Grit peppered the soles of her feet as she hit the street and kept going.

Leave me alone!

Two dark shapes tracked her down the road.

Traitors.

She stuck out her hand and waved at moving lights. A black car hit the kerb and stopped.

For God's sake, let me in.

The window squeaked as it slid down and got stuck half way.

I don't have time for this.

She grabbed the door handle and pulled. They were closing on her, their voices pounding at her ears like fists, knocking her down, sending her spinning away from safety.

Hard, wet paving. They caught her by the arms as she fell, her face already awash with tears, her body as limp as if they'd stuck in a needle.

The cabbie leant out of his window.

'You all right, luv?'

Help.

She couldn't speak.

They bundled her into the cab and sat, on either side of her.

28th April 1914, 9pm
Bloomsbury, London

Jane's father

Arthur pressed his face deeper into the pillow. *Land of Hope and Glory* was playing again next door. Doctor Fenton clearly had visitors. It seemed to have become an after-dinner ritual of his to regale the company with a grand old tune while passing round the evening tipple – brandy or possibly port. 'Britain', he would be blustering, tweaking his narrow moustache, 'is a proud and glorious nation. Every citizen must do their bit: further the cause and act the patriot.'

All very good, Arthur thought, *but has he forgotten that I am not well? He saw me this morning. Surely bed rest requires peace and quiet? Doesn't he realise that his steel horn gramophone blows holes in the adjoining wall?*

Arthur's wife Gina entered the bedroom, her long nightdress ballooning at the front, concealing the baby beneath in soft layers of satin. Arthur had given her the dress before the birth of their son, Edmond. 'This baby will be spoilt before it even arrives,' Gina had laughed when she first saw it. Now, just over a year later, she sat on the mahogany chair by the dressing table, setting her mother-of-pearl hairbrush down and smoothing out her gown over the bump of their second child.

Arthur was lying flat on his bed, his feet sticking out at least a foot over the end. He turned over. His face was red.

'You look rather hot,' Gina said.

'I feel much better,' Arthur replied, turning awkwardly onto his side and smiling at her.

He had smiled like that when they first met, a gentle beam of a smile that transformed his face and lifted his shoulders, ridding him of the insecure second son hunch that had shadowed his tall, slender shape for years. Back then he had won himself a bride. Tonight he bought himself more time. Apprehension floated like a bubble to the ceiling and popped, leaving the room clear and peaceful.

Gina was so relieved by his recovery she felt she could skip round the room with happiness; but he would think her ridiculous and girlish if she did that. She was a mother now, nearly twice over. Just a few months to go and all Arthur could think about was the new baby. He was convinced it was a girl, with curly hair just like his, and Gina knew if it was a daughter, he would adore her. He had already chosen a name for her. 'Jane'. On this she let him be. It was easier to embrace his excitement than to admit her unease. Tonight, however, was a night to rest and be thankful that she had him all to herself.

Arthur sat up in bed and Gina pushed an extra pillow behind his back. The shooting pains in his stomach had subsided. He still felt the odd twinge but nothing he couldn't cope with. He started buttoning up his striped cotton pyjamas but the buttons were slippery and refused to go through the holes.

Gina saw him struggling. 'The sooner you sleep, the sooner you'll get better,' she said, finishing his buttons for him.

'Thanks for coming up to London,' he replied, squeezing her hand gently, 'leaving Edmond behind must've been a wrench.' It was a relief to have her there. It was no fun steaming up from the countryside by himself every Monday, attending dreary meetings and spending long nights away from his wife and son. Still, they were well cared for on his parents' estate. It was the right decision to insist they stay there for the time being however painful the separation. He would have established a proper home for them by the time the new baby arrived, he had promised Gina that.

Arthur felt poised, self-assured with Gina, in a way he did not with the men at the social club, all pipes and politics. What did he care if the Germans were building a railway from Berlin to Baghdad as long as it didn't affect his family, his peaceful home. The Germans were highly efficient. Their trains ran on time. *That sounds like a model to copy,* Arthur thought, but the men at the club were irritated. British engineering was unsurpassed. This must be acknowledged or there would be blows at midnight, they blustered. It was at this point that Arthur stepped away from the group and poured himself a drink.

Gina and Arthur sat next to each other on the bed, shoulder to shoulder for a while, until they were disturbed by the patter of footsteps outside the door. The housemaid was going upstairs. Arthur got up and drew the curtains before climbing back into bed. Gina wrestled with her nightdress, its straps tight around her shoulders. Arthur leaned over and loosened them and she slipped into bed beside him. He pulled the blanket up over her bump and turned out the light.

'Stay warm, the baby is hibernating,' he whispered, kissing her cheek.

'Can I stay here next to you?'

'I'm not going to say no to that,' he said, resting his head next to hers.

She loved his forehead. High and noble, not high and mighty she liked to think. She traced his profile with her eyes, the arch of his nose, the whiskers under it, the slender mouth, the peak of his chin. His cheeks were still flushed but he was quiet. He had closed his eyes. She nestled into the crook between his head and shoulder and drew his arm over her bump. It was such a relief that the operation had not gone ahead, that it was indigestion, not appendicitis after all. He was himself again, all willowy, wonderful, well over six foot of him, intact and restored to her, and that awful sickness that had swirled and stirred in the pit of her stomach when he told her was ill, had disappeared.

His breath was warm, rhythmic, easy, calming. The tension had gone. His body softened and he slept.

12.30am

Arthur's arm was heavy, a dead weight over her bump. His hand felt clammy and hot. Gina stared at the ceiling watching headlights roll across as a late cab hummed past. She kept the blanket on for the baby but her hair grew sticky under her neck. The window was slightly ajar but there was no breeze and her mind found nothing to fix on except Arthur's slow, steady breathing beside her.

She felt the baby kick and turned onto her side. It was uncomfortable being pregnant and her ankles were already swelling up with the extra weight. She sighed. Swinging the blankets back, careful not to disturb her husband, she eased herself out of bed and headed for the bathroom along the corridor. She sponged her face and neck, letting the water dribble down before mopping it up with a towel. Leaning her hands on the sink she stared at herself in the mirror. The lines around her eyes appeared deeper, more pervasive than before, as if they had been stitched in. *I look as bedraggled as a rag doll,* she thought, dabbing eau de cologne under her neck, the fresh scent providing relief from the stuffiness of the bedroom.

She turned the brass doorknob, pulled the door back and looked over at Arthur. He had shifted. His body looked cramped, his knees were drawn up to his chest, awkward for a man his height, and he had pushed the bedcover off.

She hurried back to the bed and knelt beside him. Her heart kicked out like the baby as she listened to his breathing. It came in short, sharp rasps. His face was strained, his eyes screwed shut.

'Arthur!' A noose closed round her throat and her voice barely escaped. She hovered over him, hands fluttering to his head, his feet, his heart; jumping back in horror as the springs of the bed bounced his body into the air, arching and thrashing like a fish on a hook. She stood there, a pathetic bystander as this gasping and twitching, this terrible pain ripped through the ashen-faced man she loved, the man that she adored – that she couldn't bear to be without.

Help!

'Help!' she forced out the scream, shrill and panicked like the whistle of a train with someone on the tracks but it wasn't enough. She had to do something. She rushed to the bedroom door and flung it open, tripping over the rug on the landing and catching herself on the banister.

'Susie!'

The housemaid was up two flights of stairs; narrow and endlessly steep.

'Susie, Mr Deering is unwell. Come quickly.'

Despite her heavy feet and the load she was carrying, she got to the door before Susie, who was struggling to pull on a pair of stays.

'Don't bother with that, I need you now, he's in agony.' Susie abandoned her stays and threw on a gown, blushing slightly at her disarray.

Gina had already turned back to the stairs and was groping her way down.

'Be careful Mrs Deering, it's treacherous on these stairs in your state. Wait for me.'

'I can't wait!' Gina was already in the bedroom, flicking the light switch, next to the bed, holding Arthur's hand. It was limp but there was life in it. He was lying still now. *He's worn out*, she thought, stroking his cheek, tempting a reaction – the flicker of eyelids opening, a flutter in the fingers, anything. She pushed the damp hair back from his forehead before laying his hand back on the bed. If only he would look at her. The pounding of her heart grew louder, throbbing in her ears.

Susie entered. Her hand went to her mouth. Mr Deering did look bad, he wasn't breathing right.

'Shall I fetch the doctor Ma'am?' Susie said.

Gina drew breath. She couldn't stay here, not with Arthur like this, how could she bear to see him in such pain? She had to be certain help was coming. 'I'll go,' she said, 'I'll fetch Doctor Fenton. Stay with Mr Deering and give him some water if he wants it.' She flung on her dressing gown and rushed downstairs and out into the street.

Aware of her state of undress, she glanced quickly up and down. The street was empty. She climbed the steps next door and rang the bell.

Silence. She pressed again, a long ring. No response. She hammered loudly with her fist, paused a moment and then hammered again. *Where are they?*

A light came on a couple of floors above her. Voices. The stumble of feet. The door opened and Dr Fenton stared out blinking, pulling the cord of his dressing gown round his waist.

'Mrs Deering, what's wrong?'

'My husband's been taken ill again. He can't breathe.'

'I'll grab my gown and bag and come immediately.' Dr Fenton turned and dashed back up the stairs. He gasped at the top and clutched the banister. This was his patient suddenly taken ill. The man he had sent off with a handful of painkillers and a dose of reassurance just that morning. His hands were shaking as he fumbled over the light in his clinical room and grabbed his medical bag.

Gina ground dirt into the soles of her feet as she waited. *Why is he taking so long?* When the doctor finally re-emerged, she noted, thankfully, that he hadn't wasted time getting dressed.

'Have his stomach cramps worsened?' Dr Fenton asked as they hurried into her house and up the stairs to Arthur.

'He said he was feeling better. He was sleeping peacefully. The pain came out of nowhere.'

Dr Fenton entered the room and knelt beside Arthur, feeling his pulse, noting the heavy sweat and laboured breathing. 'I see.' He paused. His face was as pale as his patient's. A deep sense of dread ballooned in his gut.

'Mrs Deering, please wait downstairs while I examine your husband.' He pressed her hand and led her out, closing the door behind her.

She sat downstairs and picked at the hem of her dress, sick with nerves. She got up and paced round the room. She picked up a book lying on the table and put it back on the shelf. She closed the lid of the writing bureau. She stared at the small black and white photo of Arthur's family on the mantelpiece. Their expressions were stiff, taut. They weren't smiling.

Then the doctor came downstairs.

'Mrs Deering, please sit down.' Dr Fenton's hands were sticky, his forehead damp with sweat. 'I'm afraid I have bad news. Arthur was seriously unwell. It appears he had acute appendicitis. His appendix burst and his body was overwhelmed by the infection; it simply couldn't stand the strain. There was nothing I could do.' He paused. His words felt dry, meaningless but his deep-set eyes betrayed both guilt and sorrow.

'I'm so sorry Mrs Deering. Your husband …' He paused. 'Arthur is dead.'

Gina froze, her lungs slowly compressing.

'It can't be true!' She ran back upstairs. Arthur looked so relaxed, his eyes closed. She lifted a hollow hand and sobbed in disbelief. He was indeed gone. The muscles in her stomach constricted. She clutched him to her, almost dragging him out of the bed. Two arms gripped her strongly, pulling her gently backwards. She sank onto the floor. Her Arthur, her devoted, loving husband was gone forever and she was alone, with a fatherless son and an unborn baby.

Cordless

28th September 1954, 5pm
St Andrew's Hospital, Northampton
Jane is forty

Richard's tie was tight and thin, like his face. War had shrivelled him, leaving him a thread of his former self. Solitary confinement had dried him up inside and out. *Will Jane recognise me?* His heartbeat quickened, banging frantically against his ribs as if looking for an escape.

The nurse looked at him suspiciously, 'Through the double doors, down the corridor, third door on your right.'

The white-tiled floor, clean and shiny, added cruelly to his sense of guilt. He reached her room and looked in, his hand resting cold on the metal doorknob. Wind was attacking the windowpane, determined to create a draught, but the room itself was quiet and full of her.

A frosted glass figure of Madonna and Child stood on the mantelpiece. Framed William De Morgan tiles hung, slightly askew, on either side of the mirror. A faded leather-bound diary lay discarded on the bedside table.

'Jane?' His voice was hoarse.

She was sitting at the window looking out. He could see the back of her head, a multitude of grips struggling to conquer thick, dark curls, some turning grey now but just as uncontainable.

Should he go in? She hadn't moved.

He hovered, a pendulum in the doorway: caught between leaden feet and his raw, pulsing heart. A few strides and he would be there, in front of her, blocking out the darkness that spread beyond the window frame. With gentle fingertips, he touched her neck, felt the jut and rub of her cheekbones against his, blinked wisps of dark hair away from his eyes as her head rested on his shoulder, but she, what would she remember when she saw him? Would she look straight through him like the ghost he was or worse still, scream for help? His breath caught sharply in his throat as if he had swallowed nails and his hand slipped into his pocket, flicked open a cardboard lid and teased out an anti-asthma cigarette.

'No smoking in the corridors.'

The cigarette jumped through his fingers. He fumbled with the packet, shoving it out of sight before crouching down to pick up the cigarette. It had crossed the line into her room.

The corridor fell silent again. *They have eyes in the walls here,* he thought, straightening up. Still not a breath from Jane; she seemed almost immobile. She held her head awkwardly as if there was a crick in her neck, fingers clutching the arms of her chair, white knuckles. If he could just get far enough into the room before she turned. If he could just take her hands in his before she faltered.

He sensed her shiver, propped up by cushions that merely concealed her discomfort, her displacement in this room, this place. Where was her footstool, the crackle and warmth of the fire at her feet, the newspaper on her lap, slipping gently to the floor as she dozed off? Where was the decanter, the diamond-cut glass, the rippling laugh that—

Stop! he thought, *There's no point reliving the past.* What he had to know was whether there was some way, some realistic way, he could get her out.

28th July 1914, 12pm
Picketswood Hall, Surrey
Before Jane's birth

Sir Stanley twiddled his moustache, teasing it out, twisting it round. Three months since his son Arthur's death and still his widow was inconsolable. He watched her move around the house, picking things up and putting them down somewhere else: a silver-backed hairbrush placed on the hall table; a large leather blotter discovered in the dining room. If she would just be still for a while he could talk to her. His son had been gentle, sensitive – too feminine in his view – but he had provided a firm foundation for his family. Now that he was gone, it was up to Sir Stanley and his wife to shore up that foundation and so far it was proving difficult.

To compound matters there had been an escalation of tension at the Colonial Office. He kept being dragged up to London to discuss German railways of all things. *The Germans are sticking their big noses over too many borders*, the diplomats fumed. A railway from Berlin to Baghdad, connecting Berlin to the Persian Gulf, was too great a threat to ignore. Sir Stanley assured his Colonial Office colleagues that the Germans would struggle to construct a route through the great Taurus Mountains but their hackles were up and, like wolves at a carcass, they kept gnawing the issue until it became blood red and threatened to split open.

Burrowed, mole-like, in his study at Picketswood, Sir Stanley let go of his moustache and picked up his morning paper. *All most depressing*, he thought, *how's a fellow supposed to retire peacefully when the papers are full of assassinations and international quarrels? All this posturing over railways is just a fig leaf for the real trouble, and that's the diplomats themselves.*

'We're entangled in a nasty mess and instead of seeking a way out we're weaving a stronger web.' That was what his friend at the Foreign Office had said last week and it looked as if he were right. *What's the good of an alliance if it carries you into trouble rather than scooping you out of it?* thought Sir Stanley. *The quarrel next door simply becomes your own.*

A sharp knock on the door shook Sir Stanley out of his reverie.

'Come in.'

Green, the butler, entered the room carrying a silver platter with a small note at its centre. 'Excuse me, Sir. You have a telegram from London,' said Green, handing it over.

'Thank you, Green,' said Sir Stanley, glancing briefly at the telegram, 'you may go now.'

Green left the room. The telegram lay on the platter like a grenade:

"AUSTRO-HUNGARY HAS DECLARED WAR ON SERBIA – STOP – COME UP TO LONDON – STOP – MATTER OF URGENCY."

The telegram blew an even larger hole in his domestic retirement.

Sir Stanley took a deep breath and stroked his grey beard with the edge of the beastly telegram before dropping it back on the platter. He sighed. Family matters would have to wait.

Meanwhile, downstairs, Gina was in the nursery, determined to focus on her son.

'Edmond,' Gina hoisted him into her arms with effort, plastering him with kisses. He held his head away and struggled like mad, eager to get down and back to his wooden bricks. She held on. Elsie, the family nanny, gently coaxed him into submission, offering him a rusk to chew, pulling up a chair for Gina. Gina sat there, her son in her lap, staring vacantly at the back of his head.

She shut her eyes.

She saw Arthur, ducking to avoid hitting his head on the low nursery door. Her heartbeat raced. Arthur laughed, dropping his paper on the floor, sweeping his son up, planting a kiss on his cheek, and tossing him playfully in the air. She could see his deep blue eyes; smell the polish on his shoes; brush the dust of the day off his shoulders. He loved coming home. She longed to touch his hands, pull him to her, tell him how much she wanted him here with her, now. She told him her heart was in his coffin but her mind could not leave him there; it wanted to revive him, keep him with her.

Edmond yelled and wriggled irritably on her lap. She opened her eyes.

Arthur was gone.

She felt her stomach drop sickeningly through her knees. Sensing slack, Edmond squirmed out of her arms and dashed off to build a tower, tripping over scattered bricks in his haste. Arms flailing, he knocked his head on a table as he fell. Gina was flooded with guilt. She knelt beside him, squatting uncomfortably on her swollen ankles and smothered him in her arms again. Tears flooded down her face as she struggled with her son. Elsie offered her a tissue but she pushed it away, vigorously stroking her son's head, rubbing his back. Edmond's face turned red and his cries grew louder. Gina gave up, spurned and miserable, and left the room. At which point the crying stopped.

Gina's bump and ankles were fat; the rest of her was pointy thin. Sir Stanley and Lady Deering had been patient. A few months ago, following Arthur's death, they had sent their chauffeur to meet her at the station with the Cadillac and drive her to Picketswood Hall. They were all dressed in traditional mourning and they allowed her to be quiet. They sent breakfast up to her when she failed to come down. She didn't want to be traditional, she felt frosted by the formalities, she wanted to sit and cry and bellow out her grief, but it was awkward. She was staying with her distinguished in-laws and they believed in self-control.

'Gina, dear, will you join us for lunch?' Lady Deering came across her in the corridor and stretched out her hand encouragingly, her swan-like neck and beaked nose adding dignity and elegance to her manner. Lady Deering always seemed so straight, so tall. Gina felt shrivelled, her back hunched, her feet weary. Lady Deering did the same things every day at the same time. How could she go on arranging flowers on the hall table each morning, how could she go on telling the cook how many people would eat lunch that day when she had lost her second son?

'Thank you, you're very kind,' said Gina. She knew they were worried about the baby but all she wanted to do was to lie down in her room with the curtains drawn. She resented the tiny feet jabbing at her ribs. Arthur was supposed to be here, this was his dream. She had started this with him and she had loved his excitement, his attention. Now all she was left with were the physical strains of a tiresome pregnancy and the sickening fear that she wouldn't be able to cope on her own.

Lady Deering could see Gina drifting away from her again. She would have to press her harder. This self-torture was useless. Here was a woman, a fellow suffragist, a woman she had proudly marched beside, abandoning the fight to wallow senselessly in her own grief. *Lady Lytton would be horrified*, she thought.

Lady Lytton, much to Sir Stanley's concern, had gained considerable exposure following her imprisonment disguised as a working-class seamstress, and, to his horror, he had found a copy of her book on his wife's dressing table. 'At least Mary hasn't taken to the shawl herself,' he remarked, white-faced. 'I wish they would hurry up and give women the vote. Then I'll be able to sleep again. These women put themselves in terrible danger and there's precious little one can do to stop them. Force-feeding. What were the authorities thinking?'

Spurred on by thoughts of her compatriot, Lady Deering steeled herself to intervene. *After all*, she thought, *Gina has Edmond to think of and another baby on the way. Heaven knows what nourishment that little one is getting right now. Something has to be done.* She took Gina firmly by the arm.

'My dear Gina, you must join us at lunch today. Stanley has ordered ham and is determined that you try it. We have kale and potatoes from the vegetable garden,' she paused. 'Mrs Garner is making gooseberry fool for dessert.' She scanned Gina's face, hoping, though not expecting, some spark of interest.

Gina felt heat rise to her cheeks. It seemed a simple request but for her it meant at least an hour of awkward, wretched conversation. All she wanted was to be alone but Lady Deering's hand was gripping her arm and she didn't seem in a hurry to let go.

What a relief to see Sir Stanley hurrying towards them. He looked pale. Long nights of political wrangling at the Colonial Office were obviously wearing him out. He took his wife's arm and led her away with barely a glance at Gina. *Odd*, Gina thought, *for someone normally so courteous*.

Before Lady Deering could say a word, he had motioned her towards his study. He spoke in a low voice, 'My dear I've had an urgent telegram. I must go to London immediately.'

'Really?' replied Lady Deering. 'Must you? I've just been coaxing Gina to lunch. We're having the ham you asked for.'

'I'm sorry my dear but I've already asked Barrow to fetch the carriage and pair.'

'Won't you take the motorcar?' Lady Deering asked. It really was ridiculous that Stanley continued to use the carriage for the ride to Horley station when the Cadillac would be much faster and far more comfortable. *Why does he insist it is polished every day if he won't use it?* she thought.

'Maybe you're right,' said Sir Stanley. 'I'll ask Barrow to ride behind with the carriage, in case I need it. You never know with these machines, they can be unreliable.' For a successful engineer Sir Stanley could at times be stubbornly antiquated. He led his wife into the study and closed the door.

Gina was left on her own in the corridor. Her head was throbbing. She felt a sharp, shooting pain in her stomach. She grabbed the corner of the side table to support her weight and cried out in distress.

Leaning forwards on her arms, she felt something warm and wet flood down her legs.

It was too early.

The baby couldn't arrive now, she wasn't ready, no-one was ready. It was as if the baby was demanding attention, determined to get its way, make a scene. Maybe she would lose it. She doubled up with nausea. Where was Arthur? She needed him desperately, why wasn't he here? How could he leave her to suffer this torment alone? She sank to the floor, her dress and undergarments drenched in fluid, sweat beading her forehead as the first cramp squeezed her thin frame like a vice, dropping her to all fours and pressing in till she cried out in agony and the study door whipped open.

28th August 1914, 10.20am
Picketswood Hall, Surrey
Jane is one month old

She was such a gorgeous, curly haired little bundle – Elsie wanted to sweep her up into her arms every time she saw her – but she was so thin.

Such big, blue eyes in such a tiny face, it makes you want to cry, thought Elsie. She was born into a crumbling world and she seemed uncertain how to come to terms with it. She was fragile but there was fire in her. She grabbed your finger like she would never let it go. She was Jane.

Jane needed nurturing more than any of her previous charges. Jane was dependent on Elsie for everything and it was important she didn't feel the loss that had clouded her birth and was threatening to stifle her beginning. Elsie had been with Sir Stanley Deering's family since starting work as an assistant nanny over twenty years ago – first their children, now their grandchildren. She had billowed out from a slight, quiet sixteen-year-old whose father was known to have a rough hand, to a round, red-cheeked matron with a firm, kindly voice and a calming smile that mopped up tears and coaxed out an apology. She changed the flowers in her bonnet to violets when Mr Deering died, then back to roses when Jane was born.

'She's a sensitive child,' Elsie told the assistant nanny as Jane arched her back and screamed, pushing her way to the end of her crib. Jane was like a tiny green shoot in hard-baked soil, desperate for love, poor thing. Nothing wrong with her lungs certainly but she picked up the sniffles so easily and fevers came and went with the breeze. Mrs Deering had had trouble feeding her. She couldn't bear to hold her crying baby and when the colic set in, well that was that. The wet nurse managed all right but more often than not Jane coughed it all up again. The washing line was full of wet muslins.

The wet nurse came in and Elsie handed Jane over. Edmond was out with his grandmother and cousins in the garden so Elsie smoothed out her apron and busied herself folding blankets and tidying toys. It had been a strange month. Mrs Deering came in every day, brushed her son's hair, picked through his clothes and barely glanced at the crib. *Mr Deering would have loved his daughter*, Elsie thought. *He would have bounced, sung, tickled, tossed and caught her. He would have shown her how to ride, how to swim, how to fish.*

Gina knew this. It was there, in front of her, in everything the other children did, the children who didn't need the gardener to lift them on his shoulders to pick the apples that were out of reach, who didn't ask their nannies to help them build a raft. She couldn't fill Edmond's void, let alone Jane's. Jane's large eyes accused her, jellied her stomach and made her feel a failure. *I wasn't supposed to do this on my own*, she told herself.

Gina's hair fell out in clumps. Breastfeeding had brought lumps, redness and a burning heat that could only be relieved by the application of cabbage leaves. Jane was never satisfied. She scrabbled at the nipple and failed to latch on and when she did, the tugging was unbearable, so, after a few weeks of torment, Gina abandoned her to the crib, a moon face shadowed by thick, dark hair.

Lady Deering had said, 'Elsie is good with babies; she will do what is needed,' and she was right. Elsie had bathed her, clothed her, cleaned her, rocked her, cuddled her and swaddled her. She took her on daily walks for fresh air and sunshine until Jane's skin lost its yellow pallor and developed a pinkish tint. There was a glow about Elsie and a deeper purpose in her kindly eyes. Her hair was tightly curled and her clothes crisply ironed.

In the nursery, Elsie was just setting to work sweeping the train set into its wooden box when the door swung open.

'Elsie, there you are. Edmond is looking for his train. Have you seen it?' Gina's eyes swept the room, pausing momentarily on the wet nurse. She lingered in the doorway.

'Here it is ma'am.' Elsie stooped to extract the train that had come to a stop under a chair, Edmond's makeshift tunnel. There had clearly been a rock fall as it was covered with cushions.

'Thank you, Elsie.' Gina took the train and passed it to the assistant nanny who was waiting quietly in the corridor. Her eyes flicked to the baby and away again. She remembered Arthur's smile when she told him she was pregnant again. Jane was the daughter he had wanted. She saw Jane and she saw Arthur and she couldn't bear it. She left the room.

Elsie watched her go. *Give her time*, she told herself. The wet nurse finished the feed, burped the baby and handed her back. Elsie started up the nursery steps, muslin over her shoulder, one hand free to open doors, the other cradling Jane. There was nothing more peaceful, more innocent, than a baby asleep; she loved the feel of the tiny fingers, the comforting smell of lanolin and cotton wool. She kissed Jane's mass of curls, so unusual for a baby this age, stepped out the door and into the hallway, narrowly avoiding tripping on the Persian rug, carelessly folded backwards on the milk-washed marble floor. Her eyes were quick, her heart was steady and her feet didn't betray her. No child in her care would ever feel any anxiety on her account.

The hallway was long and full of mirrors. Elsie caught a glimpse of herself as she passed. A couple of hairpins had slipped from under her lace cap and a strand of dark blond hair dangled down over her ear. Wrapping her left arm firmly round Jane she pushed the hair pin back into place with her right hand. She was a good-looking woman: her chin was a little over-square and her eyebrows plain and straight, but her eyes were soft blue and her cheeks dimpled when she smiled. She felt pleased with her appearance. Not that anyone had ever noticed. Though she had thought Thompson, the head gardener, might have liked her a little. It was hard to tell. If he did, he was overly cautious. *Better to find a man who is a bit more forthright*, she sighed inwardly. Still, there was plenty to keep her occupied and anyway, she couldn't leave Jane.

Jane's pram was large and black with thin spoke wheels and a fold-up hood. Elsie tucked her in on all sides with pink-frilled blankets and pulled down the hood to keep off the sun. Jane didn't wake but yawned and shifted lazily. She had been a fretful sleeper at first but she was beginning to settle. She liked to be tightly wrapped.

The pram rattled noisily over the gravel path, leaving tracks between stones where the earth showed through. Elsie could see the other Deering grandchildren playing in the orchard. Their nannies were standing by the hedge, watching out for their charges as they hung from branches and hid behind trunks, smears of lichen flecking their clothes and faces, providing natural camouflage as they dashed around. Elsie smiled to see Edmond's curly head bobbing around with his cousins and stopped at a distance so that Jane would not be woken.

Someone came up the path behind her pushing a wheelbarrow. *It needs oiling*, she thought, the rusty squeak scratching at her ear like a nail on a blackboard. *Better push Jane on round the path.* She heaved the pram into motion but the squeak soon caught up with them. It was Alfred Thompson with a barrow full of brambles. He stopped by her so she stopped too. He was a mystery this man; he took forever to get words out, but she liked the wrinkles around his eyes and the tough, ploughed rouge of his cheeks, and he went to some trouble to be complimentary whenever he saw her. She noticed he had dandelion wisps in his beard, probably from showing the children how to tell the time by blowing away seeds. A canny spider tiptoed daintily round the brim of his hat. He had rolled up his sleeves and his bare arms were covered in bramble cuts. His gardening gloves were clearly too short – if he had worn any at all, which she doubted from the state of his hands.

'Morning, Miss Rogers,' he said, tipping his hat and the spider at her. It spun swiftly back up its line, installing itself inside as he placed his hat back on his head. *Oh well*, Elsie thought, *maybe it's a money spider, bringing him good luck.*

'Morning, Mr Thompson. It's a fine day to be working outside. I was just watching the children in the orchard and thinking how blessed we are to enjoy such sunny weather.'

Alfred smiled. She was a lovely woman. He wished he were more confident. There might not be much time for him to get his feelings out. He had to say something now. Now or never, that was the saying. Tell her how much you like her, his brother had said. Tell her in case the world goes crazy. He could feel the words catching in his throat, clogging on his tongue, congesting in his mouth. *I really like you, I really do. You're the one for me. Apple-cheeks, sweet-looking, eyes like whirlpools, drawing me in.*

Elsie waited for his reply. He seemed to be brewing something inside but it looked as if she would have to tip him upside down to get it out.

'Well, we'd better keep moving. The motion is good for the baby. I expect you're on your way to the compost heap?' she said and then wished she hadn't. She sounded as if she was trying to get rid of him.

'Oh … I mean, yes,' he mumbled, looking at his boots. The compost heap. He *was* on his way there. *Not the best time to start a romantic conversation perhaps but probably better than on my return.*

He looked up and caught her eye. His tummy lurched as it did when he rode the hay cart and they went over a bump.

'I expect you've heard the news,' he said, scratching the back of his sun-scorched neck nervously.

'You mean about the war? Something new?'

'Well yes, but no, nothing new,' he said, and paused. *What a fool I am*, he thought, *maybe I should start again.*

Elsie looked at him: a shy, awkward man, steamrolling his words and burning big holes in his sentences. She wanted to help him, steer him away from the war, back to her, or was that entirely wrong? Now it was her turn to feel flustered. Luckily, she had given him enough time to plough on.

'I mean, well, I might get called up at some point or I suppose I might volunteer,' he said, 'The men are all talking about it and—' He stopped again, unsure. She looked as if she was frowning, or was she just squinting? He was keeping her standing in the sun for too long.

The sun was in Elsie's eyes. She shaded them with her hand and looked at him, he seemed downcast, deflated. 'Everyone says the war won't last long and it won't come to that,' she said.

'Even so, I'd like the chance to do my duty,' he said, thinking, *this is all wrong, I've started by digging when I wanted to sow. What a clodhopper I am.*

'I hope you won't have to all the same,' she said and blushed. She was being more open than him. How embarrassing. He looked confused. She looked away.

'Thank you,' he said, 'I mean, it's nice to know you—' he hesitated, did she really?

'Yes,' she said and he knew she meant it.

'I have some roses to deadhead this afternoon. Do you think you might join me?' he said, taking a leap towards something new.

She paused. If Jane was asleep it might be possible but what about Edmond? No, they would have to leave it for now, she needed time. This was rushed, impractical. 'I'd like to. I really would. But the children must come first,' she replied.

'You're right,' he said, his heart tightening up as if someone had roped it with bindweed. 'I hope I haven't taken up too much of your time. I hope we'll talk again soon.'

'Of course we will,' she said. Her head felt woozy, she had forgotten to put on her sun bonnet and she needed a drink.

He tipped his hat at her again and pushed off with his rusty barrow, its rhythmic squeak painfully persistent.

That wasn't what I wanted, she thought miserably, *but I don't know what I expected and I wasn't exactly encouraging.* She wished he hadn't spoken about the war, but it was clearly on his mind, on all their minds, these men. Were they afraid, or excited or both? Please God it would be over before they were all dragged in. She looked up. Not a cloud in the sky and the heat was just too much. The baby wriggled uncomfortably. What was she doing keeping her in the sun all this time, what was she thinking?

She set off towards the house but the rattling that had soothed the baby on their way out was now an irritation; her eyes scrunched, her lips parted and she wailed. Elsie's shoulders ached, the pram vibrated through her arms up her neck and her head throbbed. She reached the back door with relief, scooped Jane out of the pram and went inside, leaving the pram in the porch.

She held Jane close, gently patting her back, calming her down. Jane coughed up some milk on her shoulder. She seemed to have absorbed the odd mix of tension and excitement in the air and it was not doing her any good. Elsie was worried for her. Here at Picketswood, tucked away in the countryside, surrounded by sturdy red brick walls and stoutly fenced meadows, with an extended family planted protectively around her, she might have a chance to grow. As long as this war didn't tear it all up. She shuddered. *Best to cool off inside for now.* She headed towards the nursery and her favourite rocking chair. At least there they had peace.

28th September 1954, 4pm
Kensington, London
Jane is forty

Edmond was getting into his car. He paused momentarily as he always did before setting off to see his sister. It was hard sometimes, that setting off, the drive from his life to hers. It hadn't been like that at first. There had still been hope. Now there was just the nagging guilt that he could only visit once a month and the depressing certainty that there would be no change.

It felt particularly difficult to leave today. His children had been so happy when he came home earlier than usual. *They will know about her when they are old enough.* The silent creeping sadness he was accustomed to now, closed in on his throat again. *When they are old enough to understand.* The journey took two hours from London, sometimes by train, sometimes by car. It was a lonely secret and it cut into his smile when the children bounced into his arms with their fun, laughter and noise. *Photos are enough for Jane. It's the right thing to do,* he thought, opening the car door and sliding into the driver's seat.

He turned the key in the ignition. The top mirror was twisted. The children were always clambering around in the front and knocking it. Whatever its faults, however many times the indicator flipper got snapped off when someone leapt out in a hurry, the Morris Minor was an improvement on the rickety old Morris Cowley he'd been driving in the 1930s, whenever his step-father had let him have it.

Before putting the car in gear, Edmond reached into his pocket, taking out the letter again. It had been gathering dust bookmarking an old copy of *Tess of the d'Urbervilles* Jane had lent him years ago for the train to boarding school. She'd always been thoughtful like that, though maybe it wasn't quite the right choice of book for the journey. It certainly hadn't helped his depression at the time.

"I hope I may always be able to share your sorrows and in this way do something to lighten them", Jane had written.

If only he could do the same for her. But her sorrows were unseen. They were buried deep within. They always had been. That was part of the problem. By the time she snapped, it was too late to help. He could see her now sitting in her room, staring out of the window and shivering as though the world's pains were her own. He wondered what she saw out there. He hoped what he always hoped when he visited her. That she would turn to him and smile. *Maybe this time*, he thought. *Maybe this time she'll remember.*

Heart Rip

10th June 1918, 3pm
Picketswood Hall, Surrey
Jane is nearly four

She was collecting eggs. Nanny Elsie had given her a small wicker basket and was watching from a distance as she rummaged around the hen house, sticking a hand, then an arm, into the straw and feeling for the smooth, warm shell. They were delicate these eggs; they had to be scooped up gently and nestled in the basket where they were comforted by a soft blanket of moss. The boys were rough. They wanted the rotten ones, the ones that floated sadly in the tub when you dropped them in. They didn't care so much about the fresh ones, though they did like to eat them. Jane didn't like to eat them, she felt sorry for them. Besides, she didn't like the way the yolk dripped out and down the side when you dipped in a toast soldier: better to have the soldier with jam; jam stayed where it was put.

Jane liked to bring the eggs to the kitchen with Nanny. Cook was so pleased to see her, she blew Jane a kiss. Jane shrank back into Nanny's skirts and smiled – a soft, shy beam that grew large and sparkled across her face like a firefly. The kitchen was full of steam; pea soup was simmering, fogging up the windows, trailing tendrils of vapour across the ceiling and out through the door, an unstoppable mist that would filter round the house, room by room. Food was home-grown now and Cook used what she had. Jane didn't care for pea soup but she put on a brave face and hid her dislike. She tugged gently at Nanny's skirt. *Time to go back outside.*

Someone knocked on the kitchen door, a heavy knock that shook the wood. George Harris stooped as he entered to avoid banging his balding head on the oak above. His trousers were splattered in mud and his cotton shirt was buttoned to the top despite the heat. He held his cap in one hand and a basket full of carrots in the other.

'Afternoon Mrs Garner, Miss Rogers,' he said, nodding to Cook then Nanny. 'I've brought the latest pickings from the garden. Shall I set them on the table?'

George was in his late fifties and smoked a pipe. His skin was crinkled and browned like greaseproof paper when the cake is turned out. He had taken over from Alfred Thompson after Alfred was called up. In a short space of time, he had planted more potatoes than pebbles on the beach – enough to feed the village he said, with some satisfaction. Cook thought it a shame to use all the space for potatoes so he had given way a little and stuck in some carrots, peas and such like to keep her happy, but he was a decidedly meat and potatoes sort of man as you could tell by the size of him. Jane thought his nose looked a bit like a potato. Maybe if you ate too much of something you started to look like it, the way people looked like their pets – though Jane was sure she didn't look like her guinea pig, whatever her brother Edmond said.

Elsie missed Alfred though she never said so. She was just a bit quiet when George was around. George, however, did not notice; his head was firmly planted in the garden where he was totally at ease.

'Thank you Mr Harris,' said Cook, as George set the carrots down on the table.

'Ah, I see someone's been gathering eggs,' said George, picking one up and examining it. Jane shifted anxiously as he turned it round in the light.

George smiled at her, 'Don't worry lass, I won't drop it, I've been cultivating a safe pair of hands for many years; they're made of moss when it comes to eggs, just like your basket,' he said, reassuringly, putting the egg back in its place. 'In fact, I've got another egg I'd like to show you if you've got time,' he continued, winking at Elsie. Elsie looked unsure. 'It's a barn swallow's egg. The boys will envy you to bits with that in your collection.'

Elsie wasn't sure this was a good thing, besides, Jane didn't have a collection, but Jane took her hand and looked at her pleadingly with her big solemn eyes and she thought, *well why not.*

'We'd like to take a look, thank you, Harris,' said Jane, squeezing Elsie's hand. She wondered if the egg would be large and spotty or small and plain. She could start a collection just like Edmond's only her eggs would be polished and kept in a glass case with straw and moss so they thought they were still outside and felt at home. Edmond's were in a dark wooden box, shut away and lonely and no-one could see them unless he let them.

George smiled. 'All right then, come this way. Afternoon, Mrs Garner,' he said, and ducked out of the room.

Jane blinked as they came out the back door into the sunlight. She decided to hop and skip her way to the barn. It was fun this egg collecting. Elsie's hand bobbed backwards and forwards as Jane swung along the path like a kite in the breeze, the blue bow in her hair bouncing up and down in her springy curls.

The barn loomed before them, huge slabs of straw stacked high at the sides like the massive stone walls of the city cathedral. The barn was altogether more welcoming than the cathedral though with loose chaff strewn across the floor and the smell of warm hay and animal droppings softening its vastness.

'Just over here,' said George, leading them towards the darkest corner. Jane hesitated in the streak of light left by the door but decided not to let the darkness put her off. She stepped forward again, letting go of Elsie's hand in case she didn't want to follow. George reached up into the corner and put his hand into a small, neat nest made of mud and grass. There, cushioned in his palm, was a large creamy egg with a splatter of brown spots as if someone had flicked it with a paintbrush. It was beautiful.

'Best take it now before the bird comes back,' said George. Jane drew back her hand. She had forgotten about the bird.

George noticed her uncertainty, 'It's all right, they lay them all the time, just like the hens,' he reassured her.

Elsie frowned but decided not to interfere; it would only confuse Jane. Jane smiled and took the egg gingerly, placing it in her basket. It was so exciting to be starting a collection. She sat down cross-legged on the floor so she could examine it better.

'There you are,' said a small voice. Edmond skipped and scuffed his way into the barn, kicking up bits of straw with his leather shoes and aeroplaning his way towards Jane and Elsie. 'We've been looking for you everywhere.'

Elsie looked round and saw the tall, thin figure of Gina hovering behind him.

'What are you doing?' said Edmond, peering over Jane's shoulder.

'I've started my egg collection,' said Jane.

'Oh, right,' said Edmond. He knew he should be pleased for her, but surely he was the egg collector of the family. 'What egg have you got there?'

'It's a barn swallow's egg. Harris found it for me.'

'A barn swallow's egg. But that's one of the eggs I need for my collection. Harris said I could have it if he found one.'

Four pairs of eyes glared at George who shrugged, 'I can't take more than one or the bird won't come back next year. I'm sure I'll find another nest soon.'

'But you said they were very rare, Harris,' said Edmond.

'Oh no,' said Jane with a determined shake of her curls, 'they're not rare, barn swallows lay them like hens, all over the place, Harris just told me.'

George said nothing, unsure how to unknot the situation, aware that he couldn't just leave, and hoping Gina and Elsie would step in quickly. He had forgotten children were so complicated; that they had memories like squirrels. Life was easier when you focused on the day-to-day. It was time to go and weed the flower beds.

Elsie looked at Gina but she seemed to be holding back so Elsie said, 'I'm not sure they're exactly like hens, they are wild birds Jane, but I am sure Harris will find another one given time and that one definitely goes to Edmond.'

Edmond did not look happy at this and he turned to Gina, 'Mummy, I don't think it's fair.'

Don't take sides Gina, thought Elsie. *Life isn't fair Edmond, you know that, you have to share with your sister* – and she was just about to tell him so, when Gina said, 'Well, it does sound like Harris promised the egg to Edmond first, Jane,' and Jane burst into tears.

Gina flushed but she had already decided on her course of action and she picked up the egg and gave it to Edmond, 'Jane there's really no need to cry. Elsie can you take her into the house, we need to get cleaned up for tea.' She turned to leave the barn but Edmond was standing sheepishly next to Jane. He knelt down and put the egg back in her basket.

'You can have the egg, Jane,' he said.

'Oh well done, Edmond,' said Gina, turning round and looking pleased. 'That is good of you. Jane, thank your brother, you can have the egg now.'

Jane's bottom lip quivered. She stared at the egg as if it was really rather rotten after all and then ran full pelt out of the barn to find somewhere to hide.

Elsie looked at Gina. *She has no idea what she has done. She'll want me to go after Jane next.*

'Goodness me! What a fuss to make over something so small,' Gina said. 'Jane must learn that she can't have everything her own way, Elsie.'

True, but she rarely does, Elsie thought.

'I'll let you find Jane,' Gina continued before turning to her son, 'Come Edmond, it's time for tea,' but Edmond was not at her side. He was edging out of the barn in the direction taken by his sister. Gina marched over to him and grabbed his hand. Then she started off towards the house, tugging her son along behind her. Edmond was still wailing as the door closed behind them.

Elsie rubbed her forehead with the back of her hand as if wiping away the frown that was brewing and hurried off to find Jane.

The egg sat alone in its basket in the middle of the barn, neglected but not forgotten.

5pm

The raft was made of driftwood, knotted together by a long piece of twine that cut into the hands when you tugged it tight. It belonged to Edmond's cousin, William, but Edmond had helped build it, he told everyone proudly. They were allowed to push off together in the duck pond but only if grown-ups were present. Jane was definitely not allowed on the raft. Edmond would have let her but Nanny Elsie said no and besides, Jane didn't like the water; her lips went purple and she shivered uncontrollably till someone wrapped her in a towel and took her inside.

They had just had tea in the nursery but the sun was still out and Edmond was inspecting the raft which had one rotten board and a section of twine that had rubbed raw on the wood and was fraying rapidly. He couldn't wait for William to come back from boarding school so that they could mend it together. Jane was sitting near him on a blanket arranging her tea set while Elsie unclipped the washing from the laundry line nearby. He had given Jane a hug before tea and made up for the egg incident. She was quiet but she had perked up when he suggested going out to the duck pond. She brought her Japanese doll in its red kimono and set it down on the blanket opposite her. Then she poured one tiny cup of tea for her doll, one for Elsie, one for herself and one for Edmond. He was forgiven.

Edmond took his leather shoes and cotton socks off, laid them on the blanket and hopped over to the pond to dip his toes in the water. He pushed them through the weeds, letting long, silky strands of duckweed slip across his feet and between his toes. He couldn't resist edging them down into the soft, gloopy mud at the side, warm at the top and deliciously cool underneath. He brushed his hands over the water's surface, skimming like the water boatmen but creating a ripple of current where they made none. A dragonfly batted busily to and fro, its diamond eyes glinting mischievously in the sunlight. It landed on Edmond's shoulder but was off again before he had the chance to tell anyone.

Edmond glanced over at the house. He could see Harris clipping back the wisteria that dripped over the sitting room windows like an overgrown fringe. In the distance, the hay cart was coming back from town. Its wheels always appeared on the point of falling off, twisting and turning through the gravel, spitting the smaller stones up onto the grass like an axe sending sparks from a grindstone as it trundled along. As it neared the front door, a stranger jumped out, wearing an old-fashioned grey suit which looked as if it had been patched up several times. *He's a grey-looking man altogether*, thought Edmond. The stranger's hair was feathery and silver like ash and looked as though it might blow away with the next breeze. His face was slate-cold despite it being summer but maybe he didn't get out much. He clearly hadn't eaten for some time, his cheeks were hollow. In his hands he held a flat cap which he couldn't stop twisting. He knocked on the front door but no-one answered so he walked over to Harris who stopped what he was doing. They went inside together.

Edmond looked over at Elsie. She hadn't noticed. She was singing *Ring-a-Ring-a-Roses* to Jane and her laundry pile was now tower-high. He pulled his toes out of the mud quickly, making a delightful slurping sound as he did so, oozing the mud out from the nooks but not his nails which were satisfyingly black, and wiping it off on the grass. The sun was starting to set, challenged rudely by a growing huddle of clouds that threatened to smudge out its glory and end the day's fun early. He decided to perform a sun dance, skipping round Jane's blanket and pulling her up to dance with him. She joined in giddily, stomping her feet and tossing her curls – until he swung her too wildly and she tripped over her feet. She picked herself up and reached out for his hands but he was looking at the house. It was strange; they were drawing the blinds in the nursery and it wasn't time for bed yet.

Elsie unclipped the last sheet and dropped the pegs in the basket. She folded the sheet roughly, to be ironed later, and placed it on the pile. She smoothed out her apron and smiled at Edmond and Jane. She was glad to see them playing together, Edmond was very affectionate but he liked to take the lead and Jane often preferred her own space, finding his enthusiasm a bit overbearing. It was almost time to take them in but they looked so happy, she didn't want to interrupt their fun just yet.

The kitchen door at the side of the house opened and Harris came out. He was an odd man but he meant well. He wasn't a patch on Alfred Thompson for skill or kindness but he kept the garden growing and did what was necessary. She certainly hadn't warmed to him on arrival when he buried Edmond's guinea pig without letting him know it had died, and dug up the buddleia bush, which had been such fun during butterfly season, to extend the herb garden still further. *He's too practical and not nearly romantic enough to be a gardener*, she thought. *You need to balance your berries with your beauties to be truly skilled.*

Harris was halfway across the lawn and clearly coming towards them when Elsie noticed the blinds in the nursery. It was far too early for them to be drawn. Her throat felt dry. She remembered the telegram that arrived from the War Office announcing the death of the children's second cousin at the Somme. He had led his men bravely and been awarded the Military Cross. It was as simple as that. Elsie guessed all telegrams read similarly. There was no knowing what was really happening but the telegrams were piling up high and painful all around them like the barbed wire used to line the trenches.

Harris approached but his eyes were lowered. He held his hat in his hand and wore a black armband. *Surely he didn't have that with him just in case he needed it?* If someone had died, he had only just heard about it, it seemed too quick, she didn't even know who it was yet, he would scare the children.

Edmond and Jane stopped playing and stared. The sun was encased by clouds and Jane was suddenly cold. Elsie knelt beside her and helped her put her blue coat on.

'Evening, Miss Rogers,' said George.

'Evening, Mr Harris.'

'Can I have a word?'

'Edmond, will you help Jane pack up her tea set and take it inside please? I will follow you both in with the laundry.'

'But what about my raft?'

'Mr Harris will bring it in for you.'

Edmond nodded seriously. He knew that he needed to do what she said; something had happened.

Elsie and George stepped back while the children packed up the toys. Elsie gathered up the laundry, delaying the conversation, making it hard for George to begin.

'Alfred Thompson is dead, Miss Rogers,' he whispered. 'I'm so sorry – I know you knew him well. His father brought us the news, poor man. Alfred was on the front line at Aisne. He died bravely protecting other soldiers they said.'

'Of course,' said Elsie and a tear rolled down her cheek. She put the laundry down and gripped her apron tightly. She wanted to collapse and scream out the grief that was shelling her heart to pieces, piercing holes in her defences and closing her in on all sides but she choked it in. She held onto it. It was there inside, trapped, stabbing wildly at her chest, trying to get out. It couldn't escape. The children needed calm. They were still packing up. She sucked in air.

'Thank you for telling me, Mr Harris. I knew something terrible had happened when I saw the blinds.'

'Can I help you with the laundry?'

'No, I can manage, thank you,' Elsie said. She had to keep ticking, get through to nightfall, to her bedroom at least.

George went over to Edmond's raft and Edmond followed him. There was a crash. Jane had dropped the tea set; it was too awkward for her. Elsie set down the laundry and swept Jane up into her arms.

She heard Edmond's voice, 'Has someone died, Harris?'

Children always knew.

George looked at Elsie. Elsie would have to tell them. She put Jane down and motioned to Edmond to join her. He perched on her knee.

'Alfred Thompson has died in battle. He died bravely defending his country and we are all proud of him,' she said, sticking to the rulebook.

'Was it a quick death?' said Edmond.

'Let's go inside and see your grandparents,' Elsie said. 'Leave the toys here for now. Mr Harris will bring them in for us later.'

Edmond jumped up and took her hand, tugging Elsie up but Jane squeezed out of her arms and ran off towards the sandpit.

'Mr Harris can you take Edmond in to his mother please?'

George nodded and stuck out a hand.

Elsie ran after Jane.

Jane was clinging to the climbing rope near the sandpit. She was half way up. Elsie knew that she could easily hang there for half an hour as she had done when they found out about Edmond's guinea pig.

'Jane, please come down, it's time for bed. There's a cup of hot milk waiting for you inside. It's getting cold out here. You can climb the rope in the morning.'

'I want to stay here. I don't want to go in and hear about Mr Thompson.'

'Come down and talk to me Jane, come on, I need a cuddle.'

Jane clung on and Elsie burst into tears.

28th September 1954, 5.05pm
St Andrew's Hospital, Northampton
Jane is forty

The visitor left the room and Jane could hear him talking to the nurse. She was scared. She didn't recognise his voice. She had been re-reading her diary and she wanted to stay there. She didn't want the watchers to come back. She had to hide, withdraw entirely, so she closed her eyes when he came in and focused on her fingers and toes but she couldn't block his voice out and she couldn't move to shut the door without alerting him.

'I'd like to talk to her but I'm worried she won't know me,' Jane heard him say.

'I'm worried she won't know you too, she's been calmer since taking the new medicine. You might just shake her up again,' replied the nurse.

'So you don't think I should have come?'

'I'm not saying that. She doesn't get many visitors. Just watch out for any signs of stress and call me if she becomes overly anxious. You may notice slight spasms in her eyes and jaw, these are perfectly normal.'

Normal, Jane thought, *what is normal?* In this place you were normal if you said and did very little but surely that wasn't normal. She spun this round in her brain for a while till it webbed over like so many of her thoughts and left her feeling lost and alone.

'Can I ask what treatment she has had? I'd like to be prepared before I go in.'

'Recently or since she's been here?' the nurse replied. She wasn't going to review the whole of the patient's history with this man, besides, she wasn't sure what he was supposed to know.

'Just an overview and what she has had recently. When I last saw her I thought she was recovering.'

'You'll have to see the doctor or talk to the family. We don't use shocks anymore. That's all I can say. She's calmed down a lot. She used to talk about …' the nurse paused. 'Anyway, now she doesn't say much at all, just reads her diary, writes in it sometimes.'

'So if I'm in her diary, she might remember me.'

'I don't know when you last saw her, but maybe. Now if you don't mind, I need to get on with my rounds, there are other patients requiring my attention.'

'Of course,' he said as she turned and walked swiftly down the corridor, her polished shoes clicking curtly on the floor as she went.

Jane turned her chair towards the window slowly so as not to make much noise. She hated that sound, the cold, clinical tapping of those shoes; it reminded her of the hospital Elsie went to, except there were many shoes there, many people and no peace. At least here it was quiet, but there was too much time to think and sometimes her thoughts twisted in her mind like a corkscrew, burrowing in and pinching her nerves, leaving her frightened and jumpy; like the time she saw faces outside the window, clouding it up with their breath; or the time she opened her cupboard and saw a man in a long, dark trench-coat inside.

She used to tell her sister-in-law about the watchers just to get them out of her head. She could tell from the look on her face that she didn't understand but then it didn't make sense to Jane either. *When did all this start*? she wondered. She felt her jaw tighten as if pulled back by an invisible elastic band, and loosen again. A spasm vibrated through her neck. Her diary might help. There could be something in there that would help her remember who she used to be, something that would help her to get out of here – get out of this space she was in, wrapped up in a spider's web of panic and medication, weaving slowly round her throat and brain until she couldn't breathe, couldn't think. *I do have a past,* she thought. *I don't want to hide from it.* She turned her head towards the door, but the man had gone.

Black Thursday

24th October 1929, 7pm
Kensington, London
Jane is fifteen

It was half-term. Jane stepped out of the car. Edmond was sitting on the doorstep, waiting. He jumped up, gave Jane an enormous squeeze and a peck on the cheek and dragged her inside immediately to inspect their new Slazenger tennis rackets, leaving their step-father to carry in her case.

'Hello, mother,' Jane said as Edmond tugged her through the hall.

'Hello, Jane,' said Gina. They were like a whirlwind when they were together, those two, hard to keep track of, not that she really tried. It was easier to tend to plants in the greenhouse than follow their giggles and whispers, scrapes, bruises and endless high jinks. Charles was coming in through the door with Jane's case. He barely lifted it over the doorstep before setting it down. Gina flicked open the lid. Jane could never learn how to pack. She was only home for a week and yet she had brought her whole bookshelf with her in amongst a raggle-taggle of unfolded clothes. Gina closed the lid, motioned Charles on and resigned herself to another week of turmoil.

In the drawing room, Jane admired her new wooden racket, its strings taut and even. She had to admit that Charles was occasionally generous but spending a whole week in his company would be testing. If she was to liken him to an animal it would certainly be a hedgehog, a ball of nerves that prickled when prodded.

Jane remembered Elsie's hand on her knee in the cab on the way back from school, when Gina told them she was getting married again. Edmond sat on his hands and pursed his lips, just as he had done a few years earlier when Gina announced they were moving away from Picketswood and back to London.

When they discovered that their step-father-to-be was none other than Edmond's deputy headmaster, the cab began to feel like a furnace. Elsie had wound down a window but Gina had carried on talking. She was sure the children would benefit greatly from a father figure. After the wedding they would all go on holiday to Scotland together. What fun that would be.

Edmond had stared out of the window. *He doesn't like Mr Cuthbert,* Jane had thought. *Why would he want to go on holiday with him?* Jane remembered the way Gina had stood nudging Mr Cuthbert at Edmond's sports day, smiling under her wide brim hat. Edmond had missed his catch. Gina had laughed at something. Edmond had stomped off the pitch.

Now they had been back in London for several years and Charles had finally retired – 'to spend more time at home with us', Gina had said – but Jane guessed it hadn't really been his decision. He became as grumpy as a toad in the sun, spending more and more time in his study or in the rockery at the back of the house, which, to be fair, he did manage to improve, planting a kaleidoscope of poppies, irises, grape hyacinths. Life was better for all when he was outside.

Charles missed playing cricket with the boys, teaching Latin, taking tea with the headmaster. At home he was no longer the umpire: he was in the stands. The children looked away when he spoke to them – he could never tell if they were listening or not – and their nanny hovered in the background like a toothache. *It is a shame,* Charles thought, *that Elsie has to live with us now that the children are at full-time school.* He was on the verge of talking to Gina about it when the children came home for the holidays and he remembered that they did need her after all.

Jane and Elsie shared a room at the top of the narrow townhouse in Kensington. The room had very little to recommend it to an outsider, a breeze ran right through it, but Elsie's photographs of the children as babies sat in silver frames on the dressing table and the tiny bedspreads she had knitted years ago lay neatly over each bed.

It was almost time for supper and Charles was a stickler for punctuality but Jane wanted to see Elsie, sit with her and unwind after the long journey home. *It's very quiet,* Jane thought as she reached the top of the stairs, *maybe she's taking a nap.* Elsie sometimes went upstairs to read and Jane had often found her asleep mid-page. She pulled off her shoes, leaving them on the stair by the banister, stepped over the creaky floorboard and turned the door handle.

The room was dark as usual, but Elsie had turned on both bedside lights and the curtains were open, letting in a sliver of moonlight. Elsie was sitting hunched on the bed. Her blouse was lying next to her and the old-fashioned stays she always wore were loose. She looked up and saw Jane, grabbed her blouse and yanked it down over her head so hard a button popped off and went flying across the room. Jane picked it up and Elsie took it back, putting it on her bedside table without saying anything. Then she reached behind to tighten her stays. As she tugged the lace she winced.

'What's wrong?' said Jane.

'I'm fine, Jane,' Elsie replied.

'But you look like you're in pain. Are those stays rubbing your skin? We should loosen the suspenders.' Jane reached over to help adjust the straps.

Elsie removed her hand and held onto it. Her blouse flapped open where the button had popped off and Jane saw a large red welt. *Why does Elsie continue to wear stays if they leave such marks*?

'You've got a huge bruise on your chest!'

'I'm sorry Jane. You weren't supposed to see that.'

'You must see a doctor.'

'I have seen a doctor.'

'But can't he give you something to help? Surely he has cream, something to soothe it?'

Elsie could see she was agitated but showing her the large red boil that had grown from pimple to volcano, erupting angrily all over her left breast, would not do any good. She had hoped to tell her without revealing her pain, but the dizzy spells were becoming difficult to control and sharing a room made concealment next to impossible.

'I have breast cancer. It's advanced. I'm quite resigned to it. You mustn't be upset.'

Jane said nothing. It was like being hit with a chisel, carving strips from her heart, shattering the peace she had felt when she slipped off her shoes outside. She sat down on the bed. The moonlight seeping into the room had a frosty feel. She could see condensation round the tiny window frame and the two lamps seemed dim and useless as the room closed in on them.

Why, Elsie? Why didn't you see the doctor earlier? You could have stopped this. Why are you asking me to accept it?

She wanted to find a quiet corner and let the grief pour out without worrying who might hear her but this was not Picketswood. There was nowhere to hide.

She put her arm round Elsie and held on. Elsie was still solid.

'Jane, supper time,' shouted Edmond from downstairs.

A wood pigeon cooed outside.

'Jane, are you up there?' His polished shoes hit the stairs.

'Coming,' she shouted back.

'Did you see the family doctor, Elsie? Does mother know?'

'Not yet. I saw a doctor from the local list. I've been paying for health insurance ever since the government started the scheme. It was about time I made use of it!' Elsie smiled broadly, trying to bolster her own crumbling courage. Jane looked so pale, her face a silver coin in the moonlight, flat, cold. *I must have faith in this family*, Elsie thought. *Jane has her brother. She has been well educated. She has everything to look forward to. Gina will realise that Jane needs her, that she will have to play a greater part in Jane's life. It will be good for them both. What am I worried about?*

'When will you tell Edmond?'

'Not yet. There's still plenty of time.'

Elsie's frosted Madonna and Child figurine sat silent and sightless on the chest of drawers. Jane glanced up at it. It would always be the same. Nothing else would ever be the same again. Her heart was ripped and the rip would scar.

New York and spreading

Black Thursday they called it. The day when the giant bubble – the American economy – floated less than serenely down onto an equally giant pin. The day of disillusion: the day the carpet was pulled up and the dank and stinking floorboards were revealed. The day the rabbit-scared stocks and shares fell right through them.

The very next day people thronged into the street, forming caterpillar queues outside the banks, demanding their money. It was all too late. Ticker tape fell in rolls around the feet of traders.

The men of the Rockefeller family weighed in heavily, shouting across the flea-pit and bashing the air with clenched fists stuffed full of dollars. Stocks buzzed overhead like wasps caught in an upturned bucket, angry and dangerous. Nothing escaped the communal sting when the market stopped and prices plummeted. Then they realised. No fist was large enough to fill the void – the treacherous vacuum that sucked pockets dry and depressed the hope of nations. Come Black Tuesday, $14 billion was gone in a day.

No soul could withstand the onslaught that followed. The loss was too great for many to bear. It opened up cracks. Cracks in communities. Cracks in governments. Cracks which matured and left a gap for rats to creep in. One puny rat, bruised and infuriated by the boots that had kicked it into captivity, sniffed the smoky smell of a barbecued bratwürst sausage and started to salivate. He poked out his nose tentatively to gauge the way the wind was blowing and was pleased to find it blowing towards him. He followed the smell to its source – the cavernous kitchens of the German Reichstag – and laughed raucously at the battered hobnails of the old boots as they left, stumbling out the door pitifully, pushing wheelbarrows of useless cash.

The rat was thrilled to find the kitchens empty at last, the food abandoned on the table. No-one was working there anymore. Green fuzz was growing like damp moss all over the bread. It was clearly time to feast. He screeched out invitations with shrill authoritarian shrieks, pushing his dark greasy hair back and combing down his whiskers. He dropped a few crumbs on the floor, at the table legs, and waited for the ravenous horde.

Not too long now, Hitler thought, as sharp claws scratched and scrabbled beneath him. *Not too long now and the place will be over-run*. He puffed up his chest.

The Great Depression had begun and the fate of the world was sealed.

10th January 1930, 10am
Hammersmith Hospital, London

'Her bed is at the end by the window,' said the nurse.

They stood, an uncomfortable huddle of gloves, coats, scarves and red noses, lingering in the doorway, sniffing. Edmond was inclined to wipe his runny nose on the back of his hand but Jane had a spare handkerchief. Three days had passed since Elsie had been admitted to hospital and the ward was the same confusing mix of noise and silence, the same science lab of drips and meds, machines and white aprons, pocket watches and curtains drawn swiftly round to hide the inmates. *It isn't a happy place, it is an efficient place*, Jane thought. Floors were scrubbed, pulses taken, people let in, people hurried out, a blur of ins and outs in fact to the background of a ticking clock and the heady smell of chlorine and camphor. But Elsie was peaceful.

She lay in her bed looking straight ahead of her.

They would have preferred to visit her in a private room but Charles had suggested that she would like to be with people rather than isolated on her own.

'Private rooms are hard to come by,' Charles had argued when Gina originally broached the topic, and she knew he meant expensive and unaffordable. 'Besides,' he had continued, 'wouldn't she rather be with people like her?'

'Elsie is part of the family. Shouldn't she be treated like it? She has been with the children since birth,' Gina had replied.

Charles was adamant. 'Elsie wouldn't object to the local hospital – after all, she has visited friends there before now. She'll be quite comfortable.' He gritted his teeth, 'You know I lost money in the Clarence Hatry debacle, your father-in-law wasn't the only one to see his investments crumble. Lucky he's got land to rent. The stock market isn't the bees' knees it was thought to be,' he muttered and stomped off into his study for a bit of peace and quiet.

Gina had hovered in the doorway before backing off to her favourite armchair where she buried herself in a book. *The children won't know,* she had reassured herself, *they won't realise. Besides, Charles has made up his mind.*

Elsie had asked for a word with the family after tea on New Year's Day. They all sat in the sitting room of their grand town house in Kensington. Jane had stood at the back behind Gina's chair so no-one could see her face except Elsie. She clutched the top of the chair, feeling the grip of her knuckles, the strength and energy that was hers and not Elsie's. Even now she felt she might stop the disease if she willed it, but Elsie had accepted it, it was just the pain that was causing her distress.

When Elsie finished there was silence in the room. The grandfather clock in the hall chimed five times. Edmond ran over and gave Elsie a hug and held her hands and sat beside her and Jane went and sat beside her too. Gina and Charles remained opposite them as stiff as a pair of waxworks in Madame Tussaud's. *Say something,* Jane thought. *She needs to know that you care. I need to know.*

'How far advanced is it, Elsie?' Gina had asked.

'Has the doctor suggested hospital yet?' Charles said.

'Wouldn't you like to stay at home with us?' said Edmond, turning to Elsie, keeping her hands in his.

'You need to go back to school,' Elsie replied. 'I will have to go into hospital soon,' she answered Charles, 'if the children are still on holiday they can visit me there, but it won't be for long.'

Jane said nothing. She moved in closer, living in the weight of Elsie's arm around her shoulder, the soapy smell that stuck to her clothes, the rise and fall of her chest and the soft tickle of Elsie's fingers through her hair, tucking away loose curls.

Elsie had gone into hospital three days later. Jane and Edmond took her in. Gina thought it might be distressing but there was no stopping them. The bed by the window was draughty, but at least it was quieter than the bed by the door that swung open and shut and let shards of light in at night time. Jane winced when the doctors put Elsie on a drip, but Edmond drew her in towards the bed and they watched Elsie's face smooth out, her eyes lose their pinched corners and regain their soft curve.

Jane and Edmond came back the next day. Gina had errands to run in town so Charles brought them in but he stayed outside. Doctors in white coats with clipboards passed them in a hurry. Nurses with caps pinned to their hair carried trays of soup to thin people who sat crooked against yellowing pillows. Their faces were lined, gaunt with wear and tear. Come to think of it, their clothes were rather thin too. They talked across beds in hoarse whispers. 'No, your insurance won't pay for your dependents, Mister Smith. They'll have to fend for themselves. Your wife's got family hasn't she? No? Well she's got two hands and feet then, she can work. Just tell her to keep down here in the south, there are more jobs. What, she already works? I'm not surprised looking at the state of you, sir! My son works shifts at the foundry in Bow. A sand rat they call him. Pouring moulds all day he is. I'm lucky to have him. Don't know how long I'll be stuck in here for. I may be leaving in my coffin at this rate. Who's this then, your daughter? Well, she's small isn't she.'

A little girl ran up to her father's bed as if there was no-one else in the room. Her eyes looked sunken, her skin the colour of cheese. Her shawl was patched. Her mother was nowhere to be seen. Had she come alone?

'I can't bear it Edmond!' Jane whispered. 'How can this be allowed? These people clearly need help.' The girl would waste away, catch pneumonia, die of a cough. 'Shouldn't the government be supporting them? What's the point of paying contributions if your family isn't protected?'

'I agree,' Edmond replied in a low voice. 'But you're talking about radical change, Jane, and that's not going to happen fast, not with the economy in such a state.'

Edmond always tried to be realistic – besides, he didn't want to enter into a hot-headed political discussion now, not in such a public place, a place that was witness to so much suffering. He could sense Jane grinding her teeth and sucking in her cheeks, ready to spit out the tirade she was chewing over in her mind. He tugged her arm, moving her on down the corridor towards Elsie.

'What will happen to that little girl, Edmond? She won't survive.'

'Come on, Jane. There's nothing we can do.'

'There's always something we can do, Edmond. If everyone thought like that nothing would ever change. There has to be some sort of public health system. The government should fund it.'

'The government won't fund anything right now.'

'How can we live in our big house when others are unable to feed their families?'

'We are born unequal.'

'I can't accept that. No-one should have to accept that.'

Edmond stopped walking.

'Elsie needs us, Jane. This isn't Hyde Park corner, it's a hospital. Everyone's looking at you, please!'

Eyes were crisscrossing the room, pinning Jane down in the aisle. A metal tray clattered as a nurse set it down on a table sending syringes tumbling, bandages unravelling towards the floor. She bent down to pick them up.

A cold wind whistled through a gap at the top of a window at the far end of the room – Elsie's window. Jane could sense her shivering beneath it. She batted away the eyes and walked over to Elsie's bed, straining across her to heave the sash window into its slot.

'Jane,' Elsie said, taking her hand and pulling her back to the floor. The window continued to rattle. Elsie put her finger to her lips and held onto Jane's hand. Edmond leaned over to give her a kiss.

A thin woman in a black fur coat entered the room at the far end. She was talking to a doctor. She waved at Jane and Edmond.

'She's got a week, maybe two,' the doctor told the woman.

Gina thought it best not to say anything to the children; they were due back at school the next day, no reason to upset them further. *Besides,* she thought, *there will be arrangements to make – it will be easier if they are not around.* There they were by Elsie's bed, huddled together as tightly as penguins on a polar icecap. *It's not that cold,* thought Gina, watching from a distance as the icecap slowly melted beneath her children's feet. *It's time for them to move on, time for them to let go.*

23rd January 1930, 9.30am
Kensington, London

"Elspeth Rogers
died 19 January 1930 aged 52"
A light frost skimmed the surface of the headstone. Jane wiped the words with her hands then cupped them to her mouth, steaming away the cold. *It should say 'Elsie'. Why didn't mother talk to us first?* Jane placed a bunch of snowdrops in a glass vase and put it down beneath the words. She had wanted daffodils. There were some at the end of their garden but their buds had remained obstinately closed.

'Jane,' Gina called through the window of Charles' car.

Jane stayed by Elsie's grave. She had been prodded from breakfast to bedtime ever since she got home. *It's as if she thinks I won't get out of bed unless she pesters me,* Jane had thought when Gina rapped on her door for the third time that morning. It was hard enough to hear Charles stomping around the house in defiance of the silence that had settled with mother fluttering feebly behind him like an ailing moth, without this constant intrusion.

It was their last day together before they returned to boarding school and Gina hadn't said two decent words to her since picking her up from the station on the day of the funeral. She had sent her up to the bedroom at the top of the house without a mention of the other bed that was there, the bed with the tiny, knitted bedspread still laid out across it. Edmond had noticed. He had offered to sleep there with Jane but Jane had wanted some time on her own. Edmond had asked Charles to take Elsie's bed out of the room but he hadn't got round to it. Still, there was only one more night to go. *Maybe I will let Edmond sleep in the room with me tonight,* Jane thought.

Back at the car, Edmond watched his sister, lingering at the foot of the earthy mound. Her legs were bare beneath her long black skirt. He picked up her black shawl.

'Edmond, find out what Jane's doing. We need to get on,' Gina said before flinging her car door open, 'Jane.'

Jane looked round. Edmond, tall and angular in his black suit was walking towards her carrying her shawl and behind him Gina's pale face was emerging from the car.

Why is she always in such a rush? Why is there never any time to think? She could see her mother tapping on Charles' window. *Why did she get out if she wanted to talk to him?* Any moment now Gina would turn and stride towards them, hustling them away from the grave, back to the car, off to some luncheon somewhere so they could all pick at their food and push it around their plates for a while. *Here she comes.*

'Time to go,' Gina called out across the churchyard.

Can't she at least walk over here before giving us our orders?

A light trail of smoke drifted out of the open window on the driver's side of the car and evaporated into the air. Charles was in no hurry then.

Edmond stood with his sister looking at the grave, but Jane was already shifting her feet. Their mother was approaching. Every time she came near, Jane felt as if a net had been thrown at her head, tangling up her thoughts, turning them sour. *She doesn't care about Elsie and I can't bear to stand here with her*, thought Jane. *I can't.*

Gina reached them but before she could say anything Jane had walked away.

4.15pm

What a wretched lunch, thought Edmond. Charles had flung his coat and hat at the stand and retreated to his study. That, at least, was a relief. He had ranted on about the need to restrict trade and impose tariffs to restore economic order and it had quite put Edmond off his ham and eggs. Fair enough: he was of a different political persuasion to the rest of the family but this was not the time to ram it down their throats. The only saving grace was the fact that all this controversial talk had provoked Jane into a response, the first time Edmond had seen her fire up since they returned from school. She had been so closed off, up there in her attic bedroom – it wasn't like her not to want to talk at all. It was wonderful to see those hackles stand up again, to see her fight off her sadness, especially if it meant savaging Charles. Jane couldn't let an argument lie once she'd started. Despite Charles' retreat, she was still engaged in a debate with their mother when they came in through the door.

'Charles *does* support women's suffrage, Jane,' said Gina, defending her husband from her daughter's outrage since he was clearly unwilling to do so himself.

'Well he certainly doesn't think much of equal pay, he made that clear.'

'We're in the midst of a depression, Jane.'

'That's no reason to give up the struggle.'

'It's hardly surprising, Jane, when unemployment amongst men is so high.'

'I'm not surprised you take that view, mother. You haven't shown any interest in the women's movement since before the war, and what did you do then? You joined a few marches.'

'Those marches were crucial to the cause, Jane. It was the militant suffragettes who held us back with their hysterical behaviour.'

'They fought for what they believed in, mother.'

'It was the peaceful demonstrators who won over the public, Jane, not the women who threw stones through windows and set fire to public buildings.'

'The same women who were brutally force-fed in prison – women who were pushed to the edge of their endurance and continued to protest.'

'Only a few of the militants carried on campaigning during the war, Jane, the rest of us united behind the country.'

'But what war work did *you* do, mother?'

'Jane,' Edmond broke in, 'leave mother alone. We all know you're hurting but this isn't right.' He had been curious to see how the argument developed; conversations didn't normally last long between them, but this was becoming an all-out attack.

Jane blanched. It wasn't fair of Edmond to rebuke her. She had asked a perfectly valid question and there was something she was building up to, something she had to say and it nagged him as much as it nagged her, she knew it did. She could feel it, taste it, bitter in her mouth. She spat it out, 'Why didn't you get Elsie a private room in the hospital, mother?'

'What?'

'She died in a dormitory surrounded by suffering – terrible, awful suffering. You visited her, mother, you saw the people in beds, the people who visited them. You know how unkind the system is and you could have lifted Elsie out of it, just this once, at the end of her life. You could have done something about it but you didn't. You gave up, mother. You don't fight for anything anymore. We could have helped her to die in peace in her own room. We could have been with her. You let Charles bully you into it. You're a coward!'

'Jane, how dare you.'

Where is Charles when I need him? Gina thought. *He ought to be here to send Jane to her room.*

Jane's right, Edmond thought. *It was hideous of them to leave Elsie in the hospital when she didn't have long to live.* It had shaken him just as much as it had shaken Jane but at least he knew who to blame. 'It was Charles, Jane. It was Charles who made the decision.'

Gina opened her mouth to defend her husband but nothing came out. He wasn't there anyway. There was no point continuing the argument. It had already gone far enough. Jane didn't know when to stop. She was relentless, she really was. Edmond had given her an answer. Best to leave it be.

Jane went quiet. Gina was surprised she didn't run upstairs to her room. That was what usually happened when they had a disagreement. Who would have thought she would have such an impossible daughter. Edmond was easier to talk to. At least he knew what boundaries were. She turned to her son, 'Edmond, I think it's time for you both to pack. Will you help Jane with her bags?' Then she turned and walked back outside, away from them both, without putting on her coat.

28th September 1954, 5.15pm
St Andrew's Hospital, Northampton
Jane is forty

Richard had the letter in his pocket. He had kept it because it was the cause of his present guilt, the excuse for his departure all those years ago and he had always known that he had been wrong to leave. The letter had dug itself into his skin deeper than the shrapnel buried in his leg. He couldn't throw it away. He had been weak. He had allowed them to convince him, gone to Australia and left no trace of his existence. He had given up. He had betrayed Jane.

"5th March 1946
Dear Mr Wright,
I have been to see Jane and I have talked to her mother and Dr Nadel. It is I am afraid clear that she has been much worse this time and the treatment will have to be prolonged. In particular the after treatment must be long and strict. Dr Nadel thinks that it would be better for Jane to cut her off from her old associates including you. It is considered very important that there should be no sex complications or suggestions. As far as possible, sex should be eliminated from her life for the next two or three years. I agree

with Nadel that it would be much easier to do this if you neither see her nor write to her at present. You are too closely associated with her past life; and it is her past life that must be exorcised. Dr Nadel does not distrust you – nor do I. But at present you would remind her of her life with Walter. This is inevitable. I hope you understand.

Yours, Dr Nell Shaw."

Richard watched the nurse walk down the corridor and turned back to Jane's doorway. Her chair was over by the window, away from him, but he could just see the bob of dark curls resting to one side. She must have woken up and moved. Maybe she had dozed off again? It might be best to see the doctor before going in. The nurse was so cagey; there could be things about her treatment he needed to know before approaching her.

He remembered the last time he saw her, back in 1940. He had replayed it in his mind so many times he wondered if it was real or not. He had been relieved to see that Jane had permed her hair again and it was looking sleek and tidy. Her blue plaid dress was tied neatly with a brown leather belt and she was wearing the silk stockings he had bought her. She looked relaxed, happy even, though the bags under her eyes suggested sleeplessness. *At last, she's on the mend*, he had thought, watching for the familiar glint in her eye as he fished greedily for that butterfly smile.

He wondered who visited her now. The nurse said she didn't have many visitors. Surely her brother and mother came to see her. He would expect them to be dedicated; certainly Edmond must come. He remembered a conversation he had had with her mother, Gina, when Jane was first admitted. She had sat in the waiting room with him, her hands clasped to her black leather handbag, as if it were the only solid thing in the room. She had looked at him with interest as if surprised to see that Jane had friends who would visit her in hospital. There was something mildly flirtatious in that first look, but he put it out of his mind. Her husband had parked his car in the street and was continually jumping up to look out of the window and check it was still in one piece.

After a while, Gina had moved a bit closer, which he had found a little uncomfortable, and said she had heard of him. 'Only after the accident,' she continued, 'Jane's so secretive about her personal affairs; it's hard to get anything out of her.' He was a bit affronted that she knew so little, but then again she was right, Jane was rather oyster-like: hard to pry open when it came to her feelings. She had never told him much about her mother.

Then Gina had asked if he had a cigarette, but he didn't smoke. Suddenly she had grabbed his elbow and whispered, 'Why do you think this has happened to Jane? She was normal, wasn't she? Do you think anything could have been done?'

Richard wasn't sure why she said 'could have been', after all, there wasn't much point looking backwards now, but she went on. 'You see she always struggled a bit with her health. I worry that she missed out as a child, you know, on milk and other things. We were never close. Her father died before she was born. It was too much to bear.'

She was clearly feeling guilty but he wasn't the person to talk to; he didn't know her. He had suddenly felt all itchy; he just wanted to get in, see Jane and get out.

This time round, so many years later, he just wanted to get out, but now he was here he really had to go through with it. Maybe there was something of the old Jane still there. He would do anything to trigger that smile again.

He walked down the corridor, pushed open the door to the stairwell and descended a couple of flights before coming out at reception.

'Excuse me, I'm visiting Jane Deering. Would it be possible to have a word with one of the doctors treating her?'

5.30pm

The footsteps got fainter then disappeared as a door banged shut. Jane felt her body relax, the pulsing in her neck subside. She had developed her routine and the voices had faded, though she was reminded by the doctor that they would come back if it weren't for the new medication that numbed. She knew her mother had hoped she could leave if the medication worked but her mother didn't realise how it ordered her days, how her peace of mind became entwined with the nurse's pocket watch and how far this removed her from the world outside. Besides, the world she knew had been through a war. It was all rubble out there for her now.

Or was it? It had surely been rebuilt. Could she be rebuilt? Sometimes questions twisted and turned in her brain and she peeled away the bandages to try and find answers; most of the time she rejected their intrusion and reached for her pills.

Her mother visited once a month and fluttered around her room arranging flowers, fluffing pillows, stacking books and talking so quickly it was hard to make out what she was saying, though that was probably no bad thing. Her brother took her out in his car but they didn't go far from the hospital, and at times they just drove around the grounds. The doctors warned him not to push it. He showed her photos but they meant little since she was never going to meet the people in them. Sometimes her friend, Evie, came too, though it was difficult to see her after what had happened and what she had done. *Why does she come here?* Jane thought. *Does it make her feel better to see me suffocating slowly?*

That day, the day she was re-admitted, just wouldn't leave her. She was petrified, screaming out loud, which was not like her, but then they didn't expect her to act rationally and they wouldn't listen. They didn't realise what she did, that the war would separate everyone. That she needed to be firmly attached or she would never recover. If she went back into hospital she might never come out.

Did they give up on me? she thought. *Or were they as scared as I was?*

Either way she could not forgive their betrayal, the way they had left her there to face the white coats alone, knowing full well that Edmond was overseas and unable to help her. *I trusted Evie. She was my best friend. She plotted against me, locked me back in.*

It was glamorous here, *like a film set*. The grounds were extensive. There were columns by the front door and a fountain circled by gravel road which visitors paraded round in their cars as if they had come to a stately home for the day. *It's a façade.* They played classical music in the wards. *A veneer of peace.* Everyone thought it was a good place to be, comfortable and the highest quality, they were paying for it after all. *A pretence at life.* The National Health Service that she had championed at Oxford was still as far away from her as it had been from Elsie. Mental health was different after all, it was best kept private: that was what everyone said. *We are all dying slowly.*

She still had an eye for art but she had given up her attempts to convince the nurses to replace the tinselly painting of flowers in their station with a bold and colourful Picasso print she once picked up at an exhibition in France.

'Paintings, after all, should be mild not challenging – this is a hospital not a gallery,' they had said.

She rummaged around in her diary when she was feeling calm enough. It was her identity badge; it had made her what she was now, there was no escaping that. If she ripped out a few pages maybe things would have been different, but the ink was permanent and it had dried.

Jane wondered about her latest visitor. *Who is he? Why is he looking for me? Why didn't he come in?* Dark thoughts attacked her like ants, biting, burrowing and swarming inside her head till she wanted to scream. She gripped the arms of her chair, scratching the fabric with her nails, clawing in. *Close the door.* She couldn't; she was tied down. They had drawn the belts so tight she could hardly breathe. *Close the door or they'll come to get you.* She closed her eyes. A panic was coming, tugging at the roots of her hair like a wire-brush, dragging her with it across the room. *Do it!* She hurled herself at the door, slamming it shut with her shoulder. Then she sank back towards her chair and curled up in it trying to still the throbbing in her head.

Friendship

25th September 1932, 10am
Lady Margaret Hall, Oxford
Jane is eighteen

It was a long, thin room overlooking the college gardens. Gardeners with spindly rakes scratched leaves off the lawn, leaving lines in the grass and removing the patchwork appearance Jane rather liked. Water was dripping gently from a crack in the guttering outside her window. Books, notepads and other academic paraphernalia lay in disarray all over the floor and bed. 'Jane, clear up this intolerable mess,' her mother would have said, but fortunately for Jane, her mother wasn't there to see it. A frosted glass figure of Madonna and Child stood solemnly on the mantelpiece. The fireguard was drawn across, hiding the remains of last night's fire behind its metal wings, a blackened poker and brush next to it in an iron basket. The creator of all the chaos slept, curled up like a dormouse in a worn-out old armchair.

A gentle knock at the door and a head peeped round.

'Jane?'

'Evie.'

'Sorry, I've disturbed you. I'll come back later.'

'No, please, come in. It's time I got moving anyway.' Jane straightened out, rubbed the crick in her neck and sloped hazily over to the mirror, grabbing a handful of hair pins on the way and jabbing them into the mop on top of her head.

'You do look pale, Jane. Maybe you should rest. I'd hoped for a game of tennis but it looks like that's out of the question.'

'You expect me to play you, with your giraffe legs?'

'Height has to have some advantages.'

'Sorry, Evie, that essay exhausted me. I'll be using it as an excuse for months to come.'

'I'm surprised you didn't set fire to the paper, the pressure you put on your pen. You can't wear yourself out like this every time you write, Jane.'

'My nanny died in a public hospital alongside men whose wives and children had to go into workhouses to survive; whose insurance wouldn't pay for the welfare of their dependents. It's so frustrating being confined to the page.'

'You want to go into politics?'

'I can count the number of female MPs on one hand. I'll work for a research bureau, campaign for equality, picket parliament if I have to. Come to think of it, maybe we should revive the suffragettes. You want to teach, but if you marry, you'll have to give it up.'

'The suffragists perhaps,' said Evie, smiling. She looked round the room for Jane's coat. There it was, slung over the back of a chair. A cluster of spots had appeared on Jane's chin and her hair looked a mess. It was the second time in a month that she had worked all night to meet a deadline. *She needs to get out more,* thought Evie, *and not just to the Labour Club or college union.* 'Will you at least walk me over to the courts, Jane?' she said.

Jane nodded and Evie handed over her coat. *We're so contained here,* Jane thought, opening her window a fraction to relieve the room of its musty smell before following her friend out into the corridor. Lady Margaret Hall was a red brick warren. There were heated debates in the common room, arguments at cocoa parties – but it wasn't enough. It was almost impossible to get into lectures, jostling with men for space only to be sneered at by the crusty Fellow behind the podium, wearing his lecturer's gown as if it were the king's robe, 'Would the women at the back refrain from poking hair pins into those students who are here to listen. If you can't find a seat, you will have to leave.'

On top of this, Jane could only get into university debates if she went with a friend. That was how she had met Karl. Her friend Rebecca had called him hugely handsome, though his eyebrows did slant down over his eyes and almost meet in the middle. *He's a man between worlds*, thought Jane: the ghostly duelling scar by his right ear an unconcealed badge of honour; the socialist literature on his bookshelf a display of progressive thought; the 17th century ancestral portrait, a reminder that he was a German aristocrat with an uncertain future.

His colleague, Philip, on the other hand, she could have done without. He had insisted on joining them after the debate and they had all gone back to Karl's rooms together.

'Women can't have it all, you know,' he had begun, taking off his topcoat and dropping it lightly over the back of a chair. 'If they want family life, they will have to acknowledge the fact that men are the breadwinners. Paid work is scarce enough without more competition.'

'What about women who don't get married?' Jane had broken in as Karl took her coat and hat and hung them on a peg. 'Don't they deserve to be paid equally for the work they do? What about teachers, civil servants?' *What's the point in going to university unless we're allowed to achieve something afterwards?* she had thought.

'You can't expect the government to pay women as much as men. Not when the economy is in a slump.'

'It's a difficult time to tackle these issues,' Karl had said, 'or at least, difficult to gain any momentum.'

'It's destabilising,' Philip had continued, 'we can't afford to focus on such things right now. Look at Germany – the Nazis are the largest party in the Reichstag.'

'The German government won't allow Hitler and his small-minded band of thugs to take control,' Karl had replied, 'but there is still so much hatred for Germany after the war. Can't we find a common humanity?'

Old resentments were indeed resurfacing. Just that weekend, they had been punting near Magdalen Bridge when they were knocked from behind. Two red-faced men in straw boaters swayed to their feet and shook their fists.

Rebecca had shouted, 'Idiots! Can't you steer?'

'He shouldn't be on the river. He's German.'

'You're disgusting.'

'You're Jewish.'

A motley crowd had gathered on the river bank like hyenas to bones, ripping into them with sharp, pointed jabs, 'German scum, go back home.'

'Miserable, murdering Fritz.'

'Hop it, Jerry.'

'Bastards,' a lone voice had shouted, 'Leave them alone.'

The conscientious objector was quickly elbowed to the back.

The men's punt had floated closer and one of them made an unsteady grab for Rebecca's arm. He wobbled and his lurch missed its mark. There was laughter from the bank. The man looked round for his pole. It had fallen into the water and floated towards the reed-strewn bank. Strands of willow whipped his face as he swept the river with his hands in an attempt to wheel the punt round.

Karl grabbed his pole and heaved.

'There goes our enemy, too weak to do battle.'

Karl had pushed on, putting water between them as quickly as he could.

The crowd had evaporated, bored by the lack of sport.

Jane breathed again.

'Jane!'

She had started. She had been gazing out of Karl's window, remembering the incident, dreaming, oblivious. Rebecca tapped her on the shoulder and motioned her to a chair. No-one was talking. Karl was pouring tea. Philip was peering short-sightedly at the tiny portrait of Karl's ancestor, hung in splendid isolation on the wall of his frugal sitting room.

Jane couldn't help but admire Karl and his stubborn patriotism. She had noticed the shift away from him in common rooms, at parties. She sensed eyes everywhere observing him, pitying him, despising him already. A German. A patriot. A Nazi?

How can you self-satisfied academics even consider that? Jane thought angrily. *He is watching Germany fall into the hands of madmen just like the rest of us, only it's his country, his future.*

Then there was Rebecca, who was in love with him; Rebecca, one of her best friends; Rebecca, who was Jewish.

Now on the way to Parks, Evie was already a couple of paces ahead. Jane's feet were as sluggish as her mind in the mornings. It was a struggle to keep up with Evie at times, let alone Rebecca who could dance all night and still attend a tutorial the next day.

Two figures were advancing towards them along the footpath.

'Rebecca', shouted Jane, waving and immediately regretting it, she was definitely not up for vigorous conversation this morning and Evie was a more sensitive, quieter companion. Then she saw that Rebecca was with Karl.

'Jane,' Rebecca broke into a jog, pulling Karl with her. He was wearing a dark grey suit, cut in the latest fashion and his shoes were buffed and shiny. *He's a foot above everyone else*, Jane thought, *that's how he keeps his head clear of all the nonsense and speculation.* Rebecca was dressed immaculately, her hair waved and pinned, the diamond broach on her lapel reflecting the flash in her eyes and the snap of her temper. Elegant and slender, she slipped in and out of a crowd with ease but, caught up in debate, she was often the loudest voice in the room.

'Evie, I don't think I've introduced you to Karl,' said Jane as they drew near, thinking, *how can someone as tall as Evie shrink away so quickly?*

Karl smiled at Jane and shook hands with Evie, 'Karl von Schulze. Pleased to meet you.'

Rebecca said, 'I see you're off to play tennis, Evie. So energetic, I don't know how you do it. Karl and I attended the Labour Club meeting last night which does wear one out rather.' She was glad to highlight her involvement in politics. Far too often people palmed her off as flighty with no serious interest except dancing. Evie on the other hand was sporty; she had no feet for the dance floor and she was far too reserved to attend parties.

Rebecca turned to Jane, 'Members are threatening to break away as part of a socialist club. The Depression is dragging us all to extremes. Karl is certain Germany will resist the Fascists but look at the way they feed off the popular resentment about Versailles; look at the government's inability to reduce their crippling unemployment. It all plays into Nazi hands.'

'Division and dissent only make matters worse,' Karl said.

'I agree,' Jane said, 'it would be a shame if the Labour Club fell apart just when it needs to stick together – but there's no point looking to the League of Nations for a response and the Depression has isolated us from the United States.'

'Economic hardship always leads to finger-pointing,' Evie broke in, 'when the only way to tackle our problems is to show solidarity.'

Karl looked at Evie. *She's the type of girl who could stand still in a storm and anchor you to the ground,* he thought. A strong jaw, firm set nose, intelligent eyes: not obviously attractive but somehow reassuring. In fact, get rid of the tennis skirt and put on a classical robe and she was the image of Lady Justice outside the Old Bailey in London.

Rebecca looked at Evie and frowned. *Why join in when she didn't attend the meeting?* Karl was gazing at her with interest. *Why? She's wearing tennis whites. Maybe he likes that sort of thing.* 'Why don't you attend next time, Evie?' she said, 'Jane could bring you. It sounds like you have some interesting views.'

Evie shrugged off the suggestion, preferring to sandbag it with silence. By now they were both grinding their feet into the path, desperate to go in different directions as quickly as possible.

'I hate to sound selfish, but it's a bit early in the day for this,' Jane said, 'You need as much energy for debate as you do for a game of tennis and I, for one, need a strong cup of tea first.'

'Quite right,' said Karl. He turned to Evie, 'It was a pleasure to meet you.'

'Likewise,' Evie said with relief, and Karl and Rebecca walked away along the river.

Alone on the path again, Evie said, 'I shouldn't have dragged you out, Jane. You look exhausted.'

'Just a slight headache, that's all,' said Jane. 'My own fault for staying up late; I never seem to get my work done in time.'

Evie looked concerned. Jane rarely complained but she did suffer from headaches a lot. Evie made a mental note to look out for her in the months ahead. She was going to struggle when it came to exams. And dealing with Rebecca.

25th October 1932, 12.05am

Knock, knock.

It's after midnight.

Knock, knock, knock.

Really?

'Jane!'

Her voice was louder than her knocking. *What will the other students think?*

Jane threw back the covers and rolled herself out of bed feet first, feeling like an elephant emerging from a cocoon. Thumping her way across the room to the door, she lifted her dressing gown off its peg and pushed her arms through, blinking and waiting for the mist to clear a bit before—

'Jane, are you there?'

She sighed and opened the door. It was Rebecca. She was wearing a velvet jacket over a long, silver evening gown and her dark hair was tied back and knotted with a glittery butterfly pin. Then Jane noticed the mud on her heels, the rip at the bottom of her dress and the bloodstain on her knee, which was being held out for inspection. Her eyes were pink-edged and she smelled of sherry.

'I didn't know where to go. I've cut my knee and everyone's shut in for the night.'

'You'd better come inside.'

'Thanks, Jane. Sorry if I woke you.'

Jane pointed to the armchair, 'Just move the books onto the floor. I'm afraid I don't have any bandages but I do have a couple of clean rags and you can wash it with my water.' She took a porcelain jug down from the shelf next to her bed and offered it to Rebecca.

Rebecca set the jug down on the floor, clearly not bothered any longer by her knee. 'It's Karl, Jane, he's unshakeably intellectual but he's a wonderful dancer. He whirls you around the floor like a water boatman. I'm all shivery and delicious when I'm with him and when I'm not I'm more fidgety than a flea. When I wake up all I can think about is where to find him. I was afraid I was becoming a bit of a stalker until tonight.'

'Oh?' said Jane.

'We kissed.'

Jane's eyes opened wide.

'I expect you want to know how it happened.'

Still no response.

'We were on the path by the river after the dance. He put his dinner jacket around me. I can still feel the kiss now. I was tingling all over. I still am.'

Jane rearranged the cushions so Rebecca could slouch backwards on the bed, create a gap, breathe. *I knew this was coming. Why do I feel so awkward all of a sudden?*

'What happened to your knee?' Jane said, pointing at the bloody scab.

'I was too late to get back into college so I had to climb the gate, only my dress tore as I was coming down and I scratched it on the spikes. The night portress was very fierce. I'll have to stay out of her way for a while I think.' She paused. 'Anyway, that's the least of my worries. I want to know what you think of Karl. Is this just a fling for him? What will happen if the Nazis continue to gain ground? He's so patriotic. He never fails to defend Germany. In fact he's irritatingly sure that his country will regain greatness, but what does that mean? Will he support Germany at any cost?'

Stop! Jane thought. *This paperchain of questions needs breaking before my brain bursts. I've never been in love. Why come to me? Why start a relationship when you already know it's desperate?*

'Let me wrap this rag round your knee,' Jane said, picking up a piece of cotton.

'But what about Karl?'

Jane put the cotton down. 'Karl won't let Germany be destroyed, which is what will happen if the Nazis take control. I'm sure he'll do everything he can to oppose them,' said Jane, thinking, *how can anyone know what Karl will do?*

'Do you think there's any hope for us? Why would he kiss me if we don't have a chance?'

Why would you kiss him? thought Jane. *Neither of you knows what will happen but you both know the risks are growing by the day.* 'Karl is wrapped up in his politics, if you take things further you must talk to him about it.' There they were again, circling round, the looks, the aspersions, the shadowy figures with their backs turned talking about Karl in the corridors. *Does he know what people are saying about him?*

'Jane, you're drifting,' said Rebecca.

'I think we both need to go to bed,' said Jane, 'You know I'm useless after midnight. You'll find me tripping round the grounds in the morning with my hair sticking up and my shoelaces untied if you don't let me sleep and you'll promptly disown me.'

Rebecca smiled at the image but stayed where she was, 'I need to know what you really think, Jane,' she said. 'If the Nazis remain in power, will Karl leave Germany? Will he leave Germany for me?'

Just go to bed, Rebecca, thought Jane, *I can't answer that.*

'Jane?'

Please.

'Jane.'

'No Rebecca.'

'What?'

'He won't leave Germany.'

'How can you say that?'

'He loves his country too much.'

'But he loves me!'

'It's an impossible choice.'

'It's an easy choice, how can anyone sane stay in a country governed by the Nazis?'

'But don't you see? Karl loathes the Nazis, Rebecca. He won't sit back and watch as they destroy Germany.' Jane felt her hands tighten; she was twisting her bedcovers into a ball. *Calm down,* she thought, relaxing her hands and taking a deep breath.

'People will think he has joined them if he stays.'

‘If Hitler becomes Chancellor any opposition will be forced underground. Karl has contacts here; so long as we support him, there is still hope.’

‘If Hitler becomes Chancellor and Karl stays in Germany, our relationship will end.’

Jane was silent.

‘I can’t bear it, Jane.’

‘I’m sorry, Rebecca. It may not happen,’ her voice faltered. *I can’t lie.* ‘We must stick with Karl for now, trust him and keep our eyes open.’

Rebecca nodded. She was staring at the grate; nothing but cold ash.

She touched Jane’s hand lightly and slipped away down the corridor.

Jane closed the door behind her. Relationships were the last thing on her mind, just another tortuous distraction, full of suffering and angst. *I may not be able to resist it when it happens,* she thought, *I’m not that strong but I need someone who will understand my commitment to politics not crush it before it has a chance to breathe. Does Karl love Rebecca more than he loves his country? He will be isolated whichever way he turns.*

She lay down on the bed. *Fascism is on the rise. If we can’t reverse the trend we must fight it before it is too late.* Her eyes began to close. *Fight it, undermine it, expose it.* Silence. Darkness. *Defy it, stand up to it.* She pulled the covers up to her ears. *Why did she ask me? What can I do? What do I know about these things?* She tossed the covers off and stumbled over to the window. No lights anywhere. *Why can I never get to sleep?*

18th September 1940, 7.30pm
The Priory, London
Jane is twenty-six

Jane followed the white coats down the corridor and Evie and Walter watched her go. Evie didn’t want to leave but they told her she couldn’t stay, she would have to come back in the morning.

‘Did she have any food or drink this evening?’ the doctor had asked Evie without explaining why.

‘She hasn’t really eaten anything for days,’ Evie replied.

‘Good,’ the doctor said and Evie’s heart lurched. *How can that be good?* But the doctor had already turned away from her and was speaking to a nurse who nodded and hurried off.

Evie couldn't bear it. Jane just stood there in the middle of the reception, her eyes staring as if not registering her surroundings. Evie wanted to go to her, give her a squeeze, bring back some sign of life but the doctor took Jane's arm and led her away.

She seems docile enough, thought the doctor as he showed her into the consulting room.

'Signs of exhaustion,' said his colleague leaning over his table and peering at her. 'Her hair's unbrushed,' he continued, 'and she's not wearing any shoes.' He looked up at the nurse who was making notes on a small pad. 'No eye contact; completely unresponsive; clear signs of self-neglect – likely insomnia, possible depression. Get her some pyjamas and a sedative. No food or drink till after ECT.' He looked at Jane again. No reaction. 'Oh and dig out her file. She's been here before.'

19th September 1940, 8am

Jane had momentarily forgotten the terrors the doctors had been planning for her. It was only when she saw the wires, what looked like an over-sized radio set on the table, that she realised what was going on, what this was all leading to. They were so well prepared they must have known she was coming. They had been watching her all this time, waiting for their chance to fry her brain; control her mind; destroy her ability to think for herself. They were in league with Evie, with Walter. They were waiting for her to reach her weakest point, when she would no longer be strong enough to resist. *They put poison in my food and water so that I couldn't eat it. They starved me out.*

Her pyjamas were grey and white striped. Jane wondered if they had come, second-hand, from the prison down the road. She lay on the trolley stiff as a corpse, waiting. Hands approached, surgical spirit was scrubbed vigorously at the sides of her head, then the smell of the sea and the touch of cold metal on her temples. She could see a doctor by the machine fiddling with the dials. The right knob and the left knob. Duration and voltage.

Four nurses closed in on the bed, their faces implacable, their hands hovering, ready to pin her down. They pulled on her chin to open her mouth and she bit down on rubber. Current whipped through her, lifting her body from the table, flipping it back down again, convulsing like a fish out of water, gasping for breath. Darkness came and went as an electric mallet smashed into her brain, driving out the light. Searing pain shot through her hips; her back arched violently and then flattened out as current rippled through her and the vibrations slowed. Then she returned to her corpse-like state, her head flopped to the side exhausted, and she felt the trolley bump as it rolled through the doorway. The lights in the corridor were piercingly bright.

Be still or they will take you back in. Don't move. Don't open your eyes.

The trolley came to a stop.

'Miss Deering,' a voice said.

No answer.

'Can you tell me your name?'

Nothing.

'The date?'

Blank.

'Do you know where you are?'

Void.

'You are in the hospital. You have had electric shock therapy. You need to rest now.'

But Jane wasn't there. She didn't feel anything anymore. She was floating towards the ceiling looking down at her body. The nurse saw her eyes roll back. 'Doctor,' she said in a shrill, nasal voice, 'We need to wake the patient. Now!'

20th September 1940, 11am
Kensington, London

Ding, dong. The brass doorbell swung backwards and forwards at exactly 11am. Dr Nell Shaw was surprisingly prompt considering she had come up that morning from Surrey. Charles retired hastily to his study.

Gina hurried to the front door. 'Please come in,' she said. 'I hope the journey wasn't too tiring.'

'Not at all,' said Dr Shaw. 'There were plenty of seats in my carriage and I took a bus from Victoria.'

'It was extremely kind of you to come,' said Gina. She hadn't seen Dr Shaw for more than ten years. Still, it was too late to turn back now; here she was.

'You said it was a family matter?' Dr Shaw said following Gina into the sitting room. Gina nodded. Dr Shaw was Arthur's cousin. She would understand the sensitivities involved. It was a risk worth taking even though what she was about to reveal would be far beyond what Dr Shaw had expected. She ushered the doctor to a seat and closed the door behind them.

11.30am

Dr Shaw's facial expressions were exemplary. She was renowned at her practice for her composure.

She sat quietly and listened as she always did, but when Gina finished she got up and paced around the room, avoiding eye contact.

Schizophrenia.

She had to order her thoughts. Pen and paper. There on the table. She picked them up and started to scribble.

Genetic? Trauma? Prognosis?

It's the sort of scandal a family can do without.

Insulin. Electric shocks.

Stigma.

When did she start showing signs of illness?

Dysphoria. Hallucinations. Paranoia.

Episodic or chronic?

What does Gina expect me to do?

She put the pen and paper down. It was a devastating blow. No wonder Gina had asked to see her privately.

'You say she recovered fully following her initial treatment?' She turned to Gina who had remained sitting down.

'I wouldn't say fully,' said Gina, 'but she did return home for a while. She began working part-time with the Information Department of the National Council of Social Service. Her doctor wouldn't pass her for full-time work. I wanted her to stay here with me but she refused. She can be impossibly stubborn at times.'

'Did she ask to be re-admitted to hospital?'

'No.' Gina faltered. It was so dreadfully awful she couldn't bear to talk about it. Thank goodness she hadn't been there to witness the scene, and they had told her there was one. 'It was an impossible situation, you understand. The bombs. People she knew dying around her. She didn't come out of her room for three days. She said someone was poisoning her food. Everyone agreed she needed help.' Everyone *had* agreed. That was important to Gina. It wasn't just *her* decision. There was nothing else that could be done. Everyone had agreed.

'Can I ask who was involved in the decision?' said Dr Shaw, wondering how many people knew about Jane's condition.

'Myself, Edmond and his wife …' Gina paused, '… and a friend of Jane's.'

'A male friend?' asked Dr Shaw.

'Yes,' said Gina, unwilling to go any further. It would come out in time, she knew, but there was no reason to unlock another scandal now. It was all so shameful. Her shame. Her daughter.

'I see,' said Dr Shaw. This was indeed a delicate situation. She knew Jane. At least she had known Jane when Jane was a little girl at Picketswood. She had been fragile, Dr Shaw remembered, prone to catching the slightest illness. Gina had had difficulty coping. She was not surprised about that now. 'Do you think it would be possible for us to visit Jane together and speak to her doctor?' Dr Shaw said. Schizophrenia was a fearsome diagnosis. Recovery was extremely unlikely but then again, there had been new developments in the treatment of mental health recently, there might be something new they could try.

'Yes, of course,' Gina replied. This was what she was hoping for – an ally, someone who could understand the medical jargon and explain it to her. Someone who could help her make decisions. Someone who could help her communicate with Jane.

Love

21st August 1934, 9.30am
Lodgings, Oxford
Jane is twenty

Richard did not realise the significance of their first meeting till it dawned on him that he was in love. He had been amused when she threw back the door, heaved an enormous suitcase a millimetre or two and promptly sat down upon it gasping. The door swung back again, hitting the suitcase with a bang.

'It's not really the weather for hard labour,' Jane said, looking up at him with a smile.

'I agree,' he replied, 'far too hot. Can I help you?'

'That would be lovely. I certainly can't manage on my own,' she said, adding, 'you look like just the person one needs in this sort of situation.'

'If you're referring to my size, I'm as large round the middle as I am head to toe, but I'll see what I can do,' he said, bending down to pick up the suitcase. 'What have you got in here?'

'Books mostly,' she said apologetically, watching as he tugged it into the hallway.

'We'd better take some out before we try to get it to your room,' he said, lowering it carefully to the floor. 'My name's Richard, Richard Wright.'

'And I'm Jane Deering,' she replied before tripping over a rug into his arms.

He caught her and helped her up. She laughed and blushed. That was the beginning for him and it was a whole month ago now.

Richard and Jane had eaten breakfast together every day since she arrived. Richard always came down first. He stood in the doorway, blocking the light for a few seconds as he scanned the room. Jane wasn't an early riser and she wasn't ruled by her stomach, but the smell of bacon floated tantalisingly over his nose each morning, rising through the floorboards and hovering over his bed like steam over a bath. The landlady was cunning. She had given him the room above the kitchen so he could hear the pans rattling on the stove, the spatter and hiss of water boiling over and the low chatter of the cook and her assistant as they worked. If the smell hadn't already reached him, the panicked whistle of the kettle did the job. He shuffled his feet to the side of the bed, threw his covers back and tipped himself into his slippers, blinking and yawning.

By the time Jane entered the dining room each day Richard had occupied the table by the window and taken his first few sips of coffee, a habit he had got into during his travels in the States. He would have loved to tell her a tale or two but she dug incessantly for opinions.

'You work for the *News Chronicle*, you must be interested in politics,' she said, astounded at his apparent indifference.

'Interested but not engaged; I don't trust politicians as far as I can spit.'

'Feel free to spit, but give me an opinion, please.'

'I have plenty, but none of them positive.'

'Well let me interview you then. I'll be the journalist.'

'Fine but I know the tricks of the trade. I can dodge pretty well.'

'Let's start with your background. You grew up in Jarrow, near the shipyard, but had to move south when your father died so your mother could find clerical work. You went to grammar school on a county scholarship and secured a place at Ruskin College, champion of working class education, on the basis of your potential rather than your grades.'

'Jane, you've got to get to the point, my coffee is almost finished.'

'Stop trying to throw me off course. I need to set the scene. You travelled to America to report on the Depression and yet you refuse to tell me what you think of the New Deal. You're a self-made man from a working class family but you won't comment on the impact of the Depression. Why?'

'Decisions are made whether the working man protests or not.'

'But surely that doesn't mean you shouldn't try?'

'I believe in information, transparency, reporting the facts. That's the only way to put pressure on the government. The unions make a lot of noise but still nothing is done to help workers in the north. Look at Jarrow. Most people lost their jobs when the shipyard closed. Soon the whole town will be unemployed. Families starve while politicians argue.'

'Exactly. So your voice does matter.'

'I'll swap you some articles for a bit of peace at breakfast.'

'Deal.' Jane smiled cheerfully. Now she was getting somewhere.

On another occasion, Jane rushed into the dining room, grasping a newspaper tightly in her left hand as if she wanted to strangle it. She slapped it down on the table in front of him, 'Hitler just proclaimed himself Führer. America will think it's none of their business but how can we sit back and watch as Fascist dictators bully and butcher their own people? They can't hold the Olympic Games in Germany now. The Nazis will use it for propaganda. They will see it as a coup.'

'Maybe hosting the Olympics will hold them back?' Richard watched her pace around her chair. 'Maybe it will force them to tone down their rhetoric? The eyes of the world will be on them after all.'

'It's not just their rhetoric that needs restraint. Besides, if they tone down their rhetoric and lock up their thugs they will gain time and consolidate their authority. That may prevent pain in the short-term but it gives them a platform for the future.'

She was still standing up. The three other lodgers in the room couldn't help but stare. Forks and knives were stilled momentarily, glasses set down. The man on the next table coughed uncomfortably and wiped the grease from around his mouth with his napkin. Jane stopped pacing. She could feel bristles springing up around her. *Breakfast should be quiet and dignified. Hitler and the Nazis are a distasteful topic at this early hour: surely she can wait till lunchtime or take it to her room?*

Jane sat down feeling flat. It was all Richard could do to stop himself reaching out across the table to take her hand, she looked so dejected.

A blonde woman with a mole on her chin waved to the landlady who hurried over, looking flustered, as if the tension in the room was too much for her and somehow all her fault. 'I'd like another pot of tea please,' said the blonde woman. 'This one's gone cold.'

Knives and forks clinked and clattered again and the room resumed the jam-and- toast routine, clearing the faux pas away neatly with the dirty plates.

It's exciting to see her provoked, Richard had thought, *but she's sensitive. I mustn't push things too far*. He could sit for hours watching her talk, watching her clip and re-clip her hair mid-sentence, twiddle her napkin in frustration, touch her chin absent-mindedly when she got to an important point. It was a shame breakfast was such a short meal, though she never seemed that keen to leave. Studying was clearly not her greatest strength: why else would she be back in Oxford over the summer?

He loved the way she blew through the door each morning, a harmonious blur of blue and white in her favourite linen blouse. She appeared so awake, so springy, like her tangle of curly hair. Then she sat down at the table with a thump and knocked off a knife or spoon; fumbled over her words when placing her breakfast order; or rubbed her eyes and covered her mouth, tell-tale signs of a light sleeper. Richard wondered what kept her awake at night: probably the world at large and its troubles – the unemployed, the uninsured and the dispossessed.

Jane was so engaged with everyone and everything else she barely spoke about herself, her life. She had mentioned her brother Edmond several times but no-one else. Was she an orphan? He didn't like to ask. Getting to know her was like painting a portrait: if you were careful and took your time, you filled in the details. He was happy to let things drift along like this, enjoying her company without making a move. It was safer that way.

That was until he heard about Karl.

'He's coming back from Germany next week,' Jane said.

Next week. Why? He had never met Karl but he sounded irritating, dangerous even. Jane described him as one of the most intelligent men she had ever met. Apparently Karl was taller than most with a duelling scar on his cheek. He sounded like he came from another era entirely.

Jane said, 'Karl is quiet and dignified.'

Richard thought, *haughty and withdrawn.*

'He is absolutely loyal to his friends.'

What does he do to his enemies?

'He is extremely patriotic. He cares deeply about international relations.'

Richard broke in, 'Can the two exist together? You say he continues to work for the Foreign Office under Hitler?'

'He understands diplomacy. Germany needs to work hard to remain stable. Leaving his post would be the easy way out.' She paused. 'He's doing what he feels is right. I have faith in him.'

What if it's more than that? Richard thought, cutting up his bacon in silence. Jane leant forward to take the butter.

'I thought you'd like to meet him,' she said, spreading her toast.

'Yes, I'd like to meet him, but won't he be very busy? I presume he's only here for a short time?'

'He's got a whole month. I'm sure he'll have time to meet up. I'm hoping to see quite a bit of him while he's here.'

A month is far too long, thought Richard. *I may have to declare my intentions sooner rather than later.*

'How long have you known him?' he said.

'We met almost as soon as I arrived at university,' she replied, thinking how quickly Karl's group of friends had shrunk after his return to Germany, how suspicious and disloyal they all were, how impossible it must be to be German right now and what difficult decisions lay ahead.

'You look worried,' said Richard. *This man is upsetting her balance. She always seemed so rational before. What sort of fascination does he hold for her?*

'Let's talk about something else.'

Tempting, Richard thought, *but I need to find out more, just a little, something to give me the edge.*

'Of course, if you'd like to. Could I ask though, as I'm going to meet him, what it is that makes you admire him so much?'

'What do you mean?' She frowned. *What is he getting at?*

'I mean you said you have faith in him but from where I'm sitting, not knowing as much as you, he's a German aristocrat who has bucked the trend and linked himself to the Nazis.'

Nazis. He spat out the word as if it were a fishbone. It choked in his throat but he wanted to shock her. He knew he was being petty, risking alienating her, but he wasn't a man who braked easily.

'If you think like that there's no point in you meeting him,' Jane replied, taken aback by the bitterness in his tone. What was Richard implying? Where had this sudden jealousy come from? She had hoped Richard would see what she saw – that Karl was a man in need of help; a man whose beloved homeland was under attack by a vile ideology that was growing in strength, an ideology that threatened them all, that thrived on hatred and division.

She hadn't expected Richard to be as narrow-minded as some of her Oxford colleagues; those back-stabbing bookworms who believed Karl's loyalty to Germany to be greater than his opposition to the Nazis, not realising that the two were absolutely linked. Now here was Richard thoughtlessly pursuing a similar line, throwing out snide remarks without knowing anything about it. Karl had not linked himself to the Nazis. He wasn't a party member. Germany needed men like him to advocate moderation or there was no hope for the future of their country at all.

Richard had come across as a liberal, free-thinking man, someone she could confide in. It had been a joy to see him there at breakfast every morning, to have him listen to her monologue as she kicked out the debris she had gathered overnight when the sky grew dark and the world's worries bit in. He wasn't political but maybe that was a good thing. She had come to believe that it was but now she wondered – his patience, his quietness, his temperance, maybe it was all a front? Maybe it was all false. He hadn't declared himself. He hadn't declared anything. She didn't really know him. She pushed her chair back from the table and set her napkin down.

'I hope you have a good morning,' she said, restraining the disappointment that was creating a crevasse between them and standing up to go.

'Stop,' Richard said, desperately. 'Please, Jane. I'm sorry.'

'No need to be sorry. I introduced a sore topic. Let's leave it there.'

'Let's not part like this. I've made a bad impression, I can't let you go.'

'I just need to go for a walk. It's very hot this morning.' A headache was coming on. She had to get out into the fresh air before it took hold, forcing her to lie down, waste the morning in bed.

'I was wrong to be judgemental, it's just …' Richard paused and looked down, not wanting to meet her gaze.

Jane had never seen him so vulnerable, so insecure before. He was such a big man: square jaw, large hands, a solid block off which ideas bounced and returned without damage. Now, all of a sudden, his brow had furrowed and his deep-set dark eyes, downward-cast, seemed shy, nervous of exposure. His barely masked hostility to Karl shocked her. It was so uncalled for. For the last four weeks, he had been her leaning post when she stumbled downstairs, still trying to pin her hair in place – always there in the mornings before her, always at a table with a seat reserved. Part of her wanted to go to him, draw his arms around her and feel the warmth, the reassurance of his heart against hers. The other part was afraid; that man, that firmness, that reality, was disintegrating in front of her.

'Nothing to worry about,' she said, wishing herself away.

Richard could tell he had snapped something. He wanted to take her hands between his and tell her he loved her, adored her, to pull her towards him and kiss her so deeply nothing would separate them again, but the confusion in her eyes floored him. There was silence between them, and a table, and she felt further away than ever before with her big blue eyes and fiery opinions. *Why am I so clunky*, he thought, *I was doing pretty well until now.*

He said nothing and she left.

I'll fix it tomorrow, he thought, hopefully. *She has to eat breakfast after all.*

30th August 1934, 6.30pm

There were roses on the dressing table. Jane breathed in. It was a dizzying, exciting feeling, having an admirer. Richard had been at great pains to patch up their differences since that dreadful argument about Karl. He had shied away from anything personal, but then again, so had she.

Was this really happening?

There was a note:

"Thanks for a wonderful summer and for putting up with my dogged distrust of politics, R."

Is that all? She turned it over.

"P.S. Can I see more of you?"

She picked it up and scanned the words again. Not a complete declaration, but then, what was she expecting? *I can't blame him, I haven't given him much encouragement,* she thought. Here, at last, was a man she could rely on, a man whose company she enjoyed and yet there was a quietness about his confession that took away some of its excitement. *What do I want?* she thought. *Why do I insist on nit-picking?* Part of her longed to be overwhelmed, submerged, hooked and sunk by love, but the sensible part said, *you need a steady man, someone who can hold you together.*

Some days she felt blurred around the edges, the fuzz of her hair reflecting the fuzz in her mind. 'Don't read last thing at night,' Edmond had told her, '*The New Statesman* will still be there in the morning. You've got a whole week to dissect it before the next issue,' but sleep never came easily.

Richard was concrete. He restored her. *I respect him,* she thought. *I trust him.*

She heard his voice in the hallway.

'Richard.'

Richard took off his hat and looked around. Jane was coming down the stairs. He would have preferred to meet her in private. He had just said goodbye to the landlady. She might come out again if she heard Jane's voice.

'Shall we sit in the lounge?' he said.

'I don't want to hold you up, I just wanted to thank you for the flowers.'

Richard longed to say, *I'd like to spend all my time with you, I can't wait for you to come down in the mornings. I love your slightly crumpled look. I love the way you conceal your vulnerability but it shows in your cheeks.* What came out was, 'I'd really like to keep seeing you. That's if your studies allow it. I'll be working in London from October, but I hope to come up to Oxford on weekends. That's if you're free. I do have other friends here too. I mean …' He petered out. He was stammering, rushing it. This wasn't like him. He needed to slow down.

Jane was nodding.

She *did* want to see him again.

Richard wanted to hug her, kiss her, lift her in his arms and twirl her around but he restrained himself. Jane still felt miles away from him, standing there quietly, unsure what to say.

A brusque knock at the door.

'Can I help you with your suitcase sir?' His taxi driver stood in the porch, eager to get going. The station would be heaving with potential customers by now, laden down with bags, tumbling out of their trains.

'Thank you,' Richard said, wishing he could delay a little longer. Seeing little movement from his client, the driver bent to pick up the case himself. *What has he got in here?* he thought, stumbling out of the door and down the steps with it, muttering under his breath.

'Goodbye then,' Richard said, his feet stuck on the step, his heart reaching out, taking hold of Jane's hand, taking her with him, but she had her hands behind her back, she looked all neat and proper framed in the doorway and she wasn't going anywhere.

A taxi revved its motor.

'I think you'd better go,' said Jane. 'Write to me.' She smiled.

'I will.'

Richard got into the taxi and drove off. It was enough for now. A smile. Something to remember. Besides, he would be stubborn and determined now he knew he had a chance.

Jane stood there, quiet for a moment, gazing at the door, at the space where his feet had been a moment ago. She felt suddenly lost. Richard had been there, as steady as an ox, and now there was nothing, a void. She looked round the room for a distraction. *I need him*, she thought. *He makes me feel safe.*

Then she saw it. 'Richard, your hat.' He had left it hanging on the coat stand. Jane grabbed it and rushed out the door, but she was too late, he had already gone.

"2nd January 1935
Dear Jane,
The trouble with the telephone here is that, though they are very efficient and call you to the floor, by the time they have done so half your first three minutes are gone. That is where the beastly awkward call-box is better, because it doesn't begin counting the time till it is paid.
I'm afraid I'm terribly in love with you. I hope it pleases you more than it embarrasses you; but it is a fact in any case.
As it is, you're pretty exceptional and worthy of love,
Richard."

28th May 1935, 2.30pm
Boar's Hill, Oxfordshire

Richard put his hand in his pocket, jangling his keys against the little square box that was in there. *Stop fidgeting.* He pulled it out again. They had driven out to Boar's Hill in his battered "flatnose" Morris Oxford, a car he had saved up for after getting the *News Chronicle* job. The plan was to picnic near Jarn Mound. Richard bemoaned the car's lack of a fourth gear as they bumped along but Jane was rather glad it couldn't go any faster. Despite its steel saloon, it was a rickety old thing. Still, the fabric seats were in reasonable repair and it was refreshing to drive along merrily with the black top flap folded neatly back. Jane was wearing a brown plaid dress with a red leather belt and her hair was held back by a silk scarf to avoid, as she put it, 'the windswept bush look'.

The picnic was a success, Richard thought as he packed it away in his wicker basket. Jane had even had a glass of wine.

'My studies couldn't be going any worse,' she had said, knocking it back and smiling that flash of a smile that bumped up his heart rate.

It wasn't like her to be impulsive but he had taken it as a good sign.

'Shall we walk to the top?' he said, 'I'd love to see the view.' They put the picnic basket and rug back in the boot and set off up the hill at a smart pace. Jane was out of breath by the time they were halfway up.

'Are you all right?' Richard said, holding out his hand. They had never held hands before. Today, however, Jane was agitated, excitable, like the breeze that kept threatening to whip away her scarf, so she grasped his hand firmly and let him lead her up the track.

His grip was firm but his heart was leaping like the rabbits in the field below, their tails bobbing white as they hopped through the patchy grass. A fox sniffed its way out from under the fence, burying its nose in the ground, biding its time. The rabbits nosed the air and scarpered, nipping into their burrows just as the sun disappeared behind some spoilsport clouds. The fox sprang up expectantly and then mooched off under the barbed wire fence and into the long grass beside the forest path, disappointed but not disheartened. He knew where the rabbits lived. It wouldn't be long. Strands of wiry red hair clung to the barbs like a warning.

Jane was relieved to see the rabbits escape. The summer air was fresh and fragrant with cowslips, foxgloves and ragged robin, a merry cascade of colour lining the path. The sun flooded jauntily back into the sky.

They reached a small kissing gate. Jane leant on it for a moment to catch her breath. Richard couldn't resist. A light breeze was twisting at her scarf and small strands of dark curly hair floated out tempting him to tuck them back in and pull her towards him.

He stole up to her as she looked away up the path ahead, spun her round and kissed her.

It felt like a hijack.

She tried to relax. She felt his arms wrap round her, his lips soft on hers. She closed her eyes and put her arms round his neck. He had taken her scarf off. Her hair blew wildly around her head. Richard had his hands in her hair, on her back. He slid them quickly down to her waist, up to her blouse. Her back was scraping the wooden gate posts. His lips felt greedy, large, and wolfish against hers. She knew how much he wanted her. How long he had waited. But she wasn't sure. Why couldn't she stop her thoughts from chopping in, stabbing back, cutting the here and now up into puzzles?

Suddenly a snap: a twig breaking in two. They weren't alone. Stones kicked to the side of the track. A whistle. Someone was coming.

She tensed. He felt her body tighten and pull away, but he was attached, he didn't want it to end, he held on, kissing her cheek, her ear, her neck. She tilted her head away. He felt her hands push his chest. He let go.

'Sorry, Jane, I love you! I want to marry you.'

He was at her feet, taking a small, square box out of his pocket.

'Will you marry me?'

A stubby, bald man and his dog appeared in the distance. The man threw a stick up the path and the dog leapt after it, spinning round, helicopter tail in the air, flicking up dust and stones and racing back with its prize. The man squinted up the path. His eyesight was failing. There were two fuzzy shapes ahead, looked vaguely like a couple but he wasn't sure. The man seemed to be on his knees in the dirt. Maybe he had dropped something. The woman was standing, pale and unmoving.

The man threw the stick into the wood.

'Fetch.'

Richard jumped and the box snapped shut. He had been so focused on the moment, on Jane, that he hadn't heard the footsteps. *Damn,* he thought, *I should have waited.* He stood up.

'I'm sorry, Richard. I can't. I don't know how I feel. I don't know what I want.'

He knew now that she would say that. The man and his dog passed them and disappeared up the track. Jane pulled a bramble thorn out of her hand. They walked back to the car in silence.

Jane walked ahead. She felt like crying. It was so disappointing – day trips, dinners, walks through town and she still wasn't ready. There were worries she hadn't discussed with him, things she had been too shy to say. There were fears for the future – how would he feel about her travelling, joining left-wing societies, picketing parliament – what if she made a spectacle of herself? It was all there in a jumble in her head whenever they met but none of it ever came out and now it might be too late. *Why can't I talk to him about how I feel? I blurt out my opinions readily enough but I can't tell him how scared I am. I can't tell him that I haven't achieved anything yet, that I need him to wait.*

Richard watched her go. She had been his for a moment, but now there was a gap opening up. *What if I've lost her?* He put the thought out of his mind. *She just needs more time.* He opened the car door and Jane got in. The colour had gone from her cheeks and her hands were linked tightly together in her lap. She twiddled her thumbs. She avoided his gaze. Their love – the potential, the desire that had built up – was rapidly fading into an awkward silence.

'I'll take you back to college.'

'Thank you.'

Richard turned the key and the car spluttered into action. He put his foot on the clutch and slid the car into gear.

'I really need to get a new car. This one drags and rattles over the roads like a rake on gravel.'

The car gave a derisory snort, black smoke puffing out of the exhaust.

'Changing the gears is a feat in itself.'

The car chuntered up the hill expressing its disgust at the steep ascent with the occasional smoker's cough.

'Maybe we should close the roof. You look cold,' Richard said, one hand on the wheel, the other craning behind him to lift the roof flap. It was too heavy so he slowed down and stopped at the top of the hill.

He had just turned to pull the roof forward when the car started to roll. He spun back and jerked the handbrake up.

It snapped off in his hand. The car picked up speed.

'Jane … get out!'

She scrambled to open her door but the handle was jammed. The car swerved and squealed like a pig in a panic. Her door fell open and she tumbled out, grazing her knees and arms and spinning painfully into the nettles at the side of the road. She scrambled to her feet as the car continued its descent, scratching the hedge, veering into the road with Richard clutching the steering wheel. There was a sharp bend coming.

Jane couldn't see round the corner, she was racing down the hill. There was a tremendous crash. As she turned the bend she saw that her car door had come off. Smoke was streaming out of the bonnet. Was Richard trapped? The back of the car was completely crushed. Had he been thrown out? Was his body in the ditch?

Her breath came in wheezy patches. It was like being inside an iron lung. She stopped still, paralysed. He was such a decent man: a wonderful, loyal, rock of a man. He couldn't be gone. He was Richard. He was ever-present. How could she have rejected him? How could she have ruined him like this? It was all her fault. He was dead and his last moments were full of sorrow and pain. *I love him. I must do. He has to survive!*

She reached the car. Then she saw him.

Witness

31st May 1935, 11.45am
Lady Margaret Hall, Oxford
Jane is twenty

The bedsprings dug into Jane's spine like hot cups, great round welts that ached and throbbed till she was forced to move. She stretched out a hand, raking the bedside table for her aspirin, knocking papers and books onto the floor before closing on the metal lid. The tablet felt furry on her tongue, its chalky taste sticking in her throat till she gulped down some water.

Broken ribs and concussion, they had told her at the hospital. They hadn't allowed her to go into Richard's room and he hadn't seen her there, outside. Dots of light had flickered then spun across her eyes, a loud banging in her head then blackout. They had scooped her off the floor, taken her pulse and ordered her home to rest. The nurse had led her to a taxi, pressed a tin of aspirin into her hand. It was then that she had seen the Blackshirt, one of Mosley's mob. Going in. Bloody nose. Bloody shirt, not that you could see the blood on the black, just a dirty great stain around the heart. He had passed a couple of white coats with stethoscopes but they didn't blink an eye and he had disappeared inside.

Is he a Blackshirt too? she had thought when she saw a copy of the *Daily Mail* on the front seat next to the taxi driver. *They're multiplying*. She had snatched at the door handle, wrenching it almost out of its socket. She couldn't stay in the cab, it was closing in on her, crushing in on all sides like the car in the ditch till she couldn't breathe and she flung herself out.

Only she didn't.

'Where do you want to go?' the driver had said.

'Lady Margaret Hall, please.' Her voice had bounced off the window back at her. Her head hurt like mad, as if someone had lit a fire in her brain.

Richard was recovering in hospital but the world wouldn't stop while he was there. *I can't ignore the danger any longer. I can't sit around and do nothing.*

The Fascists lived off prejudice and fear, sucking it up into their vacuum and spitting bile into the emptiness that was left. *I need information, facts to expose the threat.*

She had walked through college to her room without giving herself away, slammed the door behind her, wedged it shut and started to write.

Mosley was backed by Mussolini. He was receiving funds to clone Blackshirts all over the country. He must be. Fascists were spreading like weeds throughout Europe. The only way to yank them out for good was to dig for their roots. Travel to Germany. Speak to Karl. Understand the danger and begin the resistance.

That was two days ago. She had slept during the day and been up at night. She blew her nose and threw the handkerchief on the floor. Her body ached from top to toe but the aspirin was lifting the headache and she felt calmer.

She picked up the letter she had written to Richard.

I can't leave him in suspense and I can't expect him to wait for me.

The ink was smudged in places.

"Dear Richard,

I'm so terribly sorry about the accident. I wish I could change things between us but I can't. It would be wrong to lead you on any further. You deserve better than that. If we had more time I should have explained that I don't want to marry you unless I'm certain that I'm altogether in love with you and that I care for you far more than anybody else in the world and that you feel the same about me. Perhaps that's a stupid, sentimental and old-fashioned outlook. I don't know for certain; but it seems to me that any other plan would only cause confusion to you and me at present.

It's terribly difficult to be honest. It's easy enough to state what you think is the truth, but hopelessly hard to be sure that what you believe is the truth. I know that I care for you – love you, admire your mind and your character and you realise now that I think you very good looking, but frankly at this moment I don't think I'm really in love with you. J."

I can't see him, she thought. I can't think about him. The world is moving too fast. I can't be tied down.

She folded the letter and stuffed it into an envelope.

There was a knock at her door.

'Jane?' Evie turned the handle and pushed but it was stuck.

'Hold on,' said Jane, moving the table and books out of the way.

'Sorry for barging in like this Jane,' Evie said, coming in, 'I was worried about you. I knocked on your door last night but there was no answer.'

Evie drew the curtains and opened the window slightly. Jane looked like she'd smudged coal under her eyes. Her room felt as clogged up as a blocked nose. There were papers all over the floor.

'Your neck looks swollen and red. Have you eaten anything this morning?'

'A little,' said Jane, pointing to a half-eaten slice of toast and a cup of Oxo.

'Jane you look really unwell. Will you be able to take your exams?' said Evie. Finals were just a couple of days away and Jane was in no state to go to the Schools.

Jane faded back to the room, weighed down by the bedcovers. Evie was right. She couldn't afford to think about visiting Karl, or Richard. There was no point posting the letter she had written last night. It would be best all round if she concentrated on her books and got the job done, but her brain felt like a balloon. The slightest prick and she would go into a flat spin, shooting off in all directions before ending up shrivelled and useless on the floor.

'Do you want me to ask Miss Coots if you can sit the exams in your room?' Evie said.

'That would help enormously. Do you think the university would let me?'

'I'm sure they will make allowances. Miss Coots will argue your case. She says you're the champion of the underdog.'

'I always take the losing side. Anyway, I'm not sure how much she really appreciates my slapdash, last-minute essays.' Jane said, remembering the way Miss Coots peered at her handwriting like it was something out of a horror story.

There was another knock on the door.

'Can you explain that I'm not in a fit state to see anyone?'

Evie opened the door, blocking Jane from view.

'Can I help you?'

A tall man was standing outside, hat in hand. He wore a smart city suit, his eyes were blue and, though it started some way back, his hair was dark and curly, just like Jane's. 'I'm looking for Jane Deering. I'm her brother, Edmond.'

Jane's heart jumped – a welcome distraction at last.

'Edmond, come in.'

Evie stepped aside and Edmond ducked through the doorway. 'You look feverish, Jane. They said you were on the mend after the accident but I had to see for myself.'

'Accident?' said Evie.

'You know about the accident?' said Jane.

'Someone from the hospital telephoned mother. They were concerned about you.'

'How did they get her number?' said Jane.

'You gave it to Mr Wright.'

'You know about Richard?'

'No … I mean yes. We know now.'

'We?'

'Mother and I, who else?'

Jane looked at Evie.

'Do you want me to go?' said Evie.

'No,' said Jane. 'If my brother has been spying on me, I want him to come clean and tell me.' She frowned. *Spying?* The word rolled off her tongue before she could stop it. *What am I thinking? This is Edmond.*

Evie hovered like a crane fly trapped in a small space.

'Sorry, Edmond,' said Jane. 'I don't know why I said that. I'm not well. My head is thumping, my back aches, my throat is sore and I have to study for Finals. I can't think straight.'

'I can see you're suffering.'

'I've been in my room since I got back from hospital.'

'What are all these papers? It doesn't look as though you've been resting, Jane.'

'I couldn't sleep. I had to clear my mind, Edmond.'

'What's on your mind … exams … the accident?'

'I escaped with barely a scratch Edmond but Richard could've died.'

'But he didn't and he'll be out by tomorrow. He told us you were thrown out of the car. He was worried about you.'

'You spoke to him? I thought you said someone from the hospital called mother?'

'He did call from the hospital – at least he must have used a call box, we assumed he was calling from hospital.'

'I wish you would talk clearly, Edmond, don't make such a muddle of it all. Did mother talk to him?'

'Yes.'

'I expect she wanted to know why I was in a car with a man she hadn't met.' Jane allowed her tone to grind into sarcasm. 'It's not surprising I suppose. She rarely asks about my life here. I don't think she's met any of my friends. Not even Evie.' Bitter tears pooled in her eyes. She blinked them away. It had been so comforting to hear Edmond's voice. Now he had gone and spoilt it.

'What do you expect, Jane, when you rarely phone home?'

'She expects me to telephone first thing on Sunday morning, Edmond. She knows I struggle in the mornings but she barely speaks to me if I call at any other time.'

'I know,' Edmond said. Their mother could be frustratingly inflexible, particularly where Jane was concerned. It was always a challenge to get them to agree on anything.

Jane was looking increasingly miserable. 'I'm not in a relationship with Richard, Edmond, and I don't want to talk about it.'

What a fool I am, thought Edmond, *all I've done is wind her up.*

'Never mind that now, you must concentrate on getting better,' he said.

'I've decided to travel to Germany when I've finished my exams,' said Jane.

'Germany? That may not be wise.'

'You don't know why I'm going yet.'

'Sorry, Jane, but reports from Germany get worse by the day. Hitler is tightening his grip, flouting Versailles and building up the military. There are riots, boots on the streets, people abducted from what I've heard.'

'I know,' Jane said. 'I'll be travelling with Rebecca. She wants to visit a mutual friend in Berlin, Karl von Schulze. You may have heard of him, he works for the German Foreign Office.'

Worse and worse, Edmond thought.

He was relieved when Evie broke in on his side, 'Won't that be difficult for you, Jane?' Jane would be the third peg, she was sure of it, besides what was Rebecca thinking going to Germany. It wasn't safe, not with all the anti-Semitic rhetoric the Nazis were spouting.

'I need to know what's going on there. How can I help stop the rot when I have no experience of the world? I can't live in a library anymore.'

'No-one expects you to, but we don't want you to take unnecessary risks either, especially if you're not well,' said Edmond.

'I didn't say I was leaving tomorrow.'

'I think I should leave you to rest,' Edmond said, letting the conversation lie for the time being. 'Will you allow me to come up after exams and take you back to London?'

'Thank you, Edmond, sorry if I've been short with you. I do appreciate you coming all this way, I really do.'

She looked at Evie, 'Could you let me know what Miss Coots says?'

'I'll go and find her now.'

Edmond turned to Evie appreciatively. 'Thank you for looking after my sister. I didn't ask your name.'

'Evie Gray.'

They shook hands. 'Lovely to meet you,' Edmond said, bobbing his head slightly as if she was a visiting dignitary. *What am I doing,* he thought as his cheeks blistered as red as Jane's.

'Are you sure I can't bring you anything before I leave town?' he said, turning back to his sister.

'There's very little anyone can do for me I fear.' Jane smiled at him and he bent down and kissed her on the cheek.

'Will you walk to the gates with me?' Edmond said to Evie as they stepped out into the corridor together.

Evie nodded. She wasn't sure what to make of Jane's plans. Maybe Edmond wanted to discuss them with her.

'What do you think of this idea of Jane's to go to Germany?' Edmond said as they walked across the courtyard towards the porter's lodge.

'I'm not sure it's wise, but Jane won't refuse a friend even if it puts her in a hole and Rebecca has clearly asked for company. Besides, Jane is committed to crusading in some way or other. She feels removed from the causes she cares about at university.'

'I suppose it's got to happen at some point, but I don't know how much she can stand, or what she hopes to achieve. She's got a huge spirit but she's not tough. She's going to need friends like you,' he said.

They stopped by his car, an old Morris Cowley he had borrowed temporarily from his step-father. On most occasions he felt rather embarrassed by its bulky artillery wheels and frayed upholstery, the rust that was starting to accumulate around the radiator, but Evie didn't seem the sort of girl who would be bothered by material things. *At least it's an improvement on the wobbly three-wheeler Charles used to have,* he thought.

Evie wore no jewellery. Her dress was unfussy, her shoes plain and practical. Girls worried far too much about their appearance. Evie seemed comfortable with herself, reserved maybe but down-to-earth – a real English oak of a girl, calm and solid, beautifully reassuring rather than beautiful. He felt a strong temptation to kiss her, see if he could shake her roots a little.

'Would it be too forward of me to ask for your number?' he said, feeling impulsive and letting the feeling race round his mouth, pricking out the words before he had a chance to rein them back.

Evie looked surprised. Was he interested in her or did he just want to keep tabs on Jane? She wasn't sure. She hesitated.

Edmond felt his mouth clam up. They had hardly said two words to each other, how could he have been so bold? 'It's good to know Jane has a friend to turn to here. I just want to be able to get in touch. If you don't mind that is?'

Evie saw his eyes drop, heard the stammer in his voice. Heat spread to her cheeks.

'Not at all,' she said. 'I mean, yes. Yes, you can.'

15th July 1935, 7.30pm
Berlin

Jane's feet felt hot and heavy, rubbed raw at the heel till they had erupted into blisters. If she could just slip off her shoes and put her feet up they might stop throbbing – but Karl had taken them to a smart restaurant on Kurfuerstendamm Boulevard. *At least we're going to sit down,* Jane thought.

Karl seemed to think that harrying them past monuments would distract them from the swastikas and the silence that had fallen between them. They had sped round Berlin as if whipped from behind. *What's the point in being here unless we talk?* thought Jane. *Hitler has just sanctioned murder, ripped the ribs out of his own party and replaced them with Gestapo razors. Free speech is becoming more dangerous by the hour.*

Berlin was in bondage. Red Nazi banners draped the largest buildings: a gush of blood on a grey uniform. Leaderless Brownshirts wandered the streets, lingering on street corners, their belts as tight as their fists.

Meanwhile, civilians continued to dance outside cafés, floral skirts twirling and high heels rapping the pavement. They were floating around on wine and long black cigarettes: it was a false world, a delusion of freedom. It felt as if the spirit of the city were encased inside the winged Quadriga statue, slashing her horses from an immobile chariot above the Brandenburger gate.

Maybe Edmond was right: she shouldn't have come. She had fudged her exams into a papier mâché pulp and she couldn't escape the loneliness that had settled in her stomach after her rejection of Richard. On top of this she could sense Karl's helplessness as his beloved homeland darkened under the Nazi banner. *If he does try to resist,* she thought, *he will need friends overseas.*

The restaurant was busy. The waiter showed them to a table by a large glass window.

'How do you tolerate life here,' said Rebecca, 'when people are snatched from their homes and thrown into prison, when Jewish houses are splashed with foul graffiti and large parts of the population are branded and suppressed?'

'What good would I do by leaving?' Karl replied, glancing around quickly to make sure no-one was within earshot.

'If everyone who opposed the regime left the country there would be no chance for any resistance,' said Jane.

'Keep your voice down,' said Karl.

'That's all very well,' Rebecca continued, 'but how will you keep up with your friends if you stay in Germany, Karl? What about me?'

Karl looked at her. 'We were breaking up anyway,' he said. It was cruel but it was the truth. He might as well say it. They had been skirting round it all day. There were greater issues at stake. His country was falling apart in front of him. *Why can't she understand that?*

'Why have you changed? It's because I'm Jewish isn't it? I'm some exotic treasure you hoard until it becomes dangerous; then you drop me like a hot coal.'

Karl looked round, her accusation was ridiculous, offensive – he wouldn't justify it with a response. It had been a mistake bringing them here. There was no holding Rebecca back once she got started and Jane was not much better, though at least she was on his side.

Jane sensed eyes round the room turning their way then flicking away again so as not to be caught. 'It's a shame it's our last day tomorrow, Karl,' she said, changing tack, 'I would've liked to visit your ancestral home. It sounds like a glorious mix of antlers, orchards and books, worlds away from the city.' She paused, thinking, *it might have been possible to talk there.*

'It's full of musty closets and portraits of ancestors. My family is rooted in this country. We are born, moulded and buried in its earth, its traditions. That's why I can't abandon it now,' Karl said, glancing at Rebecca.

'You can't be thinking of joining the party, Karl?' said Rebecca.

'I hope I can stay out, I just don't know how long for,' he dropped his voice and leant towards them. 'I've been building up anti-Nazi connections through the old Student Korps. We have to manage the circle quietly in case things get worse.'

'How can a mismatched gaggle of scholars and aristocrats hope to resist a regime like this?' said Rebecca.

'These people are all powerful in their own way. We have to be ready to serve in a new government when the time comes. Meanwhile we will try to moderate the Nazis if we can.'

He had thought this through a million times. It was his lifeline. He had to believe it. *How could a bunch of thugs and racists take over a country as proud and cultured as Germany? There were many who would fight back, surely?* It nagged at him: the idea that the resistance represented the minority; that so many had fallen in with the Nazi way. Fear and mistrust had spread like mould over jam. The outside world was already distancing itself and the mould was getting thicker by the day.

'Things can be made to change,' Karl said. 'Your British papers are terrible war-mongers. They condemn all German citizens for the actions of a government that only came to power through bullying and manipulation. We need allies not enemies. We are universally hated wherever we turn.'

'You can't deny the persecution of German Jews, Karl,' said Rebecca. 'My own cousins have been arriving in London in droves. Why shouldn't our papers report it? It would be an outrage to witness it and not speak out.'

'No-one wants war,' Jane interrupted, 'but no-one is prepared to take any action at all. It's all formalities and diplomatic tip-toeing. It's true there's little distinction made between Germans and Nazis. If there's a resistance movement it will need to work fast.'

'We're trying to,' said Karl. 'We need partners but no-one will talk to us. They're all too bound up placating Hitler, or lumping us into one pot. Even my old tutors at Oxford are reluctant to speak to me. You don't know what it's like to be secretly despised by those you hoped would offer their support.'

'The fact that you stay in the country; that you work for the German Foreign Office and travel at will. It's all taken as evidence that you've turned your back on your friends in England,' said Rebecca. 'You can't expect to be welcomed when it looks as though you're working for the regime. Besides, it's crucial our papers report what is going on. The support you need won't materialise unless the international community is shocked into action. Germany is not what it was.'

'Don't you think I know that,' Karl said, 'but those of us who try to find help are met with outright hostility. There is no way to resist except from within but I, for one, am no longer trusted.'

Karl looks as grey and distressed as the city around him, Jane thought. *How long can he survive here?*

Suddenly there were shouts in the street outside. People were running.

Diners stood up, turning to see what the commotion was about. Just outside the window, a group of young men in civilian shirts, wearing brown Storm Troop boots and trousers had cornered an old man. Spit dribbled down his face like fresh graffiti on the wall of a Jewish shop. Someone pulled his arms down and booted him in the stomach. He fell to the floor. Boots smashed down. He was covered in blood; the raging wall of sweaty flesh that hovered over him was thick and eager – vultures at a carcass. He stood no chance. The diners stood there, horrified, unmoving.

Suddenly, a young man with dark hair and a scar over one eye barged out of the restaurant. He thudded into the backs of the attackers like a bull into the ring. They turned on him, pinioning him against the wall. He was shoved to the ground. His wife was inside. She was on her feet. She screamed, 'Eric laufen! Da raus!' The window pane was thin but her screams rebounded in her face. She smashed her fists on the window. They smashed their fists into her husband. The diners moved back fearing the mob might turn but the group outside was oblivious to them.

Screams from across the road. A chase. The group outside the window split up and raced off. The two men lay cold and bloody on the floor. They didn't move. The diners didn't move. The woman fainted. The attackers had scented another fight – a bigger one. People were coming out of the picture house opposite. They held stones. They were throwing them –at anyone on the street. *Crack.* A stone hit the window. Jane felt someone's arm knock into her head as people rushed backwards. 'Get those men inside,' someone yelled, a man, the owner of the café, his arm lifted, pointing, his feet static, motionless.

'Get them inside,' Jane cried, starting up, but an arm held her back. It was Karl.

'Wait!' he said. 'We don't want to attract attention.' He pushed Jane behind him and walked to the door. Then he dashed out and hauled the older man back in. 'I know him,' he said, bending over the man's inert form. 'He was a friend of my father. He lived in the village near our house. What was he doing here?'

Someone dragged the younger man inside. He was still breathing. Just. His wife had hit her head on a table when she fell. Jane helped her into a chair and dabbed at the cut with a napkin. Rebecca brought her water. Crowds were gathering outside. Karl stood up and stared at the picture house opposite, squinting to read the film title hanging on the wall.

'It's that Petterson and Bendel film,' he said.

'What's that?' said Rebecca.

'Swedish film. Anti-Semitic. Been in the Nazi press,' said Karl. 'We'd better get out of here. This is only going to get worse.'

The dining room exploded into frenzied action. Everyone was grabbing their belongings. No-one wanted to be trapped inside. Then again, no-one wanted to be trapped outside either. The area was full of Jewish businesses. It was pleasant and affluent. It was an obvious target. They were like corn in a pan, bursting against the walls, stuck over a flame, heat all around them and no way out.

'We can't just leave,' Jane said. 'What about your father's friend?'

'He's dead,' Karl said. The old man's body was lying next to the window.

Karl, Jane and Rebecca flung on their coats and hats and squeezed past the diners hanging back from the door.

'Where are you going?' said the waiter, 'it's not safe.'

'They're beating people!' Rebecca said, 'Do something.'

'Stay back,' warned the waiter, staring at her as if she was mad.

A sharp-nosed man with a pronounced limp straggled past the restaurant, following the mob. Seeing Rebecca, he stopped and glared, then grabbed a chair that had fallen into the road and hurled it with all his might at the restaurant window. Diners screamed and ducked, covering their faces with their arms. The chair fell harmlessly to the ground. Everyone froze. The man saw Karl. He shook his head and hobbled on to join the pack.

'I know him, too,' muttered Karl to Jane. 'He was head librarian at Humboldt University. He never said much. He fought in the war.' People were filling their vacuum with Nazi ideology like Volkswagens with gasoline: hollow, thirsty, pour in the black gunge, one spark to explode.

Outside, cars slowed to a halt, crammed in by the growing hoard.

'Raus Jude! Raus Jude! Zerstörung der Juden!' screamed the mob, dragging drivers from cars, hurling them into the throng and smashing windscreens.

Small boys with neatly combed hair and buckle shoes appeared on the streets with their mothers. They were pointing and smiling.

'Police, Karl, look at the police,' said Jane, jabbing at the window, fury rising within her like a tornado.

Karl said nothing. Truckloads of police had arrived but showed no sign of interfering. One man slouched back against his vehicle and lit a cigarette.

'Karl, I can't watch, I have to do something,' cried Jane, tears rolling down her face. The stink of sweat and blood in the air made her want to retch.

'Come away,' said Karl, pulling her back, away from the street, into the restaurant. 'Rebecca!' he said, grabbing her arm and yanking her out of the doorway. 'It's not safe for you.'

Rebecca fell backwards onto the floor, white-faced. Jane helped her up. Someone shut the door to the restaurant and urged the diners to move to the back.

The waiter turned out the lights. The screams, smashes, yells from the road felt oppressively loud, bursting on the eardrums like cymbals round the head. Stones clattered against the window pane like hail on a tin roof. They cowered in the kitchen. This was feverish. This was a tumour on the brain that grew and grew until it popped and infected the tissue around.

A migraine was developing behind Jane's left eye. She couldn't see anything but waves of light that spread in a circle round her pupil. In the waves a man was caught. He was struggling to get up. His face smashed against a window; his hands squeaked against the pane as he slipped to the floor. It was a mirage fading into a whirlpool, sucking her in. Her head felt like it was about to burst and she saw flickering dots of light. Was he real?

She felt sick. The thudding was back in her ears. She slipped to the floor and her head hit the ground with a crack.

Determination

20th August 1935, 9am
Bloomsbury, London
Jane is twenty-one

Jane's eyes flashed open and she stared upwards, blind for a moment. The nightmarish vision that had slithered into her mind, twining itself round the innocence of her dream and yanking hard till it choked and blackened, evaporated. Her heartbeat slowed as she remembered where she was. She was safe. She was home. Even so, she could still see the face of the man squashed and bloody against the window. He wasn't safe. He was German and Jewish.

She hadn't slept well. She had lain awake as she had done most nights since her return from Berlin. She had witnessed horrific brutality, cowering in the restaurant until it was all over, returning to London by train the next day as if everything were normal. She was so sick on the way home her stomach felt like it had churned butter. The Nazis scratched people's prejudices till they broke the surface and bloodied the skin. All this concealed behind a powder-puff of Turkish cigarettes and elegant parties. There had to be some way she could work with Karl to resist the regime; a way to help those who were forced to flee.

Rebecca's letter was still on her dressing table. It might as well have been written in red ink. She was a woman in torment and there was nothing Jane could do for her. Not until she calmed down, saw sense, stopped blaming her friends for her misery, for the violence they had all witnessed. For events that were out of their control.

Jane picked up the letter again. It was loud and full of fear. She read:

"I suppose I am going to hell in my own way, and you soon won't care whether I burn or not. You are wrong that I do not care for Karl's happiness …"

When did I ever suggest that? thought Jane.

"… If you really love me you would think of my happiness. Karl once said that I was the sort of person who ought to be stroked in order to be helped, not whipped fiercely. If you continue to use quite such brutal methods …"

What?

"… as you do now you will achieve your objective in driving me from you into an outer hell but may conceivably be sorry one day that you have done so. Before you both desert me – for God's sake – be sure it is the best course for all of us, R."

How does Rebecca expect me to respond to this? Jane thought. *I haven't deserted her.*

All the turmoil of her break up with Karl and the terror of the riot had solidified into a knot of anger inside Rebecca. Jane was at fault for seemingly taking Karl's side, for watching it all spiral into chaos. Her stunned silence in the train on the way home had bounced Rebecca's torrent of words back like mud from a cartwheel and this had been the result.

Karl has to stay in Germany for now, though how he can bear it Heaven knows. Rebecca must understand that in the end. She'll have to. Karl will need our help.

She put the letter back on the table, turned over and pulled the covers over her ears to block out the voices in her head – the shouts of the people outside the restaurant that wouldn't go away: 'Raus Jude! Raus Jude! Zerstörung der Juden!'

She was lucky. She really was. She tried to focus on that. Edmond had performed a miracle. He had managed to rent the top two floors of the house in Bloomsbury where their mother and father had lived during their time in London. It felt as if they had come home at last.

The smell of toast wafted upstairs. Edmond must be eating breakfast. Susie, their parent's former housemaid, was back with them again, employed to cook and clean. She lived in the East End now in her own house with her husband and children. She was tremendously loyal – domestic help was so hard to find these days.

Jane tried exorcising the horrors of Berlin by imagining her parents there, in her room, in the house. Her father had looked forward to her birth like a boy with his hand in the sweet jar, Elsie had said. If only it had lasted. Still, she had Edmond. He had been at the train station to meet her when she returned from Berlin. In fact, he had waited at St Pancras for most of the day, unsure which train she would be on. It had been dark by the time they arrived at the house. They had collapsed into the armchairs their mother and father had used and spent the whole night talking.

'There are ways you can help – refugee work, political societies. You can convince people to talk to Karl, to work with him.' Edmond had paused. 'There's no need for you to go to Germany again Jane,' he had said.

The bedside clock on the bureau ticked loudly. Rays of light cut through the gap in her curtains, slicing across her bed and forcing her eyes open. She rolled over and sat up, tugging her comb through her frazzled hair before giving up and reaching for her dressing gown.

Peering down the staircase, Jane had visions of her mother running to the door in distress to fetch the doctor.

'Jane, you've got a letter from Oxford,' Edmond shouted upstairs.

Silt in the stomach, unsettled. *Don't open it. Go back to bed.*

'Jane.'

'Coming,' she said and stumbled downstairs.

He held out an envelope.

'Open it.'

She slipped her finger under the flap and ripped upwards pulling out a letter.

'I passed.'

Edmond hugged her as if she might melt away at any moment.

'I don't deserve it though.'

'Don't be so down on yourself. You worked hard under difficult circumstances.'

'What does it mean?'

'It means you can find work, get on with life, Jane.'

The silt shifted, dissolved. It felt as though someone had picked up her puppet strings and pulled her upright. The house warmed up, light glinting off every surface, bouncing off mirrors, catching in the vase of flowers on the hall table and raking every dark corner.

'Time to wake up, you mean, to find a calling.'

As long as that calling doesn't involve overseas travel, Edmond thought, *she looks shattered, she's still not sleeping.*

'If the situation in Germany gets worse, there will be work to be done housing refugees. You could try talking to the Quakers at Friends House?' he said.

There was a loud clatter from the kitchen, a pan on the floor perhaps. Jane flinched. The light caught on a cobweb under the stairs.

'I can walk you round there today if you like,' said Edmond. 'It'll do you good to get out.'

Jane had turned her back to him. She wasn't listening. She was moving away.

'Did you open the window in the sitting room Edmond? I'm sure I closed it last night,' she said, pointing at the open sash.

'No. Does it matter?'

'Well it's open now. Who opened it?'

'Maybe Susie thought the room was getting stuffy or maybe I left it open last night. I can't remember. The fire was rather smoky. I'll go and close it now if it bothers you.'

'Leave it. I'm just feeling irritable. Little things get to me. Let's go out.'

'You're not dressed, Jane.'

'Give me half an hour and I will be. I've been cooped up inside. I need to be more decisive, feel like I'm achieving something.'

'And you need to eat breakfast,' said Edmond, 'I'll give you an hour and then I'll drag you out by hook or by crook.'

She wasn't listening. She had turned her back to him again.

She was closing the window.

21st September 1936, 11.30am
Bloomsbury, London
Jane is twenty-two

It was a quiet Georgian square: tall brick town houses surrounding a neat grassy park, railed in and inaccessible to the passing public. Only those lucky enough to live or work in the square could make use of its leafy refuge. Autumn leaves whispered their way along the pavement, blown by a whimsical wind until they got caught in a wet gutter or stuck to the bottom of a shoe and rubbed off on a doormat.

Children entering the immaculately kept offices of The Inter-Aid Committee for Children from Germany were reminded to wipe their shoes on the mat as they entered. They arrived unaccompanied, bound for boarding school or a well-funded home. Around their necks hung labels with their name and the number they had been given on arrival in Southampton. They shivered on small wooden chairs in the hallway until they were called in for interview.

Doris Palmer, the woman with all the papers, sat at a desk at the end of the corridor. She looked them up and down as they fidgeted and then wrote something in a file. She didn't ask about their parents or where they'd come from. They were glad because they didn't want to think about that. Eventually she called them over, took off the label and handed them an identity badge.

'Third door on the right dear, Peggy will show you.'

That was all she could manage. She wished the Committee had put someone with more grit in her place. *They're better off here,* she told herself each time she passed them on.

Peggy took them by the hand and led them to the third door. 'In here please,' she said, gently squeezing each small hand. They had tried to divide the office up to give the children some privacy but there wasn't enough space. The typewriters rattled and splurged and spat out paper all day and the phone just kept on ringing. As a new organisation, they were struggling to put their systems in order and each arrival was a test run for the future.

We have to establish ourselves as a safe route before things get worse, thought Jane as she answered the phone for the hundredth time that morning.

They had screened off a small area for the children to meet Matilda Jameson, the office manager, and find out where they were going. Jane, on the other side of the screen, sifted painfully through piles of letters and drafted appeals for funding. She flung open the window nearest her remembering her lonely despair returning from boarding school to her mother and step-father after Elsie's death. These children might never go back to Germany. Their parents had sent them over for safekeeping.

It was a hot, sweaty, sticky-prune day. Jane's cotton blouse quickly grew damp beneath the arms and down her back as she leaned against her chair.

Images from the Berlin Olympics stuck in her mind like dead flies to honey tape. Hitler's motorcade had sailed triumphantly through the Brandenburg Gate, 'heiled' by half-mast arms that pricked out from the crowd like chicken necks to a knife. Five interlocking rings had chained the world together. Nazi and Olympic flags hung, garish and crude, side by side.

No boycott but then there were no anti-Semitic posters in sight, the journalists had written, and there had been *one* Jewish athlete on the German team. Maybe the balmy oil of athletic prowess would soothe the tension. Maybe Hitler would bow his head to the rings and throw down his spiky swastika for good? *Ridiculous*, Jane had thought, *how can the world's leaders be so blatantly naïve?*

Four days had passed since the closing ceremony yet Jane was sitting at her desk, as hot and steamed up as a pressure cooker, contemplating the impact of all the publicity, when the door to the office opened and a small girl tiptoed in. Or at least it felt like she tiptoed. She was so light she could easily have disappeared into thin air had she not had a dark cloud of curly hair floating around her head, a bit like Jane's.

As she made her way across the room, she tripped on a frayed shoelace that had come loose. Jane helped her up. *She's not here, she's thinking about home,* thought Jane, seeing her wide, vacant eyes. She stepped back, giving the little girl space to approach Matilda.

'Hello dear, what's your name?' Matilda said.

'Ester,' said the girl. 'Ich will nach Hause gehen bitte. Ich möchte mein' Mutti.'

'You need to speak English,' said Matilda. 'I've got an information pack here for you. You'll be attending the Stoutly Roach School. Your parents have already paid. Someone will be here to collect you shortly.' The girl stared at her. 'That's all. Run along now.' The girl did nothing. 'Peggy.'

Peggy entered the office and took the girl by the hand. As they passed Jane's desk, Jane handed the girl an art book she'd bought at the National Gallery. It was called *The Wildlife of Albrecht Dürer*. There was an owl on the front. Jane wished her German was more fluent but the girl took the book and smiled, grateful to think about something other than the faces she'd left behind in Hamburg and her mother's voice the night before she left: 'England is a beautiful country. You can play in the park there.'

Ester hadn't been to the park for a while: there were big signs up and people telling her to go away. She missed playing with her friends and climbing trees.

'At least I won't have to mend the holes in your stockings,' her mother had said.

Ester left the room, escorted by Peggy, her head bent low as if still weighed down by a label round her neck.

As soon as the door closed behind her, Jane picked up the phone.

'I have a group of three children from Munich. Their father was beaten up in the street. The windows of their shop were smashed in the night. They're petrified. They say it won't be long before—'

'Will their upkeep be fully paid? Do they have a place at school?'

'They have money.'

'Is it enough?'

'For a while.'

'These children will become a public liability. They can only stay whilst they are attending school. Do you have guarantors for them?'

'Not yet but—'

'Then you must wait until you do.'

The line cut out.

Matilda poked her head around the screen. 'You must be more diplomatic, Jane. Some is better than none, surely?'

'You haven't been to Germany. People disappear. No-one turns a hair.'

'You may have travelled more than the rest of us and we don't have the contacts you do, but that doesn't make you morally superior, Jane. You need to get off your high horse and start working with us rather than undermining the Committee.'

'I'd hardly call it undermining the Committee, Matilda.'

'They want to help as many children as they can. We all do. But you have to be realistic. This country has to be realistic. We can't bring everyone and anyone in. You're all saintly and moral but you're not practical, Jane. Besides, you're not Jewish and neither am I.'

'That's got nothing to do with it.'

'And you may say we bring in non-Aryan Christians too. All minorities are at risk. But there still has to be a measure of control. I can see why the government is so strict.'

'None of the refugees want to leave their homes, their families. The reception they get isn't likely to encourage them to stay longer than they have to anyway. Fully qualified dentists and doctors will find themselves employed as domestic servants because that's the only work they're allowed to do.'

'I know that, Jane. No need to rub my nose in it.'

Peggy appeared from the hallway with another trembling applicant. Matilda and Jane retreated to their desks still bristling.

Jane listened to Matilda's interview, hoping to overhear something that would subdue the ulcer that was forming in her mouth.

'The headmaster will meet you on arrival,' said Matilda, 'and show you to your room. You'll meet the other students and I'm sure they will make you feel welcome. Make sure you speak in English at all times and try to avoid mentioning your faith, it'll only set you apart as different and you really want to blend in, don't you?'

That was it for Jane. She left the room.

5.30pm

The door banged shut. Wind whipped leaves into the air, whirling them round Jane's feet, tossing them into her hair, blowing dirt at her eyes. She bent into it and pushed off towards Russell Square with her hands stuffed into her pockets. It was cold outside but it had been unbearable in the office. *Surely there should be some reward, some sense of achievement that will make volunteering worthwhile?* she thought. There was something humiliating about unpaid work when most of the other women in the office had been taken on with a salary, trained up as secretaries.

She had promised to meet Rebecca after work. *Rebecca will understand my frustration*, she thought. *We're working for the same cause now.*

A bell jangled as she pushed open the door of the tea house. Rebecca was sitting in the corner. There was a man opposite her.

'Jane, thanks for coming,' Rebecca paused, glancing at her companion. 'Sorry I didn't warn you but I've been itching to introduce you to Walter for ages. Walter, this is Jane Deering, a university friend of mine. She works for the Inter-aid Committee. We travelled to Germany together last year.'

She turned to Jane, 'I met Walter at a community fundraiser in South London. He's one of our rare Liberal MPs and, I'm pleased to say, a supporter of our cause. In fact, he'll be travelling to Spain in November to help coordinate the Spanish Relief effort.'

'How do you do,' said Jane, holding out her hand which Walter shook warmly.

'Glad to meet you,' Walter said, 'I've heard a lot about your Committee. They debate its actions almost daily in the Commons it seems.'

'Yes, I'm afraid I find it rather exasperating. We receive letters from so many families and organisations and we're only able to help a tiny number. The government puts such heavy restrictions on entry it's all very difficult.'

'Believe me, I understand your frustration,' said Walter, pulling out a chair for Jane before sitting himself. 'This Spanish Relief racket is pretty depressing. The ball is constantly batted back. The only way to keep your sanity is to let it drop once in a while and wait for a better opportunity.'

'That's all very well,' said Jane, 'but I keep getting glued down by bog-eyed officials who refuse to give an inch.'

'I suppose it might help if you spoke to people a little higher up the chain,' Walter said. He was used to the wrangles of government and knew that if you wanted to get anywhere you had to mount a vigorous charm offensive, which, he felt, he was rather good at.

'That would certainly help,' Jane said, looking at him. Standing at over six feet, Walter was well-used to being noticed. There was an attention to detail about him, pernickety perhaps: the handkerchief beautifully folded in the upper left pocket of his suit; the dark brown hair that feathered out delicately behind his ears and combed its way across his temple; the meticulously carved sideburns. His nose was long and arched, giving him a rather haughty appearance. This distinction was, however, undermined by a rather weak chin.

'It would be my pleasure to assist you should you need it,' Walter continued, 'though I find I am more successful in the corridors of Whitehall than in the debating ring. I can't promise to make much headway there for you I'm afraid'.

He looked at his watch. 'My wife is expecting me back on the 6.30pm from King's Cross, but I hate to go when I've only just met you, Jane,' he said thinking, *I like this woman, she's not afraid to speak her mind.*

Jane caught his glance and felt the softness of his smile wrap itself round her, numbing her mind and quickening her heart.

'My wife is used to me running late; maybe I'll catch a later train home.'

'Please don't delay on my account,' Jane said. It sounded like he had little time or respect for his wife. She wasn't going to be an accessory to that. She felt her hands grow sweaty and hoped he wouldn't shake them.

Walter stood up. 'Let's hope it's not too long.' He waved the waiter over and asked for his coat and hat, 'After all, I need more information if I'm going to assist you with your cause.'

'Thank you, Walter,' Rebecca said. She nudged Jane sharply and then regretted it. It wasn't Jane's decision to bring Walter here.

'We'll meet again soon then,' Walter said, handing the waiter some money to cover the bill before making his way out of the café.

'So, what did you make of Walter?' Rebecca said.

'He seems a bit shallow, self-absorbed.'

'If you're wondering about his wife, it's a tragic case, Jane.'

'I'm not keen on gossip; it's not fair on the people involved.'

'I shouldn't worry. Walter doesn't make much of a secret of his unhappiness. He was due to get married but his fiancée died in a boating accident. I know it seems odd, but he was so grief-stricken and lonely, he married her sister.'

That was foolish of him, Jane thought, *he must've panicked.*

'That's dreadful,' she said, 'but why he would've married her sister beats me. It can't have been a love match, can it?'

'Certainly not. From the way he talks, it's a decision he's regretted ever since.'

'Even less reason to treat her badly, then,' said Jane. She was in no mood to give this man leeway, whatever influence he had in parliament. Walter had the height and slender figure of her father. *He is, in fact, very attractive*, she thought, *which makes his selfishness even more disappointing.*

'Jane, you are being harsh today. I know work is grim but you're going to have to get better at putting it behind you when you leave.'

'You introduced Walter under the guise of someone who could help win support for refugees, I could hardly stop thinking about him,' she stopped. 'I mean work, after that. All I really wanted was a quiet word with you.'

'I'm sorry, Jane. I could see when you came in that you weren't in the right frame of mind. I should've told you I was planning to invite Walter but I wasn't sure he could make it. He only confirmed this afternoon.'

'Of course,' Jane said. 'I just need to go home and rest. I'm sure he'll be a useful contact. I'll make a better impression next time.' *Though it might be hard*, she thought, *there's definitely something about him that unsettles me.*

'You do look exhausted.'

'I'll be all right.'

'Come on, Jane. If you're feeling rotten, I'd like to help.'

The waiter was lingering behind them. He looked as though he might put a pin on their chairs just to make sure they left for good. They hadn't ordered much. In fact, Jane hadn't eaten anything. A cup of tea was a poor excuse to occupy a table for so long. Jane could sense his impatience. He was standing so close to her she could feel him breathing down her neck like a dragon with a sore throat.

'Let's go,' Jane said, ending the conversation.

As they stepped outside, Jane shivered and wrapped her scarf round her neck. Leaving felt like setting off over a moor; the sense of freedom more than made up for the cold.

Why do I make life so difficult for myself? she thought. *No wonder I've got a sore head, chewing over issues and butting horns with people the whole time. Maybe Matilda's right – I'll be more convincing if I learn when to stop.*

26th October, 1936, 8.30am
Bloomsbury, London

Another letter from Walter fell with a clang onto the doormat. At least Jane felt it clanged. She hadn't asked for this attention, had she? She'd been verging on rude when they met. Yet he kept on writing to her. By now, her cheeks flushed scarlet whenever she picked up the post. She tried to get there before Edmond and so far she was undiscovered. It was like a guilty secret. On the other hand, there was nothing to reproach; they were working for a similar cause. That was all.

"Dear Jane,
The whole face of politics has changed completely in the last year, and very much for the worse. Fascism is on the offensive everywhere. The inevitability of a big war is largely treated as a commonplace by the Right, who have absorbed Winston's views.

Will you do something to get this idea of a big relief mission for Madrid going? We shall not change the Government's non-intervention – let's go out for a big relief scheme. It's wanted whoever wins, whatever happens: thousands of homes destroyed, breadwinners killed, mothers killed. Something has to be done now.

Walter."

"30th November, 1936
My dear Jane,
I wish you were in this Spanish Relief racket with me. Somehow my temper has grown shorter lately, and I am beginning to make enemies, by cursing people, or by saying the wrong thing. I have just done it again on the telephone, and that I think is another member of the committee who will be after my blood. I used to be so good at getting all these different

people to work together. They all thought I was a mild, kind man with the best intentions. I suppose one gets found out in the end!
Walter."

Jane folded the letter and put it back in its envelope. Then she took it out again. The Spanish Relief effort was being scaled up considerably. There were local fundraisers all around the country. This could run alongside her work at the office. Spanish civilians were being butchered, bombed and torn apart by Republicans and Fascists alike in a bloody battle for control. Walter had been to Spain. Working with him would mean getting something done. Something tangible. Her fist clenched around the letter as a new determination set in her mind and she sat down at her desk to write a reply.

5th February 1941, 3pm
St Andrew's Hospital, Northampton
Jane is twenty-six

Jane saw Edmond coming from her bedroom window. Then she saw herself, running towards him. *The white-coats want to use me for their experiments. I can't stay here any longer. They follow me everywhere.* Polished shoes rapped down the corridor. Hands grabbed her beneath the arms. A trestle table pulled out. Restraints. Dials. Cold metal and rubber. *No!* Jane kept her mouth clamped shut and trapped the fears inside just in time. It was her only hope of peace.

Edmond entered the building and walked upstairs to her floor. She waited for him quietly. Then she hugged him and chattered about embroidery.

'We sit together in a room. It's comfortable and although we don't talk much, we are busy. I'm trying to do a piece for mother but I may not finish it before I leave here; my hands are shaky and I find it hard to hold the needle.'

'Can I see it?' said Edmond.

'It's locked away in the activity room.'

'Oh.'

'I was in the room making a stab at it last time mother came to see me. I think she was surprised. "You never showed any interest in embroidery when you were young Jane", she said. It's one of the things they do here I told her, and I can't read books. I can't concentrate for long enough.'

Edmond's heart banged away with a vengeance like it always did when he visited his sister, not that he had been able to visit often since the war began and he was posted out to Belfast to train as an officer. Soon he would be going overseas, towards the Middle East they said. Then he wouldn't see Jane for some time. It made him feel nauseous to think that she would be here alone for who knows how long, but where else would she be cared for, kept safe, while fighting erupted all over the world? Evie was pregnant and Jane continued to exhibit symptoms of schizophrenia, or so the doctors said.

'Will you allow Evie to come and see you, Jane? I may be posted overseas and I want to know you are seeing your friends. It's important that you get better.'

Jane let go of his arm. Evie had betrayed her. Evie had brought her here. Evie didn't want her to leave. She could still see Evie standing on her front doorstep, her black coat shrouding her tall shape like a raven as she waited to tell her the news: 'He's gone.'

Evie knocking on her bedroom door again and again.

Evie shrinking away as the doctors led her off down the corridor towards the pain, darkness, confinement.

I trusted her. She was my best friend. She gave up on me.

'I don't want to see Evie.'

She loves you, Jane. Don't push her away, Edmond felt like crying.

'Jane, you must let us help you. Evie wants to help you.'

'No!' It was almost a scream. Edmond was shocked. Maybe the doctors were right. She had not improved as much as they had hoped. She had seemed calm when he first arrived. He suggested a walk in the grounds. 'The daffodils are coming out,' he said.

Men were doing sit-ups on the lawn near the golf course. Their instructor stuck a whistle in his mouth and the men leapt up and formed two rows. Next thing Edmond knew they were tossing another man into the air. It was quite astonishing. Was this some sort of exercise in trust or was it just a physical diversion? He looked at Jane. She seemed oblivious to it. She was pointing to a patch of open ground by the trees ahead.

'That's the allotment,' she said. 'The women have planted potatoes there.' She stopped. Something stirred in her memory: a man with a potato nose; a black armband; a pale egg with blotches all over it. She often tried to sew these patchwork thoughts together but she usually ended up dissatisfied. The order was never quite right and the meaning was nearly always missing.

'When I'm strong enough they say I can join them,' she continued and Edmond nodded, fighting back tears.

They walked past an old Victorian bath house, its decorative brickwork twisted up in ivy, the door hanging off its hinges. Edmond glanced in. Footprints led across the grimy slate floor towards pipes that jutted out at the back. Someone curious like him perhaps. The baths, if there had been baths, had been removed. The windows were thin and let in little light. *Thank goodness we've moved on from this,* Edmond thought, the place was so cold and damp, so far removed from any comfort.

'Edmond,' called Jane from outside, 'There's someone coming.'

Edmond ducked out of the door, blinking. Jane grabbed his sleeve and pulled him round behind the building. Two doctors in long white coats walked past.

'They don't like us coming here,' Jane said, tapping the disconnected pipes with her foot. Edmond noticed that there was still one pipe that led inside.

'They don't still use this place do they?' Edmond said. 'It's out of order, hidden away, unclean.'

Jane shrugged.

'Water shocks?'

Jane was walking away. She wasn't listening.

Edmond stared at the rusty pipework. *It's not a bath house. It's shock treatment. Water, electricity, insulin. What next?*

Jane had to get better. He was leaving her here to get better. Jane was only here because there was a war on. There was no alternative, no-one to care for her. No-one who knew how to. *But do they really know what they're doing here?*

He caught up with her. 'I'll ask mother to bring you your diaries,' he said. 'You should try to write. It'll do you good.'

'I need Elsie's statue. The one of the Madonna and Child,' Jane said. 'And the painting of the donkey on the moor.'

'Isn't that a lonely picture? I've always found it rather doleful,' said Edmond.

'The donkey is untethered, free to roam where it pleases.'

'The landscape is bleak, grey, smothered in fog.'

'It's about seeing through the fog and imagining something beyond it,' said Jane turning away from the buildings to look out over the grounds that dipped into trees, hiding the fence behind them. 'You're right. I do need my diaries.'

Torn

5th December 1936, 6pm
Bloomsbury, London
Jane is twenty-two

Walter tucked his watch back into his coat pocket. His wife was unhappy whether he was there or not. In fact, he was pretty sure she was happier when he was away.

Jane must have finished work by now. He hoped his letters had done something to impress her. He was in the right line of work, pursuing a cause she believed in but he guessed she would only admire someone whose passion for justice exceeded her own. *This might turn out to be a harder campaign than the one I ran before the election last year,* thought Walter.

He strode into the British Museum café and scanned the tables.

'Walter.' Jane was sitting near the door. She stood up as he approached.

'Jane,' said Walter, 'what a pleasure to see you again.'

She was wearing a velvet coat with a jewelled brooch on the collar, clearly making an effort to brighten up what might be seen as rather a plain outfit. *Her hair looks neater, flattened by the rain or did she straighten it before leaving work?*

'I can see from the water in the brim of your hat that it's still hideous and rainy outside.'

'I was foolish enough to leave my umbrella in the office.'

The rain had failed in its attempt to douse Jane's spirits as she dodged drips from the awnings of stalls selling trinkets to tourists outside the museum. She had just come from a meeting with Quaker friends at the Germany Emergency Committee and they had been enormously supportive. 'We'll be more effective if we join forces and work together,' they had said.

The buzz in her brain echoed the buzz in the café: a warm hum of bodies on the move, adrenaline in the veins, the clink of cups raised, caffeine injected. The waiter turned the wireless on and the voice of Judy Garland danced lightly over the crowded room.

Walter sat down opposite her and they ordered tea.

'It takes me a while to unwind from work as you had the misfortune to discover when we first met.'

'I'm glad you gave me another chance.'

Jane blushed. Her head was spinning slightly as if she'd had a glass of wine and was continuing to drink. Perhaps it was the way he was looking at her so intently as though trying to read a map that was the wrong way up.

If only Richard had the drive, the ambition that this man has to make a difference, she thought. *Walter must've worked hard to win over voters at a time when other Liberals were ousted.*

She hadn't seen Richard for well over a year but he had sent her buckets of letters to which she had occasionally tried to reply. Letters were far harder than essays. *How can I tell him how I feel when I don't know myself?* Draft after draft ended up in the bin while more letters arrived, piling up like tax receipts, less and less likely to be dealt with the higher the pile grew. *I'm being selfish. I have to tell him to stop.* It was a decision that was never quite set in ink. *He's a listener, a cautious man, he won't push me forward, might even hold me back.* She shut the letters away in her cupboard and tried to forget about them.

The tea arrived.

Walter put his hand out to pour at the same time as Jane. In fact, he reached for the pot as soon as he saw her intention.

'Allow me, please.'

He poured the tea.

'What do you think of this latest development in the Edward-Wallis scandal?'

Jane frowned. *Aren't we here to discuss Spanish Relief?*

'I'm glad Mrs Simpson has left the country for a while.'

'You disapprove of their relationship then?'

'The King couldn't continue his affair without repercussions. He knew that from the start.'

'So you don't think the King deserves to choose his partner?'

'She's still married. The King will have to bow to public pressure eventually.'

'I agree, but if the King was married and Mrs Simpson was single, would such a great fuss be made? It is quite common in an unhappy marriage for people to look for happiness elsewhere.'

'Indeed and it causes hurt and upset to all involved.'

'Surely that's not for us to judge?'

'That's not what I meant.'

'You made a judgement, didn't you?'

'No.'

It felt, once again, like they had started with a thistle and ended on a thorn. Annoyingly though, this wasn't the end; they had only just sat down. 'Betraying your partner, however difficult the relationship, is wrong,' Jane said. 'At least seek a divorce if things are that bad.'

She stopped. This was about Walter. It had to be.

'It's far more complicated than that,' Walter said.

Jane shifted awkwardly, pressing her back firmly into the frame of her chair. *Well,* she thought, *if he wants to tread on his own toes, fine, but I'm not getting involved.*

'I'm glad I'm not in Mrs Simpson's shoes,' she said. 'Shall I get the bill?'

She hadn't touched her tea.

'I'm sorry, Jane, I've upset you.'

'Not at all.'

'Please, Jane, at least finish your tea. You haven't told me anything about your work.' She wasn't looking at him. She was rummaging around in her bag, perhaps looking for her purse? *I should've started with something she's interested in. What a fool I am.*

'I want you to work with me,' he said. 'The situation is desperate in Spain. Their hospitals are simply not equipped to deal with the onslaught, food is scarce – homes, whole families have been wiped out. I'm in the process of setting up the National Joint Committee for Spanish Relief—'

The café was frantic, people coming and going, a metronome of constant movement ticking around them, but Walter's face was sharp and clear and his voice stood out from the hum. Jane closed her bag and put it down. Walter was leading a movement, establishing a team, driving the relief effort forward.

'Will you work with me, Jane?'

She paused. A moment ago she had written him off as flighty and superficial. What was behind this commitment? Had he witnessed the suffering himself, been on the front line?

'Did you go to Madrid?' she said. She had to ask, though she could feel terrors stirring her mind already: the smashed body slipping down the window, his outline stained in blood on the glass; a limping man with black swastikas in the pupils of his red-rimmed eyes. *Stop!*

She leant over the table towards Walter as if searching his eyes for a reflection of her own fear.

He didn't flinch. He said, 'A group of us did. We got out just before the shelling started while the battle was still on the outskirts. Bloody cartloads of wounded men delivered to hospital – the rip of bullets through the air, explosions in the distance. It was terrifying. We have no idea how lucky we are in this country. No idea.'

He stopped. Jane had stiffened and drawn back as though she had pulled on a mask, a plaster cast that set hard around her mouth and eyes, concealing whatever lay beneath.

'Sorry, Jane,' Walter said, 'I should have thought. You were in Berlin during that riot. You were with Rebecca. You've seen horrors yourself.'

'Did Rebecca tell you about it?' Jane said. 'It's closer than we think, Walter. It's so much closer than we think.'

Her words were half-whispered, half-lost amongst the tangle of other voices in the room yet there was no mistaking the anxiety behind them. *What have I done?* Walter thought. That magnetism that had pulled her across the table towards him had vanished. She looked small in her chair, gripping the arms as if she needed its frame for support. *She's haunted,* he thought. *Can she cope with further exposure?* He was taunted by the urge to kiss her, shock her into life again, but the table was between them; they were in public, it would be ridiculously unwise, impossible. The woman who had come into the café and sat down opposite him had a fire in her eyes, steel in her bones – it was that woman he wanted. He had to bring her back.

'Will you join us, Jane?' he said. 'You're wasted where you are. You can do so much more than banging heads; you can help us bring people out, organise transport, supplies. You can make decisions.'

Jane was looking at him now as if he was only just coming into focus but she was leaning forward again.

'What do you think, Jane? Will you join us?'

This was it: an opportunity to do something meaningful in a world that felt full of false starts and dead ends. Walter wanted her to join him. He needed her help. It was as if a window had opened somewhere and the draft had woken her up. Jane felt the tightness that had screwed her into the chair as if she were pinned into it release, the white bolts of her knuckles loosen. She could have stood up and twirled round the room with the waiter, with Walter, with anyone.

'When can I start?'

'You can come to our first meeting. I'll send you the agenda.'

Walter waved to the waiter who brought him the bill.

It was dark outside and the rain was continuing to drizzle. *Like MPs at a debate on the economy*, Walter thought, *miserable, half-hearted and depressingly unhelpful.*

'My umbrella is big enough for two,' said Jane, struggling with it.

'Here, let me,' Walter said, taking it from her before she could answer and holding it up above them both. 'Shall I call you a cab?'

'Please.' He was close to her now – she could smell the musk in his coat. They made a dash for the road.

Walter stuck out a thumb. A black cab slowed down and pulled in.

'Watch out!' said Walter, taking Jane by the shoulder and moving her back just in time to avoid the spray of water thrown up by the cab wheels. He almost had her in his arms and she wasn't resisting. He bent his head, drew her closer to him and kissed her full on the lips using the umbrella to beat off the rain and the eyes of any obnoxious passers-by.

'Can I see you again?'

She said nothing. He was so close it felt like they had merged into one, his hand on hers, on the umbrella, a tent over a fantasy that might blow away any minute with a gust of wind. He kissed her again, lifting her above the puddles, sending her shimmering into the sky like a mayfly – vibrant one minute, dead the next. She wanted more, desperately, but it was wrong. *We can't. Someone will get hurt. What am I doing?* A whirlwind entered her head and blew around wildly.

'Excuse me, guvnor,' said the cab driver abruptly, sticking his head out the window, 'do you want a ride or not?'

Walter ignored him.

The cab drove off and they were left together on the pavement, in the rain.

"6th December, 1936
My very dearest Jane,
It's such a cheerful thought that I shall be seeing you again today. If you go on looking as attractive as you were last night, you will drive me completely crazy. But without seeing you I have been growing crazier and crazier. And it was so exciting to me to feel you felt a little bit like that yourself. I've had a busy day, and things may come of it. Working for Spain like anything, working even harder when the evening papers came out (and I do hear the news is not as bad as reported).

I send you love and may the day pass quickly.

Walter."

"8th December, 1936
My dear Jane,

Victory was in your eye this afternoon. I feel certain that by now the poor fish of an MP has realised that to attempt even to resist the inevitable progress of your log in rolling to its ultimate destination was useless, unjust, and contrary to public interest.

As a result of the work you put in, Rodgers of 60 New Oxford St Museum 6115 has worked out a definite scheme for evacuation using buses. We have given him our blessing and intend to spend about £600 on his scheme, when we have it.

Franco has big superiority in the air. Hell, hell, hell. Impotent rage and no sentimentality this time. What the hell can we do to save these people?

Walter."

14th December 1936, 8.30pm
Bloomsbury, London

'... the smell of shoe polish. Nanny used to tell me he buffed up his shoes immaculately so I've always associated it with him. I think she was just trying to get me to clean my shoes properly.'

'Really? You are funny. What else do you think of when you imagine father?'

'A shy man who loved coming home to his nearest and dearest, putting on his slippers and reading the newspaper in front of the fire,' Edmond said, then he smiled, 'or is that just a reflection of me?''

'Mother always says you're the image of him so you're probably right,' said Jane. 'She doesn't seem to resent you for it though.'

'Whereas she does resent you?'

'You know she does.'

'Nanny always said father longed to have a daughter,' Edmond said. 'He named you before you were born.'

Jane patted the red velvet armchair she was sitting in, running her finger round the buttons that were buried in its sides, 'So you think this was father's favourite chair?'

'Yes,' said Edmond.

'How do you know?'

'Mother never sits in it, haven't you noticed?'

'Oh,' said Jane. 'I suppose you must be right. That's rather a sad reason.'

Edmond topped up her glass with a little more sherry. 'Don't let it put you off. Father would've loved to see you sitting in his chair.'

'Mother rarely visits us,' said Jane. 'Do you think she approves of us living here?'

Edmond sank back into his chair, the seat was rather worn but neither of them were willing to get it re-covered. 'Father died so suddenly – it took her a long time to get over it, in fact, I'm not sure she ever really has.'

'I can feel it whenever I go into the hallway and down to the front door, Edmond – her terror – running out into the street to fetch the doctor. It frightens me.'

Edmond looked at his sister but she was staring at the fire, unwilling to catch his eye. He had hoped their return to Bloomsbury would somehow help Jane to connect with their mother but Jane was right, Gina had only visited them once or twice and never stayed for long.

'You're wrong you know,' he said after a pause. 'She doesn't dislike you. She doesn't wish you were never born. Her depression after father's death was pretty severe. It left a bruise neither of you seems able to forgive.'

'It doesn't explain why she always puts you first, Edmond. She has always preferred you.'

'I know.'

'There's nothing to be done about it, Edmond.'

'It's frustrating,' said Edmond. 'She must realise how awkward she is with you but she tries to pretend it's not a problem.'

'You can't blame me for not calling her every week. She's even more distant over the phone than she is in person. We can't say more than ten words without becoming irritable or clamming up.'

'I don't blame you, Jane, you know that.'

'Let's talk about something else,' Jane said, getting up, crossing to the window and shutting the curtains. It was a cold night and they had only just lit the fire.

Edmond picked up the bellows and puffed up the flames as much as he could. Then he decided he might as well ask her. 'You've been receiving a lot of letters recently, Jane. It makes my one or two a week look meagre, I'm rather envious.'

Jane had her back to him and she didn't turn round. She wasn't sure what to say. This was definitely not a conversation she wanted to start. She went over to the bookcase, opened the glass doors and pulled out a book, delaying the necessity of a response. 'I'd like to get involved in the Spanish Relief effort,' she said at last, 'I've been in touch with a member of the National Joint Committee.' It was the truth at least, just not all of it.

'That sounds just the sort of cause you were looking for and I'm sure you're exactly the person they need to help them,' said Edmond, relieved to have got away with his probing. He couldn't bear to think Jane might conceal another relationship from him; that she didn't trust him after what had happened with Richard.

Now he thought about it, she had seemed more energised recently. Her hair was clean and bouncy. When she returned from Germany she hadn't bothered to wash it for a week, merely clipping it back to keep it out of her eyes.

'I've got the minutes of their latest meeting upstairs if you're interested,' Jane said.

'I'd love to read them,' Edmond replied. 'There's so much in the papers about the siege of Madrid, the British volunteers fighting in the Brigades. I'd like to know more about the relief operation, especially if you're going to be part of it.'

'I'll go and get them,' said Jane, going to the door. She closed it behind her and went upstairs. Her cheeks were hot.

She had lied to her brother. It would only get worse.

Unless she put a stop to it – to Walter, to his letters, to meeting up – but now she was involved in Spanish Relief and she wanted to do more. She couldn't end it now. He was part of it. She wanted to be part of it, but what would Edmond think of her?

She grabbed the papers and went back downstairs. *Focus on the work, there's no need to think about anything else yet*, she told herself, but the rapid juddering of her heart that had started with Edmond's question, refused to go away.

28th September 1954, 5pm
Outskirts of London
Jane is forty

Edmond paid for the petrol. *This fear of being watched*, he thought, *it's a delusion, surely?* Jane would describe her hallucinations occasionally: the people in the cupboard, at the window. They were real to her at the time but later she became confused. *What are the visions really about? Was it always inevitable, her disintegration? Could it have been prevented?* Schizophrenia was such a damned patchwork of a condition: you kept trying to sew things together, make sense of it, but was there really any sense to be made?

Jane had always been so secretive, so tight with her personal affairs, yet when it came to politics and the world in general, she could never hold anything back. *How long can anyone live like that?* he thought. *Why wouldn't she accept help, why did she have to be so selfless? Maybe we forced her to conceal more by fretting too much?*

I wanted to help, he thought, *but I failed. If only she could feel safe again. The world has been rebuilt since the war. There must be some hope for Jane.* The thought lifted his spirits like a rainbow, before fading away again. His visits were always the same. This one would be no different. The doctors had given up and consigned her to a purgatory of pills. There was always that flash of recognition when he came in, the glimpse of a smile, and then it was gone.

He got back into the car and drove on. It was getting dark and there was still a long way to go.

Confrontation

23rd January 1937, 8pm
Bloomsbury, London
Jane is twenty-two

Edmond was in a cab. He'd just had dinner with Evie; a straightforward delight of a woman; never mind she was more sporty than elegant, time with her was always too short. At least it would only be temporary, he was sure of that already. He wanted desperately to tell Jane. *I'll have to catch her when she gets back from work,* he thought. *We'll light the fire and have a glass of sherry like we used to do when we first moved in.*

The cab drove through Bloomsbury past Jane's office. The lights were still on. They were committed, her colleagues, he'd give them that. The divisions between home and office often crossed and tangled when you were working for a cause you believed in. Still, he knew that despite their humanitarian purpose, there was prejudice and gossip behind sweaty palms just like anywhere else.

The cab pulled up outside their flat. Street lamps lit flares in the puddles on the pavement. He dashed up the front steps and pulled out his key, tugging his hat down on his head, letting the rain bounce gaily off the top. He opened the door silently, thinking he would surprise Jane if she was there.

The hall light was on and her coat was on the peg. He slipped off his own coat, hung up his hat and put a shoe-tree into his brogues. *They need a good clean before I wear them again, I hope Evie didn't notice.*

Halfway upstairs he thought it might be better to forewarn Jane of his arrival but it was a little late to go back to the door.

'Jane?' He turned the handle gently.

There was a scream. The door fell open and there was Jane scrambling out of bed, wrapping the bedclothes round her, a semi-naked man next to her grabbing wildly at a candlestick as if to ward off an intruder. When Jane realised it was Edmond, she stiffened up like a taxidermied animal, stuck motionless in a frame.

'Sorry, Jane,' Edmond said, reaching for the doorknob and missing it several times before managing to pull it shut.

Jane sat down on the bed next to Walter, bedsheets twisted round her. She had known bringing Walter to the house would embarrass her brother but she hadn't dared talk to him about it. *It's an underhand, dishonest relationship. I deserve to be despised. I've brought this on myself.*

Walter stared at the door. It was stifling in the room. *More claustrophobic than a Catholic confessional*, he thought, not that he'd ever been into one, luckily. He said nothing but started to dress. Hopefully Jane's brother had locked himself behind a closed door somewhere. It had been risky coming to Jane's house but the danger of discovery had only added to the excitement. Now he felt humiliated and foolish like an alcoholic caught with an empty bottle.

Downstairs, Edmond flopped into his favourite armchair. His heart was tripping over itself and his hands were hot. He tried to wipe the scene from his mind but it was stamped there like a seal on wax. *So much for telling Jane about Evie*, he thought. *Why didn't she tell me she was seeing someone? Why has she made this so damned awkward?*

He heard footsteps, just one person, and then the front door opened and closed. That was a relief at least. He stayed in the sitting room, trying not to worry, knowing full well that, for the time being, Jane would close herself off and there was precious little he could do about it.

"26th January, 1937
Dear Edmond,
I'm sorry you were embarrassed the other night but I don't know what madness led you to burst into my room unannounced. You often tell me I'm too guarded on personal matters but if you insist on invading my privacy like that you will force me to become more so rather than less. I realise I should have warned you and that I have contributed to the awkwardness we both feel by not doing so. Even now I'm struggling to write, battling with the shame that constantly tempts me to put down my pen and leave you with silence. I can't do that. I can't let my mortification get the better of me. I want to be open with you but I'm terrified of the consequences.

Edmond, part of me is determined to do something meaningful with my life and the other part is continually threatening to self-destruct. I realise that I am a weak person, unable to overcome my own frailties, frustrated by my own contradictions.

Walter is married. There, I have written it down cold. Yes, I can see you frowning and tutting, anxiety marking your brow and pursing your lips, or maybe it's our mother I see and you are still standing outside in shock.

Married. It is a hollow word when it is linked to the man you desire above all others. A word that binds him to another yet lets him loose to pursue pleasure. It is my pain, Edmond, my dead end, but what will make it all worse will be your disapproval.

We are working together for Spanish Relief, Edmond. There is meaning in that. Beyond that I'm afraid I have nothing to cling to, no sense to be made, but I beg you to be kind to me because for now, I cannot turn back.

Yours,

Jane."

"27th January, 1937

Dear Jane,

It is a sorry state of affairs when we have to write to each other to express our feelings but at least the fault is mutual. I have wanted, for days, to apologise for bursting into your room the way I did and for all the discomfort it has caused us both. I only wish you had warned me. I have been feeling miserable with the thought that you do not trust me enough, that you do not come to me for help when you need it.

Jane, you are the most truthful, selfless person I know. I can see that this affair is somehow mixed up in your mind with your dedication to a particular cause – that this man's work has had a powerful influence on you and that your belief in what he is doing has blinded you to his faults. The last thing I want to do is to cause you pain but you know this cannot end well and I cannot bear to see you suffer for it. Unless he is planning to divorce his wife, there can be no joy in your future with him. I realise I am not helping by saying this but I am so terribly afraid that this will end badly and the only way to reason with you is to shock you with the truth.

I love you, Jane, and because of that I will try not to interfere. Avoidance may be the only course I can take for the moment, but please, dear Jane, do not cut yourself off from me entirely. It is not you I disapprove of; I am merely afraid that an affair such as this, barren as it must be of commitment and honesty, offers nothing but thorns and regret, and what a waste that would be.

Yours,
Edmond.

"29th January, 1937
My dearest Jane.
I have been trying to see clearly. Perhaps a day or two in Northumberland will help. But in so far as I am on my farm, I know your spirit haunts my fields and river, because I have so often thought about you there. I feel I may be making of you a romance, an idealisation, an escape, and that is selfish of me. That's why I would like to meet and talk to your brother again. I don't want to have to fight external opposition to our relationship – but maybe it's good that I should have to. I always felt and knew that he would be critical, and possibly that is not a strong enough word. There is no reason why at this particular moment we should be making any decision, except that his disapproval has made us think.

I think it was very sweet of you to tell me that you do love me. I don't know if love is the right word, but I think it is, but I don't want to claim more than you wish to give. On my side I am quite sure I want to go on seeing you as much as possible. I think of you a great deal. And I cannot distinguish between wanting you physically and being influenced by your ideas.

About my relationship with my wife, I don't want to write, but I will talk to you. I don't want to write, because there the danger is so great of my not conveying to you what I mean. I don't want to be negative. If our relationship is valuable it is because it creates something positive and creative. My crude remark last night that if it were not you it would be other people misses the real point. If our relationship is worth having, then it's a good thing – that's obvious.

I hate the thought of making things difficult for you. I hate "situations". The best thing to do with a situation is just to fade out into the landscape.

Life is worth living. I wish I could kiss you.
Walter."

15th March 1937, 7.30pm
Bloomsbury, London

Edmond's key jammed in the door. *We'll have to change the lock*, he thought, tugging it out, twisting it, jiggling till it finally turned. He flung down his bag, threw his hat at the stand and kicked off his shoes. *I filed all their papers, what more do I have to do before they give me a proper case?* he thought. He had been at the law firm well over a year but there was no sign of progress, in fact the opposite; they kept piling more bricks on the wall till there was no chink in sight.

His aching feet carried him upstairs towards his favourite armchair. He could see himself in it already, its springs sinking comfortingly beneath him, the satisfying rustle of the paper as he folded it back, the smell of ink as it rubbed off on his fingertips. An Irish painting of a donkey trotting across foggy moorland hung beside the bookshelf and a somewhat square-jawed ancestor gazed down benevolently, pen and paper in hand, from his gilded frame beside the window. It was a sparsely furnished but warm room and that was how he and Jane liked it.

He was at the sitting room door. *I need a drink.* He diverted to the pantry and opened the drinks cabinet. The sherry was missing. He looked for the glasses; definitely gone. He went downstairs and checked the coat-stand. There, displayed on the stand for all to see, was Walter's coat: a drape cut, tapered at the bottom, typical of a self-conscious man out to impress. He felt his skin itch as though he'd been bitten by horse-flies; the man had no shame. Jane left signs around the flat to prevent a repeat of last month's fiasco but it just left him confined to his room.

They couldn't go on like this – constant tension in the air as if the house were loaded with dust that choked all decent communication. Besides, if he continued to ignore it, they would only feel they could go on meeting at the flat, undisturbed. The longer Jane pursued this affair the harder it would be to end it.

He could smell wood burning. They were clearly sitting together on the chaise longue in front of the fire. *Intolerable!* he thought, banging up the stairs, seizing the door handle, striding in and blurting out, 'Well! If you must go on seeing Jane, at least you might have the decency not to do it here.'

They were sitting separately, drinks in hand. They didn't move at first; then Jane stood up. 'What a dreadful fuss to make about nothing at all,' she said.

Edmond's hand lingered on the door. Walter put his glass down. 'We were hoping you might join us,' he said.

Insufferable, thought Edmond. *This is my home. Who does he think he is?*

‘You shouldn’t be here, where’s your wife?’

Jane gasped in horror. She felt like screaming at her brother. How could he? He knew how impossible her situation was and he was making it even harder. He’d always been so kind to her, so thoughtful. Now he was tearing her down.

‘Get out.’ Jane stood up. ‘I can’t bear it, Edmond. Get out!’

‘I’m sorry, Jane,’ Edmond said and stepped out of the room, closing the door hard behind him. He hadn’t more than glanced at Walter and Jane made no attempt to follow him. He stomped off to his room and lay on the bed feeling as small and pathetic as a child in a huff. It wasn’t right, what he’d done, but they needed to know how unbearable the whole situation was. Jane needed to know. If only he could shut Walter out of her life forever. She would be happier, he knew she would, and so would he.

“18th March, 1937

Dear Walter,

I am going to Madrid. I know you have advised against it but I want to be on my own amidst strangers getting the job done. How can I truly help if I haven’t witnessed events, if I haven’t understood the conditions people are living under? I need to live and breathe this cause so that my unbreakable conviction drives others to do something when I come back: to donate funds, to provide transport, clothes, food, medicine.

I feel like I am constantly under attack and I can’t shake off this infernal depression. I see your shadow in my bedroom at night, the dent in the pillow next to mine and it makes me feel hollow and lonely.

I didn’t give Edmond the letter you wrote to him. I know he disapproves and I know he is right. He mustn’t be involved further in this. I haven’t seen him for days. Enough damage has been done.

You are too indecisive and your fidgeting is driving me crazy. I want you here with me but I can’t bear this hiding away, the underhand meetings. I feel like someone else, a different Jane, a person I do not recognise. She is a deceptive character who sleeps with you and tells no-one and attends meetings and smiles and shakes your hand as if it were the first time she met you. She horrifies me.

I don’t believe Edmond judges us unfairly as you do. He has always seen himself as my protector. He cannot see anything positive in our relationship, only endless concealment, heartbreak and a loss of self-respect. Unless you give me a sign that you will end your marriage and commit yourself to me, I cannot see any good in it either. I often feel like you have wrapped a band round us both and every now and again, when it suits you, you snap it, and I believe you love me and it hurts. I don't know who I am anymore. Sometimes at night I think I hear tapping on the window and I wake up in a cold sweat.

I need to do this work in Spain but it feels inextricable from you. From our illicit relationship. I need to tear the two apart so that I can breathe again.

Jane."

"20th March, 1937

Jane,

I have read your letter again and again, and I have been thinking all the time about you. Next day I was still dazed and work seemed an intolerable burden. It's not the sentences where you attack me that hurt most now. I see you were finding reasons for your decision, yes quite good reasons. What does hurt most frightfully are the very lonely and sad things you say. I wish I could rescue you.

I have for the last day or two felt bitter about Edmond and even angry with you. But I have never got much satisfaction by looking for scapegoats.

Jane, it seems to me certain that this letter will drive you headlong away from me. I can't think how I could write a letter more effective for that purpose. The trouble is you're two people. I have fallen in love with the fey, wild, dark-haired and blue-eyed girl; but there is another Jane that I love too, but she sets me a terribly high standard, and sometimes I'm afraid, terribly afraid, I can't live up to that standard.

Walter."

1st April 1937, 6.30pm
Bloomsbury, London

Jane was on the doorstep, shivering. It was impossible to tell whether it was the rain that had marked her face or her own tears. Her hair was matted and her eyes looked vacant as if the rain had washed away their spark.

'Come in,' said Evie, taking her friend by the shoulders and leading her into the sitting room where she had just lit the small gas fire. 'Let me help you out of those wet clothes. You're soaked through.'

Jane said nothing so Evie pulled off her sodden coat.

'You can change in the bathroom if you like. There's hot water there if you want to take a bath.'

'I'm fine, Evie.'

'You may be fine, but my settee won't be. I'll get you some dry clothes.'

Evie ran upstairs. When she got back down Jane was still standing there like a block of ice just waiting to thaw.

'I don't know what to do,' Jane said.

'Well I think the first thing is to get warm,' said Evie, hustling her into the bathroom. 'I'll leave you to it.'

She took down her silver teapot, filled it with Earl Grey and got out a couple of digestive biscuits. Jane came in as she was pouring in the water. A reassuring mix of steam and the aroma of spice filled the kitchen.

'Let's sit down next door, it's more comfortable there.'

Jane nodded absent-mindedly and Evie guided her through.

'How did you end up out in the rain without an umbrella?'

'The rain was the last thing on my mind.'

'I can see that.'

Jane's eyes scanned the room as if looking for something out of place. She avoided looking directly at Evie. 'I'm seeing a married man,' she said. 'It's tormenting Edmond and I can't bear it any longer.'

Evie bit back a gasp. This was the last thing she would have expected, but then Jane always kept her personal feelings so well hidden, a secret could burrow deep down and stay buried for ages. Edmond had said nothing about it – out of respect for Jane's privacy she felt sure – or was he really as horrified as Jane thought? Was he ashamed?

'I'm so tired all the time. I want to work but I can't concentrate. I want to go home and relax but my mind won't let me. I want to give Walter up but it's so painful. Why can't I make decisions?'

'You underestimate yourself, Jane. Your standards are impossibly high. No-one could put in as much effort as you do as a volunteer. You wear yourself out with it, that's all.'

'I'm travelling to Madrid in two weeks' time and I can't get my head straight.'

Evie looked at Jane without betraying the anxiety she was beginning to feel. 'You must travel with people you trust, Jane. Madrid is unstable. You mustn't go if you don't feel up to it.' She wanted to add *don't go!* but instead she said, 'You need to rest, Jane.'

'I can't bear Edmond's disapproval.'

'You must know he doesn't disapprove of *you* Jane. He's only trying to protect you. Find time to talk to him.'

'He's always out. He's been avoiding me.'

'No he hasn't. I'm sure he hasn't.' *He's been with me*, Evie thought.

'Why do you say that? How do you know?'

'I just assumed. I mean …' It was no good, she had to say something. 'It's not you Jane. It's me.'

'What?'

'He's been seeing me.'

'Oh!'

'We've been seeing each other for a few months now.'

What? Jane sat down. *Why did they keep it a secret? Why didn't they trust me?* My brother and my best friend; it was a betrayal of confidence, a stab to the heart. *Come on, Jane,* she thought, stamping on the feeling, *who are you to complain about concealment? It's not surprising Edmond didn't tell you. This is your own fault.* She coaxed out a smile but she had already been silent for too long. Evie looked anxious.

'That's the best news I've heard in a long while,' Jane said, taking Evie's hand and focusing on it. 'I wish Edmond had told me himself. We shouldn't keep secrets or we'll feel like we don't know each other anymore.'

'It wasn't meant to be a secret, Jane.'

'I know. It's my fault we're not talking. I just feel so guilty all the time. People look at me sideways in the street, I'm sure they do. I feel like a scarlet woman. I might as well be dressed in red so they can all fling mud at me.'

'You're exhausted, Jane, you mustn't think like that.'

'I can't give Walter up entirely but I will go to Spain without him.'

'I'm sure Edmond will support you once he's understood.'

Jane nodded. The feeling of fatigue that had been growing all day was sitting heavily on her eyelids now. She hadn't been sleeping well. The sleeping draught the doctor had given her helped but he had warned her not to take it too often. She was going to Madrid. It was all planned. She was going without Walter. It was better that way. She glanced around Evie's home. If only her own relationship was as easy as her brother's. He'd chosen well. She, on the other hand, couldn't have made things more difficult. Choice didn't come into it now. She'd made hers when she kissed Walter outside the museum. She felt her stomach mesh up as though she'd swallowed barbed wire. She looked at Evie, so clear-sighted and logical. If only she was more like that. She waited quietly, leaning her head back on the sofa while Evie cleared away the tea. Before she knew it, she was asleep.

10th September 1942, 10am
St Andrew's Hospital, Northampton
Jane is twenty-eight

'He has curls,' Jane said.

'Just like you,' said Evie. Andrew was just over a year old. She had left him with her aunts at their family home in Hertfordshire for the day. It had been an enormous relief to arrive at a place where the only sound at nightfall was the soft cooing of wood pigeons. She had fled the eerie silences, explosions and sirens of the London blackout only to be bombed in Bath, glass splinters all over the cot whilst she sheltered with the baby under the stairs in the basement.

Jane knew none of this. It had to be kept from her so that her mind had time to recover the doctors said. Still, it was strange coming here knowing that the world outside the gates was just as terrifying as the world inside Jane's head; that men were blown up and shot to pieces every second and that Jane, who had been so aware of the troubles of others, was completely in the dark.

This was Evie's second visit since Edmond had left for war. The first was the hardest. She had arrived with butterflies in her stomach, dreading a repetition of that awful night when they had taken Jane in, when Jane had pelted down the street in front of them, hair blowing in all directions, screaming at them to leave her alone.

Jane's glare as she opened the door had almost sent Evie back down the corridor but she had persisted and gradually Jane had softened. She had let Evie into her room. She had started to talk.

Today she had accepted Evie without question: perhaps it was because, besides her mother and brother, visitors were so few; perhaps she was living in the present now. Either way, it was easier. They walked down the corridor together past private rooms, past the nurse's station, past the door with the porthole. There were loud shrieks, thumps and bangs from inside. Something – or someone – was being hurled around violently.

Evie tried to walk on without turning, a queasy feeling mounting in her stomach. A burly male nurse with an enormous set of keys sauntered past them and peered through the porthole, 'Morning, luvvie,' he said cheerily as if a greeting would help, 'food will be along shortly if you quieten down.' He shot a wry grin at Evie. 'No need to worry,' he said, 'it's padded in there.'

They walked on past the insulin ward. Evie had never actually seen a patient being treated at the hospital. She could hear moans, the squeak and creak of rusty bedsprings, the low whisper of nurses and then the sound of retching. A strong medicinal smell pervaded the corridor. She didn't like to look in but for Jane's sake she felt she had to know. She glanced past the open door. There were bodies on beds. Some were twitching, some were still, with flushed cheeks and pale, sweaty brows, saliva oozing from the sides of their mouths. Rubber tubes and sterile needles lay on a tray in the corner. The patient nearest the door was propped up in bed, groping at some bread which he couldn't seem to get into his mouth. A nurse stood at the back of the room making notes in a book. A doctor was forcing a tube down a patient's throat whilst his colleague held a jug, ready to pour.

It's like something from a Hitchcock film, thought Evie.

The nurses saw her and frowned. They closed the door.

Jane was waiting by the stairs. She didn't seem concerned. *Jane must walk past that every day*, Evie thought and her stomach churned.

When she couldn't bear the feeling any longer she said, 'Jane, do they treat you in that room?'

'Which room?'

'The room we just passed.'

'No. The doctors say I'm not strong enough for coma therapy. I'm too slight, they say, "always catching cold and too many headaches."'

She was so matter-of-fact it felt as if she had absorbed all the weirdness of the place and accepted it as normality.

You have to get better Jane, thought Evie. *Get better and we can get you out of here.* She took Jane by the arm and hurried her outside into the fresh air. At least outside they were free of it all for a while. Until the gong sounded and they were rounded up that was. The grounds were fenced and the fencing was spiked – for a reason. There was no leaving here without a doctor's note and Evie had no control over that now.

5th March 1946, 10.30am
St Andrew's Hospital, Northampton
Jane is thirty-one

'Please do sit down,' the doctor said again. The woman couldn't keep still. It was impossible to concentrate on what she was saying while she paced up and down in front of him. It was like having a patient in the room. Most unhelpful. He would have to be stern with her or she would waste his time and he had precious little of it. It had been good of him to fit them in at such short notice.

'Madam, I cannot help you unless you sit down.'

There was another woman with her, a Dr Shaw, a cousin of her first husband apparently. She seemed much more together. If only she would intervene and settle Mrs Cuthbert into a seat, they could all get on.

Luckily, it seemed the thought had crossed Dr Shaw's mind as well as his. She got up, took Gina's arm and led her somewhat forcefully to a chair. Gina looked startled but accepted the intervention before taking the opportunity to lean forward across the table and wave a letter in the doctor's face.

'We received this letter a few days ago,' she said. 'We all thought he was dead.'

'What?' said the doctor. 'I have no idea what you're talking about. Who was dead?'

'Richard Wright,' said Gina.

'Jane's lover,' Dr Shaw added quickly, aware that Gina might not feel comfortable explaining further. 'He is back in London and has asked to see Jane. Mrs Cuthbert is not sure what to do. We are both worried that it might destabilise her again.'

'I see,' said the doctor, picking up his reading glasses. 'May I read the letter?'

Gina handed it over and watched as the doctor turned the pages, his face giving nothing away.

'When did the patient last see Mr Wright?' the doctor asked finally.

'Before her second breakdown. Before she was certified,' said Dr Shaw, taking over from Gina who seemed unable to go on.

'That is worrying,' replied the doctor. 'You were right to bring this to me.'

'What do you advise?' said Dr Shaw.

'No contact,' said the doctor. 'The patient is unable to tell fantasy from reality as it is. If she saw Mr Wright, it would almost certainly send her into a state of panic – a confusion from which she might never recover. As far as she knows the man is dead. Let's keep it that way.' He handed the letter back and stood up, relieved to be able to end the consultation.

'Are you suggesting we write back immediately, telling him to stay away from Jane?' said Dr Shaw.

'I am.'

Gina looked at Dr Shaw. 'I don't think I can do it,' she said weakly.

The doctor looked worried. 'You have no option, madam,' he said. 'It's your daughter's sanity we're talking about here.'

'I'll do it,' said Dr Shaw. 'I'll write to him.'

'You will?' Gina said as the doctor pushed the letter back into her hand. 'Thank you.' She put it back in her handbag. 'He would accept it coming from you, Nell. You have a doctor's authority.'

'That's settled then,' said the doctor. 'I will make a note in the patient's file. I will assume that the situation has been dealt with.' With that, he stood up, ushered them out of the room as if he was herding sheep and turned on his wireless.

Gina walked away, somewhat stunned by the speed of decision making. She could hear the crackle of the doctor's wireless as he tuned in, 'From Stettin in the Baltic to Trieste in the Adriatic, an iron curtain has descended across the continent,' a familiar voice boomed out. Gina jumped. It sounded as if Churchill were following them down the corridor.

The doctor adjusted the volume and shut the door, leaving Gina and her companion to walk in silence to their car. *My nerves can't stand this battering,* Gina thought. *Thank goodness I brought Nell with me.* They were doing the right thing. They had consulted the doctor and he was the expert after all. Still, concealing Richard from Jane entirely was going to be an ongoing headache, she knew that already.

Jane can never find out. Her anxiety mounted. *She'll never forgive me.*

Madrid

8th April 1937, 7.30pm
Bloomsbury, London
Jane is twenty-two

Jane opened the front door, kicked off her shoes and left them lying, unruly, beside the shoe rack. She flung her coat carelessly at a hook. Maybe she should ask Susie for some pea soup and lose herself in the fog for a while. Better still, run a steamy bath and blow soap bubbles like Elsie used to for her when she was little. She grabbed her towelling robe and slippers and headed for the bathroom. The front door opened and closed. Edmond was home. He would probably go straight to the kitchen to see what Susie was cooking. She heard Edmond calling her.

'Just running a bath,' she shouted back, turning on the taps. She didn't hear his reply. She shut the door and sat with her back to it while the bath filled up.

The water was hot, probably a bit too hot, but she felt like baking herself for a while. *I'll be lobster red like that pimple on Matilda's cheek, but I need the heat. Besides, it'll be cold by the time I get out: I'll have plenty of time to revert to my usual pallid self.*

She had just put a toe in the water, whipped it out again quickly and given in to the cold tap when she heard the phone ring. *That won't be for me*, she willed. *I'm definitely not at home.*

'Jane, it's for you.'

Damn it. 'I'm in the bath. Can I call them back some other time?'

'It's Richard.'

Not again, thought Jane, *it's the third time this week. He's more persistent than Walter.*

'Can you tell him I'm in the bath, please.' There was no response so she assumed Edmond had done as she asked.

She slipped into the bath and immersed herself, letting her hair float on the surface.

It was a whole hour before she emerged. There was a note outside the door.

"I've gone out to see Evie. Richard said he would call back later tonight. He won't give in. Sorry! E."

She sighed. He was committed, she'd give him that. It had been two years since she had rejected him and yet he was still pursuing her.

She flopped upstairs in her slippers and gown, threw on a nightie and collapsed onto the bed.

The phone rang.

Shall I just ignore it?

She hurried down and picked up the receiver.

'Euston 2-9-6-5.'

'Hello? Is that Jane? It's Richard.'

'Sorry I missed you earlier, I was in the bath.'

'Edmond told me.'

There was a pause.

'I'm afraid I'm rather tired tonight. It might not be the best time to talk.'

'I'm sorry to hear that. It's just a quick call. I've been in Spain, reporting on the civil war. I'm only back for a couple more days. Can I see you?'

Jane's heart thumped. Despite sending her countless letters, he had never once mentioned work in Spain. Reports sent in from Madrid boosted support for relief schemes like Walter's. Maybe Richard would be there when she arrived. He was a brave man. A man who loved her with a warm, full love, not tangled and all-consuming like her love for Walter. It was soothing somehow knowing that his love still survived despite continually being rebuffed. Yet she couldn't leave Walter. Walter, who took away her breath and then her voice whenever he was with her, whose body left an indent in her bed when he got up to leave.

I mustn't encourage Richard. She thought. *He has to let me go. I'm not the person he thinks I am.*

'I'm not sure it's a good idea,' she said. 'I'm having a tough time at work.'

'I understand,' said Richard. He paused. He knew it would be sabotage but he had to say something. 'Jane, I know about the *politician*.' The word came out like a chewed up piece of tobacco. Politicians weren't to be trusted; they made a living from broken promises. His cousin John had joined the Jarrow marchers, storming up to London, a pride of hopeful men; limping back, bruised and broken without a penny of support for the community they'd tried so hard to save. No jobs. No welfare. Nothing.

'What?'

'I wanted to warn you. You're being tracked. Luckily Walter Tenant's not high enough up the chain for it to be newsworthy but you can't trust these tabloid journalists. It'll be you who suffers in the long-run.'

Silence. *People are tracking me?*

'Jane?'

Nothing.

'I'm sorry, Jane.'

'Please, Richard. Just leave me alone.'

'I want to help you.'

'You can't, Richard! You can't.'

There was a dull buzz from the end of the line. Jane had hung up.

11th April 1937, 9am
Bloomsbury, London

Jane woke up with sallow skin and puffy eyes and despite her best efforts to pinch her cheeks pink and dab on a touch of make-up she felt as creased and dried up as a camel at the zoo.

She picked up the latest bulletin Walter had sent her:

"9th April 1937
National Joint Committee for Spanish Relief. Bulletin No.5:
The War in Spain is now in its tenth month. As the warmer weather approaches, the shortage of such things as coal, warm clothing and boots becomes less of a hardship, but the need for evacuating the civilian population, for feeding and housing the refugees and for providing medical equipment is equally, if not more pressing than it was during the winter months."

They need to be sure the aid gets to the right place, Jane thought. *They need someone who can testify to the suffering and pinpoint the areas of greatest need.* She looked at the suitcase in the corner and the clothes all over her bedroom floor. She'd never been good at packing. It was difficult to decide what to take. She wanted to blend in. She had to be practical. There was only so much she could carry without help. Then there was money. How much would she need? *Walter would help,* she thought, *but I can't ask him. I have to do this on my own.* At least her transport was arranged, the National Committee had seen to that and she was travelling with a group.

Volunteers left for Spain every day, mostly communist recruits. They joined the International Brigades, blew up munition trains, machine-gunned Nationalists, fought hand to hand with bayonets, grenades. It was a bloody free-for-all. Her heart accelerated whenever she thought about it. What if she was met by communist agents? She wasn't a party member. What if they suspected her motives? She shook her head. It was absurd all this fear-mongering, her mind was shooting off in tangents all over the place as usual.

'You have a wonderful imagination,' Elsie used to say when she worried about the monsters under her bed, but now there was no Elsie to ground her and the fears kept getting more and more extravagant. Her pillow was soaked in sweat and she had to change her nightie every day. Last night she woke up convinced there was a woman in blue overalls banging on her bedroom door with a hammer. She carried a sickle and scrawled her initials on the wall before leaving as abruptly as she had arrived.

Maybe I should stop reading reports about Spain. I'm doing myself no good by working it up in my mind and I must stop procrastinating, she told herself, sweeping the loose clothes up in her arms and jamming them into the suitcase before closing it and sitting down on the lid. *I'm as disordered and chaotic as my luggage,* she thought with a wry smile. *I need someone to put me into a cab and set me on my way. I hope Edmond gets home early.*

Edmond was worried about her going away on her own, she knew, but he was holding back. Then again, so was she. He thought she was going to Paris, to visit the art exhibitions there, to have a holiday. He didn't know she was travelling with strangers, into the midst of a civil war. *I'll tell him when I get back,* she thought, *when he can see that I'm safe.*

She hadn't told their mother about her plans either. There didn't seem much point. She had spoken to her recently. That was enough for now. She had even phoned at her allotted time. She didn't want to prolong what was already an awkward conversation with an unnecessary argument. At least Edmond would understand why she had to go. *Mother would only feel she had to stop me,* Jane thought.

She hauled her unwieldy suitcase to the top of the stairs then stopped. *It's too much! I'll have to start again.* Setting it down with a thump, she unclipped the lid and flung it open with a sigh. She hauled it back into the bedroom and rubbed her neck. There was a crick in it that wouldn't go away making it difficult to move her head to the side. *I'm non-partisan*, she reassured herself again. *I'm delivering aid. They won't be interested in me.* Still, she was worried, and she couldn't get rid of the crick.

25th April 1937, 6pm
Madrid

The gunner lit his cigarette; it glowed red like his shells as they landed in the city below. Smoke curled out of the corner of his mouth. He stood alone by the gun while militia-men scurried around loading arms onto a truck. They were all moving station but he had a few shells remaining. He looked down at the city from his hill at Carabanchel. It was distant and soundless. Peering through his binoculars he could see a black car carrying the flag of the Red Cross travelling down the Gran Via. Tiny dots moved in and out of doorways like fleas, jumpy, fast-moving. Dots in berets shook hands with dots in khaki who moved in pairs down the street, guns held tight to their shoulder, ammunition belted across the middle. Scouring the bomb-blasted buildings he saw his mark. *Café de Lisboa, that Republican hovel, crawling with communists and the sons of loose women.* Not that he could see any of them. He would wait till someone came out. He sucked in his cheeks, pursed his mouth and exhaled. The smoke blew back into his eyes and he cursed under his breath. He would have to wait for the wind to die down before using up his last shells.

Down below in the Puerta del Sol, Jane's translator Maria bought a red and black shawl from a street vendor and threw it over Jane's shoulders. The breeze had picked up as the sun went down and people were beginning to head home. The spirit of defiance that had kept the city going through the bombs last November lived on in the jutting chins and stubborn routines of the civilians under siege. They had become used to the rumbling of their stomachs and the deals that had to be done to fill them.

Jane's tired feet slipped and crunched over crumbled masonry. Great chunks of stone lay where they had fallen, torn from bullet-bitten buildings that towered defiantly above her. Yellow dust sat in the air like a thin mist long after the shelling stopped. She glanced back at the square behind her.

There was no escaping the black planes trailing disaster in huge and hellish flames behind them. "EVACUAD MADRID!" the poster blasted across the tallest block at the far end of the square declared. 'Get out, get out,' each broken lamppost and bent balcony seemed to cry. Yet the donkeys stood stubbornly beside empty wooden stalls, their enormous cartwheels making light of the rubble-filled roads and women in black-tasselled shawls and long skirts, their heads covered, dipped in and out of awnings keeping their eyes low. Weather-worn men sat on chairs by the roadside, their feet perched on footstools, watching the flat caps on the street shine their shoes, buffing busily before dust settled on them again and made a mockery of their efforts.

Jane had spent the morning at the Legation of Honduras. The rooms were packed with refugees whose closely controlled visits to the toilet had left a stench of urine and sweat that made it difficult to breathe without retching. They had just squeezed past the tight mass of desperate bodies and through a door into one of the larger rooms when Jane saw the child. He was lying on an old cot, rusty bedsprings coiling down towards the floor, patchwork blanket clutched in his tiny fist. His mother's hand hovered protectively over his matted curls. A tall, thin man slouched next to the cot, his back bent against the wall. He stood up straight when he saw Jane looking at him and glared at her as if she had invaded the tiny corner of privacy they held in that crowded space. She had smiled at him and his wary eyes had softened. He grabbed her hand and held it when she offered hers. 'He needs food,' Maria had said. 'For the child. For the mother. Here they only have beans. It's meant for animals.'

Jane had looked over at the far corner of the room. The window felt like a slit in the wall there was so little air coming through it. Dirty cushions lined the sides of the room. All colour and furnishings had clearly been removed when the refugees moved in. There were men everywhere; some muttered in low voices, some rocked endlessly on their ankles. The rug beneath Jane's feet was stained yellow in patches. She noticed a small enamel potty tucked away beneath the cot. It was full. 'They have to wait till they can get to the toilet to empty it. The queue is always too long.' Maria had explained.

Some men in long black robes shared out tins of beans which the refugees pulled open hungrily and scooped out with their fingers. A man with a scar down his left cheek and a rosary around his wrist held up his tin for her to see. She didn't want to turn away but nausea threatened to engulf her: there were maggots in it.

'They will eat anything,' Maria had said.

'We will bring them fresh supplies tomorrow,' Jane had replied. She had been in Madrid for five days but the trucks carrying food and medical supplies had only just arrived. She would instruct the drivers to bring food in the morning before they set off for Bilbao. The consul had said there was no plan to get these people out. There was talk of a boat being chartered but that would take resources, contacts. *A new campaign for me to take to the National Joint Committee*, Jane had thought.

This mission was hers. She had planned and executed it, fenced it off from her feelings for Walter. Courage and determination were hers to keep if she maintained her resolve. She had looked back at the Legation as they came out onto the street, heavy oaken doors hiding cramped bundles of people worn out by months of sweaty, sleepless nights, confined like cattle in a pen with no idea when they would be free. *How many other doors in this city hide such misery? How many other shutters remain permanently closed?* Jane had thought as she left.

Back on the Gran Via, Jane and Maria passed the Café de Lisboa. There were around a dozen men inside and a few red-cheeked women who sat on their laps drinking vermouth. A balding man with deep-set owlish eyes looked out of the window as they passed and then back at his paper. He too had a glass of vermouth in front of him, half-empty. The waiter was behind the bar washing glasses.

'That man,' whispered Maria pointing at the balding loner, 'is looking for his dead friend.'

'His dead friend?'

'He must be dead. No-one has seen him for weeks.'

'Maybe he has joined the militia?'

'When people vanish here it means they have been shot. His wife is at home crying. Her baby is crying. They know they won't see him again.'

'But who took him?'

'The Italians, or the Russians – Stalin's spies.' Maria's voice dropped even further. 'That American man won't find him but he knows who did it and no-one will help him so he comes and drinks vermouth on his own every night.'

Jane glanced at the man in the window again. His cheeks were as red as his eyes.

The glass doors swung open and two men came out of the café.

Suddenly something whizzed through the air above Jane and slammed into the building. Great chunks of stone and marble fell from the wall. The men ran in opposite directions. The gunner on the hill fired again. A sharp fragment of masonry flew off the building and hit one of them. It went right through him. His broken body lay split on the cobbles. The café window shattered. Blood splattered the engraved glass doors. The gunner stepped down for the night.

Horrendous screams ripped through Jane's head – from Jane herself; from someone next to Jane; from Maria; screaming and dragging Jane backwards, away from the body. A waiter emerged and pulled the bloody mess into an alleyway where half-starved dogs sniffed at it and howled. Another waiter hurried out with a bucket of water. Blood and water washed down the street. *Splash.* The waiter threw another bucket-load out. Blood ran past doorways and down the gutter. The engraved glass doors looked pink and jagged in the moonlight as they closed behind the waiter, shards crunching under his feet. The American had disappeared.

Maria dragged Jane along. 'We need to get inside now. Before the patrol arrives.'

The Hotel Gran Via was the grubbier stone cousin of the towering Hotel Florida, which maintained its height and most of its marble facade despite constant shells and the bombs that had knocked in the top floors. In the unlit lobby of the Gran Via, Jane's skin looked a queasy greyish-green and Maria feared she would faint, but Jane squeezed her hand and they hurried on down the back stairs and past the kitchen. By the time they had reached the basement she had composed herself enough to ask the kitchen boy for a glass of water.

Maria motioned Jane over to an alcove with a low table and pine bench and she sat down with a thump as if she'd misjudged the distance. The whole place smelt of rotting fish. Men were huddled in dark corners. Jane tried to smile reassuringly at Maria. She could sense people looking at them. Then the buzz started up again. Loud angry voices blurred by whisky.

'Whiting and spinach?'

'Hemingway drinks coffee every morning.'

'Where does he get his eggs and bacon?'

'He writes what the Russians want him to.'

'Keep your voice down.'

Someone tapped Jane on the shoulder and she spun away from them, hitting her head on the low alcove tiles above her.

A tall, bulky man towered above her blocking out the din and the fight that was breaking out behind him. 'Jane. Are you all right?'

She looked up. It was Richard. She breathed in the familiar smell of his cologne like gas and air and the thudding in her heart slowed. She took his hand and gripped it as if it was a lifebelt and she was sinking.

'Camarero, algunos camarero, por favor.' Richard pulled the kitchen boy over to Jane's table. The boy was transfixed by the group of men shouting around the long oak table in the centre of the room. They were getting up. They were shoving each other. There was going to be a fight. The boy was mesmerised.

'Now!' Richard's voice hit him like a slap across the face. Richard knelt down next to Jane and let her rest on his shoulder. The boy brought some water. Jane had closed her eyes.

'Do you know which room she's staying in?' Richard asked Maria who was hovering beside him unsure what to do.

'Sí Señor,' she said. 'Follow me.'

Richard picked Jane up and carried her out of the room.

26th April 1937, 8.30am

'I dreamt of Oxford last night,' said Richard. 'I dreamt I was back in lodgings, that I would wake to the sizzle of bacon and the whistle of the kettle on the hob, roll out of bed and into my clothes and wait at table for an hour or so until you turned up. Then I realised only half of that was true – the best half. Here you are. Earlier than usual.'

Jane sat down with a smile. His broad, honest face was exactly what she needed to see. Around him there was upheaval: the smash of a plate as a waiter slipped on rotgut whisky thrown away in disgust the night before; the hustle of correspondents packing knapsacks, drawing lots for the best escort and a pair of militiamen trying to rouse their drunken colleague who was snoring in the corner. Richard blocked it all out.

Richard's heart was not as calm as his exterior. Jane's eyes were so blue they almost looked transparent; there was a frightening kind of vacancy in them. Although the basement was lit, her pupils were fully dilated. She had brushed her hair but it straggled round her face unpinned and the buttons on her blouse were mismatched. She seemed to look through everything as if it wasn't really there; only when he caught her eye did she appear to focus.

'Were you able to sleep at all last night?' he said.

Jane had seen a man walk through her room in the night and climb out the window. His nose was broken and blood was pouring from his head. She had got out of bed to shut the window but found it open in the morning. It was a horrible feeling, not trusting your own eyes, a heady mix of confusion and fear.

'I tried to,' she replied.

His smile faded. 'I'm supposed to travel to Bilbao today to join colleagues but I don't want to leave you here on your own.'

Jane sat up. She couldn't let Richard feel responsible for her. Richard's work was crucial to raising awareness of this madness, this bloody, belligerent bullring of death. There was a spirit of survival pulsing undaunted through these bomb-blasted streets. She would draw on that.

She noticed her buttons and did them up quickly. *Pull yourself together Jane*, she thought, *you look worse than a scarecrow dragged through a hedge.* She had a mission to complete – refugees who needed rescuing before Franco machine-gunned their camp, threw grenades into the hospital or shelled their supply routes.

'I'll be fine, Richard. I'm due to leave tomorrow with a contingent from the International Brigades and some American writer based at the Hotel Florida. Besides, our trucks arrive this morning; we will unload parcels for the Legation and hospitals here and send the rest on to Bilbao. You could travel with them. That way we can be sure they reach the right place.'

The waiter brought them a hunk of stale bread and some salted ham that had curled up at the edges. Jane smiled again, 'We look like the two bad mice breaking their knives on dolls' food in Beatrix Potter's story,' she said with a giggle.

That's better, thought Richard. *Must've just been a bad night's sleep.* He looked up. A short Spanish man with a moustache and a beret had sidled over to them.

'Richard Wright?' he said in an accent so thick it was hard to make out the words.

Richard looked puzzled. 'Yes?'

'Safe conducts for you.' The man was holding out three cards.

'Thank you,' said Richard taking them.

'Use the Anarchist card when you see red shirts. Social Democrats are very quiet. Communists are well organised. You must look around and choose.'

'I understand,' Richard held out his hand but the man shook his head slightly and left the basement. 'Too many different factions,' Richard said to Jane. 'No-one knows who is watching them. The only time they fully work together is when they're fighting the Nationalists.'

Madrid was infested with wasp nests. They had smelt the sticky smell of fallen fruit and were harvesting it readily. They set up in secret in the darkest parts of buildings. Their only uncertainty was whether they would sting before they themselves were swatted. Mostly they let civilians go about their business but if anyone crossed them in any way or unwittingly disturbed a nest, then they faced a swarm from which there was no escape.

Jane looked around. There was no telling who was in the room at any one time, what their allegiances were, who they were working with. *Aid is non-partisan*, she thought. *We don't have to choose a card. Surely they will leave us alone?*

5.30pm

The trucks had been in and out and around the city countless times and Jane felt like she'd been sitting on a carousel for most of it. Dust kicked up from the road was in her eyes, hair and clothes but it was done. Aid parcels had been delivered. Richard had set off in convoy. He would reach Bilbao by midnight. She had travelled with him as far as Guadarrama where they had caught sight of an imperial eagle, circling high above the range, casting its yellow eye scornfully down on the fracas below. The slopes of the mountain were coated in pine and oak like a thick Castilian moustache. Peasants with chapped hands and faces carried bundles of firewood bigger than themselves down to their villages. The shelling was unremitting but while it was overhead they were safe. They didn't make eye contact when the trucks went past.

Jane was back in her room packing her bags. She had already packed and repacked twice but she kept leaving things out. Her toothbrush, hairbrush and stockings went in and out several times before she sat down on the rusty bed with a sigh.

Suddenly there was a commotion outside. At first Jane didn't want to look, terrified she might see something else that would haunt her, but the voices grew louder and then there was an awful wail. Jane flung open her window. The owner of the hotel had collapsed in the street. His wife was sobbing uncontrollably. The road was crammed with correspondents clutching notepads. Cars pulled up around them. Jane shoved her weary feet into a pair of low heels and opened her door. Others had done the same. 'What's going on?' she asked.

'She comes from Guernica,' the woman opposite replied, 'they say there's nothing left.'

'Franco called in the Germans,' said the man next door, 'they don't care who or what they hit as long as it can't get up again.'

'They were unprotected. They weren't allowed to escape.'

Jane felt sick. Had Richard reached Bilbao? What would he find there? Would they flatten the city too? Why had they chosen a target with no military importance?

It was terrifying. The Nazis were using Spain as a practice ground for their weapons, for their ruthless, cold-blooded tactics. They were no longer afraid of exposure. Guernica was as shredded as the empty bomb casings that littered its thermite-blasted roads and the bomb casings were clearly marked with the imperial eagle of Germany.

Foreboding

"27th April 1937
The Times, 'Telegram home', Richard Wright
It was dark as we approached Bilbao. Along the stony road coming towards us we saw carts pulled by oxen filled with limp and shattered men, women and children and anything they had managed to salvage from the wreckage they left behind them. As they saw us, they stopped and we gave them what food and help we could. They were unable to describe what had happened but it had drained their faces of colour. Many collapsed immediately by the side of the road as we hauled old mattresses off carts. They slept there until dawn."

13th May 1937, 8.30am
Bloomsbury, London
Jane is twenty-two

Bunting flapped forlornly from the window of the house next to Jane's. A bedraggled black rat sniffed round a bin overflowing with discarded cucumber sandwiches, doilies and paper hats from the street party the night before. It was spotted by a ragged-looking tom cat that landed heavily on top of the bin, screeching as it overturned it with a clang, throwing apple skins and cheese rinds all over the pavement.

Jane jumped out of bed and threw her window open but the street was empty. Yesterday's noise and celebration had died with the night. The crowds of people who had gathered to celebrate the coronation of King George VI had faded happily back home and tucked their children into bed. Jane had thrown herself into the festivities, forcing away the terrors of Spain that kept spiking her mind like a drug, bringing visions of hideous corpses and heightening her senses to every sound. She had helped her neighbours set up the long tables outside, lay plates, hang flags.

Edmond had spent the day with her. There had been no talk of Walter, no worrying over the dark rings under Jane's eyes. Jane had seemed as breezy and carefree as the children who danced down the street blowing their whistles.

Edmond can't know I've been to Spain, Jane had thought, so she had concealed her fears and floated in his world for a while. They had donned paper crowns and waved flags and drunk up the merriment until their hearts were as full as their stomachs and Jane's nerves had melted with the ice-cream. The street had buzzed and hummed all day long and the odd burst of song had lifted everyone into the clouds and left them there spinning merrily in the sunshine.

Jane had felt child-like again, hanging on her brother's arm, smiling over his shoulder at some colourful remark or other, joining in the anthem as the crowd leapt to their feet, harmonious in their joy if not in their singing. They were a ragtag bunch, some short, some tall, some young, some old, but they celebrated as one – a foot-tapping, ground-breaking earthquake of spirited revelry that swelled and shook the length and breadth of the country.

'I feel giddy,' Jane had said, squeezing Edmond's arm. 'There's something infectious about a crowd.'

'Sometimes it's good to be part of the mob,' Edmond had replied and then shut his mouth quickly, realising his slang was inappropriate. *Idiot,* he thought, *you'll remind her of Berlin.* But Jane wasn't listening; she was watching the children race down the street, eggs wobbling precariously on spoons.

It was only when the sun went down and the tables were packed away and Edmond had left to see Evie, when the people had drifted home to their slippers and nightcaps, shutting their doors and leaving the street empty and cold under a clouded moon, that Jane had felt her heartbeat slow and her high spirits wither away.

It was then that the thoughts of Spain had crept back in and the day's frivolity lost its gloss. She couldn't sleep and that mood of dark despair, that woke her up night after night soaked in sweat, had found its way into her head again.

I need Walter.

She had felt like an addict, returning to her drug.

I need to lose myself in him, let it go for a night; find sleep in the light of the morning, kill the nightmares. Visions of gore came and went like needles, piercing her mind with sharp savagery, preventing her from resting, punching holes in her sanity. *Walter has been to Spain. Does he suffer like I do? Am I a release for him too or is it just his marriage that makes him come back?*

She had wanted to talk to him desperately when she first returned but she knew she shouldn't. She had wanted to charter a boat to rescue refugees, take them to Mexico, France, anywhere but the hell-hole they currently lived in but she hadn't been able to lift the receiver. Now she knew she wanted him for another purpose – a darker one – and she couldn't resist any longer. She had picked up the phone and watched her fingers as they spun the dial his direction once again.

12th May 1937, 8pm

Walter shut the door behind him quickly as he came in.

'Lots of penny paper journalists pushing around Whitehall,' he said. 'Far too many of them idling around; the last thing I want is to be followed.'

Jane had left her slippers upstairs. A cold breeze blew under the front door and wrapped itself around her ankles. Car headlamps dipped and flashed through the stained window above the door like Morse code. She beckoned Walter in without a kiss. She suddenly felt naked, observed as if the front door were just a thin veil, not enough to block out the prying eyes of passers-by. The hall light fell on them like a spotlight, harsh, unforgiving. She thought she heard the letter box clack open and shut as if someone had pushed it upwards to peer through.

'Let's go upstairs,' she said, turning her back to the door, but Walter grabbed her arm and pulled her back, melting into her quickly and with enthusiasm. The coronation had been thrilling. Jane was back in London. She had called him. She wanted him as much as he wanted her. His nose rubbed against hers and he put his hands in her hair.

'Stop,' she leant back against the wall, away from him. 'Not here.'

'What? Is Edmond in?'

'No, he's gone to Evie's house.' She paused. 'It doesn't feel right. I need some privacy.'

'But we're inside your flat. The door is closed.'

'I just …' she paused again, 'I never feel quite private enough. I'm being watched. I can't trust my neighbours.' She thought back to their smiling faces, the linked arms and the raucous rendition of the national anthem. *That's not true. Why did I say that?* Confusion was setting in again; she could feel it taking root, feeding off the indecision that had always plagued her and turning into something darker, more treacherous.

'You're being watched or you feel like you're being watched?' Walter stepped back, alarmed by the panic that had flared up in her eyes, her voice.

Jane turned away. She couldn't tell him that she shut doors all the time and then was flustered when she came home and found them open, how a creak on the stairs brought the prickles out at the back of her neck. What she wanted him to know was that he couldn't carry on like this. She couldn't carry on like this and yet the smell of sweat on his collar, the taste of tobacco on his tongue, the certainty of his desire drew her in and forced her back to him again.

'Come on, Jane,' he said, 'we're lucky we've got a place to meet at all.'

She didn't reply. It was no use. This was it and she couldn't bear to be left alone again in the flat. Not with Edmond away, Richard still in Spain. She looked past Walter, willing away the fearful shapes that kept chasing her. There it was again – the shadow in the corridor. She screwed her eyes tight shut – *I can't bear it. Leave me alone.*

The man with the scar snarled at her, she could feel his snarl – it grated over her skin and closed round her throat. Someone grabbed her, seized her arms and shook her. They were shouting something. The sound bounced around inside her head like an echo in a cave.

'Jane?'

'Jane?'

'Jane!'

She opened her eyes. A man's shape came into focus.

'Jane, what's going on? Are you unwell?'

'No,' she shook her head. 'No.'

Walter was there – in front of her. Where had he come from? He couldn't leave her. He had to stay with her to banish the visions. She needed his body, his physical presence to fill in the holes that kept appearing in her mind and in the flat – the holes that let the dangerous shapes in.

'Walter, I love you.'

Walter said nothing but took her hand and led her upstairs. They rolled onto the bed and Walter kicked off his shoes, pulling at her clothes and drawing her in. He put his hand on her breast but she moved it away and down to her waist. It didn't feel good, his hand there;

her breast felt hard and lumpy and uncomfortable, a bit like her mind, and she didn't want him to touch it. She tried to relax into his embrace but she was as stiff as a log. Her eyes were open as he kissed her as if she was expecting to see someone standing in the corner looking at them through binoculars. *Don't be ridiculous, Jane*, she thought, shutting her eyes, but as Walter got up and undid his trousers, all she could think about was the man with the camera waiting outside the front door to catch him as he left.

He stripped off her dress and underclothes, turning her round like a doll before diving in hungrily. She wrapped her legs round him and pulled him closer, feeling him thrust his way deep inside, losing her mind to his touch, the firm, rhythmic pulsing between her thighs. She wanted him deeper still and pressed upwards as he came down, willing him to push harder into her, be one with her, stay inside forever. It was a desperate, clinging love that pulled them together like magnets till the forces of the world ripped them open and desire rushed through their veins like blood to the head. Then Walter rolled away to finish the ecstasy on his own and Jane was left lying cold without a sheet.

Afterwards, he lay beside her exhausted, his eyes closed. She folded his arms over hers. She stared at the door. She had forgotten to lock it. She had always locked it ever since the night Edmond burst in on them. She started to get up from the bed but Walter moaned, she was too restless, and pulled her back. She lay down again and listened to the voices in the street. No-one she knew. The neighbours had seen Walter coming and going but they hadn't connected him to Jane, or at least, if they had, they weren't going to intrude. Still she couldn't be sure of anything or anyone any more.

She wanted to talk to Walter but he was half-asleep.

'We can't carry on like this.'

'What?'

'I need you to make a decision,' said Jane, turning to look at him. 'I can't continue doing this. I see you but I'm never satisfied. I see you and then I want to punish myself for being weak.'

'Jane, this is feverish talk,' said Walter. 'You need to sleep. We'll talk about this in the morning. You're all over the place tonight.'

Jane's face dropped. She was fighting the urge to cry. Her determination seeped away like it always did at these moments and the great swollen bulge of unshed tears that was building rapidly behind her eyes threatened to burst.

Walter sensed aggravation in her silence. 'Come on Jane, you knew my situation when we first met,' he said, turning over towards the wall with his back to her.

'I knew you were unhappy and that your marriage wasn't likely to last long,' she replied, pulling on a nightdress and getting her head stuck as she rammed it through without undoing the buttons.

Walter pulled himself upright, putting a pillow behind his back. He couldn't rest like this. She was distressed. He couldn't just ignore it. She'd be beating around all night unable to sleep if he did. Maybe he should go. He helped her undo the buttons and straighten herself out. 'Look Jane, I can't commit myself right now. You know that. I'm an MP. I can't divorce my wife. Look what happened to Prince Edward. You have to wait until after the next election.'

'Walter, that's too long. The whole world may have changed by then.'

'Don't be so dramatic, Jane.'

'I'm not asking you to abdicate a throne.'

'That's ridiculous Jane, you know what I mean.'

'I can't go on like this.'

'Do you love me?'

'I don't know any more.'

'Jane, please. Bear with me.'

'For how long?'

'Till I'm re-elected.'

Jane sighed. Edmond was right. Walter would never go through with it.

Walter got up and walked to the window, checking outside. It was quiet. A section of bunting had blown onto the railings below the house and become trapped. A rat was sniffing around by the bin, eyeing up the cheese rinds and apple skins that were dangling irresistibly out of the top.

He turned back to Jane. 'It's time for me to go now. I mustn't leave too late or people will notice.'

'I know,' Jane whispered, feeling weak and subdued, staring at the ceiling.

He dressed quickly, kissed her tentatively on the lips, ran downstairs, threw on his coat and shoes and hurried out of the door.

She got off the bed and went to the window to watch him go. He got to the corner and waved. She waved back and blew him a kiss to make up for her foolish words. He didn't blow one in return. He wasn't looking up. A cab arrived. He jumped in. The cab sped away.

He hadn't been waving to her at all.

15th May 1937, 9am

Bloomsbury, London

Walter told Jane that she breathed in trouble like smoke; it sat, slowly defiling her lungs till she started to choke. 'You're doing yourself damage and nobody else any good by winding things up in your mind, Jane.' Perhaps he was right but it didn't matter what happened to her; over two thousand Spanish children would be evacuated from Bilbao in a week's time by boat and she was determined to be at Southampton docks to meet them.

There was a light breeze lifting the leaves of the plane trees that lined the street. She couldn't bear the office any longer with its piles of paper, endless phone calls and stuffy politics. They knew she had been to Spain but they hadn't asked her about it. They stuck to their quotas and didn't ask questions.

She pushed open the heavy oak door, painted glossy black like all the doors in the square. The carpet had worn thin at the entrance, not surprising considering the growing number of feet that had shuffled across it.

Peggy waved Jane over before she had even hung up her coat. 'Matilda's in there, she's waiting to talk to you.'

Matilda was the only person in the room. The phones were silent, all the papers in still piles on the desks. She was wearing a white blouse and black skirt. She looked almost Victorian.

'Jane. Come and sit down, we need to talk about your request.'

'I'm keen to leave as soon as possible. I was hoping to go to North Stoneham today to check preparations at the camp.' She pulled out the chair opposite Matilda, wiped off the biscuit crumbs left by nervous children, and sat down. She wondered if Matilda would give her a "leaving" biscuit at the end of their conversation too.

Matilda leant back in her chair, 'You're in early.'

'I wanted to tidy up.'

'I'm really sorry, Jane,' Matilda paused.

'Sorry for what?'

Matilda was shuffling papers in front of her, looking for something. 'The Committee's response. Here it is.'

'And?'

'Do you want to read it?'

'I'd rather you just tell me.'

'The Committee has decided it's not appropriate for you to go into the field.'

'What? Why?'

'Considering your situation Jane, they can hardly be expected to send you out as their representative.'

There was something jagged about the way she spoke.

'What do you mean?'

If she was being accused, she wanted it set out directly, not like this all veils and hints. People here insinuated, gossiped, whispered. You started to believe chewed-up rumours. *Aren't we supposed to be working together*? Whatever it was Matilda was going to throw at her it didn't come from the Committee; they had no interest in petty office politics.

'Look Jane, do you really want me to put it bluntly? Surely it would be better to leave the matter here. You can get back to what you've been doing and we can go on as normal. No-one will make any comment and none of this will go beyond the door.'

'I'm sorry, Matilda, but I need to know why. I am wholly committed to the work and I know you need people to help with new arrivals.'

'If you're that committed, Jane, you'll take it from me that you'll be more useful here.'

'I'll continue with my work if that's what the Committee wants, but I would like to know the reason behind their decision. I think I'm entitled to that.'

'You're having an affair with a married man for God's sake – a politician of all people.'

Jane blanched, 'Surely that's my own business?'

'Not when it affects the reputation of the Committee. What sort of example are you setting? How can you possibly go and check whether other people can provide suitable homes for children when you yourself are a home-wrecker?' Matilda's cheeks grew as red as the pimple by her nose. She tapped the table with her hand. Jane was morally compromised. That was that.

Jane stood up. 'Very well,' she said, looking Matilda in the eye. She walked over to her desk and sat down.

'You don't deny it then?'

Jane ignored her.

'You can't just waltz in here and expect to be given any job you ask for you know. I had to work my way up through the grades. I don't come from money like you.'

'I don't get paid to work here. I'm not taking anyone else's position. Can't we support each other? I don't want a battle every day.'

'You think you're better than the rest of us, Jane. You need to leave your airs and graces on the doormat and do the work you're given.' With that Matilda stood up abruptly, her face almost as red as Jane's, and went out.

Jane sat back and ran her hands through her hair. Then she clipped it back in place. The last thing she wanted was to appear dishevelled. She longed to open the door, run down the hallway, out into the street and never come back but she didn't want to give Matilda the satisfaction. Better to dive into the work and escape later.

It was then that she saw it: Walter's letter. Open on her desk.

Why had he written to her here? On the other hand, most people assumed private mail was just that. She wondered what excuse Matilda would come up with if she asked why they had opened a letter clearly addressed to her. But then they would assume they didn't need an excuse as the contents so deftly condemned her of a crime worse than theirs.

"My very dear Jane,
Last night the thought of you was so strong. I felt I was leaning against the table and looking at you and our eyes were trained on each other and I wanted to tell you to wait a little. Now I'm just going to bed – writing this after my bath and aching for you. Jane, darling, I want you in my arms – it hurts to be without you. I think I had forgotten that I loved so much.

Walter."

It was a violation. It had been left for her to find. *No wonder Matilda didn't feel she needed to explain.*

'They look through coat pockets. If they find a trade union card they take you away and shoot you.'

'People disappear all the time in Madrid.'

'Censor your letters or they will censor you.'

She could hear the voices in her head – spite and malice that seemed to come from nowhere. There was no knowing what people were capable of when times turned bad. What would happen if England became Madrid? What would happen if there was a war?

Jane could feel ulcers swelling uncomfortably in her mouth. She walked across the corridor to the toilet. Luckily there was no-one around. She locked the door, ran the tap and let the tears flow. Sobs racked silently through her. They were right: he was married; she was compromised. She was worthless, immoral. She hated herself for it. It was destructive. How could she help others if she couldn't even help herself?

After a while she felt her courage return. They were wrong. They were cruel. She wouldn't give in to bullying. This was private, personal, not some tawdry affair they could smear with oil, light a match and burn to the ground. It was her conscience; let them leave her to it. She was working hard. She had been to Spain and back. She had delivered aid. She wanted to do it again. That was important. Not this.

Then the guilt bit in again like a tick in the arm; she couldn't get rid of it. *Your own brother can't bear to think about it, he goes out of his way to avoid a clash but he thinks you're a fool who's going to get hurt. This is your own fault!*

She splashed her face with water and dried it with the hand towel, being careful not to rub her eyes. *I can't let this get to me. They have no right to pry,* she told herself. *Go back in and hold your head up.*

She opened the door a fraction and then closed it quietly again. *Am I ready for the onslaught, for the contempt? Can I continue working in a place where I am not trusted, where I am humiliated, where my own colleagues spy on me?* She yanked out some of the hair pins holding back her unruly mop before sticking them back in again, sharply, bringing the tears back into her eyes.

She dabbed at them vigorously with a tissue before flushing the loo and running the taps again for cover. Then she stuck out her jaw in defiance and emerged, crossing the hallway again. The door to their office was propped open. Matilda was watching from behind her desk. As Jane came in she dropped her eyes quickly and started to type something on her smart new Underwood typewriter.

Jane sat down at her desk and pocketed Walter's letter. *Self-control is the cornerstone of courage. That's what Elsie would say.* She gritted her teeth and stuck her brain and hands into other people's troubles. There were worse problems than hers to be tackled. She wouldn't let personal issues get in the way. No-one else should suffer for them and no-one else should know how much she was suffering.

23rd May 1937, 6pm
Southampton docks

Edmond watched his sister scurry in and out of double-decker buses, showing each child to their seat and placing their tiny bag in the luggage rack above their head. He had just come back from his tenth and final trip to the bakery. Bakeries, in fact, as he had visited several during the day, steadily running them all out of bread rolls.

On the docks, the men and women of the Salvation Army welcomed the last few children to shore as they stumbled off the great hulk of a boat that had provided a safe but rocky passage from Bilbao. At first the children were unsure what to make of the smartly dressed welcome committee with their white sashes, gold buckles and military tassels but when the women bent down to help them with their shoelaces and slipped sweets into their hands, they saw kindness beneath the uniforms and smiled shyly.

The seafront was cold and misty but it hadn't rained. The children gripped the knotted rope as they came down the gangplank. Some were holding hands; others clutched their only bag tightly as they shuffled along in scuffed shoes, ragged laces trailing. They looked slightly queasy as they wobbled their way to shore, the smell of salty seaweed teasing their empty bellies, the westerly wind peppering their tired eyes with spray.

Jane felt a surge of relief as she helped them onto buses but when the buses left, the thought of the journey ahead of them, uncertain where they would stay or how long for, brought back the boarding school butterflies she thought she'd long since conquered and she scanned the harbour for her brother.

Edmond was standing next to a Salvation Army banner handing out rolls from a paper bag when she found him. 'Edmond,' she whispered, 'this is twice the number of children they expected and they've only had a couple of days to prepare the camp. They had to dig open latrines yesterday. The children can't stay in tents for long, look at them – they're half-starved.' A boy with knees as knobbly as his elbows took a roll from Edmond and wolfed it down before he'd pulled the next one out. The boy was moved on by the children behind him but his eyes remained fixed on Edmond's bag.

Edmond had a quiet word with the woman next to him who smiled and relieved him of his duties. He took Jane by the hand. He could sense her desire to pull away from him, get on with the job, stop dithering but he could also see that she needed to stop, be quiet and observe the movement around them without being part of it for a while. He led her to a bench on the pier, away from the endless queue of homesick children.

'Jane,' he said, 'look how many people have turned out to welcome the children. The newspapers have really helped your cause. There won't be a shortage of help. See that woman over there, offering that girl a handkerchief. Look at that man by the bus, handing out pennies.' He put his arm round Jane's shoulders and hugged her. She was tense and stiff, as if the cold sea mist had entered her body and chilled her on the inside.

She couldn't shake the thought of Matilda, the spitefulness of her departing shot: 'You can't visit homes as our representative Jane. If you want to continue to work with us you will have to stay in the office.'

'I'm a volunteer, Matilda,' she had replied. 'If I can't volunteer for you, I'll step up my work with the National Joint Committee.' She couldn't have done it without Edmond, though, the reassurance of his support.

It was on Saturday evening, just as Edmond was getting up to wish her good night, that she had declared, 'I'm going to Southampton.' Maybe it was the glass of port she had swallowed that restored her bullish determination or maybe it was the end of a long week of fretting, either way she had finally decided and there would be no putting her off.

'When are you going?'

'Sunday first thing.'

'Then I'll come with you. It'll do us both good to get out of London and be blasted by that fearsome sea wind they've got down there.'

'That would be wonderful,' Jane had replied, going over to him and giving him a squeeze. She used to squeeze him like that every time they came home from boarding school. He told himself he would never mention Walter again if it meant he could have his sister back.

Now, on the docks, as church bells tolled in the distance, the sun slipped away and the captain of the *Habana* gave orders to pull up the gangplank, Edmond pulled Jane to her feet and led her towards the last bus. They would finish the day together. He motioned her towards the children and handed her his last bread roll.

29th May 1937, 8.30am
Bloomsbury, London

Richard was fading into the distance as the ox cart he was travelling on juddered over stones, lumbering slowly into darkly forested mountains. Or was it a truck? Jane's arms were pinned behind her. She struggled to get free, screamed, kicked, but someone stuffed rubber into her mouth and hit her round the head with a hammer. Men with guns and grim, leathery faces crowded round Richard, blocking him from view, their legs hanging over the sides, fingers on triggers, eyes scouring the horizon for movement. The wind whipped red dust into the creases at the corner of their eyes as they strained to see through the shadowy pine trees, past the endless crags and rocks that dotted the mountainside. Their frowning faces gathered dirt like war-paint, striping their foreheads and tattooing their arms as they sat, exposed to the elements on crates of ammunition and medical supplies.

The nightmare changed every night but one thing was always the same: Richard was leaving her behind.

There was the memory of his hand on her shoulder, firm, reassuring; comforting her when she woke up in a sweat. But when she tried to imagine him there with her, in her bedroom she could never see his face. *Richard can't disappear,* she told herself. *He always comes back.* Still, she could feel tension knotting tightly in her stomach whenever she thought of him, of Spain, of Guernica.

She had just finished a piece of toast, which was all she could manage, when the phone rang and a low, steady voice asked for her.

It took her a while to react, to realise that he was actually there, that it really was Richard at the other end of the line.

'Jane, I'll be in town until Tuesday, can we meet?'

Nothing.

'Jane? Are you still there?'

Jane was piecing him back together in her mind, freshly shaved, eager to see her, the shelling he had weathered night after night brushed off like the earth from his shoes.

'You're just in time,' she said. 'I'm afraid you'll find me a pale shade of my former self. I've been busy falling apart reading your newspaper reports.'

'Sorry, Jane. It was impossible to get letters through.'

'Never mind. It's wonderful to hear your voice again. You have a habit of turning up when I need you.'

'Why? What is it? Are you all right?'

'I've got an appointment with the doctor tomorrow and I'm feeling slightly nervous. It's ridiculous really.'

'What's wrong?'

'A small lump on my breast, probably nothing.'

She was suffering from severe hypochondria. Or at least, that's what she hoped it was. There was a grape-sized lump on her left breast and it was getting larger. She felt the skin, the muscle, the soft tissue and the denser matter within it gingerly with the tip of her finger.

'I'll come with you, Jane,' Richard said, 'let me come with you to the doctor.'

He had come back.

He would help her.

She would recover. She would be well again. He would stay.

30th May 1937, 4pm
Doctor's Surgery, Bloomsbury, London

He hasn't changed, thought Jane, *not on the outside anyway.*

Richard took out his paper. He guessed Jane wouldn't want to talk. Maybe she would never see him as more than a reliable presence but he didn't care. He only wanted to be next to her for now. His was an unflinching, long-term love, nothing like the shady, smoky, obsessive liaison she had with Walter. Walter: the tall, willowy flip-flop lover whose political blather and smooth self-confidence had steamed Jane's heart so thoroughly, she couldn't see past the shimmer of hot air floating above him.

Jane went to the bathroom and splashed her face with water. *I'm as pale and blotchy as the eggs in Edmond's old collection.* She smiled but a slight hysteria rose within her. Nightmares came and went but this lump had grown. It was solid. It made her feel rather faint and light-headed to look at it so she tried not to. Thank heavens for Richard and his thick-skinned persistence, his large hands and broad shoulders that had gathered her up once again before she disintegrated.

She hadn't told Walter about the lump. All this anxiety was probably what caused the swelling in the first place. She imagined popping it and watching the stress of the last few months ooze out in a malevolent trickle. Maybe it would need drawing out forcefully like poison from a bite.

Someone knocked on the bathroom door.

'The doctor's ready to see you.'

4.45pm

'She was certain it was a cyst,' said Jane. 'She took some fluid.'

'Such things are rarely serious,' replied Richard as breezily as he could.

'She advised me to see a specialist for a second opinion.'

'I'm sure they'll say the same thing. No need to worry. How is it treated?'

'I may need a minor operation to get rid of it completely.'

Richard looked at her. She looked frail, as if she was struggling to hold herself together, as if she might come unstitched at the seams any moment and collapse in a heap in front of him. All the fear, worry and pressure she'd heaped on herself and shovelled away deep within was leaching out, making her appear tired and drawn. He wanted to take her in his arms and scrunch up the hair that had lost some of its bounce, feed up the hollow cheeks and scoop her up to a sunnier place, but he was stuck in the empty zone between friendship and love and he daren't take her by the waist and kiss her however much he wanted to.

The doctor had advised Jane not to rub or crush the lump. Not that she was likely to. She was so tentative with her body these days. She couldn't bear to look at it. What if the surgery left a scar? *Don't be ridiculous*, she told herself. *Concentrate on how lucky you are.* There she was sitting on the bed next to Elsie again, the swelling on Elsie's chest so large that it couldn't be removed.

'They caught it early,' said Richard, 'so it shouldn't take long to heal.'

Why should I survive when Elsie didn't?

'You need to rest, Jane. You've had a shock. Don't let it knock you out completely. It won't be long before you can get back to work.'

He knew what she needed to hear.

They reached her flat. It felt so strange, so eerily polite standing here on the front steps of a tall London townhouse when last time they'd seen each other Richard had been wiping sweat from his forehead, heaving boxes of supplies onto a truck before heading off into a war zone.

'You look exhausted,' Richard said, noticing how pink and watery her eyes were. 'If it's all right with you, I'll call round to see how you're doing tomorrow.'

'Thank you,' Jane said. He really was a thoughtful man. The sort she should be in love with in a world where things went to plan. She pressed his hand. Then she turned the key and went in. He stood on the doorstep for a while after she had closed the door, looking, for all the world as if he was guarding the entrance.

9.30pm
Bloomsbury, London

I have to tell her. Jane climbed out of the bath and wrapped herself in a towel. She felt softer, calmer. Calm enough to speak to Gina without feeling let down, she hoped. *I need to tell her*, she thought, *she's going to find out from Edmond if I don't. Besides, I want her support. She's my mother. She doesn't even know I've been to Spain.*

She put on her nightdress and gown and picked up the phone.

The receiver felt cold and heavy in her hands as she listened to the distant dial tone. *I hope she's there,* Jane thought, *I can't bear to speak to Charles.*

A man picked up.

'Weston 2-3-8—'

Jane jumped in fast, 'It's Jane. I'd like to speak to my mother please.'

'Certainly, I'll go and get her,' Charles said then added, 'she has just gone up to bed.'

'Is she unwell?'

'Oh no, no. She's fine. Just a little tired.' *How inconsiderate of Jane to call so late,* thought Charles. *She knows we go to bed straight after supper.* Still, maybe she had something important to say: she called so rarely it was a bit of a shock to hear her voice.

'I would like to speak to her if she hasn't already gone to sleep.'

She didn't get a reply. Charles had put his receiver down and gone to fetch his wife. What a relief. The last thing she wanted was interference.

She waited. The hair on her arms was standing up. It was draughty in the hall. She wrapped her dressing gown round more tightly and hoped her mother would hurry up. She could imagine Charles telling her it was Jane, that if she was too sleepy he would ask her to phone back another day. She imagined her mother's face, her quizzical look. 'Really?' She would be curious to know why. It wasn't one of their allotted times after all.

Finally, just as she was deciding to give up, put down the phone and leave her mother to stew, Gina picked up the receiver.

'Jane, this is late to call. We were just going to bed,' she said. Then she remembered her own call to the doctor in the early hours of the morning all those years ago. Maybe there was something wrong. 'Is Edmond all right? Do you need us to come round?'

'Edmond is perfectly well, mother, thank you,' said Jane. She paused. There was silence on the other end of the phone. She imagined her mother twisting the phone cord, distracted. 'I'm calling to let you know that I've just seen a doctor and been diagnosed with what appears to be a cyst on my left breast. I will need to have a minor operation. There's no need to worry but I thought you should know.' She stopped and waited for a response. She could hear Gina breathing, misting up her receiver, adding an extra layer of fog to their already strained conversation.

'I see,' said Gina. 'If there isn't anything to worry about then that's fine.' She paused, waiting to see whether Jane would divulge anything further. Nothing. Maybe Jane expected something more from her? 'Well, a cyst is of no importance at all is it? Many women have them I've heard.'

'Yes,' replied Jane, 'the doctor did say they were quite common. There is a risk of it spreading if it isn't a cyst, if the operation is delayed.' It was about time her mother expressed some form of concern. It felt like the phone call was quickly being consigned to Gina's "unnecessary" pile. Surely she would show a little anxiety?

'You do have to be careful,' said Gina, chewing it over and coming up with a little extra, 'you must remember Aunt Winnie.'

She's so unhelpful it's almost absurd, thought Jane. *I'm not even going to reply to that.*

'She was misdiagnosed and died of cancer,' Gina went on, 'and then there was Elsie.' She stopped, realising with a jolt that she might have gone too far. She imagined Jane's face swelling, a sudden fear that she would actually hear tears drop onto the receiver.

'Really, mother, that's the last thing I want to think about right now,' said Jane. She shouldn't have bothered calling. It was some sort of self-destructive urge, a fierce hunger to shock her mother into reaction undercut by the bitter reality of dissatisfaction with her response.

'Do keep us informed, Jane,' said Gina, sensing the tail-end of the conversation. She always felt so pathetic, inadequate after conversations with Jane; it was most disconcerting.

'Good night, mother,' replied Jane.

'Good night, Jane,' said Gina, putting down the phone and standing beside it for a few minutes. What should she have said? *What does Jane expect when she phones out of the blue?*

Jane had made up her mind. She thought again of Elsie. Maybe she wanted to suffer like Elsie did, to feel pain like she had, to overcome the fear that had found a nook in her head and stuck crampons into her brain. *Should I tell Walter? What will he say? Why can't I let him go?* She felt as wobbly and unstable as jelly, incapable of setting firm in any direction.

She had Walter in one hand, Richard in the other, her mind tilting this way and that, unable to make a decision. *Let it be,* she thought. *Let it run its course. There's a plan somewhere. It's just not mine.*

"2nd June 1937
Dear Jane,
I've had the curious pleasure of being loyal to you and finding it easy. You are a good thing to be loyal to. You are a good girl according to your lights, and worthy of being loved by someone better than me. It's a pity there isn't someone better in the field. But I think I'm just good enough to qualify, and you could make me a lot better than I am, as you have made me better than I was, and that is certainly a reason for me to be utterly in love with you.

Which is a fact, whether there is a reason for it or not.

It isn't very much of a reason for you to be in love with me.

Richard."

"2nd June 1937
My dearest Jane,
It's probably just a scare, this illness of yours, but even so it makes me feel again that all the difficulties are yours in our relationship. I sometimes feel myself such a cad and a brute, and I passionately want to be a moralist living a quiet life with a garden and an intellectual pursuit and an ordered life, and stable emotions, loving you. But only a bit of me is made like that. Most of me is only good for knockabout politics, superficial in thinking, based not on intelligence but some intuitive capacity to know what people are going to do. And I am fundamentally fickle, and only garden at weekends! My love, perhaps I am not as bad as sometimes I think, perhaps I am worse, but you are a lovely person and thank you so many times for being so good to me. This letter is all about me, and it ought to be about you. But you will forgive all my selfishness, because you love me, and I love you.

Miss you, Walter."

2nd April 1954, 11am

St Andrew's Hospital, Northampton
Jane is thirty-nine

Gina flickered around Jane's room puffing up her pillows, rearranging her cornflowers, adding more water to the vase and talking at such high speed that Jane switched off and stared out of her window at the men doing press-ups on the freshly mown lawn below.

'It's a new drug, Jane,' Gina was saying, 'it gets rid of the hallucinations.' She walked over to the window frustrated at Jane's lack of attention and closed it. 'You won't need any more electric shocks.'

At this Jane turned and looked at her.

'Will I be able to leave?'

'I don't know, Jane. The doctors will have to assess you.'

'Has it been fully tested?'

'As much as any new medication.'

'How will they give it to me?'

'In a pill.'

A pill. That was all? She might be able to live a normal life again. She might be able to leave the asylum. Jane's mind bubbled with excitement before popping painfully, *Can I cope out there? What sort of life lies beyond the fence? I've been here too long.* She gripped the sink next to the window and her knuckles turned white. Gina was alarmed.

'The pill will reduce your agitation, Jane. It will prevent these panic attacks you have.'

That's all very well, thought Jane, *but will I be able to think clearly? Will it take away the fear or will it merely numb my brain so I can't focus on anything anymore?*

'Apparently you will be much calmer altogether,' Gina continued. 'You won't get over-excited like you do now.'

Jane's mouth dropped. It was definitely for them then. The white-coats. It would drain her mind of colour. She would become one of them, the people she saw outside – the wanderers, the bench-warmers, the patients whose knitting needles clickety-clacked endlessly in harmony with the clock on the wall. *Tick. Tock.* Your life has no point. You are imprisoned by the dullness of your ravaged brain. Drugs are your manacles. The doctors are pleased. Your mind clings to their cures like a limpet. There is no way out.

Then again, maybe there had been a breakthrough somewhere. Maybe this would break the cycle, the hammer blow, the fractured bone, the flatline, the emptiness and then the fear, that always returned. *What's my mother not telling me?*

'We could take you out on day trips, Jane,' Gina continued, 'You could meet the children.' She stopped. *I'm promising too much*, she thought. *We don't know whether this drug will work yet. Nothing else has.*

'What are the side-effects?' Jane asked. Swallowing a pill was too simple. There were always hidden extras, the tiny writing on the side they didn't like you to see.

'Nothing substantial,' said Gina. 'Possible twitches the doctor said.' That wasn't quite true but then she didn't want to put Jane off at this stage. She thought back to her meeting in the consulting room.

'Repetitive involuntary movements, muscle contractions – lip smacking, grimacing and the like.'

'Isn't the pill supposed to make Jane normal again?' Gina had said.

'What would you prefer? Paranoia and hallucinations or a blinking eye?' the doctor replied dismissively. 'Anyway, that's just one of many possible side-effects and Jane may not experience any of them.'

I don't know, thought Gina, *why do they make these decisions so difficult?*

Back in Jane's room, she looked at her daughter. Ten years she had been here. Ten years. She had crow's feet that seemed to deepen by the day. Bags under her eyes like storm clouds, bags of tears that never fell. The world was a different place since Jane had been certified. Every action, every decision felt like a mistake, an unknown and she'd made so many mistakes already it was impossible to know what to do about anything. *How did this happen?* she thought wretchedly. *How did Jane end up here? Why is she still here?* An awful sadness welled up inside and threatened to overwhelm her. She sat down on Jane's bed and sobbed, her hands pressing down on the mattress, denting it with the heaviness of her pain, the sorrow that was racking through her in nauseous waves, bending her double after all the years of strained silence.

Jane went back to the window and opened it. She looked out over the grounds. A car was circling the fountain on the drive, a continuous, useless, hopeless loop, round and round, again and again. The men on the lawn had gone.

Mission

"20th July 1938
Dear Jane,
My Foreign Office work has been suspended for the time being. Will you come and visit me here in Berlin? I know it's asking a lot of you but I could do with seeing a friend. I have few ties left in England.
Yours,
Karl."

1st December 1938, 8.30am
Bloomsbury, London

Jane was standing by the Elgin Marbles in the British Museum. Broken trophies of the past – looted or acquired?

She pulled out the photo again, torn from her newspaper and folded into her pocket weeks ago: looting, vandalism, cold-blooded murder; Kristallnacht; plain-clothed civilians with sledgehammers and axes. Ragged daggers of glass reflected the blood that puddled and spread from Jewish shops and synagogues onto the faces of those who took photos. Photos that would trip the wire and explode the pretence: the idea that the world could accept the Nazis; that the world could sit back and watch.

Karl needed help and there was only one way to reach him. She had to go to Germany. Even the thought of it was terrifying. She felt as if she were wearing a straitjacket that tightened with each step, digging into her ribs, squeezing her lungs till she struggled to breathe. *Isn't this what I want?* she thought. *Isn't this what I've been working towards – a way to resist the Fascists, to help those in danger?* The straitjacket tightened again. Berlin wouldn't leave her alone no matter how hard she tried to forget it. In every photo, in every news report she could see the dead man, the German Jew, his face pulped on the pavement, his broken profile carved into the German landscape, a scar on the Black Forest, sprayed in blood-red graffiti on the walls of a burnt-out Reichstag.

She had worked like a sleepwalker, setting dates, booking train tickets, hauling out her suitcase and beginning the painful process of packing without engaging her brain, without letting her mind cut in with its dreadful distortions, its visions of death.

Her cyst had been removed. It had left her with a hole in her chest like a gap in a wall, plastered over, hollow beneath. She had to fill it with something concrete, rid herself of the awful insecurity that bit in every time she went for a check-up.

Walter would be here any moment. Would he dismiss her resolve or would he help her? She hadn't seen him since her operation though he had written to her. She had been trying to cut him loose, let the feelings she had for him sweat out and wash away but it was no good. She needed his network. This was the reason they had come together. She was sure of it. Where else could she pass the information Karl would give her?

Her head was rushing again as her heart beat blood to her brain. She looked around for a bench.

A light tap on her shoulder and she jumped like a fly from a swat.

'Jane,' Walter said, 'I didn't mean to startle you.' He stopped and looked at the exhibit, assuming that was what held her attention. 'The Marbles are beautiful aren't they?'

'Can we walk round the museum and talk as we go?' said Jane.

Walter looked at her, surprised. What was she going to tell him? She hadn't suggested dinner. *Am I wasting my time?*

They walked towards the Egyptian section, with its incomprehensible hieroglyphs and heavy stone coffins. A few visitors peered blearily at plaques. The lighting was dim and the high ceilings made the space echo coldly.

A man was staring at Walter. Walter caught his eye and nodded at him before turning away. The man ignored Jane but she could feel him watching her from behind a sarcophagus.

'Who's that?'

'One of the Under-Secretaries working with Lord Runciman,' he replied in a low voice. 'I've just had a meeting with them about Czechoslovakia.'

'Oh?' said Jane, 'Isn't it a bit late for that now? How can anyone defend Czechoslovakia from the Nazis when we've given them its borders and defences?'

Walter put his hands on Jane's shoulders and gripped them firmly. 'Stop, Jane. You're frothing at the mouth before you've thought it through.' He glanced over at the sarcophagus but his colleague had gone.

'I want to go to Germany,' she said.

'What?'

'I want to go to Germany to help the resistance before it's too late.'

'What are you talking about? What resistance?'

'I can act as courier between the anti-Nazi network in Germany and ministers here,' she said. 'No-one else will do it.'

'This is madness,' said Walter, shifting uncomfortably and looking vainly for somewhere to sit down. 'Why can't you continue to work with us on Spanish Relief, Jane? Why do you need to get involved in this as well? Commit yourself to one cause. Don't try to tackle the world's problems all at once.'

'But don't you see? It's all interlinked. Franco's Nationalists wouldn't have survived without the support of Mussolini and Hitler. Hitler is scaling up the Luftwaffe. If we want to stop the suffering it is the Nazis we must go after.'

'We're non-partisan, Jane. We offer non-partisan relief. The British government opposes direct intervention.'

'Exactly. If I go to Germany, I can give you the evidence you need to convince ministers that Hitler won't be reined in and that there is still potential to remove him.'

'It's impossible,' said Walter. 'Hitler is fulfilling Germany's territorial dreams. He's spitting on the Treaty of Versailles. He has restored full employment. The Germans won't rise up against him unless he is utterly humiliated or suffers a military reverse.'

'If Britain and France act now, together, to bring down the Nazi machine, there is a network of anti-Nazis in Germany that will establish a new government. We have to start working with them rather than against them.'

'What is this network of anti-Nazis? How are we to know that this new government would be any better? The German resistance is splintered from what I hear – small groups, disparate, no solidarity.'

'If it weren't for the Munich Agreement the German generals would've carried out a putsch, Walter. You're right, the resistance is demoralised but there are still high-ranking ministers who dislike Hitler in Germany. If they were able to meet politicians, diplomats, people of influence, they could agree a plan before it's too late.'

She was speaking quickly, gabbling her sentences. She slowed down, lowered her voice, 'I have a friend in the Foreign Office, Karl von Schulze. He's been attempting to forge alliances on their behalf but he's met with the utmost suspicion wherever he goes.'

Walter frowned. 'I'm not surprised. He recently attended a Nazi training camp. What else are people supposed to think?'

'He's not a member of the Nazi party – how do you know so much about him?' Jane backed away from Walter as if he had struck a match and was holding it up to a fuse. *What does he know, who has he spoken to?*

'Calm down, Jane. You've mentioned him before. I made enquiries,' Walter said then stopped. It wouldn't be wise to reveal the extent of these enquiries but he did know that Karl had been received by Lord Halifax and Halifax had been cautious, dismissive even.

'He's under huge pressure,' Jane said. 'As a member of the Foreign Office, his ability to travel is viewed as suspicious whereas in fact it's a unique opportunity.' Her head felt hot. She had to convince Walter to help before it was too late. She took a deep breath and let it out slowly.

Walter could see she was distressed. It only added to his view that she was in no position to attempt anything this dangerous. *Is she intending to go alone? If Karl von Schulze has encouraged this he is a fool. Jane has no connections, nothing that could be of use to him*. It was implausible at best; at worst, a diplomatic nightmare with potential to disrupt the tenuous peace.

They were standing apart in the middle of the corridor, surrounded by glass cabinets, the jewellery of dead people.

'Can you put me in touch with Karl?' Walter said.

'Karl is in Berlin. I've booked my train ticket already. I can bring back whatever information, names and assurances you require if you'll agree to take it to ministers? If there are high-ranking officials to meet, he will make plans to come to London.'

'What do you think he can achieve?'

'If Britain and France stand up to Hitler, high ranking officials in the Foreign Office, Military Intelligence and Army, will stage a coup the moment Hitler declares war.'

Walter felt pale, weak. 'I'll need the evidence,' he said. *How has Jane got in so deep? I should've paid more attention to her connection with Karl.* Jane was a woman of courage, admirable but naïve. She looked so innocent with her blue eyes, her dark hair framing her face like a shadow.

Maybe he should let her go, get it over with. She was only acting as a courier after all. There was something disturbingly intense about the way she was looking at him. *She'll go anyway, with or without my blessing.*

He took her hands. They stood behind the sarcophagus; no onlookers to disturb them, just a sightless Egyptian mummy, salted, wrapped in linen strands, its heart the only remaining organ. His own heart banged loudly against the wall of his chest. He wanted to absorb some of her passion. It was more than he'd ever felt himself.

'I'll help you, Jane,' he said, pulling her towards him.

Her mouth was soft against his and he felt her relax. It was the second time they'd kissed at the British Museum and it felt like the first. He wondered, hazily, how to preserve moments like this. He wondered if they would ever kiss like that again.

28th July 1945, 3.30pm
St Andrew's Hospital, Northampton
Jane is thirty-one

Doctor's notes:

"Patient continues to experience sporadic hallucinations and periodic depression. She often refuses to take part in activities. Electric shock treatment appears to have a calming effect on her but over time she reverts to restlessness and paranoia. Recorded instances of food thrown across dining room, screaming at nurses. Spoke to patient's mother today about possible leucotomy as no progress likely with other treatments."

The doctor put down his pen and put the radio on. At least the war was coming to an end. Not that he had been involved. He had enough battles of his own at the asylum. There was the possibility of an influx of traumatised veterans, along with long-lost relatives who wanted to interfere.

"Japanese Premier Suzuki has today disregarded the ultimatum issued by the United States to surrender."

The radio set crackled. The doctor fiddled with the dial.

"A United States bomber has hit the Empire State building while descending to Newark Airport through thick fog."

Death and destruction or the fear of death and destruction. *No wonder people arrive in splinters, unable to cope with life*, the doctor thought. *If you can't take away the fear, you have to blunt the person. Otherwise you lose control.*

Failure

14th March 1939, 6.30pm
Berlin
Jane is twenty-four

Karl was standing by the fountain in front of the Nikolaikirche: its red clinker bricks, green metal spires and slender arched windows towered reassuringly above him. It was a relief to escape the intimidating, grey slab walls and hideously brazen swastikas that tattooed and oppressed the rest of the city. This wasn't an elegant building but it held a beauty and a grandeur that belonged to the past: a past that Karl was proud of. It was no surprise to Jane that he had chosen to meet here. This was the Nikolaiviertel – the historic core of Berlin. The twin clocks on the church tower had ticked on through centuries and governments. Glancing up at them, Jane was pleased to see that she had arrived on time.

Karl waved at her. He planted a kiss on her cheek and dug his arm through hers. Before she could say anything he muttered in her ear, 'This way. We're being watched.'

It was already getting dark. Jane had eaten a stale cheese sandwich on the train. She could feel her stomach digesting, lurching fretfully as they hurried along the narrow streets. Her heels were low which was lucky as she tripped and blundered over cobbles. She was relieved to see she was similarly dressed to the German women she passed: grey jacket and skirt topped by a brown banded hat, fur muff to keep the chill out, small red carry bag tucked over her arm. Karl wore a long, brown tweed coat with a dark grey suit underneath. He was carrying a briefcase. They would blend in anywhere, but someone was following them.

As they hurried along, there were moments when she thought she felt cold cigarette breath down the back of her neck, as if their pursuer was treading maliciously on her shadow, but it was just stale air gusting from the vents of half-empty restaurants. Everywhere she looked there were lurkers. Each doorway seemed to provide a leaning post for some faceless smoker, his hat tilted over his eyes, lounging casually, waiting for the brawl to start, the signal to break out, join the crowd, pull on their brown studded boots. This was a city festering slowly under Nazi law. The moon reflected the half-glow of flickering street lamps. No-one was safe. There were rumours that people were taken away at night-time and sent to camps. Jane shivered and shoved her hands further into her muff.

She was glad they weren't confronted at every turn by imperious monuments, but these thinly crafted streets somehow felt worse. This was a place for secrets not marching bands. Jane suddenly craved the hollow boom of the drums, the cracking stomp of booted feet, all the parading bluster and nonsense of this black and red regime – anything to deflect the sense of dread that was building within her.

Karl's arm was little consolation. He lived here and it was sapping him slowly. He was thinner. The beak of his nose, his deep-sunken eyes overhung by the V of his eyebrows, made him appear more careworn and sterner than before. It was impossible to know who to trust – was the woman who brushed past as she rummaged in her bag for keys a Nazi, or was she hiding someone from the Nazis? Her keys fell with a clatter onto the cobbles. Karl didn't stop. Why did the thin man in the long grey coat stare at them as they went past? Most people kept their eyes down, their souls and secrets to themselves. Her heartbeat gained pace and she gripped Karl's arm. He gave her a reassuring squeeze and they kept moving.

They had turned down so many side streets that Jane completely lost her bearings. She felt like hacking at her fears like the nettles that they were and crushing them underfoot. No-one knew she was in Germany except Walter. Edmond, her mother, Evie, Rebecca – they were all part of her other world. This was separate. It had to be hidden from view or she might jeopardise Karl's safety. Besides, she was determined to complete this mission, to see a purpose fulfilled whatever the danger. Still, as she passed a restaurant, the smell of fried meat, normally so enticing, made her feel queasy. She wished they would get somewhere soon. Somewhere private; somewhere they could talk, somewhere she would feel at ease. *Was that possible here?*

Karl stopped outside the Preussischer Hof, an unobtrusive hotel with a bar next door. They went in. It was shabby and smelt of cheese. The carpet was mouldy and frayed at the edges. There was a large black stain by the main desk. Karl leant on the counter and pressed the bell. A small pot-bellied man with a large oil-slick moustache and a bald head appeared. Karl spoke softly. The man looked over at Jane and nodded. He bent down and pulled out a pair of rusty keys from beneath the counter. Karl pointed to the stairs. Jane could feel the man's pokey, weasel eyes following her as they went up. She felt tainted by the place as if she was indeed here for some sordid liaison. They had only just come in and already she felt like she needed a long bath. It was a filthy place. Even the bannister, a metal rail, looked greasy. *Too many people gripping onto it to steady themselves after the shock of coming in the front door*. The feeling of anxiety that had been nagging her since she arrived in Berlin was closing slowly round her throat like a cheese-wire. She kept her eyes on Karl and tried to focus on his familiarity. *At least we'll be able to tell if someone follows us here – the stairs are as creaky as an old boat.* She waited while Karl opened the door.

'Wait there,' he said, going straight to the window and closing the curtains. He checked inside the cupboard, sweeping the frame with his hand.

It was a small cramped room with a double bed. The bedcover was yellow and stained like the curtains. There was a radio-set on the table. Karl plugged it in and turned it up loud.

'Sorry about all this, Jane,' he said in a low voice, 'it's a precaution in case the room has been bugged by the Gestapo.'

'Of course,' whispered Jane.

She sat down on the bed. It sank sadly beneath her. The springs had gone. She thought back to Oxford where they had bantered so freely about politics. How different this was. How unreal. The possibility of another war was unreal. They had thought at the time it was a crime of the past. They had discussed how to reduce the risks, dispose of old enmities, dissolve the tensions of nationalism – how useless it had all been, how naïve.

The radio spat out German folk tunes. Karl locked the door.

'Thank you so much for coming.' He put his briefcase down on the dressing table. 'You can't imagine how important this is. You won't be able to come back again. If the situation deteriorates that is.' He crossed to the window and peered out through the gap where the curtain met the frame.

'The man's gone. Sorry for being so cloak-and-dagger. All ranked Foreign Office staff are watched and I'm not a member of the Nazi party yet.'

'You mean you will be soon?' said Jane in a shocked whisper. No wonder he was mistrusted overseas. What assurances could anyone give under these conditions?

'I'm holding out as long as possible but I won't get access to the information I need unless I join the party. If things close down further, I'll be of no use to anyone.'

'I see,' Jane said. Karl was risking everything. His world was full of fear. Neighbours reported on you and men in plain clothes tagged your steps like snipers, ready and waiting. Everything and everyone was suspicious. There was a tall cupboard in the corner of the room. It was the size of a man. She opened its doors.

'Don't worry,' said Karl, 'I've already done that. We need to get on and get out.' He looked calm but his voice was hoarse and his manner stiff and distant.

Calm down, Jane told herself, *you saw Karl check the cupboard when you came in.* 'Let's get on with it,' she replied. 'This place is so claustrophobic. It's like being in a rabbit warren with the fox sneaking round outside.'

I shouldn't have taken advantage of her, thought Karl. It wasn't in Jane's nature, all this subterfuge and suspicion. She had always been idealistic and brutally honest. Then again, she was having an affair with a married man, a Liberal MP. He had been shocked when Rebecca had told him.

'There are substantial numbers of anti-Nazis in Germany,' he said. 'Impress that on anyone you come into contact with. If we go to war the Nazis will become patriots and the lines may start to blur. All these bloodless conquests they are making are strengthening them.'

'What do you want me to do?'

'I've got some information to pass on about Czechoslovakia. Your government needs to know what the Nazi command is intending. I can't give the documents to you today but I'll meet you at the train station tomorrow. If anyone approaches you, you'll need to get rid of the evidence.'

Jane nodded.

'We need to re-open contact with foreign sympathisers; that's meant to be my role, but I can't get anyone to listen. Munich set us back but the channels are still open. Kiep, Oster, von Moltke and von Trott are all on board. Then there are others like Israel and Solf working on emigration.' He stopped, seeing the blank look on her face. 'It's an insufferable mess,

Jane, I know that.' The gloom that was fogging up the city was eating away at him. *Focus on the plan*, he thought, *focus on the future. The Nazis won't be here forever.*

'I have to convince foreign governments, particularly the British, to act decisively. The resistance is coherent and ready, they have to believe that. You have to get that message across, Jane.'

'Can't you meet the British Ambassador, Sir Nevile?'

'My colleagues have met him but it's like talking to the gatekeeper. Besides we need to use as many avenues as we can to magnify our case, force a response.'

'I've spoken to the Liberal MP, Walter Tenant, about creating inroads at parliament,' said Jane. Karl didn't know about Walter, unless Rebecca had mentioned him? She hoped not. She knew they were back on speaking terms but Karl had specifically told Jane not to mention this visit to her, Rebecca wasn't one to hold onto a secret for long.

'That could be helpful in the long-run,' Karl said. He wasn't convinced this Walter fellow had much clout. Besides he was an adulterer. Karl wasn't sure he could be trusted. 'I'd like to meet him first.'

'I told him you'd provide concrete evidence that the resistance in Germany was both functional and essential. I thought you wanted contacts in London?' Jane looked worried. 'Was I wrong?'

'It could be useful,' Karl said. Jane was trying hard to help him but it was dangerous to send out random arrows and hope they landed somewhere. 'I hope to travel to London myself in April so I can meet him then.' *If you're still seeing him*, he thought, *I don't want to find myself in the middle of someone else's turbulent affair, there's no time for that.*

'Should I pass any information on to Walter before then so he can pursue any leads he has created?' said Jane, feeling clumsy and confused. *A courier pigeon would do a better job than me,* she thought.

'No!' Karl exclaimed. 'Please don't,' he continued, softening his tone. Why had he involved Jane in all this? He had hankered after a friendly face, someone from Britain who didn't treat him with disdain or suspicion. Now he could see that he'd placed her under enormous pressure.

'Sorry, Jane, I don't want you to get too involved.'

'You don't trust me?'

'I trust you. I just don't want to endanger you any more than I already have.'

'I see,' said Jane. *What did I expect?* she thought. Walter was right about rushing in. It felt like mining hopelessly underground without a lift back to the surface.

'Get the documents to Lord and Lady Astor, they will know what to do,' Karl said. 'But don't give anything to your friend,' he continued. 'I don't know him …' He paused. That sounded unnecessarily harsh. She was looking dejected, mortified. '… yet,' he added, 'I don't know him yet.'

'All right,' Jane said. She was praying now that Walter hadn't made any progress. She wouldn't have anything to give him. Then again, if he hadn't done anything about it, what did that say about him, about their relationship? But that was personal and self-centred. She could see why Karl was cagey. *What a fool I am.*

'Come, Jane, I'll take you to your hotel.' Karl put on his hat and picked up her small leather bag along with his briefcase. He hadn't taken off his coat since they arrived.

'You mean I'm not staying here?'

'I would never expect you to stay here. There's a nice place, close to the train station. We'll take a cab and I'll leave you for the night. There's a restaurant inside if you want something to eat. I hope you'll be comfortable there.'

'This place was just for cover then?'

'It isn't overrun by Nazis. It's somewhere we could pass for—'

'I know,' she broke in. There was really no need for him to say it.

He turned off the radio and there was silence for a moment. Then someone turned on the radio next door.

15th March 1939, 4pm

Smoke belched out from the trains in great puffballs. Whistles squealed like pigs under the knife. Porters sweated over piles of suitcases in hand-pull carts. Two tall officials and a haughty looking woman with rolled blonde hair posed for a jaunty photo in front of Jane. Jane moved away hastily. The last thing she wanted was to be captured on some private film. Any record of her journey would be wiped out entirely when the conductor collected her ticket. She felt its paper edges in her pocket and folded it unconsciously into a small ball, squeezing it between her fingers and thumb like a piece of putty. *That's if there's anything left to give him*, she thought, realising what she was doing and taking her hand out.

She stood on the platform, unrolling her wrinkled ticket, willing Karl to arrive so that she could vanish into a carriage, immerse herself behind a paper and only fold it up once she'd reached London. Never mind it would be in German. *Maybe there's time to buy one now*, she thought, looking around for a stall.

She was making her way back down the platform when she spotted Karl hurrying towards her. He was grim-faced, out of breath, puffing like the trains.

'Have you heard?'

'No? What is it?'

'We've invaded Czechoslovakia.'

Jane stared at him, horrified, 'No!'

'We knew it would happen,' Karl replied, trying to suppress the sourness in his tone, 'but no-one would listen. It was inevitable …' he paused.

'After Munich?'

'Yes. You know what this means?'

'No,' she said, dreading his answer. It was too depressing.

'This has been a waste of time.' The despair in his tone was so emphatic Jane felt like shrivelling up then and there.

Karl turned anxiously, looking over his shoulder to make sure no-one was close enough to hear.

'I have nothing to give you.'

'Oh,' was all she could say, her voice sticking in her throat.

'Hitler's got the survival instincts of a viper. Plant a bomb under his table and he'll stick his teeth into you and leave before it goes off.'

He was crumbling. 'It looks like war,' he said.

'Isn't that what you wanted – decisive action now?' Jane said. 'Won't this trigger the endgame?'

'That's if the military commanders hold their nerve. If they don't, we're in for a long struggle.'

'If Britain and France denounce the Nazis and declare war there'll be a coup won't there?'

'Let's hope so,' Karl replied.

'You need to stop, Karl. Rest. Breathe. You're part of a network. You have to keep it going.' Jane paused. Karl needed a jolt, 'Or you could just leave before things deteriorate further?'

'I won't desert my country, Jane. You know that.'

I need to get back to my flat, he thought suddenly, his mind starting to refocus, *Jane's right. I need to get back to the circle. Talk this through. I can travel to Britain in a month's time. There will be a clear plan by then.*

Two men walked past them talking in low voices. They wore dark belted coats.

'We're being watched,' Karl muttered with annoyance. Everywhere you turned the Nazis were there. It was like living in a termite mound, crawling with bugs.

He pulled Jane towards him tightly. She was the only genuine friend he had spoken to in days and she was leaving. He kissed her warmly on the mouth. She pulled away as he knew she would but he pressed harder. It was selfish but he needed it.

The men in coats turned away. Karl von Schulze was an intellectual. He travelled a lot. He was handsome in the Gothic German mould. He wasn't Aryan but his lineage was sound. If he wanted to keep moving though, he would have to prove his loyalty. There had been concern at camp about him. He had been too quiet. No-one knew what he stood for. Then there was his mother who had refused to fly the Nazi flag outside their family home during a march. They were right to follow him. At least they knew one thing about him: he loved women. There was nothing wrong with that.

Karl looked at Jane. She seemed unwell. Her hands were cold. There was something hollow about the way she looked back at him. His stomach turned like a runaway cart wheel. He felt like a man in limbo with no safe direction to fall.

Train brakes protested loudly, applied at the last moment by harassed drivers. The noise penetrated Jane's ears and jarred through her body. The din in the station was overwhelming: door slams, wagon clatter, steam spouts; a witches' cauldron of sound to submerge and suffocate. She was flailing. So was Karl by the look of him.

Jane's train pulled in. She hadn't moved since the kiss.

She picked up her bag.

She boarded the train.

She found a seat.

The lingering men disappeared and the train pulled out.

She sank back into her seat and closed her eyes. It was over. Why were her relationships so complicated, so dishonest? Everything was so transient, so fickle. Except Richard. She sat up and looked out the window and locked onto that thought.

"17th March 1939
Dear Jane,
I have read your letter a dozen times now. This last Czech business is bloody awful. Tonight I feel like joining the Communist Party. A thing I haven't felt before and probably won't again. But we are all so bloody spineless. Anyhow no-one can believe now that the Nazis ambitions are limited to German racial minorities.

Can I see you?

Richard."

Cracks

20th March 1939, 8pm
Bloomsbury, London
Jane is twenty-four

Susie's mother died suddenly so she went home for a while. Jane wasn't coping well with the mess. There was a dead fly in the glass on her bedside table. They were all over the window sill like shrivelled sultanas, covered in dust. Jane grabbed a brush and swept the flies into the bin. One was still moving. She imagined it climbing out of the bin and landing on her face. She shivered and rubbed the back of her neck nervously. *Where are they all coming from?*

Karl had sent a note:

"For some time yet – the friendships that still reach across the channel will be stressed by further tests. But about ours I do not worry a bit. Tell me occasionally how things are going and to what degree the temper of the metropolitans around is running. But don't join them. Love K."

He was asking her, in his rather stilted English, to keep him informed about public sentiment in London, which he was concerned was increasingly hostile towards Germany. It was meant to be reassuring but somehow it made her feel more isolated, as if the city around her was full of prickles, people who had to be watched, observed, people who didn't understand there was a thin sheet of glass between them and the horrors in Berlin.

At work she had been quiet but people were too busy to notice. The Kindertransport was underway. Lonely, homesick children were being farmed out all over the country. Addresses had to be double-checked, identity cards stamped. The speedy rattle of Jane's fingers over the typewriter kept her mind, ears and eyes occupied. She kept her distance from the children. She didn't want to think about what they had left behind: the parents, silent in the attic; the neighbours smearing 'Juden Heraus' on the house in dirty yellow paint; the men in plain clothes who made use of the information; the shoulder to the door after midnight.

It was only when she got home at night that she dropped her guard. Then she began to notice things. The bathroom door was ajar; she had left it closed. There was water on the floor; she was sure she had mopped it up after her bath. The carpet was coming away from the stairs; she almost tripped over. Little things but they kept happening.

The image of Karl peering sideways past the curtain kept coming back to her. She kept her curtains slightly ajar at night so she could see out if she needed to without pulling them back. There was the chug of a car engine slowing down. Her body stiffened; her hands gripped the sheets. The cold, deliberate slam of the car door. The hard, rhythmic knock of heeled feet on the pavement. Her heart pattered faster than the rain on the roof above her as she listened out for the scratch of a lock being picked or the rattle of a sash window being forced up.

She had phoned Edmond as soon as she arrived at St Pancras. She had wanted to see his face and glue it firmly over the others. The faces from Germany. The men in coats. Karl.

She hadn't told him about the mission or where she had been and he didn't press her. He had taken her out to supper at a fancy restaurant with art deco furnishings and convex metal corner windows but her mind was elsewhere. She had picked at her food as if it were birdseed.

Rebecca had sent Jane a letter. It had been waiting for her when she returned home from Germany. It was on the table next to the dead fly glass. *It's about Walter,* she thought, *I know it is.* Walter, to whom she had nothing to pass on. Walter who had been right all along: Germany was full of shadows; nothing could be achieved in such a dank and dismal climate.

Jane looked at the envelope again. Rebecca was over-exuberant and careless at times but she was loyal to her friends. *Why don't I want to read it?* She unpinned her hair. The grips were tight. She tugged them out, catching strands of dark hair as she did. It felt like it was coming out in clumps. She dropped the nest of clips onto the floor and looked round her untidy room. Her travelling bag lay where she had thrown it that first night, stockings flipped out over the side. The bedcovers had fallen off the bed. She hadn't changed the sheets since before she left. There was dust on her mirror. She smeared it with her finger. It came off grey.

She grabbed the stockings in disgust and shoved them into her laundry basket, dusted the mirror and table, pulled off her sheets and opened the window a fraction to let in some cool air. Finally she sat down on her bed and opened the envelope:

"14th March 1939
Dearest Jane,
I hope you are well. I am worried about you! It's been too long since we last met. You simply must get back in touch. There's work to be done. The Kindertransport is underway. You don't need to go abroad to make a difference, you know!

The other reason I have for writing so urgently is to warn you. I don't want to cause you pain prematurely but I can't bear for you to be deceived. I have found out that Walter is having an affair with an old school friend of mine, Molly Harker. I don't know when it started. I am so sorry to have been at the root of all this. I wish I hadn't introduced you to Walter in the first place. He has let you down. He has let me down. He is doing nothing in parliament right now, at least nothing to help our cause. You must give him up Jane, before he selfishly drags you into the quagmire with him. You deserve better than Walter. He is a conceited, irresolute, self-absorbed …"

Jane could read no more. She put the note down. Walter was having an affair with Molly Harker. Walter had dropped her like a pair of socks that were wearing thin. He thought nothing of it. Then again, she had set this pattern. She had stopped seeing him. She had wanted to end it. He must've sensed that. Still, he could have told her. *Why did he kiss me?* she thought. Her eyes stung as she fought off tears. She lay back and closed her eyes. She was still dressed but she didn't have the energy to strip off. She just wanted to lie still and wait for sleep to swallow her. She concentrated on the soft downy swell of her pillow around her head. A couple of goose feathers poked their way through the cotton lining and scratched the back of her neck. She threw the pillow to the ground.

Walter doesn't know that I've found out, she thought. *What if he tries to see me? What if he comes to the house? Or is he with Molly?* Suddenly she felt sure that he was. He was betraying her right now, like he had betrayed his wife, lying in another bed, with another woman. He had never intended to help her or Karl. She felt sick. He had used her. Why had she trusted him? *What's wrong with me?* she thought. *Why am I such a fool?*

11pm

The door swung back on its hinges. It badly needed oiling. She woke with a start. *Walter?*

A man was in the doorway. He seemed hesitant. His shadow fell heavily across the floor, blocking out the light. He stepped inside and she saw his face. A high forehead and deep blue eyes not unlike hers. A man so tall his head almost hit the doorframe as he entered. It wasn't Walter. It was her father.

'You've made a mess of everything,' he said. 'You're pathetic. I'm glad I never met you.'

A cold draught crossed the room. It seemed to gather pace. It was racing for the door.

Stop!' Jane cried, leaping out of bed. She had to get to the door before the wind, before he left. She had to change his mind about her.

'You should never have been born,' her father said. 'Your mother didn't want you.'

'I know,' she cried. She wanted him gone again. He had left her before. He was dead. She closed her eyes, willing him away. *You're seeing shadows. You're going mad,* she thought, battling with the voice that was penetrating her mind, sinking in like a needle.

The voice stopped. She opened her eyes slowly. He had gone. The door was solid, wooden, closed. There was something rough under her feet. She looked down: a rug. Her legs were bare but she was wearing a skirt and blouse. Where was she? Was this her home? The window was open. Why? Had she opened it? There was a turmoil inside that was gathering pace like a tornado.

Get back into bed, Jane, she said to herself. *You mustn't be caught wandering like this.*

She looked around the room for the bed. It was too dark to see. She scrabbled for the light. She needed to feel safe. It felt as if the walls of the room were moving closer, squeezing in till she couldn't breathe. She tried to think about Elsie; a red lump had grown on her chest. She cried out in pain.

Footsteps on the stairs. Someone was coming.

Edmond flung her door open and held her in his arms. She sobbed relentlessly as if some control mechanism deep inside her had suddenly snapped.

21st March 1939, 5.30pm

I can't concentrate at work anymore, Jane thought. She felt as if she had been sitting in the middle of a boxing ring, thick red gloves punching at her ears, her head swollen and heavy. The phone was ringing as she came in through the front door. The sharp, insistent rattle of the telephone on its hanger dug into her brain like a scalpel. She had to make it stop so she picked it up.

She was too tired to say anything.

'Richard Wright here,' a disconnected voice said. 'Can I speak to Jane, please?'

Silence.

'Hello?'

She didn't have the energy.

'Hello? Is anyone there? It's Richard. Calling for Jane.'

She dragged out her voice.

'Hello, Richard. Sorry, I'm exhausted. Is it anything specific or can we talk some other time?'

She was brushing him off but at least it was a response. He was hardened to her reluctant replies anyway. He would phone back another day.

'I wanted to check you were all right. You didn't reply to my letter. I've been back for over a week. Can I see you?'

'No!' She couldn't help herself. *Leave me alone,* she thought, then realised she had said it out loud.

'I see,' he said dismayed. She sounded slightly out of control.

He wondered what she was thinking. He wished there were some sort of visual device on his receiver so he could see her. It was impossible to read anything past the complete rejection in her tone.

'The paper is sending me back to Spain,' he said. 'I leave tomorrow.'

Silence.

'It looks as though the Republicans will surrender to the Nationalists.' *Surely that will provoke a response?*

'Jane?'

He could hear her breathing. Could she hear him? Was she even listening?

'Well, goodbye then,' he said.

He put the phone down. How could he leave now, without a word from Jane? She was no good at replying to letters. He stared at the phone, the wires, the false sense of connection it brought when really there was nothing there, nothing solid between them, nothing he could rely on anyway.

Jane heard a dull buzz on the other end of the line. It felt like the buzz in her head. She was glad Richard had rung off, or was she? She sat down on the stairs and gazed at the front door. A key turned in the lock. She jumped up, knocking the receiver off the phone again.

Edmond came in. She sank back down. The phone dangled beside her.

Edmond looked at his sister. The buttons on her coat were uneven. *How long has she been sitting on the stairs? She looks distraught.* Now was not the time to tell her that he had broken off his engagement to Evie.

31st March 1939, 10am

Edmond was away from home. His law firm had sent him up north to visit an important client: his first real break at work yet he was desperate to get back. His separation from Evie was tearing wretchedly at his heart but he wasn't ready for marriage. *How can I support a wife when I can't even support my sister?*

Jane had been struggling to get out of bed in the mornings. She'd always been a bit sluggish but it wasn't normal even for her. *Is she depressed?* His stomach turned just thinking about it. Something was wrong with her; he couldn't ignore it any longer. *How will she cope while I'm away?*

Before he left, he had knocked on her bedroom door. No answer. He had pushed it open gently. A sharp intake of breath: Jane was splayed out over her bed like a starfish, one arm hanging limply over the side, mouth open, pillow soaked in drool. His heart had skipped a beat as he bent over her. She was breathing heavily. A glass medicine bottle lay on the floor next to the bed, *'Nembutal'?* It was half empty. *Some sort of sleeping draught?* He unscrewed the lid. It smelt mildly alcoholic. *Mother used to take something like this,* he thought, *till she met Charles and he weaned her off it. What did Jane say to the doctor? Why won't she talk to me?*

His feet tapped the floor impatiently as he waited for his colleague at their client's office. *I need to get back to Jane. Hang the work.* It was all a waste of time anyway; they wouldn't raise his salary or his position, not with so many partners in the firm already. He looked at the pile of papers in front of him and thought about throwing it out of the window. *What good will that do anyone?* he thought, gritting his teeth.

Back at home in Bloomsbury, Jane was in the sitting room. She had spent the last few days wrapped in blankets. She felt as if she was trapped in a bunker, throwing out grenades that hit her friends till she wasn't sure she had any friends left. Edmond was away. Richard had gone overseas again. Her eyes were pink and puffy as if she'd been trying to get sand out of them by rubbing hard. The rain had been coming down for days. She watched the droplets merge and fall. It felt like she was slowly rotting away. Her feet were smelly. She hadn't bothered to have a bath. She just wanted to sit in her nightgown and do nothing.

The doorbell rang and Jane almost fell off the sofa. Edmond was due back that evening. Surely he wasn't early? Anyway, he had a key. It must be someone else. She hauled herself over to the window, unlocked the sash and heaved it upwards, craning her neck awkwardly over the frame. There was a woman at the door. She was excessively tall.

'Evie.'

Evie looked up and saw Jane waving from a window towards the top of the house.

'I'll come down. You'll have to wait a moment. I'm not dressed yet.'

Evie was surprised. It was past ten. Jane's voice was loud. Evie glanced down the street. A few people had stopped to look. They moved on as the window shut with a bang. Evie felt nervous. It was an unusual feeling for her and it took time to register. Jane must already know that the engagement was off but perhaps this wasn't the best time to talk to her. She couldn't delay though; her tickets were booked. There was no changing the situation now.

Evie stood on the doorstep and waited. The rain penetrated her thick hair and edged its way down her face, dripping off her long nose and landing on her shoes. She re-opened her umbrella. What was Jane doing? She was a patient woman but it was all she could do to stop herself ringing the doorbell again. Her high heels ached. She hated wearing them but no-one in London would be seen in gym shoes except on a tennis court. If only women could wear flat shoes and trousers every day. It was impossible to run in a skirt. She had to buy her clothes from the 'Tall Girls' store in town, utterly humiliating.

Evie was just considering whether it was worth sitting down on a soggy bench in the square when the door opened.

'There you are.'

'Sorry, Evie. I had to whip round the house. I've been extremely slovenly since Edmond left.' Jane smiled. It felt good to smile. It felt good to be dressed again, receiving visitors. 'Come upstairs. Just kick off your shoes. You'll be much more comfortable without them.'

Evie followed Jane upstairs. Jane took her umbrella and opened it out to dry in the bathroom. Evie went into the sitting room and sat down. Perhaps Jane wouldn't take it badly after all. She certainly wasn't treating her any differently since learning of the broken engagement. Jane came into the room.

'Can I get you a hot drink?'

'No thank you … unless you're having one that is?'

'I wouldn't mind. I'll go and put the kettle on.'

Jane went out again. *She's restless,* thought Evie. *Not surprising if she's had a few days at home.* She noticed the blanket on the sofa opposite; a couple of empty wine glasses balanced on a stool; piles of ash in the fireplace.

'I'm glad I came,' she said when Jane got back. 'It looks like you've been hibernating.'

'I know. It's a mess. Edmond should be home tonight. I'll get things clear by then. Stay and have dinner with us.'

'Hasn't Edmond told you?'

'No?'

'He's broken off our engagement.'

'What?'

'We're not engaged anymore.'

'Oh, Evie! Why?'

'I don't know, Jane. We didn't argue. He just made a decision and that was that.'

'But it doesn't make any sense. I know how committed he was to you. Something must have happened.'

'Whatever it was, it doesn't change things and however much I try I can't quite bring myself to forget about him.'

Jane sat down next to Evie.

'I've accepted a job as a teacher in Wales. I'm leaving tomorrow.' Evie said.

'No!'

'There aren't many positions available. It seemed the most sensible option.'

'Evie, you can't go. What if Edmond changes his mind?'

'I don't think he will. He was quite deliberate.'

'At least wait until I've had a chance to talk to him.'

'Sorry, Jane, I can't. I can't linger around, it won't help.'

Evie was always so straightforward. *It's Edmond's fault – he's driven her away*, thought Jane, *he has to see sense. I can't let her go. She can't leave.*

'Won't you stay for supper?'

'Too awkward. I'm sorry Jane. I have to go.'

Jane was silent. Her skin looked a sickly shade of yellow as if she hadn't seen sunlight in a while. 'I will write to you regularly. I'll be back in the holidays.'

Jane was staring blankly at the floor. *They're all leaving me,* she thought. *Walter, Edmond and now Evie. Even Richard hasn't written for a while. Has he given up?*

'You must promise me you'll get out and about, Jane,' Evie said. *I can't leave her like this,* she thought, *she won't even look at me.* 'You need a new project, Jane, something that'll get you out of this rut. Have you ever thought about volunteering for the New Fabian Research Bureau? Your travels in Germany and connection with Karl will be very useful to them.'

Jane looked up and tried to focus on Evie. Evie was trying to help. Evie was still her friend.

'Thank you, Evie. I'll think about it,' she said, 'Just don't desert me will you? I need to know you'll come back.'

'I will,' Evie said, 'I'll call you as soon as I get to Wales.'

Jane went upstairs to get Evie's umbrella. 'You can have this back then,' she said. 'I was considering holding you captive but I'll let you off this time.'

Evie wobbled down the front steps in her heels, as unbalanced as a giraffe wearing stilts. A cab stopped and she clambered in, pulling in her legs and skirt awkwardly before shutting the door. Jane waved at the cab till it rounded the corner. The world was turning so fast it was in danger of splitting open, sucking humanity into its great molten core and spitting out a hard, solid mass of dead matter. That was if the Fascists continued their assault unchecked, if the Nazis stepped up their persecution, their infernal rampage over everything that was good and feeling. *Come to your senses, Jane,* she told herself, *stop fretting your life away and choose to act.* She shut the front door with a bang and went upstairs to clear up the mess.

28th July 1945, 4pm

St Andrew's Hospital, Northampton
Jane is thirty-one

Gina was eating cake. Jane hadn't touched hers.

'When will Edmond come and visit?' Jane said.

'As soon as he is released from service.'

'When will that be?'

'I don't know, Jane. Soon. I'm sure he will write to you.'

'I haven't had a letter in two weeks.'

'Jane, it's your birthday, have some cake.'

Jane pushed the cake around on the plate but didn't look interested. They were sitting in an open dining hall at a long trestle table. Other patients were eyeing up Jane's plate. She pushed it towards them. Gina looked alarmed.

'Let's cut it up and pass it round,' Jane said.

'I'm not sure,' said Gina. 'Aren't some of them on strict diets?'

'The nurses will have to take it away then,' Jane replied. 'Look at them whispering over there. They're taking it in turns to watch us from the corner. There's no escape in here you know. From being watched.'

Gina sighed. She couldn't get Jane away from this idea that she was being spied on. She'd had endless shock therapy but it hadn't rid her of any of it. Sometimes it felt like the hospital with its locked doors and exposed lavatories fed Jane's anxiety rather than relieving it. Then again there were oak trees in the grounds, a golf course at the end of the lawn. Normality was clearly within reach, patients could venture out into it and they did, though some looked a bit tentative as if they might burn their toes on the grass.

'I want to meet Edmond's son,' Jane said suddenly. 'I want to meet Andrew.'

'You know that's impossible, Jane. It's too expensive, too difficult to get him here. It's a four-hour round trip. He might be frightened. You never know what the patients are going to do.'

'Exactly,' said Jane. 'I can't stay here mother. I don't want to stay any longer.' Jane had raised her voice. Gina could see the nurses teetering on the sidelines.

'There is a treatment that might work, Jane,' she said hurriedly to grab Jane's attention. 'Something they've been testing in America. Apparently a doctor called Walter Freeman is treating hundreds of patients there. It produces immediate results.'

She stopped. She hadn't planned to bring this up now. It would've been better in private. Still she couldn't take it back. She had to go on now she had started.

'Your doctor says the effect is quite astonishing,' she continued. 'He called me into his office earlier to talk about it. He said it would take away your hallucinations. That they wouldn't come back.'

Jane was quiet, waiting.

'It's some sort of surgery on your brain.' Gina found the thought of it quite disturbing but she kept going, 'It's over very quickly they say. You don't even need anesthetic. The doctor says it is painless.'

Jane stared at her. *Painless?*

Heat was prickling the back of Gina's neck now. The palms of her hands felt sweaty. It felt odd talking about it like this, but she had to go through with it now. She had to finish the conversation. Not that it was a conversation. Jane was giving her that dead-eyed stare that she really disliked. It was so disconcerting.

'The doctor assured me that it wouldn't affect your intellect or your creativity.'

She paused again, waiting for a response, a gesture, anything from Jane. This was awful. Worse than expected.

'Help me, Jane,' she whispered weakly. 'I can't decide this for you. It's too much for me.' She glanced nervously around the dining room. It felt as if everyone was looking at her, giving her the same dead-eyed stare as Jane. *I can't do this any longer*, she thought with desperation, *this can't go on. I can't bear it. God knows, I can't cope. Give me an answer, Jane, please! I can't do this alone.*

Collapse

7th August 1939, 5pm
Kensington, London
Jane is twenty-five

Sunlight spilt out in glittery paths across the round pond in Kensington Gardens. It looked as if the sun was dipping its toes in the water and wriggling them around. A teasing breeze nipped the feathers of the swans. Orange beaks dipped hungrily as children in striped shorts and neat summer dresses threw chunks of stale bread into the water.

Jane had left the offices of the NFRB early to meet Rebecca. She felt lifted by the sunlight as she walked along the path towards the pond but the breeze was chasing her, parting her hair at the back, whipping it round her face, exposing her neck. Surely it was too cold for August?

If only Edmond would come back. The flat felt hollow without him, full of creaks and drips. His contract in York had been extended indefinitely, he had said last night. Empty pauses had dotted their conversation making it stilted and uncomfortable. *Is he avoiding me, Evie, or both of us? Why can't we talk about it?* she had wondered before another thought stabbed her, *He doesn't trust me.* Edmond's voice had faded to a crackle, giving way to other voices, an ever-growing mob of bullies that yelled at her and drowned him out. *He doesn't care about you or Evie. He left to get away from you.*

'Goodbye then,' had popped up out of nowhere, sending the receiver spinning out of her hand. 'Jane?' a sharp cry from the dangling end.

She had picked the receiver up again. It had felt heavy in her hand. She had twisted the cord round her finger so that it wouldn't escape and pushed it up to her ear in an attempt to banish the rest of the noise. *Come back soon, I miss you,* a lonely voice inside her had said, but the words had balled up in her mouth like over-chewed meat and she couldn't spit them out. Faced by impenetrable silence he had eventually put the phone down.

How long will he make me wait before he calls again? Jane thought as she stood by the pond, letting the sun warm up the back of her neck, watching her shadow flicker and wave across the water.

It was a relief to leave the office, the repetitive tapping of fingers on keys, slap and fall of pamphlets from the press, the whole place as volatile and determined as a beehive. Democracy was under threat. Fascism had to be refuted, exposed and condemned. Time was squeezed tighter than an orange in a press. Anyone could see that there would be war before a new world could begin.

Recently there had been meetings, suggestions, prods. People had buzzed around her like flies to meat. The ardent socialists of London were desperate to reach out to the beleaguered socialists of Berlin and her contact with the German resistance made her useful. Plans had been made, papers arranged. She had nodded, shaken hands but when she got home she had run upstairs to her room, locked herself in, picked up her medicine and then struggled to undo the lid. A glass of water had slipped out of her hands and spilt all over the floor. She had sat down in front of the mirror then turned it round so that she couldn't see her face.

Rebecca, she had thought. *Rebecca will help me. I need someone I can trust.*

Rebecca clutched her netted hat to her head as she came out from under the trees. It wasn't pinned on tightly enough and she had visions of it landing on top of a swan, catching a few fish in the pond perhaps. Jane had never replied to her letter about Walter. *Why would she? I should never have sent it,* she thought as she walked towards the figure in blue, standing on her own by the water's edge. *For all I know, she's still seeing him. At least she knows how it feels to be in an impossible relationship, that's something we've got in common.*

A nanny with an unwieldy black pram trawled along the path past Jane who jumped backwards, surprised to find her toes on the verge of being steamrollered.

'Jane!'

Jane turned. Rebecca was right behind her. *How did she get so close without me hearing her?*

'It's so good to see you,' Rebecca said, 'Listening to your voice on the phone felt like picking up a treasured gramophone record – a long-lost comfort.' Rebecca moved instinctively to embrace, but Jane edged away.

'I'm sorry,' said Jane, 'I've been so tired recently.' It was pointless giving excuses. They both knew it had been difficult between them.

'Your work at the NFRB sounds excellent,' said Rebecca. 'You must be in your element. Tackling some of those old issues we used to discuss in halls – a more comfortable environment for you than our work with refugees?'

Jane felt herself frown. Was that what Rebecca thought: that she had run away from the work? Then again, there was some truth in it. She had never been at ease working with the Inter-Aid Committee however much she tried and she hadn't been able to make the difference she had hoped to. That was why this new assignment was agitating her so much. She wasn't convinced she was the right person for the job. Then again, it was depressing to admit that it might be too much for her. *I can't just pick and choose projects that suit me,* she told herself.

'I need to talk to you about an assignment I've been given,' she said, 'I need your advice.'

'How can I help?' said Rebecca, wondering what it could be. Jane had been so secretive, so closed off since her affair with Walter had begun. Now she was asking for advice, was it a good sign, or was she just desperate?

'The Foreign Office wants to strengthen its contact with the German resistance. They want me to travel to Berlin, pass on papers.' Even as she said it, Jane felt tension pour into her spine like concrete, setting in hard nuggets around the bones. *Is Rebecca still in touch with Karl? How much does she know? How would she react if I told her I had already been to see him without her knowledge?*

'Really? You are in deep Jane. How did you get so involved?' Jane's face tightened. 'Sorry, Jane, I only wish I were as intrepid as you.'

That's not true, Jane thought, *you'd go out there in a blink if you could. But you're Jewish. It's not possible.*

'There are so many restrictions,' she said, 'when you're not caught out by any of them it's your duty to make the most of it, don't you think?'

'I wouldn't say it was your duty, Jane.'

'It's something I have to do,' said Jane. 'They've asked me to meet Helmuth von Moltke.'

'Karl's friend? The Count?'

'He's been in contact. He's offering information. He wants to assist with emigration.'

'Excellent news,' said Rebecca. 'I had to choose sixteen children from a group of forty today. They all face persecution if they stay in Berlin but there aren't enough sponsors. Can your contacts get them out of the country?'

'I don't know,' Jane said. A young couple went past. They were deep in conversation. They stopped at a bench nearby and sat down: too close. Jane backed away from them.

'Jane, watch out,' Rebecca said, grabbing Jane's arm to stop her backing off the path entirely and into the long grass.

'I don't find undercover work very easy,' Jane said. 'I'm not your typical secret agent am I?'

'I'd say you're perfect for the job, Jane. Who would suspect you? The most upright, sincere, dedicated person anyone could ever meet.'

'When I get to Berlin I'll meet Frank Seaton at the British Embassy. If you give me the information, I'll pass it on to him.'

'Thank you, Jane.' Rebecca paused. *I have to say it,* she thought, *I can't ignore it.* 'I'm sorry about the letter, Jane,' she said, 'It wasn't my place—'

'Please don't mention it,' Jane said quickly.

'Have you seen Walter recently?'

Jane looked out across the pond. Two Canadian geese were fighting over a hunk of bread. 'No.'

'Probably for the best,' said Rebecca, taking her friend's hand.

Jane pulled away. The geese flapped their wings and spat at each other. A man threw a stick at them and they scattered, honking angrily. The noise was intolerable, it felt as if they were flapping and honking in her face.

'I wrote Walter a letter,' she said, 'some simple questions, yes/no answers.'

'Oh?' Did he reply?'

'He needs time.'

'He doesn't deserve it.'

'I know I should hate him. I should despise him for his betrayal, his selfishness, his weakness but how can I? I'm just as guilty as he is.'

'Don't compare yourself to him.'

'I'm worse than him. I'm worthless, pathetic. I've pushed Richard away again and again and now he's gone and I don't know if he'll ever come back and why should he? I've kept secrets from Edmond, embarrassed him in his own home, humiliated myself at work, and still I can't keep on a straight course. I can't make up my mind to anything, it feels like soup in there and it only gets worse at night.' She tried to stop but the beating of her heart wouldn't let her. 'I can't stay at home anymore, Rebecca. I can't bear it.'

It felt like a scream. A trapdoor had fallen open and all the loose chaff she'd been holding back was blowing out in every direction.

'Jane!'

She needed two firm hands on her shoulders, gripping her, holding her together. The scream gathered pace like a geyser, shooting up from her lungs, reaching her mouth, but she could feel Rebecca shaking her … Rebecca's hands … Rebecca's voice.

'You're not well Jane.'

'They've all abandoned me.'

'What do you mean?'

'I've driven them away.'

Jane tried to sit down but there was nothing to sit on, nothing to catch her.

'Who are you talking about? Is Edmond not at home? What about Evie?'

'They've left me Rebecca and they're not coming back, I'm sure of it. I'm on my own and I can't cope anymore.'

Why did I mention Walter? Rebecca thought. *She was fine until then. She needs to focus. She can't give in to this despair.*

'Jane,' she said. 'Look at me.'

Jane looked up. Her face had changed as if a veil had been ripped off. The sunlight fell on her like a spotlight. She looked haggard and pale.

'Come and stay with me,' Rebecca said.

'What?'

'Come and stay with me, at least until you leave for Germany. You need to rest or you'll be no good to anyone.'

Jane looked up. 'Really?'

'I won't take no for an answer.'

The heaviness in Jane's head remained but she nodded and let Rebecca steer her back along the path. *If she's really going to travel to Germany she needs to calm down,* Rebecca thought, *otherwise it's a suicide mission.*

Jane felt her heels crunch along the dirt track. Bike wheels spun past, tracing a rut through the soil. She was following Rebecca's feet, wherever they were going. A squirrel scurried off a bench as they passed and hid in the grass. They stopped at the road. Jane heard Rebecca say something about catching a bus. She nodded again. *Just stay quiet*, she thought, *otherwise they won't let you go.*

A bus pulled in. She felt the cold metal pole in her hand, the swing and jolt that threw her into a seat as the bus pulled away. *I'm off,* she thought. *There's no stopping it now. I'm going back to Germany.*

She can't go in this state, thought Rebecca, *they must be desperate, she's desperate, the mission, whatever it is, will fail.*

Jane was staring out of the window.

Why did she come to me? thought Rebecca. *Did she want me to stop her or help her? Is there no-one else who can go in her place? Time is running out. The Nazis are relentless. How important is this? Is there no-one else she can talk to, I can talk to?*

Jane was resting her head against the glass now. She looked shattered.

Should I really let her go?

28th August 1939, 8am
Belgian-German border

The ticket conductor stooped badly as though he'd been collecting tickets for far too long. Even though she had hers ready in her hand, Jane felt uneasy as he approached. Her eyelids were leaden. She'd woken with a headache. A large English woman with fat hands and a nasal voice was sharing the wagon-lit berth with her and she hadn't been at all friendly. The woman had insisted on opening the blind before they reached the Belgian border and the early morning rays had bounced straight into Jane's eyes.

Jane noticed the woman's rings: they glared in the sunlight – blood-red rubies, sunken into the skin, wedged tight like jewels in the hilt of a dagger. She had a sharp nose that looked misplaced, a ridge in the middle of her puffy face and she wore what appeared to be half a fox around her neck. Jane wondered what she was doing travelling to Germany.

As the conductor ducked his head into the next-door berth, the woman tied her long plait into a bun and pulled on a plain grey jacket. She took a mirror out of her handbag and checked her appearance. Glancing at Jane surreptitiously, she took a badge out of her bag and pinned it to her jacket. The badge portrayed an eagle killing a snake. Two initials stood out, "P.J". *That's 'Perish Judah'*, Jane thought with a start. The woman must be a member of the 'Right Club', a London-based movement she had heard about recently through colleagues at the NFRB. No wonder she hadn't made much effort to speak to Jane. The club was both secretive and exclusive. Its pamphlets were venomous, laden with anti-Jewish rhetoric. The woman was probably travelling to Germany to meet members of the Nazi party. Jane shuddered. This was the last person she wanted to share a carriage with. Jane kept her bag firmly out of sight. Who knows what this woman would do if she discovered Jane's mission.

The conductor punched her ticket and moved on. Border officials entered. The woman spoke to them in German and laughed loudly. Jane didn't speak much German so she looked out of the window. The woman pointed at Jane. *Did she look in my bag while I was asleep*? Jane thought. *Why is she pointing at me?* A greasy-haired official stood in front of her blocking out the window light. She felt shaky and cold. A hand was held out in front of her nose. *Any minute now he'll ask to look in my bag.*

'Der pass, danke sehr.'

She reached into her bag and took out her passport, hoping he wouldn't notice the fear tingling through her fingers as she handed it over. *He's looking at it for too long. He suspects something.* The large woman opposite shifted in her seat, flicking the fox fur back over her shoulders and fiddling round in her bag again. *At least she's ignoring me. They haven't checked her passport yet.*

The official handed back Jane's passport, giving her what she felt was a withering look as he did so. He said something in German to the woman and they went out together. *Thank goodness for that. It's another few hours to Berlin. I really don't want to be in the same compartment as her all the way.* She drooped back into her seat and rubbed her eyes. She shoved her passport back in the front pocket so she wouldn't have to open the main bag until she reached the embassy. Then she got up and closed the blind.

28th August 1939, 11am
Berlin

Frank Seaton sent one of his colleagues to meet Jane at Berlin Friedrichstraße station. She had just passed through the checkpoint and was feeling a sudden surge of relief when someone took her by the arm.

'Jane Deering?'

Her heartrate accelerated. She might have been walking round on ice skates, she felt so insecure. The man had short dark hair and wore a suit.

He looked like most other men in the station: nondescript, ordinary. She had seen photos of Frank. This was not Frank. Frank wore glasses and was in his fifties. This man was young. He pulled her to one side and showed her his embassy pass. There was something dubious about him despite the innocence of his face. *How long had he been watching me before he decided to approach?* she wondered, anxiety streaming round her veins like nicotine.

'Frank was unable to come himself,' he said. 'I'm William Watson. Frank asked me to take you to the embassy.' He stopped, sensing Jane's discomfort. 'I'll take you straight to Frank, promise.' He smiled at her but her nerves refused to die down.

They walked down the long tunnel to the underground. Yellow tiles stretched on endlessly. It felt rude, not making conversation, but she didn't know what to say. There were eyes everywhere. Hordes of people crowded past and all of them seemed to be looking at her, shouldering her, grabbing for her bag. She held it close. It was locked but that wouldn't stop them if they wanted it.

William Watson was worried. Frank had instructed him to look out for the woman in the photo and given him the train time. He hadn't said much more than that. William presumed she would be a diplomat of some variety but the woman he met didn't have the confidence for that. She had the sort of dazed, panicky look he was used to seeing on the face of people leaving the embassy – people heading for the border as fast as they could.

He wondered what her business was. She looked pale. Maybe it was just the mass of dark hair edging her face that made her look washed out. He hoped so. The last thing he wanted was a sick woman on his hands, especially a woman he knew nothing about. He wished he'd pressed Frank for more information before agreeing to escort her. Frank was so inscrutable and at the same time so determined; he wasn't a man you questioned.

They got onto a train. Jane could smell the sweat on people's hands as they clutched the metal rails, leaving smudge marks. Passengers were stuffed in like hens in a coop. The doors shut with a clunk. *Like a trapdoor closing*, thought Jane, scanning the carriage. No-one could be taken at face value here, she was sure of it. They all had a hidden agenda just like her. The woman opposite was scratching her neck as if she had fleas. The man holding onto the rail by the door had his hat pulled low over his eyes. He was scanning the paper but he didn't look like he was actually reading it.

He turned the pages too fast. As the train jerked to a stop, he almost fell on top of Jane. She clamped her hands over her bag hastily, feeling his breath on her face. He was a smoker. She imagined him puffing away, his face slowly turning as grey as the fumes he was letting out. He mumbled some sort of apology and went back to his paper.

'We're getting off at Berlin Unter den Linden,' said William, relieved to be arriving at last. It felt like an age, travelling with a stranger who didn't talk and looked as if she might faint at any moment. Still, she was pretty in an understated way. She had violet eyes but she kept them so low he could hardly get a glimpse of them.

Jane nodded, her neck and throat too tense to reply. She would talk to Frank and he would introduce her to von Moltke in the morning. She would hand the documents over. It felt like a long time to keep them with her. She hoped she could hold her nerve till then. They were almost at the British Embassy. Not much further now.

The train juddered and jolted and threw a few more people around before coming to a slow stop. Someone opened the door and what seemed like the whole carriage piled out. Jane was swept along with the crowd and William had a hard job keeping up with her. He took her by the elbow and steered her to the side.

'Through here,' he said, pointing to the ticket barriers.

They came out of the underground and into the rain.

'We'll have to make a dash for it. I haven't got an umbrella, sorry. It wasn't raining when I left. I'm sure the sun will come out again soon.'

Jane nodded and drew her coat round her more tightly. Then she saw the woman with the fox fur. *She's followed me.* She grabbed William by the wrist and he looked at her with surprise. It felt as if she was trying to monitor his blood pressure, she was gripping so hard.

'Let's get to the embassy,' he said. 'You can have a hot drink when we get there and Frank will make you comfortable.'

She said nothing. The woman with the fur disappeared round the corner but Jane couldn't relax. *She's watching me.* Her left eye was flickering. *Not now,* she thought. It felt like someone had planted a tree in her brain and it was starting to take root. She allowed William to lead her along the street towards the embassy building. She noticed that the bushy green trees along the boulevard had been brutally cut down. Jane imagined Hitler posing on a stump, joining the other statues that dotted the street, short and ugly, spitting out phlegm where they were silent and dignified. A man brushed past her, spinning her round. He was in a brown shirt, carrying a violin. A strange whining sound was coming from the gigantic neo-classical building that loomed in front of them. It grew louder till her ears were filled with it and she felt like putting her hands over them and screaming, 'Stop!'

William suddenly realised that Jane wasn't with him anymore. He turned this way and that in a panic until he spotted her. She was standing outside the Staatsoper with her hands over her ears as if the sound of the orchestra inside warming up was drilling into her brain. She looked like she was about to scream. He rushed over quickly and took her by the arm.

'Miss Deering?'

She looked at him or at least she looked in his direction. She didn't appear to be focusing very well.

'It's just the orchestra getting ready,' William said, 'We'd better get to the embassy.'

'The same orchestra that played at the Olympic Games and the Nuremberg rallies?'

'Yes.'

That building is full of Nazis, Jane thought. *At any moment they might come out and see me.*

'That's the Humboldt University,' said William, pointing across the road, trying to distract her whilst hurrying her past it. *The sooner we get to the embassy the better*, he thought.

She went pale. The Head Librarian of Humboldt University. That was what Karl had said. The sharp-nosed man with the limp. She could see him coming out of the gates now, picking up a stone, hurling it at them and limping off. Where was the mob? The street was wide and crowded. At any moment the mob might gather and hem them in. She could feel her heart gathering pace, echoing the speed of her feet along the pavement. She was almost pulling William along now.

There it was, the British Embassy, but before they could reach it, out of nowhere, a patrol of troopers appeared, marching down Unter den Linden, high black boots beating the ground beneath their feet, asserting their ruthless authority. William ushered Jane over to the side of the street as the troopers went past. They seemed innumerable, an endless column of tight collars and high belts, their minds as narrow and sucked-in as their uniforms. Was that a skull and crossbones on the caps of the men at the front?

Death was here in Germany. Terror rose inside her like acid from the stomach. She wasn't sure why she was here anymore. The bag in her hand felt heavy. It was something to do with her bag. She clutched William's arm like a safety rail. Her head felt like it was going to burst.

The embassy looked like a miniature Buckingham Palace, all straight lines, classical columns and balustrades. William took her inside, helped her off with her coat and sat her down in the reception room. He went to get Frank.

There was a woman sitting typing at the desk opposite. Jane felt as though she might keel over at any moment. She had to get hold of some paper, write to Evie. She stumbled over to the desk.

'Are you all right?' said the woman, looking up at the tottering stranger with the glazed look in her eyes.

'Can I borrow a pen and some paper please?'

'Certainly,' the woman replied, taking out a sheet or two and handing them over with an embassy pen. 'There's a table over there.'

'Thank you,' said Jane, feeling more and more incoherent. She sat down at the table and wrote a brief note to Evie. It had to be done. This was out of her control. *What if the woman in the fur is lingering outside, waiting for me to come out?* she thought. 'Stop being paranoid, you're fine!' she heard herself say.

The woman at the desk looked up surprised. Did the visitor say something? Jane was bent over the table. She must have misheard. People generally kept to themselves when they came in. There was a lot of fear around these days. The apprehension was palpable. It was as if there was a plague of locusts hovering above Berlin waiting to descend in a great buzzing swarm. This woman carried tension all over her face – the tension of someone who'd been on the edge for some time but supressed it. She was scribbling now as if the pen was attached to her fingers. In fact she was pressing into the paper so hard it looked as though she might tear it.

'Jane Deering, I presume?' said Frank, entering, filling the room with the quiet confidence that he traded on so well. 'Frank Seaton. Pleasure to meet you.'

Jane looked up. Frank walked over and shook her by the hand, ignoring the anxiety in her eyes. He was used to setting people at ease and a master at concealing insecurity, in himself as well as others. He'd been running secret service networks since the Great War and had already assisted thousands of Jewish families to escape Germany. He realised Jane was in distress the moment he saw her. Best to get her somewhere private quickly. He escorted her out of the room and into his office.

Frank's office was lined with bookshelves. A pile of tatty folders lay stacked up on his desk next to a glass of water. Two chairs sat opposite his which was a red leather monster that declared him master of the room and all who were in it. He motioned Jane to one of the chairs and took the other, sensing a need for reassurance rather than authority. He handed her the glass of water but she didn't take it. *She's got the shakes*, he thought as she slipped her hands under her legs as if to hide them.

'You're not well, I can see that,' said Frank at last, wondering how to start. 'You must have had a long journey to get here. Perhaps you need to rest. We can do this tomorrow if you like.'

'Thank you,' said Jane. 'I don't think I can wait till then.'

'von Moltke arrives tomorrow,' replied Frank, 'I expect you want to see him?'

'I'm sorry, but I can't,' said Jane. She had to get out of here, give the documents to Frank and leave.

'Can I help you then? What can I do?'

'Take the documents and give them to von Moltke,' replied Jane, mustering all her strength. 'I'm sorry. I don't know what has come over me but I need to go back to London. I have to get home. Can you help me get to the station?'

'Of course,' said Frank. 'I quite understand. It was exceptionally brave of you to come in the first place with the situation as it is. I will keep the documents in my safe tonight and let your colleagues in London know you're on your way back. William will take you to the station.' He was calm, clear, direct.

'Can't you take me?' she said, 'I don't feel safe.'

Frank looked at her. Was she fretting, unaccustomed to undercover work, or was she in fact being followed? He had to find out.

'There's nothing anyone could suspect you of,' he said. 'To the Nazis you're an embassy worker, sent out by London, that's all.'

'A woman in fox fur. The Right Club. She was here then she disappeared.'

Jane was mumbling. Frank couldn't get a clear picture.

'Someone followed you?'

'She was on the train. In my berth. She may have looked at the papers.'

'You've made it here. You haven't been arrested or questioned. The papers are safe. We'll get you back to London. You'll be fine.' He was right. He was sure of it. She couldn't have been followed. They would have taken her in. She was just overwrought, perhaps even hallucinating.

'Thank you, Mr Seaton.' The dizziness was subsiding. She could go home now. She had passed on what she had to. It would be over soon.

'I'll call William.'

To Frank's relief she didn't object this time. He had so many visas to process he didn't have the time to take her to the station, but she looked so vulnerable and coming here had clearly been a huge strain. It was his duty to make sure she got back safely. William would see to that. He rose and left the room.

Jane felt empty and alone. It was cold in Frank's room but her hands were sweaty.

Frank came back in and Jane remembered her letter. She pulled it out. It was crumpled. She must have sat on it in her attempt to steady her hands. 'Can you post this for me please?' she asked him. 'I have written the address at the top.' Frank glanced at the note. She had given it to him open without an envelope. He read a few words and looked alarmed.

'We will do what we can,' he said, folding it up and putting it in his pocket. 'Now let's get you onto the train and headed for home.' *The sooner the better*, he thought. *It's some sort of breakdown. Why did anyone put her in this position? She must've concealed her distress well. Maybe that's why they chose her. Then again, someone with this level of adrenalin is liable to stretch too thin very quickly. They still haven't realised the stakes here.*

He helped her up and guided her to the corridor where William stood waiting. They would have to sit for a few hours in the station café. The next train wasn't till evening.

As they walked out of the room, Jane felt a shadow fall across her feet. She looked up and saw Richard. He looked ghostly, unwell. She moved towards him to support him but a voice behind her said, 'He's not who he appears to be Jane,' and she looked again and saw a young man with short black hair. She turned away in horror and reached out for the door – anything to steady her – she felt as if she was falling. Then she saw her father. He was reaching out for her.

Frank caught her as she collapsed.

War

2nd September 1939, 4pm
Bloomsbury, London
Jane is twenty-five

"Thank God you exist, and will be home soon."

She read them again.

Nine words. Written in distress.

Simple. Clear.

Desperate.

It didn't make any sense. The postmark was German. It had only been sent a few days ago. It was amazing the letter had arrived so quickly. Then again the envelope had a diplomatic seal. What had Jane been doing? Why had she gone to Germany again? Was she back yet?

Evie felt she should warn Edmond. She hadn't spoken to him since they parted. He had written. He had apologised. She felt terrible. She hadn't replied.

She rounded the corner, long legs carrying her along at a rattling pace. There, standing by her front gate, was a woman in blue. Her hair sprung out in all directions like a bird's nest attacked by a cat. She was staring at Evie's door. With a jolt that pulled her up sharp, Evie realised that it was Jane. It just didn't look like Jane. She was unkempt, all over the place. As she drew closer, Evie could see that one of her stockings had fallen loosely around her ankle. Her jacket was unbuttoned and her blouse had slipped out from her skirt.

'Jane!'

Jane turned round but made no move towards her.

'Let's go in,' said Evie, taking her arm and guiding her up the steps.

Evie opened the door and dropped her bags in the hallway. She motioned Jane inside and took her jacket, flinging it over a peg before leading Jane into the sitting room. It was lucky it was a sunny day. She had been away such a long time, the place had a castaway feel about it, cold and bare.

Thank God I came back today. Who knows how long she's been standing there or how long she would have waited.

Jane sat down in the faded green armchair by the fireplace.

'I got your letter, Jane.' Jane's eyes had a disconcerting blankness about them. 'You sent it from Germany?'

Jane frowned. Clearly that wasn't a useful start. 'Do you want to talk or shall I get you something warm to drink?'

Jane stood up.

'Really Evie, I'm fine,' she said briskly as if there was nothing unusual about her appearance on the doorstep. 'I need to get to the train station. I'm meeting the children there.'

'The children?'

'Yes, they're arriving from Germany. I need to meet them.'

Maybe she's continued the refugee work, thought Evie, *alongside the NFRB? Maybe she does have to get to the train station? But she's in no state to go out alone.*

'Have a hot drink first and a warm bath. You'll want to straighten yourself out before you leave.'

'There's no time for that Evie, I'll be late!'

'At least let me help you with your clothes and hair. You must let me do something. You did come to me after all.' Evie smiled at Jane, waiting for her face to soften, her jaw to unclench.

'Evie, you can't keep me here. I can do what I like and this is what I want to do.

'Let me come with you at least.'

Jane shrugged as if it was irrelevant.

I'll walk her to the train station, talk to whoever is there and then take her home to Edmond. I hope he's in, Evie thought, *she looks as though she hasn't slept in days.*

Jane was standing by the fire staring at the grate as if she wanted to light it with her eyes. The voice in her head was directing her. She had come to Evie. She needed to go to the station now.

Evie helped her into her jacket, tucked in her blouse and pulled up her stockings. She tried to rearrange her hair slightly but Jane pushed her away, so she linked her arm through Jane's, scooped up her handbag and they left the house together. King's Cross was not far. They could walk there in ten minutes – anything to help Jane to relax.

Evie walked at her usual brisk pace until she realised that she was almost dragging Jane along the pavement. She slowed down. They were drawing attention. Jane's hair was so wild. It bobbed around, unclipped, like a bale of straw on a donkey cart. Women with neatly curled, scooped and tucked hair stared rudely as they walked past. Evie kept her eyes ahead.

Jane whispered, 'We're being watched.'

Evie thought, *I know.*

Kings Cross was a crawling hive of luggage tags, steam, heels and overcoats. Moving through it was as testing as clambering over a pile of logs in a river. Evie let Jane lead. After all she had no idea whom they were meeting or where they'd agreed to meet. Eventually they emerged from the throng into a pocket of space next to the newspaper stand. Platform eight. Jane stopped. She looked around expectantly. A train pulled in. Jane turned towards it. Carriage doors banged out and people began to get off. *Groups of frightened children will be here any moment*, thought Jane, *carrying bags, wearing labels. Where is everyone? Where is the welcome party?* She turned around, and around again. It was too terrible. She recognised no-one in the crowd but they all seemed to be glaring at her.

Evie was increasingly anxious. It didn't look like anyone was here to meet Jane. She was clearly distressed. She had to get her home but she couldn't force her to come against her will.

'Jane,' she said, 'Jane, let's go. It doesn't look like the children have arrived. Let's go to your flat. We can phone your colleagues from there.'

Jane was still staring at the train. Its doors were all open. Guards were busy closing them again. There was no-one left on board. An old woman with a cane walked slowly past them. She had fox fur around her neck. A porter carried her bag.

'Take me home, Evie,' Jane cried suddenly, clutching Evie's arm. 'We have to leave now. We can't stay any longer. It's her!' She pointed wildly at the old woman.

Evie decided she'd left it too long. She swept Jane out of the station and into a cab. She needed to get help and quickly.

3rd September 1939, 11.15am

"I am speaking to you from the Cabinet Room at 10, Downing Street. This morning the British Ambassador in Berlin handed the German Government a final note stating that unless we heard from them by 11 o'clock that they were prepared at once to withdraw their troops from Poland, a state of war would exist between us. I have to tell you now that no such undertaking has been received, and that consequently this country is at war with Germany."

'This country is at war with Germany,' the radio crackled, spitting electricity.

'At war.' The voice in her head echoed angrily. She was still in her nightdress. The voice on the radio, Chamberlain's voice, was small, fractured.

"We have done all that any country could do to establish peace, but a situation in which no word given by Germany's ruler could be trusted and no people or country could feel themselves safe had become intolerable. And now that we have resolved to finish it, I know that you will all play your part with calmness and courage."

The voice on the radio sounded like it was speaking directly to her, but there was nothing she could do. She had no energy left. They were at war and she wanted to tear out her hair and cry.

Jane allowed Evie to settle her into a cab. She had lost her key. Edmond was not at home so she had stayed at Evie's. Now they were on their way to the hospital. The Priory, Evie said it was called. As they drove up Jane was relieved to see that it was a beautiful building. *A bit like a castle without the turrets, an imaginary world.*

It was some sort of mental breakdown they said in the little room with the narrow door. Evie was in there with her. She was grateful for that. She remembered that she wanted Evie's help. People were all so hostile and their eyes seemed to chase her around.

It could be schizophrenia the doctors had said when she told them about the voices, the visions. She didn't like the sound of that. It was a harsh word. It cut her off and cast her out.

It could be treated they said. That was better. She wanted them to treat her. She said, 'Yes,' and agreed to put herself in their care.

'You won't be on your own, Jane,' Evie said. 'The doctors will help you and I'll come in the morning with Edmond to see how you are.'

Evie had managed to get in touch with Edmond. It was a relief. Jane was grateful.

When Evie left, Jane felt frightened. She was on her own. Isolated. It was a familiar feeling. One she had locked away inside. A feeling she had grown used to. A feeling she had had for months now.

She had tried to remain calm but when they took her into the treatment room her eyes burned in the bright lights and she opened her mouth to scream. They shoved a rubber bit between her teeth and she gagged violently till they threw the switch and electricity pinned her head backwards, like a spool of barbed wire shot through the brain. The room they used was white, like the doctors and nurses, and her face when they wheeled her out and in again next morning.

She could see it coming – the needle. Someone was holding her arms down, her legs. They stuck on the electrodes and turned the dial. She watched them turn it until her body whipped into the air like a rag doll on springs and shook the sight and sound out of her.

Afterwards, the voices were gone and that was a relief but so was everything else. She lost her memory; it was like shards of glass now, impossible to piece together. That was why she wanted her diary. Thoughts were less painful on the page, they made more sense. Then again, maybe she was better off without the worries of other people, the fears that had stacked so high in the past. Maybe the watchers would leave her alone for good. There wasn't much point tracking her in here. She felt quiet and still on her own in the room with nothing in it except a bed. She needed to sleep. She closed her eyes and accepted the emptiness inside.

"3rd September 1939
Dear Richard,
My family and my doctor say that I'm suffering from violent persecution mania, but whether or not that is the case at least it has made me think about my personal relations and I have now decided that I do not wish to see you ever again since I can never marry you. I know what Walter has done to me, but I know also that it is Walter who I am still in love with and entirely love. You knew roughly what was going on – though no doubt not the details – and so you are in a position to find out from my 'friends' many things which should cure you of your love for me, if it exists. Walter, I realise, may hate me and certainly despises me but that makes no difference to my love for him.

I genuinely regret any pain I have caused you.

Jane.

NB: Perhaps by this time the love you had for me has changed to hate. If not you ought to realise that I'm abnormally sensitive about anything to do with W. and that you are treading on v. dangerous ground when you do or say anything connected with him."

"4th September 1939
Dear Jane,
When I knew you first in Oxford, your friend Rebecca used to say 'It can't be altogether a bad world, because Jane's in it.' If the premise were true, the conclusion would follow. But it won't – you're not in the world – you have one foot in the world and the other on a blind alley with W.

This is a rotten letter. I want to see you. I hate that it should be under these circumstances.

Richard."

"6th September 1939
Dear Richard,
I wrote you a cruel letter in the night and called my friends 'frauds' because I disliked their methods and thought them foolish but in fact I know them to be entirely benevolent and therefore shouldn't have objected so strongly. That I have loved you very much and that I continue to respect, care and admire you is well known to you. You are very, very good and worthy to be loved by someone much better than myself. Don't answer this letter.

Jane."

"8th September 1939
Dear Jane,
The usual solution of such tension is pity; but I am too close to you to pity you. Pity is incompatible with solidarity and a tremendous solidarity between us does all but exist. Damn you. I'm going to walk northwards this afternoon – can't work. The wind may blow something away. Objectively, I hate these wasteful crises. Not that I want to be wanting you like that often – it is a tearing, incapacitating thing most of the time, though sometimes by help of illusions it seems splendid.

I've tried dutifully to love other people.

It hurts like hell to love you so much and be so shut out from your life.
Richard."

Recovery

9th September 1939, 10.30am
The Priory, London
Jane is twenty-five

Can't he sit still? thought Richard irritably. *He's hopping up and down from that chair like an impatient father shut out of the maternity ward. I'd understand if he was anxious about Jane but he seems more concerned about his car.*

Richard was waiting at the hospital. He had rung Jane's house and Edmond had told him, reluctantly, where she was. *I guess he must be in two minds about visitors*, thought Richard, *fair enough, but he knows what Jane means to me.*

Jane's mother and step-father had arrived shortly after Richard. Gina had introduced herself but Charles was too busy checking his car hadn't been trifled with, stationed, as it was, outside an asylum. Richard was attempting to be polite to Gina, who looked rather stunned to see him. 'Oh!' she said, 'the man who crashed the car.' He was trying not to feel too upset by that. He had hoped he was more than 'the man who crashed the car' but Jane was private by nature and she wasn't close to her mother. Her ignorance of Jane's affairs shouldn't really be a shock.

Gina edged uncomfortably close to him. She was clearly nervous. She asked him shakily for a cigarette. He didn't smoke. She looked disappointed then tried another tack. *Maybe I can find out something about my daughter from this man.* She couldn't understand why Jane had become so ill so suddenly. She assumed there wasn't anything she could have done. She hoped it wasn't something genetic. She prodded Richard's elbow and whispered, 'Why do you think this happened to Jane? She was normal, wasn't she?' He looked uncertain how to respond so she continued, 'You see she has always struggled a bit with her health. I worry that she missed out as a child, you know, on milk and other things.'

What do you say to that? thought Richard. 'Let's wait and see what the doctors tell us,' he replied and got up. He couldn't stay sitting any longer, he needed to pace around, get away from Gina. Her presence was somehow suffocating. He felt sorry for her but he couldn't help but think she hadn't been much of a support to Jane. She seemed to realise she had let her daughter down in some way but it was too late to make up for it now.

Gina remained seated, watching Richard pace; watching her husband peer fretfully out the window at the car parked outside. *It's good to see that Jane has male friends*, she thought. Jane had never mentioned anyone special. She was frustratingly difficult to talk to on that score. Gina had warned her that she might end up on her own. The man pacing the room seemed solid enough. He was a big man, tall and square-looking. He had a reassuring pair of hands. She liked him though he hadn't been very forthcoming.

The door to the waiting room opened and they all turned expectantly, hoping one of the doctors had arrived to call them through. A tall, slender man walked in with a large bunch of purple chrysanthemums. Gina was startled. His height and size, matched with the dark hair and arched nose struck her immediately. He was the image of Arthur. Arthur, who was never that far from her thoughts despite Charles' best attempts to remove him.

Charles, had recently uprooted Arthur's portrait from the library and replaced it with a country landscape. 'It's just not appropriate,' Charles had said, 'far too prominent in the library.' The portrait had been placed in Edmond's bedroom, which, Charles asserted, 'was far more satisfactory.'

Anyway, it gave her somewhere to go when she was feeling particularly low. She liked to let loose a tear or two and indulge in tawdry moth-eaten regrets when Charles became too obnoxious to bear.

Walter walked over to Gina and shook her hand. 'You must be Jane's mother,' he said, letting her soak blissfully in the ease of his manner. 'Walter Tenant, I'm pleased to meet you. I only wish it were under better circumstances. How is Jane?'

'We don't know yet. None of us has seen her,' Richard interrupted gruffly. It was most irritating of Walter to visit. He had made no effort to see Jane in months and it had clearly torn her apart. Her letters had become increasingly irrational. Walter wasn't here to help; this was a token gesture. *But it will re-establish her commitment to him*, Richard thought bitterly. And he had brought chrysanthemums –an enormous bunch. Richard had brought roses. *Both conventional at least but Walter's will last longer. How annoying.* Walter was a hollow type of man in his view: all words and no action. It felt as if he had been waiting to reappear when it would have the biggest impact; waiting for a moment that suited him. Then again, maybe he was being overly resentful. Walter had just as much right as him to be there. Except that he was married and where was his wife?

Walter guessed the broad man with the ill-fitting and rather shabby suit was Richard. Jane had talked about him but they had never met. *He's clearly more of an admirer than Jane admitted*, Walter thought, looking at the flowers condescendingly. They wouldn't last as long as his.

'Richard Wright, I presume,' said Walter, stretching out his hand loosely for a brief handshake. 'Jane has told me about you.'

Richard took his hand lightly. There was silence as the two men looked at each other. *Two suitors,* thought Gina. *That is unexpected.* The waiting room started to feel small and tight. Even Gina felt squeezed. Charles, meanwhile, paid no attention to any of them, reducing the options for an outlet still further.

Richard knew he must say something to Walter to avoid looking like the bitter lemon of the two, but he couldn't bring himself to strike up a conversation, it was too much to expect – the man was an adulterer with a ridiculous sob story. He may have lost his first love in a tragic accident but marrying her sister was always going to be a mistake. The man was a fool. Worse than that, he was playing with Jane's love like a ball of wool, tossed around, strung out and then wound up again. If Richard did say anything, it wasn't going to be flattering or polite.

Sensing an impasse, Walter looked around for a seat. He didn't really want to sit next to Jane's mother in case she asked uncomfortable questions and he definitely wanted to avoid her step-father who was loitering awkwardly by the window. He was on the verge of taking the chair next to the door when it suddenly swung open, almost knocking him sideways. Richard restrained a smile. A short man in spectacles and an immaculate white coat came in.

'You must be waiting to see Miss Deering,' he said. 'You'll be glad to know that she is able to receive visitors now.' He surveyed the silent group. It felt like talking over someone's grave, they all seemed slightly on edge. Then again, he was used to that. 'I must ask you to go in separately or in pairs,' he continued. 'More than that would be too much for her. She needs to rest and remain calm. Keep conversation to a minimum and let me know if she says anything that appears out of the ordinary. We are monitoring her closely. She has experienced delusions and we are not sure if or when they will return.'

'Can you tell us why this has happened?' said Gina. 'How long will it take her to recover?'

'When can she come out?' Charles broke in, 'We don't want her to stay here for long.'

The doctor frowned. 'What caused the breakdown? I really can't say. It's likely this has been building for some time.'

'So it wouldn't be hereditary then?' mumbled Gina as if she wasn't quite sure she wanted to be heard.

'I'm not saying that,' the doctor replied. 'Schizophrenia is complex – there are likely to be multiple factors.'

'Will she recover? Can it be cured?' Walter couldn't contain himself any longer. He felt partly to blame but what was his role now? Visiting a sick woman would not be possible long-term. His passion for Jane was already more nostalgic than anything else but he couldn't bear to lose her entirely. She was still the most loving, adoring woman he had ever known.

'I'm sorry but this must be discussed in private with the family,' said the doctor. There were far too many people in the room. It wasn't clear who the men were. 'Mr and Mrs Cuthbert, you can come through now. Your son was with Miss Deering yesterday. I'm sure he told you what to expect.' He turned and left the room without waiting for confirmation. Charles looked as if he'd rather leap into his car and leave but he followed Gina obediently down the corridor, closing the door behind him.

Richard and Walter were alone together. *This is unbearable,* thought Richard. It felt like being boxed into a cargo hold with limited air. Richard began to pace again – anything to relieve the pressure.

Walter stared across the room, wishing he hadn't come. Jane meant a lot to him, she really did, but he couldn't bear this man's restlessness. Richard's constant turning was giving him a headache. It was worse than watching a merry-go-round at the fair with all its jangly music. Jane had described Richard as a calm, reliable sort of man, yet he appeared more itchy-legged than a child with mosquito bites.

'Would you mind sitting down?' Walter said. 'This is difficult enough as it is.'

It was like releasing a spinning top. Richard felt himself explode uncontrollably.

'Why are you here?' he said. 'If you find it difficult, you should leave now.'

Walter stood up, putting himself on a level with Richard. They were about the same height.

'Jane will want to see me. You have no more right than me to be here. You know that.'

'You haven't been to see her in months. You let her down but you haven't got the courage to let her go. You're the cause of this distress. Can't you see that? You'll only make things worse for her. You've only ever made things worse for her.'

'Whereas you haven't?' retorted Walter. 'You can't let her go either. You've called her almost every day since she rejected you. Don't you know when to give up?'

Jane had told Walter. It was the one thing Richard would have expected to remain private. He felt like he'd been strung up and exposed like Prometheus on his rock. That initial rejection was a pain that kept repeating itself and now Walter was the vulture pecking at it.

'That's none of your business. I'm there for Jane when she needs me; unlike you with your women on the side, your loose morals, your pathetic political posing.'

'You're a petty stalker. She doesn't want you around. She doesn't need you around. Don't you think it's stressful fending off unwanted calls? You heard the doctor. It's you who should leave.'

'Let's leave that to her to decide.'

'It'll be obvious whom she wants to see the moment we walk into her room,' said Walter. It was what Richard was most afraid of: Jane's reaction. 'We can go in separately,' Walter continued, prodding the cut further, holding it open for more salt. 'If you're worried that is.'

There's no way he's going in on his own, thought Richard. *No way.*

'You know that's not going to happen,' he replied.

Walter shrugged dismissively and sat down as if he didn't care either way.

Richard felt a strong urge to yank him out of his seat and hurl him out of the room. Tension tightened his fists like boxer's bandages. He could only just contain himself. It was a horrible feeling. He was, by nature a placid, relaxed type but he had been so patient. He had waited so long to win Jane. He didn't even need her love: just to be allowed to help her; support her;

be with her. Now this man – this philanderer with a politician's treacherous tongue – had brought her crashing down.

Still, whatever Jane's feelings, whatever her reaction, it would be Richard who would last the course. He just had to steady himself. Walter might impress her more but he was as flimsy as a blade of grass and he wouldn't want any responsibility. If he didn't get what he wanted from Jane, he would disappear. Richard had the upper hand – in the long-term. Jane would see that when she was well again.

They sat there a long time, in opposite corners, gloves off, waiting. The doctor opened the door. Both men were ready, both were pale-faced. They walked down the hard-tiled corridor towards the little room at the end. The doctor left them.

Richard went in first. Jane was sitting in a small armchair by the window. She was wearing a dressing gown and slippers but quite presentable. Her hair had been neatly brushed and pinned back from her face. She smiled. She was still Jane. He should have had more confidence. If she didn't want to see him he would've seen it immediately in her eyes. She seemed pleased with the roses. She pointed at the table in the corner. Evie had brought her a couple of glass vases and Edmond's flowers were almost over. Richard could replace them with his.

Jane had opened the window slightly so she could hear the birds outside. It was a relief to see her mother and step-father drive off in their car. She hoped to be well enough to leave soon. Then they wouldn't need to come back. The men in dark leather coats hadn't returned since the treatment but she was worried they might be inside that new pine cupboard in the corner of the room or under her bed, waiting to creep into her head again.

Overnight her fears had grown again. She had felt like a bed-wetting infant, on her own and vulnerable to terrors. It reminded her of the first few nights at boarding school without Elsie; only this was worse. This was a waking reality. She had asked the nurse to leave the cupboard doors open so she could be certain there was no-one there. The nurse knew this wasn't a good sign but it was important to keep her patients calm. The nurse had left them open.

Walter gave Richard a few moments to put his flowers in the vase before entering. He didn't want to hang around too long. It was gracious of him to let Richard go first after their spat in the waiting room. It also gave Richard time to turn round and see Jane's face as he came in.

'Walter,' she cried, her eyes open wide like a child given candyfloss. He had come. He did love her. Chrysanthemums all over the floor. She didn't care.

The doctors have no idea, thought Walter. Surely such joy was something to be hoarded, something to swim in fearlessly, not something to fear? Walter felt her love rush through him and weave its way round his body like wool round a reel.

Richard, meanwhile, was out in the cold.

He stooped to pick up the chrysanthemums for Jane. His time would come. His love would last. He put the flowers in the second vase and quietly left the room.

"10th September 1939

Dear Jane,

This is the letter which you may never see, written as a remedy against isolation and to clear my mind. I cannot eliminate you from my thoughts – that would be to mutilate and degrade myself. But actually there is no cause for the thought of you to be disturbing. I have now this new certainty of my love for you, and that means I need not think any more about the rightness or goodness of my loving you. It is firmer than any rock, and is going to be the centre of me. This certainty is independent of circumstance and – I think – independent of you loving me. On the certainty I can build a sad but honest life without you, or a splendid life with you. The certainty will, I think, do a great deal for me.

Richard."

15th September 1939

Dear Jane,

This is a strictly rationed letter, unemotional by order. It is very good that you are autonomous again.

Edmond and Evie tell me that you are very tired, and will need a complete rest from emotional strain and from taking decisions for a good while still. This seems reasonable, and I should have independently come to the same conclusion. I have been cursing myself continuously for my share in making you ill, which consisted in pestering you with letters and calls. So until you are ready for a full life, I'll leave you alone.

Even in an unemotional letter I must say that I love you utterly and completely, and that the whole incident of your illness, in all its effects, has confirmed and authenticated that in all sorts of ways. You can safely have the same feeling of the stability of this.

I've asked Evie to tell me of your progress. Apart from this, I don't know where you're going after hospital, and I shan't ask. So you can feel entirely unpestered and unwatched, though not un-thought about and anything but unloved.

Richard."

8th October 1939, 6.30pm
Bloomsbury, London

'Jane,' Edmond called upstairs. 'It's mother … on the telephone for you.'

He had just settled Jane back into her room, helped her unpack and was boiling water for a pot of tea when Gina called. *I know mother is worried about Jane,* he thought, *but we've only just arrived home, she could've given us a bit of time to find our feet.*

There was a pause and then he heard Jane coming downstairs. She had rather a heavy tread. *I don't think this is a good idea*, thought Edmond, *maybe I should ask mother to phone back tomorrow?*

It was too late. Jane picked up the phone.

'Hello, mother,' she said.

'Jane,' said Gina, 'are you all right? Have you settled back in?'

'We've only just got home.'

'I see. I wanted to make sure you arrived safely. I'm glad Edmond is there with you.'

'He would hardly have gone out, mother. Don't worry, we'll be fine.'

'I'm not worried. I just wanted to let you know that we are at home. You can call whenever you need to.'

'I'm rather tired.'

'Yes, of course. Make sure you get lots of rest. If you want to come and stay here in Kensington, you need only say.'

'Yes, mother.'

'In fact, it might be better if you stayed with us. It's quieter here.'

'It's that why you're calling? It's a bit late now, mother, besides, I'm not sure Charles would see it that way.'

'Charles has nothing to do with it, Jane.'

'I'm sure he doesn't,' sighed Jane. 'I'd rather be in my own home though and Edmond is here now, he will look after me.'

'What will happen when Edmond goes away, Jane? You know his work may take him out of London.'

'I'm sure I'll be all right. I promise I'll call you if I need to.'

'You are sure then?'

'Yes, mother. I'd like to go now. I'm exhausted.' It was good of mother to call and offer her support but Jane didn't want to have to think about anything right now. It was all she could do to stop herself hanging up the receiver without waiting to say goodbye.

'If you change your mind, Jane—"

'Mother!'

'Goodbye then.'

'Goodbye.'

Jane hung up.

"15th October 1939
Dear Richard,
This is just to let you know that Jane is very much better and now living at home again. She has been de-certified, and is really very nearly well again. She is still convalescent, and needs a bit of shielding, but if nothing goes wrong I think in a few months' time she will be able to stand on her own feet again. Till then she will probably, at her own wish, remain at home, but it is difficult to make plans for any length of time. I hope you are able to enjoy parts at least of your present life. I have not told Jane that I am writing to you. At present anyhow I do not think old friendships should be re-intruded upon her, unless she makes a move herself – but if you want definite advice, ask her doctor.

Yours, Evie."

"24th October 1939
Dear Jane,
I had faith all through that if you survived the incarceration, your character would survive intact and from our conversations I'm sure it has. It is all there for you to use, if ever you can get through the mess and mash of circumstance. It would be surprising if you could cover the distance all by yourself, but you may be able to, because you've pulled off some pretty surprising progress already. If you need to lean on anyone, don't be afraid to do so.

I was a bit depressed because I love you too much to bear your being hostile with equanimity, but now that I've had a moment to settle down I'm very happy, because you are so much better than I expected and the real core of you, which is what, as I now know, I am in love with, is still there untouched.

To that essential you, my love, and to you as you now are, my love and a terrific lot of solidarity, which for the moment you won't appreciate but is there all the same.

Richard."

"30th October 1939
Darling Richard.
Thank you for your letters – good letters. I sometimes have a desire for you to save me from myself. You mustn't ever pander to that desire although its existence gives me a feeling of unity with you.

My love to you,
Jane."

"5th November 1939
To be read in the event of us being separated for some time by war.
Dear Jane.
I hope you will see no more of W. because it seems clear that if you do there will come again conflicts which are beyond your power to solve, and you will become schizophrenic again. Deliberately to do anything which will probably upset your mental balance seems to me to be morally equivalent to suicide, or rather worse. I did not want to write this to you boldly in a letter, and only do so because this will not come to be read unless there is no hope of our meeting for a good while.

I love you entirely, and want your body and your mind, and your advice and your loyalty and your children. One ought not to promise that this state of feeling will persist, but it has for a long time now, and I can see little chance of its changing.

Jane, I love you. Everything about you that I've loved at any time, I love now.

Richard."

8th November 1939, 5.00pm
Munich

Fog ran smoky coils round the wheels of the airplanes stationed at Munich airport, tying them to the ground more effectively than a metal chain. The pilots were pleased. They could go home for the night.

A man with no wrist watch and splinters buried deep in his chapped hands drew his hat tighter down on his head and left Munich on the train to Switzerland. His name was Elser. He left behind no clues to his involvement but he carried with him a well-thumbed postcard – a postcard of a beer cellar. He might change the course of history. The mechanism was simple: a time bomb, waiting for Hitler.

5pm
Bloomsbury, London

Jane had been back at the flat in Bloomsbury for a month. The voices had vanished, for the moment. The doctors prescribed rest and tranquillity: no sudden shocks, no confrontations, no work. Of course there was the war to contend with.

'No newspapers? That's ridiculous,' Edmond said to the doctor, 'you can't keep Jane away from the news. Besides, isn't it important for her to get back to normality?'

Then again, no-one knew what that was anymore.

'Who will look after her when I leave for the army?'

'Haven't you got relatives in the countryside?' replied the doctor, resisting the temptation to walk away and leave him to figure it out. Jane was no longer in his care after all. 'Put her somewhere safe and get someone to keep an eye on her. She needs time or she may relapse.'

'I'll see what can be done,' said Edmond.

His first thought was to persuade Jane to stay with their mother and step-father. He wished Picketswood Hall was still the haven it used to be but it belonged to his uncle now and they rarely visited. Anyway, Jane would have none of it. She wouldn't leave their flat.

'I don't want to hide away,' she said. 'This is my home.'

She found she couldn't focus very well. She flipped through the paper, from article to article, finding the narrow print constricted, unreadable. Besides the Nazis and Soviets were crawling all over it, smudging the ink into great blotches as they trooped their red and black way across the page and into new territory. They seemed to occupy every crease and fold. It was most depressing.

She hoped reading the news would trigger some washed-out memory. She had no idea why she had travelled to Germany all those months ago. She remembered getting on the train but nothing more. It was distressing to think so much of her mind was grey, indecipherable. Clues would be helpful. Edmond rang her colleagues at the NFRB but they wouldn't tell him anything. Then again, maybe it was better not to probe too far.

At first she didn't want to leave the flat.

'I look terrible. My hair's a crow's nest. My eyes are sunken. I'm not sure I can even walk straight anymore.'

'Just take your time, Jane,' Edmond replied. 'You don't need to rush. Your confidence will come back.'

'I don't have time. There's a war on.'

'Just concentrate on getting better,' Edmond said, but she was right, there wasn't much time. Their neighbours had already received their corrugated steel shell from the government and were busy planting it in their garden. There was room for six. Edmond made sure there was space for Jane. He hoped she would remember to go down in the event of a raid. They hadn't practised yet. Anderson shelters hadn't been available in the early days of the blackout, back in September. Besides, going inside was less tempting than a cold cup of tea. The drainage sump was continually blocked. They had to fit wooden benches to keep the puddles at a distance. They were more successful at decorating the outside surface. Jane said the sweet peas would look beautiful next summer. That cemented her spot and Edmond was relieved. Evie visited them at the flat almost every day. She and Edmond were engaged again. It was as if they had never broken up. In fact the whole break-up was so ridiculous they would've laughed about it together if it weren't for the seriousness of Jane's condition and the way they were reunited. Evie helped Jane dress and untangled her hair. She reminded her how to clip it back so it didn't slip into her eyes.

Jane began to take pride in her appearance again. She soaked luxuriously in the bath, letting her toes curve around the taps, hoisting her hair up above the water and resting her head. She hadn't seen Walter since the hospital but the days were so similar she couldn't tell how long it had been. She wasn't even sure she cared. He had visited. He had brought chrysanthemums. They had drooped, turned the water in the vase yellow, lost their petals. The smell of their decay, mixed with the sickly, sweet taste of the tea brought in by the nurses, had turned her stomach.

She had held her hands out to him when she saw him, rising from her chair, joy pulsing through her veins faster than the insulin they had pumped into her: but his hands had been hot, clammy to the touch. Beads of sweat, gathered on his forehead, had caught in the light as he leant towards her. She had shuddered and slipped her hand out from beneath his. She never wanted to feel the sticky dew of sweat on her skin again. Not after the injections, the black terror that had sent spasms through her till every pore in her body wept with fear. Clean, dry, light, clear. She was on a beam, balancing on tiptoe. The slightest wind could blow her off. Walter had left and she had been glad of it. To be free, to put a lid on the voices, the plague of frightening thoughts that ate into her mind till it was full of holes, she had to focus. She was eating well again. She was at home. She was quiet but she was more at ease. It was where she needed to be.

Then Richard turned up. He rang the doorbell and waited. He was just about to pull the cord again when Edmond opened the door.

'Richard!'

'I just wanted to check how Jane is,' said Richard, shifting his feet like a gawky teenager, not the six-foot-something genuine giant of a man that he was.

'Of course,' said Edmond shaking his hand. 'Come in. She'll be pleased to see you.' *Richard's safe enough. It's Walter I have to watch out for*, he thought.

Jane appeared at the top of the stairs. Richard could just see her past Edmond's shoulder. She was wearing a slender green dress with a butterfly collar. Her hair was decorated with what looked like daisies but turned out to be small yellow and white clips, dotted around so as to contain the curls. She even had a pearl bangle on her wrist. Richard wondered if she was going out. She still looked fragile and paler than the wall she was leaning against but she was beautiful. That was clearer than ever.

Suddenly it struck him that she might be dressed up to go out with Walter; that Walter might turn up any minute and scratch out his raw, aching heart once again.

He hesitated on the doorstep. He took off his hat and mangled it in his hands.

Jane ran downstairs to the door. This was the man she was waiting for, not Walter. He was as big as the doorframe but he looked so gentle, so diffident standing there. He had been to the hospital to see her. She remembered that. She remembered because he had picked up the flowers. He had left without saying goodbye.

'Richard,' she said, taking his hand. 'Please come in.'

9.20pm

They popped the champagne. It gurgled and fizzed happily in their glasses, reflecting the warm lamp light and spitting merry bubbles up their noses. It was a toast to Edmond and Evie. The tall flutes chinked harmoniously. The wedding would take place tomorrow. Then Edmond would leave to join the army. All a bit rushed but what were they to do with a war on? 'Besides,' said Jane, 'separation is bearable if there's someone waiting for you.' They looked at her but her face was smiling, happy. Richard was here beside her again and her brother was marrying her best friend. The flat felt snug and full of joy. Jane reached out a hand from the sofa and turned on the wireless, flinging her cushion to the side and leaning back contentedly as The Andrews Sisters sang *Roll out the Barrel.* Edmond reached for the cards and suggested a game of bridge before bed. Evie turned on the table lamp. The curtains were drawn. The blackout had to be preserved. It was late but no-one wanted the evening to end. Not yet.

Munich
9.20pm

Across the sea, in Munich, beer tankards were flung upwards and cracked violently against each other in a fiery 'heil' to Hitler's rousing screech. A thunderous bang: the air in the Buergerbrau beer cellar fractured. Gunpowder ripped through the enclosed space. There was no time to react. Plaster, wood and concrete smashed down, splitting swastikas and heads as it fell. Brown-shirted men in ties were hurled from the balcony as it ripped from the wall and crushed those beneath. Hitler's podium was flattened beneath the rubble. Dust and ash smothered mouths. Men stumbled around blindly scrabbling for a door, a way out to that smell: sausages burnt to a crisp by startled street vendors outside. Anything was better than this acrid, choking stench and the bodies already buried in it, their blood seeping out and staining the charred black floor scarlet red. One man squeezed his broken body out of a jagged Gothic window. Two hands emerged from the debris and heaved bricks off a purple face. Scrabbling around, the hand picked up a trumpet from the splintered bandstand and blew out the dust. No sound. Party membership cards lay, soiled and worthless, under the grime. The lights went on outside the building. The blackout was lifted. The streets around the cellar hummed with electricity. Cheers went up a block away. Peace! The streets loaded up with noisy chatter. People shouted and danced with joy.

Stony-faced policemen silenced them with guttural threats and cut-off cordons.

Munich fell quiet again apart from the occasional thud of falling plaster, the foaming spit of those pulled out alive, faces black with soot. The neighbourhood peered into the pit. The black guards mined the hole for survivors. 'Was he in there?' one man whispered.

'A man must have luck,' Hitler said at the station, unperturbed by the explosion, ready to board the train to Berlin. The party faithful followed him in. The carriage doors shut. 'Blame it on the British,' he had said. 'Prepare for a long war.' The night had only just begun.

Relapse

"25th November 1939
Dear Jane
I am afraid that in this place I need a photo of you. You say that there is one extant: please send it to me. All I have of you is the initials "J.D" in indelible fluid, put on the wall by the builder or the previous occupant, and, to an unimaginative person like me, they aren't particularly evocative. It would be a good life if we could take the step we discussed a few nights ago. I can't go long without thinking of the way you curled up with me on Sunday night. It is a curious gift you have of making yourself seem very small and very lovely. Every cubic inch of you infinitely precious.

The sun was out yesterday afternoon or this morning, and the hills were very green, almost like the hills of Ireland opposite, which we can't quite see. Ailsa Craig looked like a very benevolent haystack and over on the Arran coast there is a fine spiky mountain that I haven't yet identified, not having a map that covers it. It will be fine country to fly in.

Tell me if you are offered the Gloucestershire job. I think you should take it, if you are offered it, unless the doctor absolutely forbids it on what seem to you reasonable grounds. I can see nothing to disqualify you except general diffidence.

I love you truly. Richard."

"2nd February 1940
Dear Richard,
Thank you very much for your letters. You have helped me tremendously, and I believe still could help me a great deal. I'm glad you chose the Air Force, which to me seems the wisest type of service in this war, anyway for you. I wish women were allowed to go into it as well, not merely as WAAFs, but flying and fighting as well.

I am working part time in the Information Department of the National Council of Social Service, and at present can generally take Fridays off. It is not a job which I would have been likely to take but for ill-health, but the Ministry of Labour seem to approve, and by the end of this week I'll enjoy it more.

With best wishes and love, Jane."

"20th August 1940

Dear Jane,

I'm sorry the doctor didn't pass you for full-time work; but he was pretty certainly right, if you get as tired as you say. It is a pity, from the point of view of getting a new job. But need you mention your health, where no form of medication is prescribed?

I gather that it is a bad thing for one's operational flying to get married in the early part of one's operational tour, though it may be a good thing later on in it. So you may for, say, a month, regard me as not an urgent suitor. But I certainly shall be after that. You need fear no WAAFs!

My true love to you,

Richard."

15th September 1940, 4.30pm
Bloomsbury, London
Jane is twenty-six

Planes droned through the sky like demonic dragonflies, slashing across the sun and casting malicious shadows on the city below. Anti-aircraft guns swatted them down, spattering the clouds with pellets and the ground with burnt metal. It felt strange to see the attacker, brazen in broad daylight, hurling fireballs at the earth, hammering holes through brick and mortar like a blacksmith's hammer on hot metal. The city burned but so did the planes. People wondered why they attacked in daylight. Were they so convinced they had the upper hand? Little did the enemy understand the fierce determination of the city to withstand the onslaught, the bonds that were forged even as the ground split apart. Now that the monster was visible the people could cheer its destruction. Such arrogance would not go unpunished.

Jane was sitting against the wall of the tunnel. The tiles felt cool against her back. Her knees were drawn up to her chest. The woman in front of her was sitting between her toes. Workers had made a beeline for Warren Street as soon as the sirens went off. They had been there since midday. It was hot and stuffy inside the tunnel. The trains had stopped running and the air hung heavy with the breath of the masses gathered nervously on the platform.

It was hard to tell what was going on in the skies overhead. The odd runner would take a peek above ground. Air Raid Wardens, their steel helmets and Wellington boots authorising their defiance, spat at the bombers in the sky and shooed the runners back into the tunnel like desert rats. The man next to Jane had been swigging from a flask since he arrived. She knew him. His name was Bill. He often came to the canteen where she worked as a volunteer. He had been sheltering in this very same tunnel when his house was flattened. 'Like an 'ob-nail boot on a mole'ill,' he muttered, shaking his head.

Now he lived in a makeshift shelter set up by the Women's Voluntary Services near Euston. He looked about seventy. His hands were gnarled, his fingernails grimy and jagged. He smelt of sweat and urine. The wardens caught him peeing onto the track one night. He was terrified. Others had done it but they took risks: they slipped into the blackness and wandered down the tracks.

Bill's back was bowed from osteoporosis. He couldn't get onto the tracks. He told the wardens about his house. He showed them the photo of his grand-daughter (evacuated) and daughter (dead). Someone had pulled it out of the rubble for him. He didn't say when his wife had died. It might've been the bomb. It might not. They told him not to pee on the tracks again and left him in peace.

'Well I'm 'appy to be alive,' Bill mumbled to anyone and everyone. His breath stank so badly Jane had to turn her head away. 'I'm 'appy to be 'ere with the 'oi polloi of London in the great, gurgling belly of the city.' He stood up. 'Let's raise our fingers together. Raise 'em skyward and bring those planes crashing down.'

He tapped the woman at Jane's feet on the shoulder. 'Let's 'ave a song.' She shrugged him off but smiled. He was encouraged. 'Let's 'ave a song and live a l'il longer.' He stood up. 'What shall we sing?' he shouted above the swarm of heads. Faces turned expectantly. Comedy. Companionship. Crumbling city, heaving heart.

'I've got the Deepest Shelter in Town,' he croaked, 'Please don't be mean, better men than you 'ave been—'

'Filthy like you,' Someone shouted. 'Get down!' Someone tugged him to the ground.

'Hey, he's got the right idea, wrong song.' A woman said, standing up. 'How about, *Somewhere over the Rainbow*?' A cheer went up. Jane felt herself lifted by the crowd, the ramshackle choir, roaring out the tune, rocking the ceiling with greater effect than any of the aircraft above.

Edmond had been so worried about her; about how she would react to the bombs, to the flash and smash of the explosions at night-time, the unpredictability of the strikes. She didn't even bother to go down to the Anderson anymore. She sheltered in the old servant's room below the stairs. She was bolder than the bombers. She had come through her crisis. She was thriving again, electrified by the spirit that coursed through the city. It was easier now that the enemy was outside rather than in her head. Each blast was like a shock to her system, the wires to the brain: a revival of consciousness. She was alive and she was part of it all.

Besides, she had Richard. It was almost a year since that day he had turned up on her doorstep. Almost a year since she had dared to admit that she loved him. He had visited her every day since his reappearance until, fearing the call-up, he took matters into his own hands and volunteered for the RAF Reserves. He was now a pilot officer, acting as observer and rear gunner in a Beaufighter squadron, engaged on reconnaissance over the North Sea. The separation was hard but he always came back and she wasn't afraid. He was more solid than the ground. He always had been. She had taken him for granted for too long; blended him into the walls of her life. Now he was in the forefront. It was a secure love, a love that bandaged and filled the holes. It was a love that stayed even when he was gone.

Before he left they had gone away together for the weekend. She had permed her hair. Her blue plaid dress was tied neatly with a brown leather belt and she was wearing silk stockings. She had felt peaceful, rested for once. She had put away the Nembutal.

Richard had spun her round in his arms when he saw her and she had smiled. He had kissed her then as if he would never kiss anyone again. His touch was gentle for such a big man. Even now she couldn't restrain a giggle when she remembered how he had explored her as carefully as an archaeologist, digging deeper as his excitement rose. Her body filled with joy and softened as he pushed hard against her and she kissed his neck and mouth again and again, high on the love that was coursing through her, faster and faster until he pulled out, breathless, panting, stroking between her legs till he swooned downwards, pulling her into his arms. And there they lay, happy, together.

She glanced quickly round the tunnel as if to check she hadn't been found out – that her thoughts were still her own. The singing was in full swing. No-one was paying attention to her blushes. She was free to dream.

He phoned her from his base whenever he was there. He used every possible method of communication to be with her: letters arrived in bundles; postcards in packs. He was as patient as ever. He had spent his week of leave with her, coaxed her out of her depression: the daggers that dug into her mind and darkened her daylight, fishing at her fears and casting nets over her self-confidence. He had praised her dress, her hair, her figure. He didn't want to change her. He asked her what she wanted, what she needed. He made her want to be clean again, to be tidy, to take care of herself.

He wanted to marry her. She knew that. But he didn't pressure her. There was no rush. He could wait a decade if she needed it.

There was a shout, a cheer. Jane looked up, her thoughts interrupted, her mind whirling and unsteady as if she'd got up too quickly. Everyone was on their feet. The tunnel was emptying. Someone reached down and pulled her up. She looked around wildly. She'd forgotten where she was.

The bombing had ceased. An ARP Warden was ushering the crowds out, back to the surface. Adrenaline pulsed through the huddled bodies as they rose and bustled along. The tunnel filled with chatter, whistles, relief, and swept its heaving, breathing load up the stairs and out into the heady half-light of the city after dusk.

As the mass of bodies drifted apart and the makeshift community evaporated into the side-streets, Jane felt her loneliness return. It was merely an echo of her illness, a reminder that she was still vulnerable but it felt like a stone, turning painfully in her stomach. She wanted to get home. There would be a letter there from Richard, she felt sure of it.

The streets grew dark as she walked, scuffing her feet on paving stones and tripping slightly in her hurry to get back. She passed the back entrance of the British Museum and kept her eyes ahead. She didn't like being reminded of her meetings with Walter. That was a part of her she had to conceal. Those feelings were burnt but not extinguished; like a cigarette butt on the arm, they only caused her pain. They lived in the dark side of her brain – the side she was trying to shut down.

She thought again of Richard: the stubble on his chin after two days without a shave; how it rubbed against her cheeks and reminded her that he was real – genuine, faithful. She wanted more than ever to see him again, now. If he were there, waiting for her on her doorstep, she would love him forever.

Jane turned the corner and passed the bombed-out buildings in the street two blocks from her own. She stood and stared for a minute. She could see the arm of a paisley sofa poking out from under timber floorboards. She could make out the shape of the rooms from the walls that remained, jutting up like the bones of a carcass. Either that or a giant had taken a bite out of the building, spitting out the crumbs. The void left behind was black, cavernous.

The warplanes were indiscriminate in their appetite for destruction. *No-one died here,* she told herself. *No-one died. They were all under shelter.* But she didn't know for sure.

She started to run. She could sense the planes in the sky again. She knew they were coming. Any moment now the sirens would start. Then she had to be inside, blacked out, at home. She would pick up Richard's letter from the door mat and feel her way to the servant's room where she would be safe … calm.

Crossing the road, Jane saw a figure sitting on her doorstep. She wondered who it could be. No-one would usually be outside now, certainly not on a doorstep, locked out. Not after the shock of a daytime attack.

The trickle of excitement grew into a wave, pulsing through her. Was it Richard? Had she willed him here? Was he on leave? Could he stay? Her heart was jumping wildly now. She was sure it was him.

Closer now, the person on the doorstep saw her and waved and stood up. It wasn't Richard. A sense of nervous tension stilled the thumping of her heart. The figure was almost the same height as Richard but extremely slim. Long legs, large shoes, low heels.

Evie.

What was Evie doing here at this time?

It was good to see her. It was a relief that it was her. But there was something unnerving about her standing there, waiting. Something anxious about the way she had jumped up on seeing Jane approach.

It couldn't be Edmond, could it? Edmond was in Ireland, at a training camp, waiting to be posted to Africa. He wasn't in any danger surely?

She had just reached the doorstep when the sirens went off, smashing all other thoughts out of her head, sending her scuffling for her keys.

'Shouldn't we go to the neighbours?' asked Evie.

'I've been using the room under the stairs. Come on, it's quicker,' Jane replied, grabbing Evie's arm.

They huddled together under the creaking floorboards as the wails came and went like a ghostly gramophone, stuck during winding. The small window was open a fraction and Jane reached up to close it, flicking on the light once she'd sealed out the searchlights and preserved their blackout.

'Jane, you're not safe in here,' said Evie, looking around at the room.

'Maybe not but I'm a lot more comfortable.'

Evie let it pass. The last thing she wanted was an argument. Not now. She had to tell Jane the awful news but the blasted sirens were ringing in her ears, making it difficult to talk, let alone say what she had to say.

At last the sirens ceased and silence fell like a cord between them, both separating and binding in its heaviness.

'I think we can go upstairs now,' said Jane. 'They can't have much ammunition left after today's mindlessness. You should stay the night, Evie. You can't go home now.'

'I would like to stay,' said Evie. Jane looked at her and noticed the small tartan bag in her hand. She had clearly expected this.

'Let's crack open a tin of beans then,' Jane said, desperately trying to deflect whatever was coming. It was good to have company, it really was, no need to know why Evie was here.

She hustled Evie out of the room but Evie hesitated at the foot of the stairs, wondering how to approach what might be a knockout blow. She had to handle it right. She couldn't leave it any longer.

'Jane, there's something I need to tell you,' she said. 'Let's sit down again.'

'I'd rather go upstairs, Evie,' said Jane, 'it's rather dusty in there if you hadn't noticed. Every time a plane cuts low it shakes more grit out of the ceiling.'

'We really must sit down,' Evie replied.

Jane looked at her. Her head started to throb. She didn't want to know. It was better not to. Couldn't Evie see that?

Evie's face was paler than the flakes of paint that had fallen on her during the raid.

'It's Richard.'

'What?'

'His plane was shot down over the Norwegian coast.'

'How do you know?'

'His mother sent a telegram.'

'To you?'

'To Edmond.'

'Why?'

'She couldn't get hold of you.'

'When was this?'

'A couple of days ago.'

'A couple of days ago! But I received a letter from him yesterday.'

'But when did you last speak to him?'

Jane was silent. It had been a week.

She ran to the front door.

No letter on the mat.

It couldn't be. Richard was ever-present. He was as stable as four walls.

She stopped. The image of the burnt-out house seared into her mind.

The world was so confused. Richard was real. He had stubble. It grazed her cheek. If he wasn't real, nothing was.

She turned round. Evie had followed her to the door.

'There must be a mistake,' Jane said.

It felt as if someone had tipped petrol over her head and was holding out the match, tempting her to strike. Was it possible to stay sane when street by street the lights went out every night, and sometimes they failed to come back on?

She could feel holes opening up, all the trauma that she had buried, fragmented, cemented, cracking her open, leaving her raw and vulnerable. *How could Richard let this happen? I accepted his love. I let him in. I love him.*

Evie was looking at her, waiting for a sign; a sign that she had absorbed this and was dealing with it.

'Jane?'

'I'm fine, Evie,' she said. She couldn't reveal the panic that was building inside, 'I'll phone Richard's mother in the morning. Let's go to sleep now,' she said, fighting it, slotting words into place, building a dam.

Evie let her lead. She might be in denial but she was calm. That was the best Evie could hope for.

They parted at the top of the stairs. Evie would be there in the morning if she was needed.

When she got to her room, Jane took out the bottle of Nembutal from her bottom drawer. If the sirens went off again, she would be dead to them.

"17th September 1940
Darling Jane,
Is it true that Richard has been killed? Is he perhaps missing – in which case there is hope? Either way it must make you miserable since you had seen so much of him and he loved you so much. Is there anything I could do to help or comfort you? You know I would gladly come to London any day you chose – or you if you prefer it come here any time. But I assume the worst – perhaps there is still some hope. Let me know please. It gives one an awful feeling of desolation that so good a person should go. I will write more when I know what has happened.

Much love, Rebecca."

"17th September 1940
Dear Jane,
I am terribly sorry to hear about Richard Wright. I have been moving around England and Scotland, so I have been rather useless for making enquiries, but those I have made have not produced anything useful yet.

The RAF are good about helping people who are lost. And many airmen have turned up after a long time. So it is not hopeless yet. Please write to me and let me know any further information which you now have.

My dear, I wish I could help, but I have done the very little I can do.

Good wishes, Walter."

18th September 1940, 4pm

Evie felt she couldn't wait any longer. She had spoken to Edmond and he had spoken to Gina. They had agreed that they had to act but Edmond was away and Gina was unwilling to do it. 'Jane would never forgive her,' Edmond had said. That had only made Evie feel worse. Edmond tried to reassure Evie but he knew just as well as she did, that they were relying on her; that it was terribly unfair. Evie would have to take Jane back to hospital. She might not want to go.

The last few days had been hellish. Jane had kept mostly to her room. When she did come out she had shadows under her eyes, clumps of hair matted to her clothes. She hadn't bothered to wash. She wasn't interested in her work at the canteen or at the National Council any more. She seemed aware that something was wrong but unable to do anything about it.

She said little at first and Evie left bowls of soup outside her door. They remained untouched, cold like her hands when Evie reached out to her. She didn't shake Evie off but she said, 'Evie, I dreamt people were looking at me through the window last night. I couldn't get them to go away. They were still there when I opened my eyes.'

'Do you want to see a doctor, Jane?' Evie said.

'No!'

She didn't say much the next day.

'Will you come downstairs and take tea with me?' Evie asked, hoping to draw her out of solitary.

'I'd like some peace,' Jane replied but then the sirens went off again.

There was no stopping the war.

'I opened my door and started to drink my soup,' Jane said on the third day, 'but then I heard a voice. It told me not to. It told me I deserved to starve; that they would come and put poison in if I didn't stop drinking. I put my spoon away. I can't eat it, Evie.'

'I made your soup, Jane,' Evie replied gently.

'I know.'

'You can drink it. There's no-one else in the house.'

'I know,' said Jane. 'But I don't believe it.'

Evie knew she had to do something.

'Won't you come out with me, Jane?' she said. 'If we see a doctor we could find a way to make sense of this.'

'Sense of what?' Jane snapped back. 'I'm not leaving the house. It's not safe. You can go if you want. This is my home. I don't want to go out.'

'All right,' said Evie. She couldn't reason with her, not like this.

She spoke to Edmond. She could hear the tension in his voice. This was his worst fear. He couldn't be there for Jane – when she needed him most.

'It feels like watching her through a long-range telescope, clinging to a window ledge,' he said, 'I'm totally useless from here.' He paused a moment, thinking things through. Then he said, 'Phone Walter.'

'Really?' Evie was shocked. This was the last person she expected Edmond to think of.

'Phone Walter. He may be able to convince her she needs help. There's no-one else.'

Silence over the phone. They both knew it was a gamble.

'I'll speak to you tomorrow. We leave in a couple of days. I don't have long.'

Evie found Walter's number in Jane's address book. She dialled slowly, listening to the whirr of the ring as it swung back round after each turn. The operator put her through.

Walter was hesitant at first as she knew he would be. She'd never thought much of his swagger. He wore the waistcoat but there was little beneath it as far as she could see.

'Walter,' said Evie, 'I need you to persuade Jane to go back to hospital. She won't listen to me.'

'What makes you think she'll listen to me? I haven't seen her since her first admission,' he replied. 'That was over a year ago now.'

'You can influence her. You always have.'

'Seeing me might make things worse. After all she may resent me for …' he tailed off. He didn't want to admit anything. He hadn't known it would turn out like this. It had always been Jane's choice, being with him. He had left it open for her. Breaking it off entirely might have tipped her out of her cart even sooner. Enough time had passed now for him to avoid responsibility. This was the last thing he wanted on his conscience or his mind right now.

'It's worth a try,' said Evie. Walter needed to step up. He was a dreadful coward. This was the least he could do. Jane needed him now. He had never fully broken with her. He had left a tie that was damaging. It was time for him to justify his position in her life.

Still he hesitated. There were no controls here, nothing to guarantee success.

Evie sighed. 'You don't need to continue seeing her if it's difficult. I just need you to convince her that she needs help.' Even as she said it she felt it was wrong. Who was she to suggest that Walter could pick Jane up and then toss her aside again, shirking his responsibilities as he had always managed to do? Jane was not his plaything to manipulate and then discard. A flicker of uncertainty edged the firmness out of her voice. 'Just meet me at the house and we'll take it from there,' she said, wishing she had never phoned him. Jane was delicate. There was no telling how she would react. What if this sent her even further over the edge? What if returning to hospital was more than she could bear? The treatment, from what she understood, was extreme. *Then again,* reasoned Evie, *she got better last time. She can get better again.*

But she still couldn't shake the feeling that kept tweaking away, tugging at her logical mind like a chess player at end game – the feeling that this might be the wrong move; that she might in some way be betraying Jane; that if Jane didn't want to go to hospital she shouldn't be forced. *Richard isn't here to carry her through it this time.*

'All right,' Walter said, breaking through the torrent of misgiving sweating through Evie's pores and tempting her to put the phone down. 'I'll come tonight and see what I can do.'

There was no turning back.

18th September 1940, 6.45pm

Walter turned up on foot. He had walked all the way from Whitehall. He needed time to think. This was a woman he had been in love with; a woman who became obsessed with him against her reason; a woman he had dropped but never fully parted from.

The last time he saw her, she was in a mental institution. It had been hard to swallow, the fact that she was so ill; that he hadn't noticed anything during their time together; that he might be partly to blame for her collapse; that he had escaped. He didn't need to look after her. No-one had asked him to. He had been relieved to disengage.

When he thought about the time they had spent together he couldn't help but add dark twists to her behaviour: all the idealism, the dedication, the drive to help others. She had been his romantic heroine. Now her fragility was exposed: the secrecy, the sensitivity, the desperation in her eyes when he left her at night time. It wasn't love. It was madness.

She was mad. It made him shudder. He didn't understand it. How could someone he had been so close to, intimate with, break down so completely?

Schizophrenia: no-one understood it. He wasn't alone.

At first he had expected to play the hero. When he visited her in hospital he had turned up like a knight, albeit in tarnished armour. He was ready to rescue her with promises and a morsel of hope.

He hadn't wanted Richard to steal his moment, Jane was still his.

But when he left he realised he didn't want to wait for her to recover. The image he had in his mind was not what she was now. It would be better for her if he simply vanished. Her family would be relieved, he was sure of that. He was grateful to Richard for removing any suggestion of responsibility from his dust-free shoulders.

Now Richard was dead.

What did that mean for him?

What did Evie expect?

He knocked at the front door tentatively. Footsteps clattered down the stairs; a yelp of pain. Evie opened the door.

'Sorry Walter,' she said, 'stubbed my toe. That'll teach me.' She stopped. Walter was edging away from her as if still considering flight. 'Come in, please.'

They went upstairs together without another word. Neither could think what to say. They'd never had much to do with each other till now.

Evie tapped gently on Jane's bedroom door.

'Jane, Walter's here.' She had warned Jane that Walter was on his way. She didn't want it to come as too much of a shock. Then again, it was difficult to know how much Jane was taking in.

Jane pulled back the door a fraction and peered out. It was Walter. She felt sick.

'Jane,' said Walter tentatively, 'Evie tells me you're unwell. I want to help. It's been too long since I saw you.'

'I've missed you,' he added after a pause. This was damned awkward, especially with Evie hovering behind him.

'Can we talk?' He was searching for a light in her eyes but she just looked bewildered as if she couldn't quite believe he was there.

'I could do with a stiff drink, I don't know about you, Jane.'

'Why are you here, Walter?'

'To see you.'

'Why?'

'I care about you.'

'I don't understand. You haven't written to me. You haven't spoken to me since—' She broke off. She couldn't bear to think about it: the white hospital room; the flowers on the floor.

'Can we go downstairs, Jane? It's more comfortable there.'

'I don't want to go anywhere.'

'Please, Jane. We need to talk.'

'We can talk here.' She was stubborn. She always had been.

'You seem on edge here. Let's go to the sitting room. Come on, Jane, I walked all the way from Whitehall to see you!'

'I can't, Walter. The thought of going out frightens me. I hear voices telling me they are looking for me. I'm scared they will come and take me away.'

'Who will take you away?'

'The men at my window, trying to get in; I can't get rid of them. I can't control anything anymore.'

'You can, Jane. You can choose to get better. You can choose to have treatment.'

'I don't want treatment.'

'Can we just go downstairs?'

'Don't push me, Walter, I don't want to.'

She sounded panicky. He didn't know how to talk to her. She wasn't normal. The situation was horrific; best to get it over with.

'You're not well, Jane. The doctors at the hospital can help you. Won't you come with us and we'll take you to them?'

'I'm not going back to hospital!' She sounded frantic. It was unnerving. She was standing there in the doorway, her face mottled and grey, terror in her eyes.

'Why not?'

'I won't go back there.'

'But they will help you,' said Walter, trying to remain cool.

He looked at her. Love had been tainted with pity – pity and shame. He had to understand her point of view if he was going to charm her out of this hole. Then again he wasn't a psychologist and that was what she needed.

'We're here to support you, Jane,' he said. 'I'm here to support you. Please, won't you trust us and let us help?' He was pleading with her now, white-faced. There was no plan. Her buttons were all confused. The wires were already cut. He didn't want to be here. He wasn't doing any good. It was useless.

'You're trying to trap me.' Jane sounded edgy as if she was holding it together by a hair.

'Just come with us,' said Walter, tension creeping into his voice. This was taking too long. He couldn't bear it. He reached out to take her by the shoulder.

It was too much for Jane.

'Get off me,' she screamed. 'Let go.'

'I'm only trying to help.' Walter sounded weak. He felt weak. He knew he was weak.

'Leave me alone.'

'You need help, Jane.' struggled Walter, trying to push through it, make sense of his presence.

'Get away!' Jane brushed off his hand and fled her room. Next moment she was downstairs and in the street.

They were shocked. Then they rushed after her.

'Stop, Jane, wait!' shouted Evie but her friend was already half way down the road, hailing a cab. 'Where are you going?'

The cab driver pulled over and slid his window down. It got stuck half way. The woman on the pavement looked odd. Then he noticed her feet. She wasn't wearing shoes. Two figures appeared in his back mirror, racing towards her, shouting. They took her by the arms and she fell to the ground sobbing. Maybe she had lost someone. Her house had been flattened. Her husband had died over in France. There was so much trauma around these days.

'You all right, luv?' he said, leaning over the passenger seat towards the window. The woman looked so frightened. Her eyes were glazed, unfocused. Her hair was sticking up all over the place.

'We need to take her to The Priory, Roehampton,' said Evie. *If we're going to do it, we need to do it now*, she thought. *I can't handle this and neither can Walter.*

Walter opened the door of the taxi and helped Jane in. She didn't say anything. She seemed exhausted, as if the fear that had driven her out the door had drained her of all energy. The struggle was gone.

They drove to the hospital in silence. Jane stared straight in front of her.

They arrived at The Priory.

The doors opened and she was swallowed up. Evie and Walter faded away and wilted into nothing – two parched travellers outwitted by a mirage.

She wanted to swim out again, up the throat and out but something was pinning her there. Wires attached to her head.

She didn't want to be there but what option did she have? She was a void now – an empty space, like the black hole in the bombed-out house where the furniture had once been.

She couldn't forgive them. They hadn't listened.

She didn't want to be in hospital because this time she knew she would not be leaving.

Hope

28th September 1954, 5.30pm
St Andrew'+s Hospital, Northampton
Jane is forty

Leucotomy. The pickaxe to the brain. The hole in the head. The loss of personality. The loss of a person.

Fear had kept him away from Jane for over a decade: fear that his imprisonment during the war had left her a prisoner for life, locked inside her shattered mind, irreclaimable. He had said he would wait a decade or more, however long it took, to marry her. It was too long. Too long without contact.

He was holding out a newspaper article, crumpled, well-thumbed. The doctor was staring at him as if he were one of the patients, slightly lopsided, weighing him up.

'Is this …' he began, '… is this what you did to her?'

'Sorry Mr …?'

'Wright.'

'Mr Wright. I don't know what you're talking about.'

'Your patient. Jane Deering. Is this what you did to her?'

"Human vegetables"; that's what the article called them – the tragic victims of a brutal and guinea-pig-led science. As if those with an illness of the mind were disposable. He couldn't bear it. It stuck in his chest and gummed up his throat like a gag in the mouth. Confinement within a body. The dark room flashed into his mind again. No space to move, caught in the spotlight, shoved into solitary. The thought of her had kept him alive but she had always been how he had left her, in his dreams.

The doctor glanced dismissively at the mangled piece of paper.

'I don't know what you're talking about,' he said again. Visitors were often worse than the patients, more demanding. This one seemed particularly irritable and irritating. He didn't have time for this. The job was stressful enough. Treatment wasn't to be questioned. He wasn't that familiar with Miss Deering. He had only recently begun work at the unit.

He did know that she had been in hospital during the war; that she was stable but that there was no chance of her leaving.

'Are you a member of her family?' the doctor asked.

'No.'

'Then I'm afraid I can't discuss the case with you.' The doctor turned to go.

The case, thought Richard, *is that all she is now?*

'Wait,' he exclaimed. Then, toning his voice down, steadying himself, 'We were engaged to be married before the war. Please. I just want to know what happened to her before I see her.'

'When was the last time you saw her?' asked the doctor, softening a little. His sister had lost her fiancé during the war. She had fallen into depression and never married.

'June 15th 1940. The day Hitler took Paris,' Richard replied, keeping it short, trying to stop his hand from shaking.

'Do the family know you're here?'

'Yes,' said Richard without hesitating. He'd come too far to worry about a small fib now.

'I'll have to look over her file. Wait here and don't expect too much.'

He disappeared down the corridor and through a door at the end, letting it bang loudly behind him.

Richard walked over to the window and looked out over the extensive grounds. It was a beautiful place at a glance, no denying that, but it had no soul. Inside was cold and clinical. There were single rooms for those patients well enough off to afford them but no escape from the perimeter without consent. There were no guards with guns but plenty of access to restraints. You weren't imprisoned: you were institutionalised. Would Jane want to leave even if she could? Maybe it was better to be closeted away than face a world that had moved on without you?

A car ground slowly down the drive as if reluctant to arrive at its destination. It crunched to a stop near the main entrance and a man in blue slacks and a grey wool jumper hopped out and slammed the door. Richard squinted through the glass like a seasick sailor through a porthole, steaming it up in his anxiety to see the shore, or in his case, confirm the man's identity. *It was him, surely?* He was tall with dark curls like Jane's cropped close to his head. Richard's finger squeaked noisily as he rubbed out a section to peer through, then gave up and picked another pane. *Could it be?*

He rushed down the corridor to the front hall. He had to get there quickly before the man disappeared upstairs. He had to do it. He couldn't be found creeping around unannounced.

He flung open the double doors in front of him.

The man brushed his shoes vaguely on the bristly mat before entering the building. He looked up expecting to be accosted by a nurse or official of some sort.

'Edmond?'

'Richard!'

Edmond dropped the bundle of photos he was carrying, open-mouthed. The man was back from the dead. He looked like it too. He seemed half the size he had been and stooped. He walked as if one foot were shorter than the other. This was incredible, unbelievable.

'Your plane was shot down.'

They were standing metres apart. Neither approached the other.

'I've been in limbo,' said Richard truthfully. Anxiety was starting to mount an attack on his chest. He wished he hadn't left his inhaler in the car; it was too cumbersome to carry around but he needed it now. He was wheezing already, each breath was a battle. He sucked in air and blew it out through his mouth slowly, calming down, trying to slow the barrage. Edmond had every right to be angry. He would know now that Richard had deserted Jane; that he had been alive but hadn't come back for her. He would see that Richard was a crumpled coward of a man.

Edmond wasn't thinking about Richard. He remembered Evie's call that night. The night Jane had gone back into hospital. She hadn't said much. She was matter-of-fact as always, except this time it sounded like she was holding something back. Jane hadn't wanted to go back to hospital. It was a truth that condemned them all.

Another concern spiked his mind. If Richard's death had shattered her so completely, what would his inexplicable return do now she was stable? Jane had been taking chlorpromazine for several months now. There were side-effects: spasms, numbing. It seemed to suppress the hallucinations though. She appeared peaceful, resigned. This might be more than she could handle.

'Have you seen her?' Edmond said, sounding harsher than he meant to, his voice catching in his throat slightly. He noticed that Richard's hands were quivering.

'No.' Richard spoke quietly. 'I mean, yes, I've seen her but she didn't see me. We haven't spoken.'

'Good,' said Edmond, a little too emphatically. Richard frowned. Was he going to be banned from seeing Jane? His heart squeezed painfully as it had done when they tied his hands behind his back and shoved his face in the snow – the day his plane went down; the day he was captured.

'I was waiting for the doctors to advise me. I don't want to cause her any pain.'

'Right,' said Edmond, relieved. The man had clearly suffered. He took him by the hand. 'It's amazing to see you. Really it is.'

'I'm sorry,' was all Richard could say.

Edmond shook his head. 'I don't know what you've been through. Let's talk to the doctors and see what can be done.'

Richard had always been patient. It took guts to turn up like this after such a long absence. Whatever had happened to him, it had beaten him for a while.

They walked back through the double doors together and down the corridor to the reception. The doctor Richard had spoken to was already there clutching a file. It was dauntingly large. The doctor put it down on the desk with a loud thump as though reprimanding Richard for having forced him to drag it out. He looked at the two men questioningly.

'And you are?' he said to Edmond in a voice that asserted his authority.

'Edmond Deering, brother of Jane Deering.'

'Fine,' said the doctor, pulling spectacles out of his breast pocket and perching them on his nose, 'You must know the history then,' he continued, leafing through the file half-heartedly. 'No point repeating what you already know. I expect you've filled Mr Wright in yourself?'

'No actually. I've only just arrived. Until a few minutes ago I thought Mr Wright was dead.'

The doctor looked up momentarily and frowned, then shook it off as if he'd heard it all before and nothing would surprise him.

'But I will fill him in, if that makes it easier,' Edmond continued, looking at the heavy file and raising an eyebrow.

'I can put your mind at rest on one point,' said the doctor, turning to Richard and ignoring Edmond. 'It states here that the patient was due to have a leucotomy in September 1945. Late in fact for someone with her condition considering the prevalence of the technique. She must have been relatively stable. Anyway, it seems the family refused it on her behalf. It was her mother who made the decision.'

So Jane's mother has achieved some sort of redemption then, thought Richard, remembering that painful conversation in the waiting room, the letter he received when he contacted her after the war, the one that sent him away.

'As the success rate was questionable,' the doctor continued, 'the doctors working on the case agreed to defer. Had they been certain of success, they might have gone ahead without needless consultation.' Richard looked horrified.

'The drugs she's on now are sedative. They're new to the market but patients are responding well: less wandering at night; fewer screams and hallucinations. I have to say, we're pleased. The wards are far quieter. We don't have to use restraints as much.' He stopped as if he'd revealed more than he meant to.

'If you want more information you'll have to make an appointment,' he said, finishing abruptly and slipping his half-moons back into the crisp white breast pocket of his overcoat.

'Wait!' exclaimed Richard, a note of desperation in his voice. Fourteen years could not be summed up like that. 'We need to know whether it's wise for me to visit. I mean, she thinks I'm dead. How should I approach her?'

'With great care I should think,' said the doctor, clearly wanting to end this conversation and get on with his rounds; these visitors had taken up far too much of his time already. He started to walk away then remembered the file, lying forlorn and abandoned on the desk. Richard accosted him, taking him by the arm lightly as he turned to retrieve it.

'Is it possible for a patient to recover from schizophrenia given the right conditions, the right care?' he asked.

The doctor shrugged him off impatiently. 'It's uncommon. Highly unlikely. Patients receive the best treatment possible here,' he said. What was this man suggesting now?

'I'm not questioning that,' said Richard quickly, thinking, *but I would if I could.* 'I just want to know if remission is possible. You see, Jane recovered last time. Then the war started. There was no-one to care for her full-time, she was lost in the debris. I want to pull her out again. I believe I can.'

Edmond looked worried. The doctor looked at Richard sternly. This man had no idea what he was dealing with. He was a naïve fool. He was setting himself and the patient up for disillusion and potential disaster.

'If you really thought that you would have come back before,' he said, raising an accusatory eyebrow,digging at Richard's guilt, taunting the pangs of misery and loss that had haunted him for years.

'So you don't think there's any hope that I can—'

'Cure her?' the doctor broke in. 'Certainly not. The patient has been in hospital for fourteen years. There's no chance of recovery now. It's unheard of. The best you can hope for is that she remains steady. She's between two worlds now. Her brain finds it hard to distinguish what is real from what is not. It's a chemical imbalance you understand, not a trauma that can be worked away. She depends on the drugs to keep her sane. Unless you want her to live her life in constant fear, there's no way out for her.'

I can't believe that, thought Richard, *I have to hope for more. That's why I'm here.*

Seeing the pain haunting Richard's face the doctor softened his tone slightly, 'I'm afraid it would be inadvisable for you to visit the patient with any hope of a miracle. I would suggest Mr Deering accompanies you and if you see any sign of distress you leave immediately.' He looked at Mr Deering for his agreement. 'I really can't allow you to visit on any other condition.'

They both nodded silently. The doctor left and they were alone. The office was cold.

Richard looked at Edmond. Was this wise? He couldn't leave now. Besides, some small light still flicked on and off inside him like an SOS flare, urging him on, refusing to give in – the flare that had supported him through years of post-traumatic stress that had bent his bones and spirit into angles so distorted he didn't know himself when he looked in the mirror.

'Is there anything left of the Jane I knew?' Richard asked, thinking, *there's only a fragment left of the Richard she knew. She may not even recognise me.*

'When she smiles,' Edmond replied thoughtfully, 'you can see the old Jane when she smiles.'

6.30pm

Jane turned the pages of her diary absentmindedly. It was exactly fifteen years since her first admission to hospital. Just over fourteen since re-admission. She was forty. She didn't bother to pull out the grey hairs, they were too deeply entangled; twisted in a fuzz of darkness just like her thoughts. Not that she cared about such things anymore.

The nurse had just brought her a pill. She looked at it. Too large to swallow without water hence the tall glass beside it. Always the screwed-up eyes and the gulp. She used to worry it would lodge in her airway and that maybe they had designed it to do so. Then the paranoia returned and the room warped into a cell with bars on the windows and a man with a hacksaw outside desperately trying to get in and at her. At first she had screamed and the doctors had come and taken her to lockdown, sending bolts of electricity through her scared and stiff body. Finally, with practice, she had learned that forcing the pill down was the safer option.

She reached for the glass. There was a knock at the door. Water spilt over the table. The glass crashed to the floor and rolled under the bed. She snatched up her diary, its pages wet through and sodden. The door handle turned and two men entered. Her eyes went woozy. She felt a spasm pass through her jaw, grinding through her teeth. Their faces appeared full of resentment. They saw the diary dripping in her hands. They were coming for it. She clutched it to her and screamed. They were getting closer. They were reaching out to take it.

A nurse burst in through the door and rushed towards Jane. Edmond and Richard stepped away. Jane was shaking. Her hands were locked firmly over a brown leather book. Richard looked at her face full on for the first time in over fourteen years. It was pale and lined. Her eyes were still large and violet but wracked by fear. Her jaw was twitching slightly. It was terrifying to see her like this – in pain.

The nurse glanced at the glass on the floor, the pill on the table. She swept up the glass and poured more water in from the jug beside the bed. She took the pill and pushed it into Jane's mouth, prising the book from Jane's hands. Jane was staring vacantly at her but she took the water and swallowed. There was silence in the room. Then everyone breathed again.

'You must have scared her,' said the nurse. 'The pills keep the delusions at bay. You should have known better Mr Deering.' She looked sourly at Edmond who was standing quietly just inside the door. It felt like someone digging their nails into his back, seeing his sister like this. Every time he hoped she would be better and recently she had been, but then he would be reminded that she wasn't cured and the sadness returned.

Like Richard, he longed to see the Jane he grew up with. He found fragments of her but it was difficult to piece them all together. He was grateful to the pills for restoring her to calm at least. He was aware that they wouldn't do more than that. He was aware that they didn't restore her to herself; that they continued to trap her in her illness.

Richard watched as Jane's body relaxed. He could still see tension behind her eyes and in the way she gripped the arms of the chair but she did look more restful. *There's no pleasure in this life*, he thought. *It's a cycle of function and dysfunction, relapse and remission. Where are the interests? Where's the drive? Where's the love?*

She looked up and saw him. Was this man real? That was her brother in the corner, by the door. He was real surely. The man with him must be a hallucination. The pill had not done its work. This hallucination was comforting though, it wasn't like the others. It looked like Richard.

Maybe she was dying. Maybe this was the last projection of a withered brain: a Richard who mirrored herself in his stunted frame, his tired demeanour; someone who had borne a lot of pain, a lot of isolation, a lot of fear.

He looked crushed, bent over as if someone had squeezed the juice out of him till he was half the size he used to be. He was coming over now. She wanted to take his hand but she assumed it would melt right through hers. He looked so sad. She wanted him to appear happy, like she was to see him.

So she smiled. She could embrace this vision. If only they were all like this.

'Richard?' she said quietly, knowing he wouldn't reply.

He went to her then and took her hand. He knelt down next to her, willing the love that he still felt to spread from his fingers to hers, warming her, tickling her into life with butterfly wings, transforming them both in a moment.

She looked at him closely. He had a pulse. His pupils were dilated, earnest.

He wasn't dead.

She had been here all these years and he wasn't dead.

What was going on?

Fear started to stream through her body again. This couldn't happen. It was a cruel ploy to trick her into happiness only to snatch it away again.

Edmond was here. Edmond had known Richard was alive. Evie must have known. They were in it together. They had told her he was dead. They had made her believe it. The old resentment returned, biting savagely at her heart. She had to block them out to stave off this hurt, the terrible sense of betrayal. They had shut her in here and so she had shut them all out for years.

Edmond sensed the hostility. He remembered it well. It had taken time to heal and it was still there, lurking, leeching out the joy from their relationship, from seeing her.

'We didn't know Richard was alive,' he said. 'We didn't know, Jane.'

Richard nodded. Jane felt the tightness in her neck and hands loosen a little. The pulsing terrors subsided. Maybe it was all right. Maybe this was something she could accept. She was accustomed to confusion. She didn't have to understand. He had stepped out of the pages in her diary and returned to her. She needed him. He would help. She put her hand on his and pressed lightly.

'I'm sorry Jane,' was all he said.

She felt a tear trickle down her face.

'Will you stay?'

'I will stay as long as you need me. I will come every day until we can take you out of here. You've been here too long already.'

'Will they let me?'

'When you're ready.'

She nodded.

Not yet.

Edmond smiled at her. Maybe there was hope here.

She would be happier now. This was better than a pill.

Edmond left the room, peace in his heart. He left the bundle of photos of his burgeoning family on her bed. He would wait for Richard outside.

Richard stayed.

For half an hour more.

Jane stared out the window as Edmond's car drove away carrying Richard with it.

She knew he would be back. That this was not the end.

That her history, his, had somehow been altered.

She sat down in her armchair, ran her fingers over the bare patches where she'd rubbed it raw with her elbows, glanced up at the painting of a donkey, crossing the foggy moor. She imagined the fog lifting, sunlight catching in reedy puddles. Red heather, a thin path made by sheep through the scrub, setting off at a run. Freedom, there to be imagined, there to be chased.

Richard was alive and the room was no longer four square walls closing in on her. He had taken her hands in his and she had touched his face, worn to leather and bristle with years of neglect. He had gone out. He had left her door open.

A cold draft was coming in from the corridor but she wasn't shivering. She was sitting quietly, in her chair, looking out of the window.

Grandad's Poem

If you should come again,
Stand in the door and smile,
What should we speak of then,
For you have not known meanwhile
All the years that are passed between?
What should we play, or do,
Whom time has lamed and lined,
Who can no more run, as then we ran,
Seeming to leave our limbs behind,
When our clear stream days began?
Yet in the play of my children
It is your laugh that still I hear,
And know that if you smiled
We should love again with the love we knew,
The dawn light love of a child.
So from your darkness come, smile again,
Oh dear, dear Jane.

Jane. September 1914

Afterword

Biographical Reflections

This work, although, fictional, is inspired by the life of my great-aunt. My narrative ends with hope but sadly, before the pages have settled, I must upset my version of events and shatter my fictional rehabilitation of Jane - a woman I have come to love as much as my grandfather hoped I would when he picked up his own pen to tell her story.

The sad truth is that Jane died in 1991 after nearly fifty years in hospital.

Over ten years ago, my grandmother gave me a box full of large brown envelopes, each one stuffed full of letters, alongside photos of a girl with a mass of dark brown curly hair. Most of the letters were ones that had been sent to my great-aunt, a few were written by her. On my bookshelf I also had a hefty and intriguing spiral-bound book titled simply 'Jane', written by my grandfather. I started thinking about retelling my great-aunt Jane's story the moment I opened my grandfather's book and read his introduction.

Letters and biography combined told the story of a woman whose life, like her mind, was splintered. Her beginning was spirited but fraught, full of intellectual intensity and the determined pursuit of social justice: her later years, a black hole. All this was framed by two terrifying wars between which the whole world collapsed into chaos.

It felt as if Jane's mind, bent on tackling inequalities, despaired at her own fragility and that of the world around her. She was a woman whose passion and determination were undermined from birth by events outside her control, whose eager honesty and desire to resist evil took her to the limits of her endurance. Could anything have prevented her from developing schizophrenia? How could someone so bright, so full of promise, break down so entirely?

My grandfather did not try to answer these questions but he clearly wondered about them. According to the Royal College of Psychiatrists, one in a hundred people will be affected by schizophrenia during their lifetime but as yet, no clear cause has been identified. One in five, recover completely. For others, cycles of remission and relapse are common. It is thought that a combination of genetic and environmental factors may increase the risk of developing the illness. With this in mind, I looked for stresses and strains in my great-aunt's life and relationships that might have increased her vulnerability to schizophrenia and began writing my novel.

Jane's continuing illness had been heart-rending for my grandparents as they watched their flourishing and increasingly sprawling family grow up in an era of peace and stability: a joy that Jane was not able to share. Jane's existence was never purposefully hidden but until we were given her biography, the youngest generation of the family was unaware of her existence. My mother, uncles and aunts, on the other hand, grew up knowing that their father and grandmother visited Jane in hospital at least once a month. As children, they would not have been taken to a secure hospital and they were too young to ask questions. By the time they were old enough to be curious, it was clear that Jane would never leave.

Every time a new drug was issued or a treatment discovered, my great-grandmother hoped it would be a miracle cure. Relatives, at the time, were given little information about the possible side effects or likely outcomes of treatment. Consent forms were basic: a signature was needed, the doctors knew best. Even by the 1950s, according to Ronald Senator's book, *Requiem Letters*, (Marion Boyars, 1996), patients were certified and treated against their will.

When Jane was first admitted to hospital in 1939, suffering from a 'nervous illness', she was treated with Electroconvulsive Therapy, deep Insulin and Cardiazol. Each of these treatments induced intense fear in the patient as they were carried out, and yet, somehow, they were supposed to reduce the patient's paranoia. All, with the exception of ECT (which is now approached humanely and strictly regulated), were disproven and discontinued within the decade. All, including ECT, which was given without sedatives or relaxants, had the potential to cause further damage to patients who were already vulnerable.

Given this, it is not surprising that my great-aunt violently resisted doctors when she was detained in 1944 and again when they told her they were going to operate on her brain. At the time, she was experiencing delusions and hallucinations, believed that Nazi agents were plotting against her, that she was the recipient of state secrets and that her food was being poisoned. She was not violent before she entered hospital: she was vulnerable, suspicious and fearful. The doctors, in effect, became her torturers, forcibly restraining her whilst doing her irreparable harm. Two weeks after her detention, she was given a leucotomy against her will.

The results of this were devastating. Jane continued to experience hallucinations and her distrust of those treating her only grew stronger. Doctors judged her to be aggressive and difficult, an unpredictable patient whose behaviour could not be calmed except through further shocks and drugs. It could be that her self-control and impulse inhibition were damaged by the operation on her frontal lobes; it was probably a combination of this and the panic created by her confinement that led her to strike out. At other times she was subdued and selectively mute, perhaps terrified of further treatment should she communicate her feelings. She seemed to lose much of her motivation and some of her interest in politics, isolating herself from others and communicating through noises and gestures when taken out of her room.

Although schizophrenia is often associated in the public mind with violence and disturbance, researchers agree that the vast majority of those with schizophrenia will never be violent. It seems likely that my great-aunt's 'violence' was not a result of her illness, rather a reaction to her treatment. She was left with no familiar faces in an institution with long, cold corridors, locked doors and doctors and nurses who would restrain patients if they didn't do what they wanted: of course she was desperate to escape.

When my uncle and aunt visited Jane towards the end of her life she was suffering from muscle spasms, lashing out at my grandfather with her arms and jabbing at photos with a finger. She had been confined to a wheelchair since the late 1950s when she developed contortions in her posture and legs. It is likely that these physical changes, brought on by a fall, were worsened by lack of good nutrition and exercise and also by the side effects of first generation anti-psychotic drugs.

By the late 1970s to early 1980s, my great-aunt was calmer though her mood still fluctuated. She took part in occupational therapy, went out into the community, started swimming and developed more positive relationships with staff she knew. Her care plan changed considerably as doctors and nurses focused on how best to support her and improve her quality of life. The judgemental and negative descriptions of her symptoms and behaviour disappeared, replaced with a more humane approach.

Having read through my great-aunt's records, I can categorically say that if she had been diagnosed with schizophrenia today, and without the horrors of the second world war to contend with, her prognosis would have been different. Decisions about her care and treatment would have been discussed openly with her family and her consent gained whenever possible. She would have been protected by safeguards that didn't exist in the 1940s. Tragically, by the time the dignity and humanity of each individual patient began to be considered, my great-aunt's physical and mental health had deteriorated to such an extent that the flash of a smile and the brightness of her eyes were nearly all that remained of the woman she had been.

The sorrow my grandfather suffered, watching his sister edge into old age, a shell of her former self, unable to use her intellect, voice her opinions or influence the trajectory of a world that moved on so quickly without her, led to his determination to write her biography. His unconditional love for Jane was evident in his pride in her life, her character, his relationship with her. Despite refusing to speak to staff or other patients, Jane spoke to my grandfather in whispers whenever he visited and took great pleasure in seeing him. He was dedicated to helping her in hospital and developed strong relationships with doctors and nurses in her later years in order to ensure she was well looked after and protected.

As I finished my novel, I worried that I had betrayed my grandfather's confidence by focusing on the impact of Jane's illness on her life and the insecurities that fed it, rather than her personality and her achievements. Now I realise that the two were always inseparable. In fictionalising her story, I had to choose events and focus on relationships that I felt had the greatest impact on what ultimately happened to her. I had to reconcile myself to the idea that a biography and a novel are entirely different and some drift away from real life was inevitable.

I wove a plot that loosely followed the path of Jane's life but omitted huge chunks of material about her travels, a year spent teaching in America, her love of horse riding and her eye for art. No-one in the family, including my grandparents, knew what Jane was doing when she got on a train to Berlin via Belgium on the brink of World War Two but we do have her train tickets. Return tickets from London to Paris and on to the Belgian frontier are torn. Tickets from the Belgian frontier to Berlin and back again are untouched. My grandfather believed Jane had a breakdown near the Belgian border and turned back before she reached Germany.

In researching a credible hypothesis for this trip, I found links between the German resistance movement, especially the group later labelled the 'Kreisau Circle', and the New Fabian Research Bureau (where Jane was a volunteer). In amongst the collection of letters my family inherited from Jane was a note introducing Jane to Helmuth James Graf von Moltke, lead member of the 'Kreisau' circle. Jane was apparently heading into Germany with no training in espionage but with introductions intended to help her establish contact on arrival.

I often spoke to my grandmother about her relationship with Jane. Jane had been her best friend at university and she had the utmost respect and love for her but, being an extremely rational person, she found it hard to relate to Jane during or after episodes of paranoia. When she visited Jane in hospital, Jane would tell her about the men under her bed or at her window. She seemed to know they weren't real but she couldn't dismiss them entirely. Jane also felt strongly that my grandmother had betrayed her by taking her back into hospital against her will. Given the intrusive and damaging nature of the treatment Jane received, it is obvious to us why she did not want to return but at the time her family believed it was the only way to help her. She had gone into remission before, there might still be a chance she could find peace again. The problem was, at the time of her final admission, my grandfather was away at war and Richard was no longer there to offer support.

My reintroduction of Richard in the 1950s was designed to answer the 'what if' question my grandfather posed, reviving a protective relationship that could hypothetically have made a difference to Jane's chances of remission. Even without a leucotomy, the likelihood of this would have been low given the level of stress and anxiety caused by her treatment in hospital. However, I did feel that I could, by changing a few facts, offer some light, if only a flicker, at the end of my novel.

The ethics of using extracts from real letters in my novel has led to some soul-searching on my part. I wondered if I had gone too far, invading the privacy of my family and their friends. The first few drafts of my novel did not include them. Was I right to use private and highly emotional letters to my own ends? I concluded that the same question could be asked of the whole novel. The more I diverged from reality the greater my insecurity became. The letters are stunningly beautiful, more intense than anything we would write today. They are of their time. Without recording them, typing them up and passing them on, they would fade away in their hundreds, stuck in a box in the corner of a cupboard. They are memories of a turbulent past. In a biography they would have had a more secure place. In a novel they have greater anonymity but they also become extracts, set out of context: person, date and place.

Not all the letters in the novel are real. I had to invent a couple from Jane, one from Karl, one from Edmond and two from Rebecca. All the letters from Richard and Walter are extracts from real letters as is the letter from Dr Shaw to Richard; Bulletin No.5, National Committee for Spanish Relief; and the note Jane sends Evie before her breakdown in Berlin. Richard's 'Telegram home' for *The Times* was inspired by George Steer's 'Telegram from Guernica', 1937. There are also a couple of scenes in which characters use words recalled by my grandfather, specifically during his collisions with Walter in the flat. The poem at the end of the novel was written by my grandfather and Jane's silhouette is on a family postcard given to me by my uncle.

This novel, in the words of my mother, is a gift that has come out of a tragedy. I believe, as do the rest of my family, that my great-aunt and grandparents would have thought of it that way too. I can only hope that, despite steering a rocky and, I'm sure, at times unrecognisable course through their lives, I have written a book that does some justice to Jane's legacy.

Pippa Beecheno, January 2018

Acknowledgements

This novel has been a collaborative journey through family history and beyond. It started with my grandfather's book, painstakingly put together and printed after his death by my grandmother. In it, he sought to honour his sister's memory and to give his children and grandchildren an account of her that we could understand. At the beginning of his book, he included a note stating that he felt his sister's story might be retold one day either as fact or fiction by one of his descendants.

I often spoke to my grandmother about my desire to write a novel loosely based on my great-aunt's life and she was extremely supportive of this, supplying me with letters to and from my great-aunt and her own insights. My parents and grandparents have always encouraged my love of reading and writing. I explored glass cabinets full of beautifully bound books, burst into their rooms in the early hours of the morning with my latest find and sat listening to them read me stories and poems for hours on end. They watched me develop my story box full of neatly stapled paperbacks, praised even my most comical works and fostered my writing spirit. I can't thank them more.

I am also grateful to my aunts and uncles and my wider family, all of whom have been highly supportive of this project, from start to finish. For such intimate, emotional work, that includes excerpts from private letters and my grandfather's poem, the backing and understanding of my extended family has been essential. Thank you all.

My parents were my first reviewers, providing the constructive criticism I needed to develop my novel and helping me realise how far positive feedback can help a writer to improve their work. They have also looked after my children on many an occasion when I was desperate to get some more lines on paper.

To my mother and father-in-law, Liz and Francis Beecheno, thank you for your encouragement and support and for taking care of my children when I needed that little bit of extra time.

Sorrel Wood, thank you for believing in the story, pushing it forward, giving me an edge in the competitive world of publishing. Celine Hughes, for all your moral and practical support and for telling me to keep going and not lose confidence.

Ali Thomas, Elizabeth Foster, Richard Crawley and Jane Crawley, for your thoughts and ideas as I was starting out. Sanna Karolszyk and Anne Moule-Schlag for helping with scenes set in Germany and for checking my German. Kim and Christian Bjurstedt for your enthusiasm and interest all the way through.

I would like to thank Marisa Locke for your enthusiasm and for pointing me in the direction of my brilliant agent, Laura Macdougall. Inez Munsch for reading my book at short notice in amongst so many other commitments and for propping me up and sending me out again with my head held high. Twinky Mellor for looking at the novel from a professional angle, checking the sensitivity of my portrayal of schizophrenia and giving me the benefit of your knowledge and understanding. Jasmin Kirkbride and the team at Endeavour Press for taking that leap of faith - publishing my novel and for working so hard behind the scenes to give it the best chance of success.

I am grateful to my tutors at the Writer's Bureau who nurtured my writing in the early days, providing the input I needed to kick-start my novel. Most importantly, I would like to thank my agent Laura Macdougall, who worked with me to develop and hone the novel to the point when we felt it was ready to send out. Thank you Laura, for providing your expertise at a moment's notice, being swift to respond to all queries, believing in my writing and my novel, and taking it out into the world.

Finally, my husband, Dominic, for being so supportive of the whole project and enabling me to pursue writing as a career. My sons, Danny and Joey for being, until recently, fairly oblivious to my writing, and for the joy of listening to you tell your own stories. My lovely sisters, three: Tess, Sally and Lisa, for being my cronies, allies, henchwomen. All the wonderful friends who have taken an interest and leant me their support along the way, thank you. I hope you enjoy the result.

About the author

Pippa Beecheno has a first class degree in English Literature from the University of St Andrews, and an MA in Social Anthropology from the SOAS, University of London. After university, she worked as a Community Development Manager for various charities. With a growing family to look after, she began writing fiction whenever the opportunity arose, combining this with copywriting and proofreading. She is married and lives in South London with her husband and two young sons.

You can find photos of Jane and behind the scenes information on the author's journey to publication at www.pippabeecheno.com.

Follow Pippa Beecheno on:

Twitter: https://www.twitter.com/PippaBeecheno
Instagram: https://www.instagram.com/pippabeechenoauthor/
Pinterest: https://www.pinterest.com/pbeecheno/

If you enjoyed *A Thin Sheet of Glass*, please share your thoughts on Amazon by leaving a review.

For more free and discounted eBooks every week, sign up to our newsletter.

Follow us on Twitter, Facebook and Instagram.

Printed in Poland
by Amazon Fulfillment
Poland Sp. z o.o., Wrocław